THE SPECIAL COUNSEL

Introduction

Dear Attorney General Barr:

I previously sent you a letter dated March 25, 2019, that enclosed the introduction and executive summary for each volume of the Special Counsel's report...

I did not want to go to paper with this. That is not how I handle my business. That is not what any of us do as a general practice. We know the game as lawyers, as professionals, as people in the government, as officials who have worked in the intelligence community. We meet. We talk. We consult. We work things out and keep the details under wraps. We do not want to draw attention to ourselves. We do not want to show someone up or to back someone into a corner.

We avoid going to paper.

A paper trail is significant. They know this. You do not go to paper just to write things down. You go to paper to create a historical record — because you think one is necessary. You are making history, and you are not confident about how it would be written otherwise.

I never wanted to make history. If my time in public service — as a marine, a US attorney, director of the Federal Bureau of Investigations (FBI) for twelve years, and finally as special counsel for the US Department of Justice — could have been of zero historical significance, that would have been optimal. But it was not to be.

They should have been happy that I occupy this position. There are many people, particularly in the District, who *do* seek attention, who seem to be acting out roles in the movies they expect to be made. The president is fond of discussing central casting, but if he were an astute man, he would desire me in this role. Mind you, I do not mean to comment upon someone else's powers of perception. I'm merely addressing this particular point, and I leave it to you to draw any further conclusions.

What I am saying is that they could have had a showboat sitting in this chair. A Democrat could have been appointed — not that a Democrat inherently would have been any less fair as long as he or she was devoted to the law and to the Constitution. But we are living in highly partisan times, and in the president's mind, having a Democrat as special counsel would have been his worst nightmare.

I know this because he has said repeatedly that I *am* a Democrat.

Which, of course, I am not.

So perhaps I should walk back that last statement. Maybe having a Democrat as special counsel is not his worst nightmare. Maybe having a registered Republican devoted to the law and to the Constitution is — which is why he must pretend that I am a Democrat. He must place his adversaries on the other side of the fence. That side of the fence, I am compelled to note, has grown rather crowded.

The president's team shows no appreciation that I play everything by the book. They do seem not particularly interested in books.

For almost two years after I was appointed special counsel to oversee an investigation into the Russian government's efforts to interfere in the 2016 presidential election — and to explore any possible coordination between Russia and individuals in Donald Trump's campaign — I kept silent. I did not comment. I did not leak information. I made no television appearances. I issued no statements. I said nothing.

When the president of the United States publicly called the investigation a "witch hunt" in excess of a hundred times, I did not respond.

When he tweeted that the probe was "a big Hoax by the Democrats based on payments and lies" and concluded, "There should never have been a Special Councel [*sic*] appointed," I did not respond.

When he posted fourteen tweets about "the 13" — which later became 17 — "Angry Democrats" pushing/rigging/leading/heading/working on "the Russian Witch Hunt," I did not respond.

When he complained that "Mueller & his gang of Dems refuse to look at the real crimes on the other side" and called my investigation "McCarthyism at its WORST!" I did not respond.

When he accused me of having conflicts of interest with him, including "the fact that we had a very nasty & contentious business relationship," I did not respond.

When the president's lawyer, former New York mayor Rudy Giuliani, was asked about this alleged dispute, offered no details yet claimed it remains unresolved "even to this day," and called on me to "stand up and be a man," I did not respond.

When Mr. Giuliani, who had established his legal reputation prosecuting organized crime cases as US attorney for the Southern District of New York, boasted about the president's efforts to discredit my work ("Mueller is now slightly more distrusted than trusted, and Trump is a little ahead of the game. So I think we've done really well. And my client's happy"), I did not respond.

When I met with the president's lawyers, I did not do so at the White House, where reporters would note my presence. Instead I invited them to conference rooms in my own offices in the southwest part of the District, the address of which remains unknown to the press.

I did not dine in restaurants where I might be recognized.

When a CNN reporter asked me point-blank in a Senate hallway, "The president thinks it's a 'witch hunt.' Is there any way you can respond to that?" I continued walking and offered not even a change of expression.

Then, on March 22, 2019, I submitted to Attorney General William Barr a 448-page report capping 675 days of work, 2,800 subpoenas issued, about five hundred witnesses interviewed, almost five hundred search warrants executed, thirteen evidence requests made to foreign governments, thirty-four people indicted, and more than $25 million spent. And I offered detailed summaries of this work, no redactions necessary, to be released to Congress and the general public.

Instead, the attorney general characterized the report to Congress and the public in a way that was strictly his own. An initial appeal from me that he modify his message was rebuffed.

The president declared the report "complete and total EXONERATION" and continued to repeat, "No collusion! No obstruction!"

So here I am, committing words to paper, no matter how loath I am to do so. I thought my report was exhaustive and that no more needed to be said. It appears I was incorrect.

> As we stated in our meeting of March 5 and reiterated to the Department [of Justice] early in the afternoon of March 24, the introduction and executive summaries of our two-volume report accurately summarize this Office's work and conclusions. We communicated that concern to the Department on the morning of March 25. There is now public confusion about critical aspects of the results of our investigation. This threatens to undermine a central purpose for which the Department appointed the Special Counsel: to assure full public confidence in the outcome of the investigations.

I sent that letter to the attorney general on March 27. A little more than three weeks later, on April 18, the attorney general released our report to the public with numerous redactions. Book-bound versions of it became instant best sellers, and hundreds of thousands of copies were sold. But like another topical publication that flew off the shelves long ago, Salman Rushdie's *The Satanic Verses*, it was unclear whether the people buying and downloading the report were actually reading it. The way that the president and his supporters portrayed its contents indicated that they, at least, had not — or that they were willfully misrepresenting its findings in the hope that their audience would not read for themselves what my office had uncovered.

Indeed, the website Politico reported in July 2019 that many Congress members still had not read the report.

"What's the point?" asked Tim Scott, a Republican senator from South Carolina.

"It's tedious," said Lisa Murkowski, a Republican senator from Alaska.

"I've got a lot on my reading list" is how Fred Upton, a Republican representative from Michigan, shrugged it off.

Even Hillary Clinton's vice presidential nominee, Virginia senator Tim Kaine, had an excuse: "I didn't have to read it. I lived it."

"You can't expect people to read lengthy documents in large numbers," Jerry Nadler, a Democratic representative from New York City, told Politico. "They have their own lives to lead."

Nadler, I will note here, is chair of the House Judiciary Committee.

On May 29, 2019, I finally did something that I hate to do: I held a news conference.

I stood in front of the cameras and spoke for less than ten minutes. I did not take questions. I directed people to seek any answers *in our report*.

I reiterated the seriousness of obstruction-of-justice allegations: "When a subject of an investigation obstructs that investigation or lies to investigators, it strikes at the core of their government's effort to find the truth and hold wrongdoers accountable."

I also explained that my office determined that Justice Department policy prevented us from bringing criminal charges against a sitting president, but we still collected evidence regarding possible obstructions of justice because there are other mechanisms for dealing with alleged crimes from the executive branch. "The Constitution requires a process other than the criminal justice system to formally accuse a sitting president of wrongdoing," I said.

Yes, these potential remedies include a congressional pursuit of impeachment. I do not like saying that last word because then it gets blown up in headlines, but we are all intelligent adults here. This is what we are talking about.

Also, as I thought we made clear in the report, we did not exonerate the president. "If we had had confidence that the president clearly did not commit a crime, we would have said so," I said.

Finally, I drew people's attention back to volume 1 of the two-volume report. This perhaps is the less sexy part of the report, as it does not explore behind-the-scenes White House dramas and eruptions but instead the painstaking, deliberate, highly detailed work of Russian forces to disrupt our presidential election via social media, computer hacking, diplomatic back channels, and other means. The idea that a hostile foreign power can attack something as central to the American identity as our elections should be setting off alarm bells across our country. But those bells have been difficult to hear amid all of the other noise.

"I will close by reiterating the central allegation of our indictments — that there were multiple, systematic efforts to interfere in our election," I said. "And that allegation deserves the attention of every American."

I made myself clear on one additional point: there would be no reason for congressional Democrats to compel me to testify before them.

"The report is my testimony," I said.

Read. The. Report.

So, naturally, on July 24, 2019, I found myself on Capitol Hill, compelled to testify before the House Judiciary and Intelligence Committees. The Democrats wanted me to read aloud what I had written in the report. I declined. What was this, story time? The same Republicans who had celebrated our report for exonerating the president were now excoriating it and me for being part of a vast conspiracy that victimized the current president and covered up the Russians' efforts to try to get Hillary Clinton elected. Which, of course, is pure malarkey.

I was not expansive in my answers. I was a seventy-four-year-old man sitting there in my dark suit and blue tie, being forced to be the center of attention, which, to put it mildly, is not my preference. This report was not about me. It was about actions being taken against our Constitution and elections.

So I continued to state the obvious. When asked whether it was "fair to say" that the president's only-in-writing answers to our office's questions were incomplete and not always truthful, I replied, "Generally." No, our work was not a "hoax" or "witch hunt." Yes, a presidential candidate encouraging the leaking of hacked documents was "problematic," and that was "an understatement." No, "the president was not exculpated for the acts that he allegedly committed." And, yes, Russian attacks on our democracy remain a serious issue that is not going away.

"It wasn't a single attempt," I said. "They're doing it as we sit here."

I also told the representatives, "We spent substantial time ensuring the integrity of the report, understanding that it would be a living message to those who came after us. It is a signal, a flag to those of us who have responsibility to exercise that responsibility, not to let this kind of thing happen again."

My "performance" was not well reviewed.

The *New York Post* called my testimony "a stammering, stuttering mess." The *New York Times* referred to my "Labored Performance" in its headline and said I was "excruciatingly awkward" as I "stumbled" for an answer. Politico offered quotes that I was "struggling" and perhaps not "up to" testifying.

President Trump was all but popping the champagne, telling reporters, "It was a very big day for our country, it was a very big day for the Republican Party, and you could say it was a great day for me."

So here I am, going to paper again.

In general, I do not look at what I do as storytelling. I see it as investigative work with the purpose of determining facts and possible bases for legal action. The way I present these facts is, by its very nature, *lawyerly*. This is what I do.

Yet for lawyers' work to be meaningful, it must connect with its intended audience. When prosecuting or defending a criminal case, an attorney must convince those twelve people inside a jury box of someone's innocence or guilt. That is the basis of the American legal system, the best, fairest system in the world. We must make a grand jury's decision easy by handing them an airtight case. What we present and how this material is received must be in sync. And storytelling is involved.

I have worked my entire career to avoid the specter of politics. The pursuit of facts, the pursuit of *truth*, is not a political act. I believe that deep in my bones.

But the audience for my office's report is not twelve people in a box or a grand jury. It was, first, an attorney general appointed to replace the attorney general whose actions, indirectly at least, led to my appointment. One might argue that the first attorney general, Jeff Sessions, was fired because he did not prevent my appointment and that the subsequent attorney general, William Barr, was named because the president viewed his attitudes toward this investigation to be closely aligned with his own.

The political implications there are unavoidable.

The report's other intended audience is Congress. As you know, there is no way to remove politics from Congress.

Then there is you, the American people. You are the basis of our government — a "government of the people, by the people, for the people," as the great President Lincoln declared on the battlefield of Gettysburg. You have not only a right to know of threats to our democracy but also a *responsibility* to know.

The members of our government, in all three branches, are there to represent you and the values contained in our Constitution.

Members of Congress report to you.

The president reports to you.

You are their boss. This point must not be forgotten.

So please, sit down. Let me tell you this story in a way that I've never told it to you before. It is not a legal brief, an academic paper, or some sort of treatise. I will spare you much of the analysis, so you can focus on what people *did*. This is, at its root, a story with lots of characters and action.

Pay attention.

Part One

BEFORE THE ELECTION

1

"Putin's chef"

Let us begin by introducing a seemingly minor player who nonetheless would play a major role in much of what followed.

You might say that Yevgeniy Prigozhin was living the American dream, if not for the fact that he was a Russian conducting cyberwarfare against the United States. When he was a young man, he pursued a skiing career, but that did not work out. Soon he was serving a nine-year prison term for organized criminal activities including robbery, fraud, and involving minors in prostitution, according to an extensive profile published by the Russian online news site Meduza. Then the rags-to-riches part of this tale began.

After emerging from prison around the time of the Soviet Union's collapse, Prigozhin started a hot dog business in Leningrad/St. Petersburg with his stepfather. Apparently he sold a lot of hot dogs; in an interview, he discussed not being able to count all of the rubles that piled up in his mother's apartment. Soon he was becoming the manager of the city's first grocery store chain, Contrast, in which he maintained a 15 percent stake.

Media accounts indicate that by 1995, he was partnering with Contrast's commercial director to open one of St. Petersburg's first high-end restaurants, the Old Customs House. A couple of years later, he and his partner remodeled a run-down ship docked on the Vyatka River into a fancy restaurant called New Island. This was where the elites came to dine — businesspeople, city and federal government officials, and one especially important guest: Vladimir Putin.

You may know plenty about Putin already, but given what a major figure he is in this story, let us take a moment to refresh our memories. The future Russian president and prime minister was born October 7, 1952, making him more than six years younger than Donald Trump. His sixteen years serving as a Committee for State Security (KGB) foreign intelligence officer culminated in his becoming a lieutenant colonel before he entered the world of politics. He took positions in St. Petersburg and then Moscow, and in July 1998, President Boris Yeltsin appointed him director of the Federal Security Service (FSB), the Russian Federation's successor to the KGB. A little more than a year later, in August 1999, Yeltsin named Putin as acting prime minister and announced that Putin eventually should replace him as president. This happened sooner than most people expected; Yeltsin resigned on December 31, 1999, and Putin, as prime minister, rose to acting president. Putin won the presidential election the following March and a second four-year term in 2004.

As the Russian Constitution barred Putin from seeking a third consecutive term, Dmitry Medvedev succeeded him as president in 2008 and appointed Putin prime minister again, thus maintaining Putin's hold on power. After his four-year term, Medvedev stepped aside so that Putin could regain the presidency in 2012 for a six-year term. Putin was reelected in 2018.

After the more West-friendly regimes of Boris Yeltsin and Mikhail Gorbachev, Putin's time in power has been marked by an increase in tensions with the United States and European countries. Putin drew widespread outside criticism for his crackdowns on protesters, most famously following the 2012 election when the three members of the feminist Russian punk band Pussy Riot were sentenced to two years in a prison colony for hooliganism. (One member was soon released on two years' probation, while the other two served most of their sentences before being freed by a Putin amnesty proclamation.) Dozens of journalists and political opponents have been killed during Putin's reign, and human rights advocates opposed his 2013 anti-LGBT legislation known as the "gay propaganda law," which criminalized the "propaganda of non-traditional sexual relationships," such as the display of a rainbow flag or public displays of affection.

Putin also has found himself in conflict with the West over his military support of Syrian president Bashar al-Assad as well as the incursion of Russian forces into Ukraine and the forced annexation of Crimea.

This is not the last you will hear of the Russia-Ukraine conflict.

Back in the summer of 2001, the year after Putin was elected president for the first time, French president Jacques Chirac visited Russia, and Putin took him to that fancy restaurant on the rehabbed boat, New Island. Then forty years old, Prigozhin turned on his patented charm as he served the two heads of state. He must have made a good impression because Putin kept returning to the restaurant with other world leaders. Putin and US president George W. Bush dined together on the converted boat in 2002, and Prigozhin served the Russian president many times after that, earning the nickname "Putin's chef."

Prigozhin's duties extended beyond his restaurant, much to his benefit. In 2008, he was hired to feed the guests at Dmitry Medvedev's presidential inauguration. More lucrative contracts were sent Prigozhin's way, such as the food contract for Russia's schools, a job so big that it required the building of a factory. Prigozhin got to work, with a state-owned bank loaning him the bulk of the $53 million in construction costs, according to media accounts. When Prigozhin opened this Concord Culinary Line factory in 2010, Putin was there.

After a while, though, St. Petersburg parents were not feeling too celebratory about Concord. They complained that the food being served to their children was too processed and full of preservatives, and a television news show reported that Concord had failed to provide several St. Petersburg schools with *any* food. The factory was shuttered after just a year, Meduza reported.

Yet Prigozhin and Concord continued to thrive. The company won large catering contracts to serve Moscow's schools, the Moscow mayor's office, and, most significantly, the Russian military. In 2012, Prigozhin's companies became responsible for more than 90 percent of all food orders for soldiers in a two-year deal worth 92 billion rubles (about $1.45 billion in mid-2019 dollars).

As Prigozhin made his riches through these government contracts, his service to Putin came to involve far more than food. In early 2012, the year in which Putin recaptured the presidency, Concord personnel delivered tea and cookies to anti-Putin protesters who were rallying "For honest elections!" Soon Concord came to an agreement with this group to provide security for their rallies.

Little did the protesters know that Prigozhin's people, according to subsequent reports, actually were collecting information on the protest leaders to use in a TV documentary that accused the opposition of plotting a coup against the Russian government. Concord's workers infiltrated the organization electronically as well. Dmitry Koshara, Concord's development director who oversaw these efforts, later revealed that every fifth account on the protest's website was one of his bots, according to the Meduza report.

Here was the future of warfare being played out: battles fought on screens. Prigozhin and Concord backed other propaganda efforts to boost Putin and to denigrate his opponents. They staged a bogus "gay" demonstration when US president Barack Obama visited in 2013. ("Obama is our president," one sign declared.) Prigozhin also supported the founding of the pro-Russian news agency Kharkov in the Ukraine three months before the overthrow of the Putin-friendly Ukrainian president Viktor Yanukovich in February 2014.

But Prigozhin's biggest project was a virtual weapons factory called the Internet Research Agency (IRA), the existence of which was revealed in 2013. Funded by Concord and colloquially known in Russia as "Trolls from Olgino," after the St. Petersburg historic district where the headquarters were located, the IRA employed hundreds of people to work around the clock posting social media messages. These often-scripted posts supported the Kremlin and branded critics as traitors and liars tied to the West.

"Alexey Navalny, who calls himself a 'truth seeker' and a 'freedom fighter,' has earned himself a reputation as a liar, a fraud, and a traitor to Russia," went one such post, as reported by Meduza. "Meeting with representatives of foreign intelligence services, Navalny once again proves that he's on the West's payroll."

When Putin critic Boris Nemtsov was murdered in 2015, the troll farm came out to blame his death on the Ukraine and its Western supporters, all of whom were accused of drumming up hostility against Russia. Meduza reported that the propagandists received an assignment that read,

The main idea is that we're cultivating the view that Ukrainian players might have been involved in the death of this Russian Oppositionist…that now Russia has once again become a country that faces the West's hostility. This is an obvious provocation, and an effort to create a surge of discontent among the opposition's leaders, who will begin calling for protests and demonstrations with the aim of overthrowing the government.

The Russian government kept feeding Concord huge contracts, such as 26 billion rubles (about $411 million in 2019 dollars) to provide housing and services to the military in 2015. Prigozhin, in turn, redirected millions of rubles to the IRA, which churned out propaganda to support Putin and to tear down his opponents.

His work was having the desired effect; Putin solidified his power while controlling his message. So Prigozhin and the IRA, with money flowing from the Russian government, extended their ambitions.

Why limit themselves to influencing people within the Russian Federation?

There were bigger battlefields to conquer.

2

"An improbable quest for the Republican nomination"

So, ladies and gentlemen, I am officially running for president of the United States, and we are going to make our country great again.

Thus began Donald J. Trump's run for the White House on June 16, 2015. Trump, a high-profile New Yorker known for developing (and putting his name on) large-scale real estate projects and purchasing prominent properties (such as Manhattan's Plaza Hotel) from the 1970s onward, had considered previous presidential runs. He launched a campaign for the 2000 election to represent the Reform Party, which Ross Perot had founded for his own presidential run four years earlier, but that effort was short-lived, and Trump dropped out of the race in February 2000. He registered as a Democrat in 2001 and as a Republican in 2009.

His fame escalated with his popular NBC reality competition show *The Apprentice*, which he hosted for fourteen seasons (seven in the form of the offshoot *Celebrity Apprentice*), starting in January 2004. His signature line was "You're fired."

The social media platform Twitter was launched in July 2006, and Trump's first tweet, posted on May 4, 2009, promoted one of his TV appearances: "Be sure to tune in and watch Donald Trump on Late Night with David Letterman as he presents the Top Ten List tonight!" But as Barack Obama remained in the White House, Trump posted an increasing number of political tweets. In 2012 alone, he made twenty tweets devoted to the "birther" theory that Obama was born outside the United States and thus was ineligible to serve as president. "An 'extremely credible source' has called my office and told me that @BarackObama's birth certificate is a fraud," went one August 6, 2012, tweet.

Trump's June 16, 2015, announcement speech laid out the us-against-them anti-immigration themes that would persist in his campaign and presidency:

> *Our country is in serious trouble. We don't have victories anymore. We used to have victories, but we don't have them. When was the last time anybody saw us beating, let's say, China in a trade deal? They kill us. I beat China all the time. All the time....*
>
> *When do we beat Mexico at the border? They're laughing at us, at our stupidity. And now they are beating us economically. They are not our friend, believe me. But they're killing us economically.*
>
> *The U.S. has become a dumping ground for everybody else's problems....*
>
> *When Mexico sends its people, they're not sending their best. They're not sending you. They're not sending you. They're sending people that have lots of problems, and they're bringing those problems with us. They're bringing drugs. They're bringing crime. They're rapists. And some, I assume, are good people.*

Much of the mainstream media reacted with skepticism to Trump's throwing his hat into the presidential ring. The *New York Times* story ran the headline "Donald Trump, Pushing Someone Rich, Offers Himself," and the article began,

> *Donald J. Trump, the garrulous real estate developer whose name has adorned apartment buildings, hotels, Trump-brand neckties and Trump-brand steaks, announced on Tuesday his entry into the 2016 presidential race, brandishing his wealth and fame as chief qualifications in an improbable quest for the Republican nomination.*

CNN.com used a nickname in its headline: "Donald Trump Jumps In: The Donald's Latest White House Run Is Officially On." The story referred to his "lengthy and meandering 45-minute speech" and noted,

Many Americans now view him primarily as a reality TV star after 14 seasons of his "Apprentice" series, and his numerous flirtations with a presidential run — first in 1987, then 1999 and again in 2004, 2008 and most recently in 2011 — have left voters eye-rolling as he prompted yet another round of will-he or won't-he speculation.

The Democrats also took a mocking tone, with Democratic National Committee spokesperson Holly Shulman saying in a statement,

Today, Donald Trump became the second major Republican candidate to announce for president in two days. He adds some much-needed seriousness that has previously been lacking from the GOP field, and we look forward to hearing more about his ideas for the nation.

But despite being one of seventeen Republicans vying for the presidential nomination, Trump polled well and soon established himself as one of the party's viable candidates. He rallied behind the slogan "Make America Great Again" and campaigned on fighting illegal immigration and Islamic terrorism, reducing the national debt, and keeping jobs in the United States.

By early 2016, he had carved out another position that distinguished him from the rest of the Republican field.

He was praising Russia and its leader, Vladimir Putin.

3

"I will get all of Putins team to buy in"

The Republican Party had not typically sought close ties with Russia. Ronald Reagan, the party's most revered president of the past few decades, had labeled the Soviet Union "an evil empire" and accelerated an arms race that some credited with leading to the union's breakup. At the height of the Cold War a few decades earlier, Wisconsin Republican senator Joseph McCarthy led a crusade against communists and Soviet spies in the United States, with future Trump lawyer Roy Cohn at his side.

Early in the 2016 presidential campaign, Jeb Bush, then considered a strong contender for the Republican nomination, was advocating a harder line against Russia. In an October 2015 Reuters interview, Bush called Putin a "bully," pledged to counteract Russia's military support of Syria, and favored an extension of sanctions to punish Russia for its military aggression in Ukraine.

Donald Trump, a political outsider compared to the brother and son of two presidents named Bush, was taking the opposite tack, calling for closer relations with Russia and saying he would get along well with Putin. "He is a strong leader. What am I gonna say, he's a weak leader?" Donald Trump said of Putin on NBC's *Meet the Press* on December 20, 2015. "He's making mincemeat out of our president."

In a March 2016 tweet, Trump called the NATO alliance, which excludes Russia, "obsolete." Press accounts reported that Russian political analysts considered Trump pro-Russia, and in an April 4, 2016, article, the conservative magazine *National Review* referred to him as "The Kremlin's Candidate."

Trump's dealings with Russia far predate his run for president. His first reported visit was a trip to Moscow in 1987, and he pursued projects in Russia in the 1990s and early 2000s. The 2013 Miss Universe pageant, then co-owned by Trump, was held in Moscow that November, with Trump present. Soon afterward, his real estate company entered into talks with people involved with the pageant to build a Trump Tower Moscow.

The Trump Organization, which Donald Trump runs, oversees real estate ventures across numerous countries. Some of these are licensing deals in which developers and management companies pay to apply the Trump name to the project. That was the case with Trump Tower Moscow (also known as Trump Moscow), which was discussed at various times between 2013 and 2016, sometimes involving individuals with high-level connections to the Russian government.

The first of these talks took place between the Trump Organization and the Crocus Group, a Russian real estate conglomerate owned by Aras Agalarov, an Azerbaijani Russian billionaire. The Agalarov-owned Crocus City Hall hosted the 2013 Miss Universe pageant, and Agalarov's son Emin sang there. To get the Trump Tower Moscow project off the ground, Emin Agalarov and Irakili "Ike" Kaveladze negotiated on behalf of Crocus, with the occasional help of British music publicist and manager Robert Goldstone, while Donald Trump Jr. was the Trump Organization's point person.

All looked positive in the beginning. Kaveladze and Trump Jr. signed a preliminary agreement of terms in December 2013, and Donald Trump OK'd the deal, which would give the Trump Organization a flat 3.5 percent commission on all sales, with no licensing fees or incentives. The two sides continued to discuss development plans after that. In January 2014, the Crocus Group proposed building an eight-hundred-unit 194-meter high rise to be situated on the Crocus City Hall site in Moscow, where the Miss Universe pageant had been held. Ivanka Trump, Donald

Trump's daughter, became involved in these talks and toured the site with Emin Agalarov in February 2014. From March through July, the two organizations hashed out design standards and other aspects.

But in September 2014, the Trump Organization quit responding in a timely fashion to the Crocus Group's communications, and contact between the two organizations became less and less frequent until November 24, 2014, the date of their last apparent correspondence. Trump Tower Moscow appeared to have stalled in the planning stages, never reaching the point of construction.

Still, the idea of a Trump Tower Moscow was far from dead, and a complicated figure in our tale was about to revive it.

Felix Sater was a Moscow-born real estate advisor based in New York. He also was a two-time convicted felon with Russian mob ties who became an informant for US intelligence agencies. Sater was convicted of first-degree assault and spent fifteen months in prison after a 1991 bar fight in Manhattan in which he stabbed another man in the face with a broken cocktail glass, busted his jaw, severed some nerves, and caused 110 stitches' worth of lacerations. In 1998, he pleaded guilty to fraud for his involvement in a Russian Mafia stock scheme, but instead of serving prison time, he became a secret informant for organized crime investigations. Loretta Lynch, who had been the US attorney in the Eastern District in New York before becoming attorney general under President Obama, credited Sater with "providing information crucial to national security and the conviction of over 20 individuals."

Sater's information gathering extended to unearthing an al-Qaida assassination plot against then-president George Bush and helping the military track down the mastermind of the 9/11 terrorist attacks on the World Trade Center and Pentagon. "He provided the telephone number of Osama bin Laden," US District Court judge I. Leo Glasser said at a May 2019 hearing that addressed the unsealing of Sater's criminal records. "He has done an awful lot of very interesting and dangerous things."

As Sater told the *Los Angeles Times* in a 2017 interview, "I was building Trump Towers by day and hunting Bin Laden by night."

Sater had done work for Donald Trump as managing director of the high-end real estate firm Bayrock Group, which was located in Trump Tower in Manhattan. Sater collaborated with the Trump Organization to develop numerous Trump-branded buildings. Some, such as proposed projects in Phoenix and Denver, never happened, although, Sater told the *Washington Post*, he and Trump traveled together to Denver to evaluate plans. But the organization did construct the Trump International Hotel & Tower Fort Lauderdale and, in Lower Manhattan, Trump SoHo, which broke ground in 2006. Around this time, Bayrock moved its office to the same floor as the Trump Organization.

As early as 2005, Sater also had eyes on developing a Trump Tower Moscow, and he located a shuttered pencil factory as a potential site. Sater told the *Washington Post* that he worked closely with Trump as architectural plans were drawn up and the developer brought Russian investors to Trump's office to discuss the project. "It's ridiculous that I wouldn't be investing in Russia," Trump said in a 2007 deposition for a defamation suit he had filed against a former biographer. "Russia is one of the hottest places in the world for investment."

Acting, he said, on Trump's request, Sater accompanied the developer's children Ivanka Trump and Donald Trump Jr. on a Moscow trip in the mid-2000s. He said that he even arranged for Ivanka to get a private Kremlin tour, which culminated in her sitting in President Vladimir Putin's chair.

At the height of their activities together, Sater told the *Post*, he would speak with Trump "sometimes more than 20 times in a single week."

In a deposition for a 2013 lawsuit, Trump said of Sater, "If he were sitting in the room right now, I really wouldn't know what he looked like."

In September 2015, Sater, then forty-nine, contacted Michael Cohen, the Trump Organization's executive vice president and Donald Trump's personal counsel. Now working on behalf of a Russian real estate corporation — I. C. Expert Investment Company, controlled by apartment developer Andrei Vladimirovich Rozov — Sater relayed a proposal to the Trump team: I. C. Expert would license the Trump name and brand to construct a Trump Tower Moscow.

By this time, Donald Trump was running for president of the United States and, in theory, had to be more mindful about accepting foreign monies and engaging in business that might be considered a conflict of interest down the line. Nonetheless, he gave Cohen approval to negotiate with I. C. Expert, and Cohen provided project updates directly to Trump throughout 2015 and well into 2016 as the candidate moved toward locking up the Republican nomination. Cohen also discussed the project with Ivanka Trump and Donald Trump Jr. over the fall of 2015.

In the meantime, yet another Russian party was interested in getting into the Trump Tower Moscow business. Russian businessman Giorgi Rtskhiladze had worked on a development deal with the Trump Organization in Batumi, Georgia, and now he was communicating with Cohen about developing a Trump Tower Moscow. On September 22, 2015, the same month in which Sater reached out to Cohen, Cohen sent preliminary Trump Tower Moscow designs to Rtskhiladze.

"I look forward to your reply about his spectacular project in Moscow," Cohen wrote in an accompanying note.

Rtskhiladze passed along Cohen's note to an associate, emailing, "If we could organize the meeting in New York at the highest level of the Russian Government and Mr. Trump, this project would definitely receive worldwide attention."

This was the first known linking of the Russian government to Trump Tower Moscow.

Rtskhiladze sent Cohen two emails on September 24, one with an attached letter addressed to the mayor of Moscow. The letter, as translated by Rtskhiladze, called Trump Moscow "a symbol of stronger economic, business and cultural relationships between New York and Moscow and therefore United States and the Russian Federation." Another Rtskhiladze email sent three days later proposed that the Trump Organization partner with Global Development Group LLC, which was controlled by a Russian architect and his business partner.

But Cohen turned down Rtskhiladze's proposal because the Trump Organization was moving ahead with I. C. Expert and Felix Sater. The

Trump Organization and I. C. Expert completed a letter of intent between October 13 and November 2, 2015, for a Trump-branded Moscow building that would include about "250 first class, luxury residential condominiums," a "first class, luxury hotel consisting of approximately 15 floors and containing not fewer than 150 hotel rooms," and office units. The Trump Organization would receive 1–5 percent of all condominium sales, 3 percent of rental and other commercial revenues, and, on the hotel side, a base fee of 3 percent of gross operating revenues for the first five years and 4 percent after that, plus 20 percent of the operating profit. The letter of intent also provided for the Trump Organization to receive a $4 million "up-front fee" before breaking ground.

A lucrative deal, estimated to be potentially worth $1 billion, it would provide the Trump Organization with significant earnings over Trump Moscow's lifetime without requiring major financial commitments or liabilities.

The Trump Organization transmitted its letter of intent on November 2. The following day, in an email to Cohen, Sater explicitly linked the project to Trump's presidential campaign.

"Buddy our boy can become President of the USA and we can engineer it," Sater wrote to Cohen. "I will get all of Putins team to buy in on this. I will manage this process.... Michael, Putin gets on stage with Donald for a ribbon cutting for Trump Moscow, and Donald owns the republican nomination. And possibly beats Hillary and our boy is in.... We will manage this process better than anyone. You and I will get Donald and Vladimir on a stage together very shortly. That's the game changer."

About thirty-five minutes later, Sater added in another email,

Donald doesn't stare down, he negotiates and understands the economic issues and Putin only want to deal with a pragmatic leader, and a successful business man is a good candidate for someone who knows how to negotiate. "Business, politics, whatever it all is the same for someone who knows how to deal."

I think I can get Putin to say that at the Trump Moscow press conference.

If he says it we own this election. Americas most difficult adversary agreeing that Donald Trump is a good guy to negotiate....

We can own this election.

Michael my next steps are very sensitive with Putins very very close people, we can pull this off.

Michael lets go. 2 boys from Brooklyn getting a USA president elected. This is good really good.

4

"Sanders and Trump — we support them"

Let us skip ahead for a moment to August 2, 2016. Donald Trump had officially become the Republican presidential nominee a few weeks earlier, and the party was rallying around the still-controversial candidate. So it was that the Florida for Trump Facebook page received this message from someone named Matt Skiber:

> *Hi there! I'm a member of Being Patriotic online community. Listen, we've got an idea. Florida is still a purple state and we need to paint it red. If we lose Florida, we lose America. We can't let it happen, right? What about organizing a YUGE pro-Trump flash mob in every Florida town? We are currently reaching out to local activists, and we've got the folks who are okay to be in charge of organizing their events almost everywhere in FL. However, we still need your support. What do you think about that? Are you in?*

Matt Skiber was not a real person. He was concocted by the Russia-based Internet Research Agency to appear to be a US-based pro-Trump activist, and now this fictitious persona was reaching out to actual Trump workers to organize events. This is how the Russian government was pulling the virtual strings on the 2016 presidential election: creating fake accounts and fake people to convince real accounts and real people to do their bidding to help Donald Trump get elected president.

The IRA employed such manipulative tactics well before Trump announced his candidacy. By the spring of 2014, the organization had established an entire wing devoted to influencing US public opinion through online media. Internally they called this the Translator Department. Its employees did their work on computers, but some also traveled to the United States to gather intelligence, including four IRA workers who applied for visas with the US State Department claiming to be friends who had met at a party. Two of them, Anna Bogacheva and Aleksandra Krylova, were allowed entrance to the country on June 4, 2014, under these false pretenses.

IRA specialists focused on Facebook, YouTube, and Twitter — and eventually Tumblr and Instagram. By 2015, the IRA was creating larger social media groups and public pages that pretended to be aligned with US political and grassroots organizations. So although one might assume that @TEN_GOP represented the Tennessee Republican Party, it actually was an IRA-run Twitter account. Likewise, the IRA created accounts that appeared to be affiliated with the anti-immigration push, the Tea Party, the Black Lives Matter movement, and other causes across the political spectrum.

By February 2016, internal IRA documents were pushing support for the Trump campaign and opposition to the campaign of Hillary Clinton, who had served as secretary of state under President Obama and was seen as continuing his relatively hard line against Putin's intervention in Ukraine and alleged human rights violations. Before Clinton had secured the Democratic presidential nomination, the IRA backed Bernie Sanders, the Democratic Socialist challenging her in the primaries. An IRA memo to employees was explicit in stating the organization's preferences: "Main idea: Use any opportunity to criticize Hillary and the rest (except Sanders and Trump — we support them)."

When the IRA produced an internal critique of the Facebook group it had created called Secured Borders, the chief evaluator complained about the "lower number of posts dedicated to criticizing Hillary Clinton" and instructed the specialist in charge of that page that "it is imperative to intensify criticizing Hillary Clinton."

As the US election grew closer, the array of IRA Facebook groups grew, representing such supposed conservative organizations as Being Patriotic, Stop All Immigrants, Secured Borders, and Tea Party News; such purported black social justice groups as Black Matters, Blacktivist, and Don't Shoot Us; as well as other affinity groups like LGBT United and United Muslims of America. The IRA promoted these groups through ads that popped up on Facebook users' newsfeeds. Facebook reported that the IRA spent about $100,000 buying more than thirty-five thousand such ads.

As of March 2016, many of these Facebook ads were attacking Hillary Clinton. A March 18 ad depicted Clinton with a caption that read, in part, "If one day God lets this liar enter the White House as a president — that day would be a real national tragedy." An April 6 Black Matters Facebook ad called for a "flashmob" of Americans to "take a photo with #HillaryClintonForPrison2016 or #nohillary2016."

At the same time, other IRA ads were promoting Trump. An April 19 Tea Party News Instagram ad encouraged people to "make a patriotic team of young Trump supporters" who would upload photos with the hashtag #KIDS4TRUMP. Over the next few months, dozens of pro-Trump Facebook ads followed, often from the groups Being Patriotic, Stop All Invaders, and Secured Borders.

The IRA social media accounts wound up reaching tens of millions of Americans and attracted hundreds of thousands of followers. The United Muslims of America Facebook group had more than three hundred thousand followers before Facebook took it down in mid-2017. Also on Facebook, Don't Shoot Us had more than 250,000 followers, Being Patriotic had more than 200,000 followers, and Secured Borders had more than 130,000 followers. Facebook reported that by the time of their deactivation in August 2017, the IRA accounts had produced more than eighty thousand posts, reached at least 29 million people in the United States, and "may have reached an estimated 126 million people."

The IRA's expenditures on these ads were not reported to the Federal Election Commission, and the people behind these efforts did not register, as required by law, as foreign agents with the US Department of Justice.

Then there was Twitter, where IRA bots did their work. The Translator Department created fake accounts to post original material, to promote these posts, and to communicate with actual US Twitter users via tweets and private messages. Aside from @TEN_GOP, the IRA produced such Twitter accounts as @Jenn_Abrams, a supposed Virginia Trump supporter who accumulated 70,000 followers; @Pamela_Moore13, a supposed Texas Trump supporter who also drew 70,000 followers; and @America_1st, an anti-immigration account with 24,000 followers. Another IRA account, @MissouriNewsUS, gathered 3,800 followers for its pro-Sanders and anti-Clinton posts. Some IRA tweets went viral, such as this one from @Jenn_Abrams that elicited more than forty thousand responses: "To those people who hate the Confederate Flag. Did you know that the flag and the war wasn't about slavery, it was all about money."

US media outlets quoted tweets from these fake accounts and presented them as comments from actual people. Michael McFaul, who was the US ambassador to Russia for two years under President Obama, responded to @Jenn_Abrams tweets in 2015 and 2016. People supportive of the Trump campaign — including Trump advisor Roger Stone, Fox News personality Sean Hannity, and Michael Flynn Jr. (son of Trump campaign advisor Michael Flynn) — also retweeted and responded to Russia-created tweets, as did people officially affiliated with the Trump campaign.

In January 2018, Twitter publicly identified 3,814 accounts associated with the IRA and said that in the ten weeks leading up to the 2016 presidential election, these accounts posted 175,993 tweets, "approximately 8.4% of which were election-related." The company also said it had identified 50,258 automated Russian accounts, or bots, that produced more than a million tweets over those ten weeks. Twitter announced that it notified about 1.4 million people that they may have been in contact with an IRA account.

Here are some of the messages that the IRA pushed in 2016:

April 6: "You know, a great number of black people support us saying that #HillaryClintonIsNotMyPresident."

April 7: "I say no to Hillary Clinton/I say no to manipulation."

April 19: "JOIN our #HillaryClintonForPrison2016."

May 10: "Donald wants to defeat terrorism…Hillary wants to
sponsor it."

May 19: "Vote Republican, vote Trump, and support the Second
Amendment!"

May 24: "Hillary Clinton Doesn't Deserve the Black Vote."

June 7: "Trump is our only hope for a better future!"

June 30: "#NeverHillary #HillaryForPrison #Hillary4Prison #Hill
ary4Prison2016 #Trump2016 #Trump #Trump4President."

July 20: "Ohio Wants Hillary 4 Prison."

August 4: "Hillary Clinton has already committed voter fraud during the Democrat Iowa Caucus."

August 10: "We cannot trust Hillary to take care of our veterans!"

October 14: "Among all the candidates Donald Trump is the one
and only who can defend the police from terrorists."

October 19: "Hillary is a Satan, and her crimes and lies had proved
just how evil she is."

As minority voters were considered a Clinton stronghold, the IRA
worked to discourage them from turning out on Election Day. The Instagram account Woke Blacks posted a message on October 16 asserting
that a "particular hype and hatred for Trump is misleading people and
forcing Blacks to vote for Killary. We cannot resort to the lesser of two
devils. Then we'd surely be better off without voting AT ALL."

The IRA paid for an Instagram ad promoting this November 3 post on
its Blacktivist account: "Choose peace and vote for Jill Stein. Trust me, it's
not a wasted vote." Jill Stein was the Green Party's 2016 nominee for president. She wound up receiving just 1.07 percent of the popular vote, but in

the crucial states of Wisconsin, Michigan, and Pennsylvania, her vote totals eclipsed Trump's margins of victory over Clinton.

United Muslims of America posted antivote messages claiming that American Muslims were "boycotting elections today. Most of the American Muslim voters refuse to vote for Hillary Clinton because she wants to continue the war on Muslims in the middle east and voted yes for invading Iraq."

In the summer of 2016, the IRA's fictitious US personas started spreading the message that the Democrats were engaged in voter fraud. On August 4, they bought Facebook ads promoting a post from their Stop A.I. account that alleged, "Hillary Clinton already has committed voter fraud during the Democrat Iowa Caucus." A week later, the group's @TEN _GOP Twitter account stated that North Carolina was investigating voter fraud allegations against the Democrats. On November 2, that same account alleged "#VoterFraud by counting tens of thousands of ineligible mail in Hillary votes being reported in Broward County, Florida."

These claims were not true.

The group worked to spread its messages in the physical world as well as the virtual one. In November 2015, the IRA promoted a "confederate rally" in Houston, announcing on its Stand for Freedom Instagram page, "Good evening buds! Well I am planning to organize a confederate rally....in Houston on the 14 of November and I want more people to attend."

From June 2016 through the election (and beyond), the IRA regularly organized US rallies, almost all centered on the presidential race, with the purpose of promoting Trump or opposing Clinton. IRA employees posed as US grassroots activists who enlisted help from actual Trump supporters and campaign workers without ever meeting them in person; IRA specialists often claimed they could not personally attend the events due to preexisting conflicts or being located elsewhere in the United States. The IRA pushed these events through their fake social media accounts and also reached out to administrators of large political social media groups to get them to promote and advertise the rallies.

So United Muslims of America, the same IRA account that would urge blacks to boycott the election over Clinton's supposed desire to "continue the war on Muslims," promoted a July 9 Washington, DC, rally called "Support Hillary. Save American Muslims." The group bought Facebook ads to publicize the rally, ordered posters, and recruited an actual American individual to depict Clinton at the rally displaying a sign that read, "I think Sharia Law will be a powerful new direction of freedom."

More bogus accounts, including the Being Patriotic Facebook group and the @March_for_Trump Twitter handle, promoted two New York political rallies: "March for Trump" on June 25 and "Down with Hillary" on July 23. Not only did these accounts buy Facebook ads to promote the events, but they also used false US personas to send messages to actual people asking them to help organize the rallies and to participate, offering money to cover expenses. A Trump campaign volunteer agreed to provide signs for the "March for Trump" after being contacted by the @March_for_Trump Twitter account. The email address allforusa @yahoo.com sent "March for Trump" news releases to members of the press. A Facebook account for the fictional Matt Skiber contacted people to serve as recruiters for the rally, telling one he would "give you money to print posters and get a megaphone." The group used the email address of another false US persona, joshmilton024@gmail.com, to send press releases to more than thirty media outlets for the "Down with Hillary" rally at Trump Tower.

These same forces pushed a series of "Florida Goes Trump" rallies that took place on August 20. Again, they used fake personas to communicate with Trump campaign staffers as well as local grassroots groups to solicit help in coordinating and participating in the rallies. @March_for_Trump tweeted that it was seeking volunteers for "a series of rallies across the state of Florida," and good old Matt Skiber sought help from the actual Florida for Trump organization. Around the same time, the IRA used the stolen identity of an actual US person with the initials "T.W." to send emails to Florida grassroots groups that read,

My name is [T.W.] and I represent a conservative patriot community named as "Being Patriotic."…So we're gonna organize a flash mob across Florida to support Mr. Trump. We clearly understand that the elections winner will be predestined by purple states. And we must win Florida.… We've got a lot of volunteers in 25 locations, and it's just the beginning. We're currently choosing venues for each location and recruiting more activists. This is why we ask you to spread this info and participate in the flash mob.

Facebook ads bought to promote "Florida Goes Trump" reached more than 59,000 Facebook users in Florida, and more than 8,300 Facebook users clicked on them and were routed to the Being Patriotic page. The Russian-created Instagram group Tea Party News purchased ads to promote the rallies as well. The so-called Matt Skiber enlisted an actual person to acquire signs and a prison uniform, another pro-Trump worker agreed to build a cage on a flatbed truck, and the @March_for_Trump account recruited a woman to appear in that cage as Hillary Clinton wearing the prison uniform at a West Palm Beach rally. These people were all paid for their efforts.

An official-looking poster for October 2 rallies in Pittsburgh and Philadelphia — in the important swing state of Pennsylvania — depicted a serious-looking, dirty-faced miner above the message "MINERS FOR TRUMP. BRING BACK OUR JOBS. How many PA workers lost their jobs due to Obama's destructive policies? HELP MR. TRUMP FIX IT! #TRUMPPENCE2016." In April 2019, the *Philadelphia Inquirer* reported that the miner in the photo, Lip Hipshire, actually died at age fifty-seven in 1987 from black lung complications. His son Ronnie Hipshire complained in the paper, "How in the world did they steal that picture and use it for a campaign poster for Trump? It was something my dad would have never went for. I mean, he was a staunch Democrat, my dad was. He always believed that Democrats [were] for the working people and Republicans [were] for the companies, and to see his picture supporting

Trump, it made me right sick in my stomach, knowing that Dad's picture had been used like that."

Even after Trump was elected, the IRA continued to stage rallies driven by fictitious US personas. They coordinated a November 12 New York rally to "show your support for President-elect Trump" as well as an *anti*-Trump New York rally that same day called "Trump is NOT My President." They also organized a November 19 "Charlotte against Trump" rally in Charlotte, North Carolina.

Posing as Americans, the Russians enlisted other Americans to do their bidding. They also sought to work closely with a more select group:

The Trump campaign itself.

5

"Consent of the person of interest"

By the fall of 2015, with Trump's presidential campaign well under way, it was clear that the Trump Tower Moscow deal was not just about real estate. It was engaging the top levels of Russian government.

"All we need is Putin on board and we are golden," Felix Sater emailed Michael Cohen on October 12, 2015. For a project of such size and scope as Trump Tower Moscow, Sater said that he needed approval from the Russian Federation government and its president. He told Cohen that a "meeting with Putin and top deputy is tentatively set for [October] 14th."

Sater later said Putin factored into his and Cohen's plans in ways that went beyond gaining the Russian president's approval. "My idea was to give a $50 million penthouse to Putin and charge $250 million more for the rest of the units," he told BuzzFeed News in November 2018. "All the oligarchs would line up to live in the same building as Putin."

Two weeks after the project's letter of intent was finalized on November 2, Ivanka Trump received an email from Lana Erchova, who said she was writing on behalf of her then-husband Dmitry Klokov. Klokov was a Russian electricity company communications director and former government official who happened to share his name with an accomplished Russian weight lifter.

"If you ask anyone who knows Russian to google my husband Dmitry Klokov, you'll see who he is close to and that he has done Putin's political campaigns," wrote Erchova, who identified herself as Lana E. Alexander and said that her husband could assist the Trump campaign. Ivanka

Trump forwarded the email to Cohen, who assumed Klokov was the famous weight lifter.

On November 18 and 19, Klokov and Cohen exchanged emails and had at least one telephone call, with Klokov describing himself as a "trusted person" who could provide "political synergy" and "synergy on a government level." Klokov suggested that Cohen travel to Russia to meet with him and an unidentified intermediary in order to facilitate a later meeting with "our person of interest," a.k.a. Russian president Vladimir Putin.

(Erchova, or someone purporting to be her, sent an email to our office in July 2018 saying, "At the end of 2015 and beginning of 2016 I was asked by my ex-husband to contact Ivanka Trump...and offer cooperation to Trump's team on behalf of the Russian officials." Erchova's email stated that the Russian officials would offer Donald Trump "land in Crimea among other things and unofficial meeting with Putin." We emailed back seeking further details, but Erchova did not answer.)

Cohen responded to Klokov that he was willing to meet with him and the intermediary, but any Russia meetings involving him or Trump would need to be "in conjunction with the [Trump Moscow] development and an official visit," which required a formal invitation. Klokov, who had proposed an informal visit, advised Cohen not to combine discussions about the Trump Moscow project with a potential meeting with the "person of interest."

"I would suggest separating your negotiations and our proposal to meet," Klokov emailed Cohen on November 18. "I assure you, after the meeting level of projects and their capacity can be completely different, having the most important support."

In another email to Cohen the following day, Klokov said there was "no bigger warranty in any project than consent of the person of interest." Stressing that he was not reaching out on behalf of any business, Klokov wrote that such a meeting, if well publicized, could have a "phenomenal" impact "in a business dimension."

But Cohen ultimately turned Klokov down, saying that talks were under way with the project's developer — that is, Sater and I. C. Expert — to arrange "a formal invite for the two to meet." After that, Klokov apparently disappeared from the picture.

Yet by the end of 2015, Sater had yet to set up his promised meeting with Russian government officials, so Cohen texted him on December 30, saying he was "setting up the meeting myself." In mid-January 2016, Cohen emailed Dmitry Peskov, the Russian government's press secretary, seeking to be put in contact with Putin's chief of staff, Sergei Ivanov:

Dear Mr. Peskov,

Over the past few months, I have been working with a company based in Russia regarding the development of a Trump Tower-Moscow project in Moscow City.

Without getting into lengthy specifics, the communication between our two sides has stalled. As this project is too important, I am hereby requesting your assistance.

I respectfully request someone, preferably you, contact me so that I might discuss the specifics as well as arranging meetings with the appropriate individuals.

I thank you in advance for your assistance and look forward to hearing from you soon.

Although Cohen initially told Congress and our office that he did not recall receiving a reply to this inquiry and that he abandoned Trump Moscow in January 2016, that was not the case. Cohen continued to push the project forward through June 2016 and updated Trump, who was closing in on the Republican presidential nomination, throughout the process. Cohen received a response to his email to Peskov and spoke with the press secretary's personal assistant, Elena Poliakova, on January 20. He described the project to her and asked for help in, among other things, securing land and financing.

Cohen later said that he could not recall any direct follow-up from

Poliakova or other Russian government officials on this matter, and our investigation found no evidence to the contrary. But that conversation between Cohen and Poliakova still may have had an effect, given that Sater texted Cohen the following day, "Call me when you have a few minutes to chat.... It's about Putin they called today."

Sater and Cohen soon were swapping drafts of a formal invitation to be issued to Cohen for travel to Moscow to discuss the Trump Tower. Sater sent Cohen the final version of the invitation on January 25, signed by Andrey Ryabinskiy of the company MJH. It invited Cohen to travel to Moscow "for a working visit" about the "prospects of development and the construction business in Russia," "the various land plots available suited for construction of this enormous Tower," and "the opportunity to co-ordinate a follow up visit to Moscow by Mr. Donald Trump." Cohen later said he did not take this trip because the land plot situation remained unsettled.

Yet opportunity after opportunity kept arising for Cohen and Trump to visit Moscow. Sater emailed Cohen in December 2015 trying to work out logistics to bring the two of them to the Russian capital, with Russia's VTB Bank to issue this invitation because "politically" neither Putin's office nor the Ministry of Foreign Affairs could do so.

"VTB Bank CEO Andrey Kostin will be at all meetings with Putin so that it is a business meeting not political," Sater wrote.

Sater requested copies of Cohen's and Trump's passports to facilitate their travel, and Cohen must have been seriously considering the trip because he texted back an image of his passport and requested a copy of Trump's from a Trump Organization executive assistant.

Sater and Cohen still were discussing a Moscow trip in the spring of 2016. Sater wrote on April 20, "The People wanted to know when you are coming?" Sater asked about it again on May 4, wondering about the trip's timing in relation to the Republican National Convention, set to take place July 18–21 in Cleveland:

I had a chat with Moscow. ASSUMING the trip does happen the question is before or after the convention. I said I believe, but don't

know for sure, that's it's probably after the convention. Obviously the
pre-meeting trip (you only) can happen anytime you want but the 2
big guys where [sic] the question. I said I would confirm and revert....
Let me know about If I was right by saying I believe after Cleveland
and also when you want to speak to them and possibly fly over.

"My trip before Cleveland," Cohen replied. "Trump once he becomes the nominee after the convention."

The next day Sater tried arranging for Cohen to travel to the St. Petersburg International Economic Forum, which he described as Russia's version of the prestigious World Economic Forum in Davos, Switzerland, on June 16–19, as a guest of Russian press secretary Peskov.

"He wants to meet there with you and possibly introduce you to either Putin or Medvedev," Sater said in a text, later adding, "This is perfect. The entire business class of Russia will be there as well. He said anything you want to discuss including dates and subjects are on the table to discuss."

"Works for me," Cohen replied the following day.

But although plans for this trip progressed through early June, Cohen ultimately lacked confidence that the Russian officials would meet with him. When he met Sater on June 14 in the Trump Tower lobby in New York, Cohen told Sater he would not be traveling to the forum after all.

Other chances for Trump to visit Russia didn't pan out either. Trump had told Cohen he might make such a trip if it would push forward the Trump Moscow project, and Trump asked Cohen to coordinate his schedule with then–campaign manager Corey Lewandowski. But Cohen knew that Trump's volume of campaign activity would make such a trip near impossible before the convention, and the matter fell through the cracks.

Trump also was invited to the St. Petersburg International Economic Forum by Sergei Prikhodko, a Russian deputy prime minister, via one of Ivanka Trump's fashion industry contacts. Citing his packed campaign schedule, Trump declined that invitation in March 2016.

Yet another party desired Trump's presence at that forum as well.

Around the same time that Prikhodko was inviting Trump, a New York–based investment banker, Robert Foresman, began reaching out to Trump's people on behalf of Russian presidential aide Anton Kobyakov to try to get Trump to speak at the St. Petersburg International Economic Forum. After an introduction from Mark Burnett, who produced Trump's NBC show *The Apprentice*, Foresman emailed Rhona Graff, Trump's executive assistant at the Trump Organization, and touted his expertise with Russia and Ukraine; he wrote that he had established an early "private channel" between Vladimir Putin and former president George W. Bush.

Now Foresman was saying that "senior Kremlin officials" had approached him about Trump, so he wanted to meet with the candidate, campaign manager Lewandowski, or "another relevant person." Foresman followed up with emails in April and early May suggesting that he might convey his information to Donald Trump Jr., Eric Trump, or policy advisor Stephen Miller.

Were these overtures ever acted upon?

We do not know. We tried to determine the answer in our investigation, but nothing came up.

Investigations can be frustrating that way.

But do not worry about losing this thread. Those would be far from the last communications between the Russian Federation and the Trump Organization.

6

"Mr. Trump posted about our event in Miami!"

I'd like to pause here to interject a note about a term we have heard often in discussions of this investigation: "collusion."

The president has repeated it constantly on Twitter and in other public pronouncements; one might say that "No obstruction, no collusion!" has ascended to the level of mantra with him. The word has surfaced in countless media reports and much commentary as well. Did the Trump campaign *collude* with the Russian government to interfere in the 2016 presidential election? That question keeps getting asked.

But technically speaking, "collusion" is not a word that was relevant to our investigation. The United States Code — that is, this country's code of laws — does not include "collusion" as a specific offense. Federal criminal law also does not employ the term. Our office's mission, as stated in the special counsel appointment order, was to determine whether the Trump campaign *coordinated* with the Russian government's election-interference activities. "Coordination" means that two sides have come to an agreement on a matter, either directly stated or implicitly understood. They are working together. They are in sync. Discussing a situation does not necessarily mean coordination. Even acting in response to another's party's actions does not necessarily mean coordination.

I trust you grasp this distinction.

My office was involved in a legal process. We were addressing what we could prove. That is the threshold for pursuing legal action. So we asked whether we could establish beyond a reasonable doubt that the Trump campaign and the Russian government coordinated election-interference activities.

If we could not prove such coordination, that does not mean such coordination did not take place. It just means we could not prove that it did.

Understand?

What is *not* in doubt is this: the Russian government worked to support the Trump campaign and to oppose the Clinton campaign.

Also not in doubt: the Russian government, in various ways and guises, made contact with the Trump campaign, and the Trump campaign used the Russians' work to try to win the election.

Was that the right thing for the Trump campaign to do?

That is for you to judge. My office was investigating the legality of the campaign's actions, not their morality, ethicality, or any other aspect.

Why was the Russian government so helpful to the Trump campaign? Did they view a Trump presidency as the likeliest route to overturning the Obama administration's sanctions? Were these actions linked to the Trump Organization's business dealings in Russia at the time?

We have tried to connect as many dots as possible, but you may have to fill in some of those blanks as well.

I hope we are clear on all of that.

Now we can get back to the Putin-backed Internet Research Agency's interactions with the Trump campaign.

The Internet Research Agency and the Trump campaign became connected in two different ways. Members and surrogates of the Trump campaign retweeted, reposted, and linked to pro-Trump/anti-Clinton material that the IRA published through its social media accounts. People associated with the Trump campaign promoted dozens of IRA-created tweets, posts, and other materials. Donald J. Trump Jr. and Eric Trump, the president's sons, cited or retweeted posts from the IRA's @TEN_GOP account.

For example, on October 26, 2016, Donald J. Trump retweeted,

"BREAKING Thousands of names changed on voter rolls in Indiana. Police investigating #VoterFraud. #DrainTheSwamp." And on November 2, 2016, he retweeted, "BREAKING: #VoterFraud by counting tens of thousands of ineligible mail in Hillary votes being reported in Broward County, Florida."

On the day before the election, November 7, 2016, Donald J. Trump Jr. also retweeted the IRA-created @Pamela_Moore13's tweet about Detroit residents speaking out "against the failed policies of Obama, Hillary & democrats."

Eric Trump retweeted this October 20, 2016, @TEN_GOP post: "BREAKING Hillary shuts down press conference when asked about DNC Operatives & #VoterFraud #debatenight #TrumpB."

Again, I must interject that these claims were *not true.*

Also retweeting @TEN_GOP were Kellyanne Conway, the third Trump campaign manager ("Mother of jailed sailor: 'Hold Hillary to same standards as my son on Classified info' #hillarysemail #Weiner Gate"); Michael Flynn, the Trump advisor who led the "Lock her up!" chants against Hillary Clinton at the Republican National Convention ("@realDonaldTrump & @mike_pence will be our next POTUS & VPO- TUS"); and Brad Parscale, the Trump campaign's digital media director ("Thousands of deplorables chanting to the media: 'Tell the truth!' RT if you also are done w/biased Media! #FridayFeeling").

Meanwhile, Trump himself posted a collection of photos on Facebook from the IRA-organized August 20 rallies in Florida with the note: "THANK YOU for your support Miami! My team just shared photos from your TRUMP SIGN WAVING DAY, yesterday! I love you—and there is no question—TOGETHER WE WILL MAKE AMERICA GREAT AGAIN!"

The IRA-created Matt Skiber posted a screenshot of Trump's Face- book page and sent a message to a US Tea Party activist that "Mr. Trump posted about our event in Miami! This is great!"

IRA employees, presenting themselves as US-based individuals and organizations, also contacted Trump campaign members to help execute rallies in the United States. These messages and emails included requests for signs and other materials as well as help in promoting and organizing the events. The IRA-created joshmilton024@gmail.com carried on an extended exchange with someone with a @donaldtrump.com email address about supplying Trump/Pence signs for the Florida rallies, getting Trump campaign affiliates' phone numbers, and adding rally locations.

So the Trump campaign worked with the IRA. But did Trump campaign officials *know* that these requests and social media posts were coming from foreign nationals? Even as these Trump campaigners were promoting numerous IRA-originated claims that had no basis in fact?

That remains hard to prove. But our office collected enough evidence to conclude that Yevgeniy Prigozhin ("Putin's chef"), his companies, and IRA employees had violated US law by using deception to undermine the federal agencies that regulate foreign influence in US elections. A grand jury handed down indictments on February 16, 2018, against the Internet Research Agency, Concord Management and Consulting, Concord Catering, Yevgeniy Viktorovich Prigozhin, and eight other individuals variously on counts of conspiracy to defraud the United States (by not registering as foreign agents or reporting election-related spending to the US government), conspiracy to commit wire fraud and bank fraud (in part by opening US accounts under false names to move money in and out of the country and to support and enrich the organization), and aggravated identity theft (by using actual people's names, Social Security numbers, and birth dates to commit bank and wire fraud, among other offenses).

So that was that. But aside from social media, the Russian government was pursuing other aggressive means to disrupt the 2016 presidential election and to work with the Trump campaign.

7

"Please tell me if i can help u"

The Russian military attacked the Hillary Clinton presidential campaign.

That sounds dramatic, but it is true. In the months leading up to the election, at a time when the Russian government was trying to forge connections with Donald Trump through his business dealings and political ambitions, it was conducting cyberwarfare against Clinton and the Democratic Party. And the Trump campaign reaped the benefits.

Here is how it worked.

The Russian Federation's Main Intelligence Directorate of the General Staff, otherwise known as the GRU, oversaw the military wing that carried out this offensive. Military Units 26165 and 74455 were responsible for the actual attacks.

Unit 26165 — a catchy name, I realize — was a cyberunit that targeted military, political, governmental, and nongovernmental organizations outside Russia, including in the United States. The unit boasted such specialties as developing malicious software ("malware"), conducting large-scale spear phishing campaigns (which often involved sending an email from an apparent trusted source that, when opened, gave the sender access to an account or network to steal data or to install malware), and mining for bitcoins. Unit 74455 focused on releasing documents stolen by Unit 26165 and hacking into entities such as state boards of elections, secretaries of state, and tech and software companies.

Unit 26165 began hacking the Democratic National Committee (DNC) and the Democratic Congressional Campaign Committee (DCCC)

in March 2016. Seeking access to such Democratic websites as democrats
.org, hillaryclinton.com, dnc.org, and dccc.org, the GRU officers sent
hundreds of spear phishing emails to the work and personal accounts of
Clinton campaign employees and volunteers. Between March 10 and
March 15, the unit sent about ninety spear phishing emails to hillaryclinton
.com email accounts, and on March 15, it began targeting Clinton workers' Gmail accounts as well as some dnc.org email accounts.

As a result, the GRU hacked many Clinton Campaign employees' and
volunteers' email accounts, including those of campaign chair John Podesta, junior volunteers on the campaign's advance team, informal campaign advisors, and a DNC employee. The GRU stole tens of thousands of
emails this way, including many Clinton Campaign–related communications.

By April 12, Unit 26165 had, via spear phishing, stolen a DCCC
employee's credentials to gain access to the DCCC computer network.
From there, it was able to compromise about twenty-nine different computers on the DCCC network. The GRU broke into the DNC network six
days later through a virtual private network connection that had been
established between the DNC and DCCC networks. Between April 18
and June 8, the GRU compromised more than thirty DNC network computers, including the DNC mail server and shared file server.

Unit 26165 then began installing various types of malware onto the
two networks: a credential-harvesting tool; a tool to compile and to com-
press data before it is removed from the network; a tool that enabled the
hackers to log keystrokes, to take screenshots, and to gather other data
from the infected computers; a tool to enable large-scale data transfers
via an encrypted connection between the targeted computers and those
controlled by the GRU; and something called X-Tunnel, which allowed
the stolen data from the targeted computers to be imported.

The thievery began soon after the GRU gained access to the DCCC
network. Unit 26165 downloaded malware onto the DCCC document
server on April 14, and the next day searched for files that included the
terms "Hillary," "DNC," "Cruz," and "Trump." The GRU compressed and

grabbed more than seventy gigabytes of election-related data from the DCCC shared file server on April 25.

The GRU stole DNC documents, including opposition research on Trump, after breaking into that network as well. Between May 25 and June 1, Unit 26165 accessed the DNC's mail server and swiped thousands of emails and attachments that later would be released by WikiLeaks.

But before WikiLeaks got involved, the GRU was releasing stolen documents to the public via two fictitious online personas: DCLeaks and Guccifer 2.0. Unit 26165 registered for the dcleaks.com domain on April 19 via a service that kept the registrant anonymous, and the GRU paid for it using bitcoin it had mined. The dcleaks.com landing page pointed to tranches of stolen documents, arranged by victim or subject matter, while other pages indexed the stolen emails being released. Sometimes these pages were password protected, at least until the GRU lifted the restrictions to allow public access.

The GRU began posting stolen documents, including those taken from people involved with the Clinton campaign, on the dcleaks.com site in June 2016. This material apparently came not from the DNC or DCCC networks but from the personal email accounts of, among others, a Clinton campaign advisor, a former DNC employee, a campaign employee, and four campaign volunteers. Thousands of documents were made public, offering up individuals' personal and financial information, internal campaign correspondences, and fund-raising information. DCLeaks also released a "United States Republican Party" portfolio containing about three hundred emails from Republican Party members and employees, political action committees, campaigns, state parties, and businesses.

The GRU operated a DCLeaks Facebook page to promote these releases and to communicate privately with reporters and other US individuals. It did the same using the @dcleaks Twitter account and the dcleaksproject@gmail.com account. GRU employees sent links and passwords to certain reporters to allow them early access to stolen files not yet made public, using the DCLeaks Facebook account on July 12 and

Twitter direct messaging on September 14. The DCLeaks website was not taken down until March 2017.

The DNC and its cyberresponse team announced on June 14, 2016, that representatives of the Russian government had breached its network and stolen documents. The following day, GRU officers created a WordPress blog under the name Guccifer 2.0, and after searches on a Moscow-based server managed by Unit 74455, they published a post claiming that the DNC hacker actually was a Romanian working on his own. The Guccifer 2.0 blog also began releasing stolen DNC and DCCC documents on that day.

Among the thousands of documents released on the Guccifer 2.0 site between June 15 and October 18 were DNC opposition research on Trump, internal documents discussing ways to approach politically sensitive issues, fund-raising documents, and analyses of congressional races. Guccifer 2.0 also released documents to reporters and news outlets. A June 27 email to the Smoking Gun website offered "exclusive access to some leaked emails linked [to] Hillary Clinton's staff," followed by a password and link to a locked portion of dclinks.com that contained an archive of emails stolen by Unit 26165. As had become apparent, the efforts of DCLeaks, Guccifer 2.0, and the GRU's hacking units were being managed together.

The GRU released more materials via Guccifer 2.0 through August 2016, sending a congressional candidate material about his opponent, a Florida blogger a chunk of stolen DCCC data, and a reporter documents concerning the Black Lives Matter movement. Guccifer 2.0 also exchanged private Twitter messages with Roger Stone, a former Trump team official who was still informally advising the campaign.

"Thank u for writing back…do u find anything interesting in the docs i posted?" read an early August Guccifer 2.0 message to Stone.

"Please tell me if i can help u anyhow," read another one, sent August 17. "It would be a great pleasure to me."

On September 9, 2016, the Guccifer 2.0 persona asked about a stolen DCCC document that had been posted online: "What do u think of the info on the turnout model for the democrats entire presidential campaign?"

"Pretty standard," Stone responded.

In addition to its operations against the Clinton campaign and Democratic organizations, the Russians cyberattacked offices administering US
elections and the election apparatus. They hacked state boards of elections, secretaries of state, county governments, and individuals who
worked for these entities. They also targeted private technology firms that
manufactured and administered election-related software and hardware,
including voter registration software and electronic polling stations.

By the summer of 2016, the GRU had attacked state and local computer networks via software vulnerabilities in their websites. They sent
malicious codes to websites to break into registered-voter databases, such
as in June 2016, when the GRU compromised the Illinois State Board of
Elections' network, gained access to a database containing information
about millions of registered Illinois voters, and extracted data about
thousands of voters. Russian forces attempted to hack into more than
two dozen states — that is, at least half of the United States — in this
manner.

After spear phishing employees at a voting technology company, the
GRU's Unit 74455 installed malware on its network. In the days before
the election, the unit also sent spear phishing emails to the accounts of
more than 120 Florida county officials who were administering the election. Attached to these emails was a Word document infected with malware that gave the GRU access to each computer. The FBI determined
that the GRU hacked into at least one Florida county government network this way.

To put this all in simple terms: an adversarial foreign government was
conducting war against the United States and the integrity of its
elections.

And it was escalating.

8

"A bright, well-connected, sadistic sociopath"

WikiLeaks founder Julian Assange, whose international organization was devoted to leaking confidential and classified documents, was no Hillary Clinton fan. Living in asylum in London's Ecuadorian embassy to avoid a Swedish international arrest warrant on sexual assault allegations, the Australian provocateur expressed his antipathy to the Democratic presidential contender in a note to WikiLeaks colleagues about the 2016 US election:

> We believe it would be much better for the GOP to win...Dems+_ Media+Liberals woudl [sic] then form a block to reign [sic] in their worst qualities.... With Hillary in charge, GOP will be pushing for her worst qualities., dems+media+neoliberals will be mute....She's a bright, well-connected, sadistic sociopath.

Assange's organization thus found its interests aligned with those of the Russian military cyberunits working to torpedo Clinton's presidential aspirations and to boost Donald Trump's. In March 2016, WikiLeaks released a searchable archive of about thirty thousand Hillary Clinton emails obtained through the Freedom of Information Act. In a private message to another WikiLeaks staffer, a WikiLeaks tech worker wrote that the goal of these releases was to be "useful" and to "annoy Hillary" — and for WikiLeaks "to be seen to be a resource/player in the US election, because eit [sic] may encourage people to send us even more important leaks."

That message was received.

After the GRU released its first batch of stolen materials on the DCLeaks site, a representative of that Russian branch sent a direct message from @dcleaks to @WikiLeaks on June 14:

You announced your organization was preparing to publish more Hillary's emails. We are ready to support you. We have sensitive information too. In particular, her financial documents. Let's do it together. What do you think about publishing our info at the same moment?

While DCLeaks was reaching out to WikiLeaks, WikiLeaks was reaching out to the GRU's other leaking persona, Guccifer 2.0. "Send any new material [stolen from the DNC] here for us to review, and it will have a much higher impact than what you are doing," WikiLeaks told Guccifer 2.0 in a Twitter direct message on June 22.

WikiLeaks wrote again to Guccifer 2.0 on July 6, "If you have anything hillary related we want it in the next tweo [sic] days prefable [sic] because the DNC is approaching and she will solidify bernie [Sanders] supporters behind her after."

"ok…I see," the Guccifer 2.0 persona replied.

"We think trump has only a 25% chance of winning against hillary… so conflict between Bernie and hillary is interesting," WikiLeaks wrote.

I must make an admission right here. The GRU and WikiLeaks are technologically savvy organizations, and they worked to hide their communications. When our office attempted to collect all of their exchanges, we soon became aware that we were falling short. So what I am presenting here is what we were able to retrieve. We cannot state definitively what we are missing.

But this much is known: the GRU transferred the documents it had stolen from the DNC and John Podesta to WikiLeaks. The Guccifer 2.0

email account sent WikiLeaks an email on July 14 with the subject "big archive," the message "a new attempt," and an encrypted attachment with instructions on how to open it.

And on July 22, three days before the Democratic National Convention began in Philadelphia, WikiLeaks released more than twenty thousand emails and other stolen DNC documents. Its one-paragraph introduction began,

> Today, Friday 22 July 2016 at 10:30am EDT, WikiLeaks releases 19,252 emails and 8,034 attachments from the top of the US Democratic National Committee — part one of our new Hillary Leaks series. The leaks come from the accounts of seven key figures in the DNC.

The press reported on and quoted from the leaked emails, which were seen as highly embarrassing to Clinton and the Democrats. There was much focus on tensions between the Clinton and Bernie Sanders camps at a time when Clinton was hoping to pull the party together at the Democratic National Convention.

"Wondering if there's a good Bernie narrative for a story, which is that Bernie never ever had his act together, that his campaign was a mess," one DNC communications official, Mark Paustenbach, wrote in a May 21 email to DNC communications director Luis Miranda.

Another DNC official emailed Miranda asking whether questioning Sanders's faith might be an effective strategy in states such as Kentucky and West Virginia. "It might may no difference, but for KY and WVA can we get someone to ask his belief," wrote DNC chief financial officer Brad Marshall. "Does he believe in a God. He had skated on saying he has a Jewish heritage. I think I read he is an atheist. This could make several points difference with my peeps."

The leaked emails also included discussion of strategies to be used against Donald Trump, including a proposed mock Trump Organization recruitment ad that would read,

Seeking staff members for multiple positions in a large, New York–based corporation known for its real estate investments, fake universities, steaks, and wine. The boss has very strict standards for female employees, ranging from the women who take lunch orders (must be hot) to the women who oversee multi-million dollar construction projects (must maintain hotness demonstrated at time of hiring).

WikiLeaks was just getting started — and soon their people would be communicating with not only the Russians but also the Trump campaign.

9

"Dirt"

Certain parties, generally those supporting Donald Trump, have asserted that the FBI investigation into Russian interference in the 2016 presidential election began with Hillary Clinton's campaign and the Democratic Party funding something called the Steele dossier, an intelligence document from a former British intelligence agent named Christopher Steele that addressed the possibility that Donald Trump was being used as a Russian asset. Some critics of this report have called for an investigation into its origins to discredit the work of the FBI and our office, which they deem to be politically driven.

But the FBI investigation, which led to ours, was not triggered by the Steele dossier.

It was triggered by George Papadopoulos.

This young man, who grew up in a leafy Chicago suburb and later described himself as an "oil, gas, and policy consultant," joined the Trump campaign as a foreign policy advisor in March 2016 after working on Ben Carson's failed presidential campaign. He was twenty-eight years old.

A week after signing on with the Trump campaign, Papadopoulos, who also recently had taken a position with the London Centre of International Law Practice (LCILP), traveled to Rome as part of his LCILP duties. There he was introduced to Joseph Mifsud, a Maltese national and London-based professor at the London Academy of Diplomacy — and someone who boasted of contacts in Russia, including people involved in the social media campaigns related to the 2016 US presidential election.

After being fired as FBI director, James Comey would refer to Mifsud as "a Russian agent."

Mifsud showed little interest in Papadopoulos until the American mentioned his position with Trump. At that point, Mifsud brought up his substantial connections with Russian government officials and began the process of making Papadopoulos the latest conduit in the Putin regime's efforts to get Trump to meet with the Russian president.

On March 21, in a meeting with the *Washington Post*'s editorial board, Trump announced Papadopoulos's appointment to his foreign policy and national security team.

"He's an energy and oil consultant, excellent guy," Trump said.

Three days later Papadopoulos met Mifsud in London along with a Russian woman, Olga Polonskaya, whom Mifsud introduced as a former student of his with connections to Putin. Papadopoulos mistakenly believed her to be Putin's niece.

After this meeting, Papadopoulos emailed the Trump foreign policy advisory team, using the subject line "Meeting with Russian leadership — including Putin":

I just finished a very productive lunch with a good friend of mine, Joseph Mifsud, the director of the London Academy of Diplomacy — who introduced me to both Putin's niece and the Russian Ambassador in London — who also acts as the Deputy Foreign Minister.

The topic of the lunch was to arrange a meeting between us and the Russian leadership to discuss U.S.-Russia ties under President Trump. They are keen to host us in a "neutral" city, or directly in Moscow. They said the leadership, including Putin, is ready to meet with us and Mr. Trump should there be interest. Waiting for everyone's thoughts on moving forward with this very important issue.

In addition to the fact that the woman was not Putin's niece, Mifsud had not introduced Papadopoulos to the Russian ambassador in London, and the ambassador did not serve as Russia's deputy foreign minister.

Trump's campaign national cochair Sam Clovis responded to Papadopoulos and others on the email chain:

This is most informative. Let me work it through the campaign. No commitments until we see how this plays out. My thought is that we probably should not go forward with any meetings with the Russians until we have had occasion to sit with our NATO allies, especially France, Germany and Great Britain. We need to reassure our allies that we are not going to advance anything with Russia until we have everyone on the same page.

A week later the campaign's foreign policy advisory team met with Trump and Jeff Sessions, the Alabama senator overseeing the campaign's national security issues, at the Trump International Hotel in Washington, DC. The press was invited into this meeting, and Trump posted a photo to his Instagram account that showed Trump and Sessions sitting at opposite ends of an oval table, Papadopoulos two seats to Sessions's left. At the meeting, Papadopoulos mentioned that his London contacts had passed along Putin's desire to meet with Trump. Trump expressed interest in meeting with Putin as well.

Papadopoulos moved forward with the understanding that the campaign supported his continued efforts to try to arrange a meeting between the Trump team and Russian government. Returning to London in April, Papadopoulos met with Mifsud and Polonskaya, who later emailed him that she "would be very pleased to support your initiatives between our two countries" and "to meet you again." Papadopoulos said that he thought it would be "a good step" for him to be introduced and to speak with "the Russian Ambassador in London...or anyone else you recommend, about a potential foreign policy trip to Russia."

"This is already been agreed," Mifsud, who had been copied on the email exchanges, replied on April 11, 2016. "I am flying to Moscow on the 18th for a Valdai meeting, plus other meetings at the Duma. We will talk tomorrow." The Valdai Discussion Club is a Moscow-based organization with close ties to Russia's foreign-policy establishment, and the Duma is a Russian legislative assembly.

Polonskaya also responded, "I have already alerted my personal links to our conversation and your request... We are all very excited the possibility of a good relationship with Mr. Trump.... The Russian Federation would love to welcome him once his candidature would be officially announced."

Papadopoulos and Mifsud met the following day at the Andaz Hotel in London, and Mifsud subsequently left for Moscow, where he introduced Papadopoulos via email to Ivan Timofeev, a Russian International Affairs Council member whom Mifsud said was connected to the Russian Ministry of Foreign Affairs. Papadopoulos and Timofeev had multiple Skype and email exchanges over the next several weeks to lay the "groundwork" for a possible meeting between Trump campaign and Russian government officials.

When Papadopoulos and Mifsud met again on April 26 at the Andaz Hotel in London, Mifsud said that not only had he met with high-level Russian government officials during his Moscow trip but that he had also learned that the Russians had obtained "dirt" on Hillary Clinton, in the form of "emails of Clinton."

"They have thousands of emails," Papadopoulos reported back to the campaign.

When members of our office later asked who in Trump's campaign had been told about the Russian acquisition of "dirt" on Hillary Clinton, Papadopoulos and other members of the campaign experienced collective amnesia. Papadopoulos said that he could not clearly recall having told anyone on the Trump campaign about Mifsud's bombshell, and he wavered in his memory of Clovis becoming rattled when Papadopoulos told him, "They have her emails." Senior policy advisor Stephen Miller could not remember hearing from Papadopoulos or Clovis that Russia had obtained Clinton emails or "dirt" about her. Clovis could not recall Papadopoulos or anyone else telling him that a foreign government possessed derogatory information about Trump's chief opponent.

It must be said also that no one connected to the Trump campaign thought to contact the FBI about the prospect of the United States' chief global rival working to disrupt a presidential election.

Papadopoulos did remember telling at least one person outside the campaign about Russia's obtaining Clinton's emails, but that was a Greek foreign minister. Yet a diplomat from another country had a clear memory of Papadopoulos sharing this information with him as well.

On May 6, ten days after his revelatory London meeting with Mifsud, Papadopoulos was visiting with an Australian diplomat named Alexander Downer at a London wine bar. During their conversation, Papadopoulos mentioned that the Russian government had indicated that it could help the Trump campaign by anonymously releasing damaging information it had collected about Hillary Clinton.

This conversation went unreported for more than two months. But on July 26, 2016, after WikiLeaks had released more than twenty thousand Clinton-related emails and DNC documents in the lead-up to the Democratic National Convention, the Australian government contacted the FBI to report that a Trump official had informed an Australian diplomat about a Russian scheme to hurt Hillary Clinton's candidacy while boosting Donald Trump's.

A few days later, the FBI quietly opened an investigation into potential coordination between the Russian government and the Trump campaign.

10

"No official letter/no message from Trump"

Was George Papadopoulos an important figure in this ongoing dance between the Russian government and the Trump campaign, or was he just an overreaching not-quite-somebody, as the campaign would later claim? He certainly served as a nexus between the two parties, someone who would not be discouraged in his efforts to set up a meeting between top Trump campaign officials and those representing the Russian government. He kept the Trump team in the loop all the while.

"The Russian government has an open invitation by Putin for Mr. Trump to meet him when he is ready," Papadopoulos wrote to Trump senior advisor Stephen Miller on April 25, 2016. "The advantage of being in London is that these governments tend to speak a bit more openly in 'neutral' cities."

On April 27, the day after Mifsud told him about the Russians having "dirt" on Clinton, Papadopoulos wrote to Miller about "some interesting messages coming in from Moscow about a trip when the time is right." Papadopoulos also emailed campaign manager Corey Lewandowski that day to say, "I have been receiving a lot of calls over the last month about Putin wanting to host [Trump] and the team when the time is right."

Russia-related communications between Papadopoulos and campaign officials continued through the spring and summer of 2016. On May 4, Papadopoulos relayed to Lewandowski, Sam Clovis, and senior campaign official Paul Manafort an email from Ivan Timofeev suggesting a Moscow meeting. Papadopoulos also sent Manafort an email on May 21 with the subject line "Request from Russia to meet Mr. Trump."

"Russia has been eager to meet Mr. Trump for quite sometime and have been reaching out to me to discuss," Papadopoulos wrote.

Manafort forwarded this email to another campaign official, saying, "Lets discuss. We need someone to communicate that [Trump] is not doing these trips. It should be someone low level in the Campaign so as not to send any signal."

But the emails about a possible Russia visit did not let up, with Lewandowski at one point telling Papadopoulos to "connect with" Clovis, who was "running point" on this topic. Papadopoulos sent another email to Lewandowski on June 19, saying the "Russian ministry of foreign affairs" had contacted him and asked whether a campaign representative such as Papadopoulos might attend meetings if Trump was not available to travel to Russia.

"I'm willing to make the trip off the record if it's in the interest of Mr. Trump and the campaign to meet specific people," Papadopoulos wrote.

But June 19 turned out to be the day that the Trump campaign announced it was parting ways with Lewandowski, putting Manafort in charge of the campaign. Lewandowski later would tell NBC's *Today* show that Papadopoulos was "a low-level volunteer" who "was not a person who was involved with the day-to-day operations of the campaign, or a person who I recall interacting with on a regular basis at all."

Papadopoulos continued to be in touch with Clovis and Walid Phares, a fellow member of Trump's foreign policy advisory team, about arranging an off-the-record meeting between Trump campaign and Russian government officials, or with Mifsud and Timofeev. When Papadopoulos attended the Transatlantic Parliamentary Group on Counterterrorism (TAG) on July 16, he sat next to Clovis and, at the event, discussed with him and Phares the prospect of a foreign policy trip to Russia.

Ten days later, Papadopoulos emailed Mifsud, listing Clovis and Phares as "participants" in a potential meeting at the London Academy of Diplomacy in September 2016. As Papadopoulos's handwritten notes indicate, the "Office of Putin" would be involved in this meeting, as well as "Walid/Sam me." Although one note read, "Explore: we are a campaign," the meeting was intended to take place on the down-low with "No official letter/no message from Trump."

Papadopoulos said that he also had received requests from multiple foreign governments, "even Russia," for "closed door workshops/consultations abroad." Clovis wrote to Papadopoulos on August 15 that he could not "travel before the election," but he encouraged Papadopoulos and Walid "to make the trips, if it is feasible."

Apparently they were not feasible, because these trips never happened, as far as we know.

Nonetheless, Papadopoulos continued to be a magnet for Russian outreach. After the TAG Summit, he was connected via LinkedIn to Sergei Millian, a Belarus-born American citizen who introduced himself as "president of [the] New York–based Russian American Chamber of Commerce." Millian told Papadopoulos that he had "insider knowledge and direct access to the top hierarchy in Russian politics." The two met in New York City on July 20 and August 1, and afterward, Millian invited Papadopoulos to speak at two international energy conferences, including one in Moscow in September 2016.

Papadopoulos did not wind up attending either conference but stayed in touch with Millian and relayed information to the Trump campaign, emailing campaign official Bo Denysyk about having been contacted "by some leaders of Russian-American voters here in the U.S. about their interest in voting for Mr. Trump." He asked Denysyk whether he wanted to be put "in touch with their group (US-Russia chamber of commerce)."

Denysyk thanked Papadopoulos "for taking the initiative" but asked him to "hold off with outreach to Russian-Americans" because by then there were "too many articles" portraying the campaign, as well as Trump and then–campaign chair Paul Manafort, as "being pro-Russian."

It turned out that Millian already had experience with Trump regarding Russia and business. Millian told ABC News in July 2016 that he met

Trump and Michael Cohen in 2008 during a marketing meeting to boost a Trump-branded development in Hollywood, Florida. "Trump's team, they realized that we have lots of connection with Russian investors. And they noticed that we bring a lot of investors from Russia," Millian said. "And they needed my assistance, yes, to sell properties and sell some of the assets to Russian investors." Millian said he signed an agreement "with his team so I can be his official broker," though Cohen and the Trump Hollywood later denied having any record of a signed agreement with him.

Millian sent Papadopoulos a Facebook message on August 23, 2016, promising to "share with you a disruptive technology that might be instrumental in your political work for the campaign." Papadopoulos later claimed not to remember this matter.

The Trump campaign dismissed Papadopoulos in early October 2016, after he drew criticism for an interview he gave with the Russian news agency Interfax in which he criticized the Obama administration's sanctions and its approach to Russia and touted Trump's "willingness to usher in a new chapter in U.S.-Russia ties."

But neither Papadopoulos nor Millian quit talking about business and Russia. On November 9, the day after the presidential election, Papadopoulos arranged to meet Millian five days later at Chicago's Trump International Hotel & Tower to discuss potential business opportunities involving Russian "billionaires who are not under sanctions." Papadopoulos later told our office that in Chicago the two discussed partnering on business deals, but Millian cooled on him upon learning that Papadopoulos was pursuing strictly private sector opportunities and not a position in the Trump administration. Nonetheless, the two of them kept in touch and arranged to meet again in a Washington, DC, bar when both were in town for Trump's inauguration in January 2017.

In 2017, Millian was identified as an unwitting source for information contained in the Steele dossier, including salacious unverified claims about Trump's activities with prostitutes in Moscow (which our report does *not* get into) and allegations of the Trump campaign's cooperation with the Russian government. The *Washington Post* reported in February 2017 that Millian "also offered to serve as a conduit to the Trump campaign for a Belarusan author in Florida with connections to the Russian government."

Millian remained out of the country for the entirety of our investigation. The House and Senate intelligence committees were unsuccessful in trying to get him to testify as well. So we will move on.

11

"If it's what you say I love it"

This is not a quiz, but you no doubt have noticed that there are a lot of names and moving parts in this story. If you would like to stop and take a breath, I would not blame you.

OK. So…do you remember Aras Agalarov?

He is the Azerbaijani Russian billionaire owner of the Crocus Group real estate conglomerate who worked with Trump on the 2013 Miss Universe pageant in Moscow and pursued the Trump Tower Moscow project until talks with the Trump Organization apparently were tabled in November 2014.

Agalarov and Trump stayed in touch afterward, and the two exchanged gifts and letters in 2016; in April of that year when Agalarov wrote a letter, Trump sent back a handwritten note. Agalarov expressed interest in Trump's campaign for president, congratulated him on a primary victory, and, according to an email drafted by Robert Goldstone, passed along an "offer" of "support" from him and "many…important Russian friends and colleagues, especially with reference to U.S./Russian relations."

Goldstone was the publicist for Emin Agalarov, Aras's singer-businessman son, from late 2012 till late 2016, and during that period, Goldstone facilitated contact between the Agalarovs and the Trumps, including extending Trump's invitation to Putin to attend the 2013 Miss Universe pageant. On June 3, 2016, Emin Agalarov called Goldstone to discuss having information that might interest the Trumps. It involved

Hillary Clinton. Goldstone emailed Donald Trump Jr. shortly after this conversation:

Good morning

Emin just called and asked me to contact you with something very interesting.

The Crown prosecutor of Russia met with his father Aras this morning and in their meeting offered to provide the Trump campaign with some official documents and information that would incriminate Hillary and her dealings with Russia and would be very useful to your father. This is obviously very high level and sensitive information but is part of Russia and its government's support of Mr. Trump — helped along by Aras and Emin.

What do you think is the best way to handle this information and would you be able to speak to Emin about it directly?

I can also send this info to your father via Rhona [Graff, Trump's executive assistant], but it is ultra sensitive so wanted to send to you first.

Best

Rob Goldstone

Trump Jr. emailed back within minutes:

Thanks Rob. I appreciate that. I am on the road at the moment but perhaps I just speak to Emin first. Seems we have some time and if it's what you say I love it especially later in the summer. Could we do a call first thing next week when I am back?

Goldstone then emailed Emin Agalarov, saying that Trump Jr. "wants to speak personally on this issue."

On June 6, Emin asked Goldstone, "Any news?"

Goldstone responded that Trump Jr. probably was still traveling for "the final elections... where Trump will be 'crowned' the official nominee."

Goldstone circled back to Trump Jr. to ask when he was "free to talk with Emin about this Hillary info," and Trump Jr. replied that they might "speak now." Goldstone then set up multiple brief calls between Trump Jr. and Emin Agalarov that day and the next.

Meanwhile, Aras Agalarov was calling Ike Kaveladze, Crocus's chief negotiator of the Trump Moscow project, to ask him to attend a meeting in New York with the Trump Organization. Kaveladze told our office that Aras Agalarov said the meeting's purpose was to discuss the Magnitsky Act.

The Magnitsky Act is another pretty significant factor in our story. Russian tax accountant Sergei Magnitsky was a whistle-blower who exposed fraud by Russian officials before being arrested, denied medical care, and finally beaten to death in 2009 in a Moscow prison. In 2012, the US Congress passed, and President Obama signed into law, the Magnitsky Act, which punished Russia for Magnitsky's death by allowing the United States to sanction human rights violators worldwide, including freezing their assets and banning their entry to the United States. Calling this statute "a purely political, unfriendly act," Putin retaliated by barring a list of current and former US officials from entering Russia and prohibiting US citizens from adopting Russian children. The Russian president wanted these US sanctions overturned.

For this New York meeting with members of the Trump Organization, Aras Agalarov was asking Kaveladze to translate for Natalia Veselnitskaya, a former Russian prosecutor who had lobbied against the Magnitsky Act and did legal work for a defendant alleged to have laundered money as part of the fraud that Magnitsky had exposed. Veselnitskaya also apparently was involved in offering a US congressional delegation in Moscow in April 2016 "confidential information" from "the Prosecutor General of Russia" about "interactions between certain political forces in our two countries."

"Emin asked that I schedule a meeting with you and the Russian government attorney who is flying over from Moscow," Goldstone emailed Trump Jr. on June 7.

Trump Jr. responded that he, along with "campaign boss" Manafort

and Jared Kushner, likely would attend. The attendees surprised Goldstone and "puzzled" Kaveladze, who asked one of Emin's assistants about
the meeting's purpose. He was told it was for Veselnitskaya to pass along
"negative information on Hillary Clinton."

The meeting was set for 4:00 p.m. on June 9. Trump Jr. forwarded his
complete meeting-related email correspondence with Goldstone to
Manafort and Kushner under the subject line "FW: Russia — Clinton —
private and confidential." In a note, Trump Jr. added, "Meeting got
moved to 4 tomorrow at my offices."

"See you then. P.," Manafort replied.

Kushner, who had previously told his assistant about a 3:00 p.m. meeting with Trump Jr., emailed her again to say, "Meeting with don jr is 4
pm now."

In the days before the June 9 meeting, Trump Jr. told a regular morning meeting of senior campaign staff and Trump family members —
including Eric Trump, Paul Manafort, campaign press secretary Hope
Hicks, and a late-arriving Ivanka Trump and Jared Kushner — that he
had a lead on negative information about the Clinton Foundation.

As a point of information, Hicks, who would turn twenty-eight a couple of weeks before the election, was often the youngest person in the
room for Trump team meetings but turned out to be one of his longest-
serving aides. She was a former teen model employed by a New York–
based public relations firm when she did some work for Ivanka Trump's
fashion line in 2012. The Trump Organization hired her full-time in
2014, and she continued to help Ivanka Trump with her brand before
Donald Trump named her press secretary for his presidential campaign
in January 2015. She had done no previous political work.

Rick Gates, then the deputy campaign chair, recalled that at this campaign staff meeting, Trump Jr. said that the information about the Clinton Foundation came from a group in the former Soviet republic of
Kyrgyzstan to whom he was introduced by a friend. Manafort warned his
colleagues to be careful, because the meeting likely would not yield vital
information.

Michael Cohen later recalled to investigators that he was in Donald Trump's office on June 6 or 7 when Trump Jr. told his father that a meeting to obtain damaging information about Clinton was moving forward. Cohen did not remember Trump Jr. mentioning Russia in connection to the meeting, but he had the impression that the two Trumps had discussed the meeting previously. Trump Jr. later testified before the Senate Judiciary Committee that he did *not* tell his father about the emails or upcoming meeting, and Manafort and Kushner had no recollection of anyone, including Trump Jr., informing Trump about the meeting. In written responses to our office's questions, Trump said he had "no recollection of learning at the time" that his son, Manafort, or Kushner "was considering participating in a meeting in June 2016 concerning potentially negative information about Hillary Clinton."

Yet on June 7, the day when top campaign officials discussed the prospect of obtaining damaging information about Hillary Clinton two days later, Trump announced that he would give "a major speech...probably Monday of next week" (June 13) to address "all of the things that have taken place with the Clintons."

Veselnitskaya was the defense attorney for Prevezon Holdings, a real estate company accused by prosecutors of laundering stolen Russian money by buying up high-end New York properties. This was one of the schemes that Magnitsky had uncovered, and in January 2019, federal prosecutors would charge Veselnitskaya with obstructing a federal investigation into this matter. Veselnitskaya was attending appellate proceedings about Prevezon civil forfeiture litigation in New York on June 9, 2016, the day of the meeting with Trump Jr. et al.

First, she had lunch with Rinat Akhmetshin, a Soviet-born US lobbyist who worked on issues related to the Magnitsky Act, and Anatoli Samochornov, a Russian-born translator who had worked with Veselnitskaya on the Prevezon case and Magnitsky-related lobbying. They discussed what she would say in her Trump Jr. meeting, and she pulled out a document alleging financial misconduct by Bill Browder and the brothers Dirk, Edward, and Daniel Ziff. Browder was an American-born

British financier who had been a major investor in Russia until the country barred him in 2005 as a security risk after, he said, he uncovered corruption there. Browder had lobbied for the Magnitsky Act, and in 2013, Russia tried and convicted him (in absentia) and Magnitsky (who had been dead for four years) for tax fraud, sentencing Browder to nine years in prison. Interpol rejected Russia's requests to arrest Browder, deeming the case political. The Ziff brothers also had done business in Russia and supported Democrats.

After lunch, the three Russians went to Trump Tower for the meeting, where they were joined by Goldstone and Kaveladze on their side and Trump Jr., Manafort, and Kushner on the other. (All but Veselnitskaya and Trump Jr. agreed to be interviewed by our office later, and their combined account is what is represented here.) Veselnitskaya started the twenty-minute meeting by discussing Browder and accusing the Ziff brothers of tax evasion and money laundering in Russia and the United States as well as donating their profits to the DNC or Clinton campaign.

"How can these payments be tied specifically to the Clinton campaign?" Trump Jr. asked.

"I can't trace the money once it has entered the US," Veselnitskaya replied.

"Well, what do you actually have on Hillary Clinton?" Trump Jr. pressed.

When Veselnitskaya could not supply a satisfying answer, an aggravated Kushner supposedly asked, "What are we doing here?"

Akhmetshin then brought up the Magnitsky Act and related US sanctions, and Trump Jr. responded that as his father was still a private citizen, there was nothing they could do at that time, although they could revisit the issue once he had taken office.

During the meeting, Kushner sent Manafort an iMessage saying, "waste of time," and then he sent separate emails to two assistants at Kushner Companies asking them to call him so that he would have an excuse to leave. Kushner made his exit before the meeting ended.

After the meeting, Goldstone apologized to Trump Jr. Aras Agalarov called Kaveladze to ask how it had gone, and with Veselnitskaya sitting next to him, Kaveladze said that it had gone well. Later, however, Kaveladze told him that pushing a meeting about the Magnitsky Act had been a waste of time because it was not with lawyers, so they were "preaching to the wrong crowd."

In a June 14 phone call, Kaveladze's teenage daughter asked him how the meeting had gone.

"The meeting was boring," Kaveladze replied. "The Russians did not have any bad info on Hillary."

Veselnitskaya later gave a different account of the meeting to the press and Congress, saying that she had no connection to the Russian government and had not passed along any derogatory information about the Clinton campaign to Trump's team. The meeting's purpose, she said in a written statement to the Senate Judiciary Committee, was "to have a private meeting with Donald Trump Jr. — a friend of my good acquaintance's son on the matter of assisting me or my colleagues in informing the Congress members as to the criminal nature of manipulation and interference with the legislative activities of the U.S. Congress." No one else present recalled any reference to Congress during the meetings.

Trump Jr. told Fox News's Sean Hannity in a July 2017 interview that if "someone has information on our opponent…maybe this is something. I should hear them out." In September 2017 congressional testimony, he said that he thought he should "listen to what Rob [Goldstone] and his colleagues had to say." Then he could "consult with counsel to make an informed decision as to whether to give it any further consideration."

Again, no one involved with the Trump campaign informed the FBI that a hostile foreign power was attempting to influence the US election as well as to bypass the current government to cut a deal on US sanctions. In contrast, when someone on Al Gore's 2000 presidential campaign was anonymously sent George W. Bush's stolen debate prep book before a key debate, the Gore campaign immediately turned it over to the FBI, and the recipient declined to participate in Gore's debate preparation.

Following the June 9 meeting, Trump changed the subject of his planned speech from the Clintons to national security. In his written answers to questions submitted by our office, the president stated that he altered the speech's focus "in light of the Pulse nightclub shooting," in which a security guard fatally shot forty-nine people at a gay club in Orlando on June 12. He also said his intended Clinton speech would have referenced "the publicly available, negative information about the Clintons, including, for example, Mrs. Clinton's failed policies, the Clintons' use of the State Department to further their interests and the interests of the Clinton Foundation, Mrs. Clinton's improper use of a private server for State Department business, the destruction of 33,000 emails on that server, and Mrs. Clinton's temperamental unsuitability for the office of President."

The week after the Trump Tower meeting, the Democratic National Committee announced that it had been hacked by the Russians.

12

"I think he is an idiot"

Here is something you should know about intelligence officers, also known as agents or spies. They are always seeking sources of information, people to recruit, ways to gain advantage on behalf of the countries or groups they represent. They are playing a confidence game as they work to earn the trust and friendship of their targets, aiming to obtain leverage and, ultimately, other assets. They may double-cross someone in spectacular fashion, as spy novels like to portray, or they may go about their business quietly and maintain relationships that on the surface appear normal but in reality may exist to create a back channel to bypass aboveboard diplomatic communications.

Do not be fooled. These agents want something.

Many are fooled.

Russian intelligence officers were interacting with Americans long before Donald Trump ran for president and will be interacting with them long after he has left office. One such American was Carter Page, who had spent much time working in and with Russia by the time he was introduced to Victor Podobnyy at an energy symposium in New York in January 2013, when Page was forty-one years old.

Page was deputy branch manager of Merrill Lynch's Moscow office from 2004 to 2007 and became involved in transactions with the Russian energy company Gazprom. In 2008, Page founded his own energy-related investment-management company, Global Energy Capital LLC, and asked Gazprom deputy chief financial officer Sergey Yatsenko to be a senior advisor. That same year, Page met Alexander Bulatov, a Russian government official working at the Russian consulate in New York. Bulatov was a Russian intelligence officer, although little has been revealed about his interactions with Page.

Page met Podobnyy, who was working covertly in the United States under diplomatic cover, five years later. Podobnyy also was a Russian agent, and after meeting at the energy symposium, Page and he struck up a relationship. They exchanged emails and got together several times, with the American offering his views on the energy industry's future and providing documents about the energy business. Page apparently thought that Podobnyy could assist him in his efforts to reap riches in Russia. Page did not realize that Podobnyy viewed him as a foreign source to be recruited, probed for information, and discarded.

Podobnyy, in turn, did not realize that the FBI was surveilling him and two other Russian intelligence officers, Evgeny Buryakov and Igor Sporyshev, and recording their conversations. In 2015, those three would be charged in the Southern District of New York with conspiracy to act as an unregistered agent of a foreign government. The criminal complaint cited Podobnyy's interactions with "Male-1," a.k.a. Page, and included a transcript of an April 8, 2013, conversation between Podobnyy and Sporyshev that made clear how these agents felt about their target:

Podobnyy: [Male-1] wrote that he is sorry, he went to Moscow and forgot to check his inbox, but he wants to meet when he gets back. I think he is an idiot and forgot who I am. Plus he writes to me in Russian [to] practice the language. He flies to Moscow more often than I do. He got hooked on Gazprom thinking that if they have a project, he could be rise up. Maybe he can. I don't know, but it's obvious that he wants to earn lots of money....

Sporyshev: Without a doubt.

Podobnyy: He said that they have a new project right now, new energy boom....He says that it is about to take off. I don't say anything for now.

Sporyshev: Yeah, first we will spend a couple of borrowed million and then....

Podobnyy: [laughs] It's worth it. I like that he takes on everything. For now his enthusiasm works for me. I also promised him a lot: that I have connections in the Trade Representation, meaning you that you can push contracts [laughs]. I will feed him empty promises.

Sporyshev: Shit, then he will write me. Not even me, to our clean one.

Podobnyy: I didn't say the Trade Representation.... I did not even indicate that this is connected to a government agency. This is intelligence method to cheat, how else to work with foreigners? You promise a favor for a favor. You get the documents from him and tell him to go fuck himself. But not to upset you, I will take you to a restaurant and give you an expensive gift. You just need to sign for it. This is ideal working method.

When Page later spoke with a Russian government official at the United Nations General Assembly, he identified himself as "Male-1" and told the official, "I didn't do anything." Years later, after opening its investigation into Russian election interference, FBI officials interviewed Page, and Page told them that he understood that he had associated with Russian intelligence agents but did not view his relationship as a back channel. "The more immaterial non-public information I give them, the better for this country," Page asserted to the FBI agents.

Donald Trump chose to name this man to his foreign policy team at the same March 21, 2016, *Washington Post* editorial board meeting in which he introduced Papadopoulos, Walid Phares, and others. Trump referred to him as "Carter Page, PhD." The *Guardian* later reported that University of London examiners twice rejected Page's PhD thesis about central Asia's transition from communism to capitalism, noting that it was "characterised by considerable repetition, verbosity and vagueness of expression." One of the two academics who had read his thesis, Gregory Andrusz, told the *Guardian* that Page "knew next to nothing" about social science and seemed "unfamiliar with basic concepts like Marxism or state capitalism." After failing on his second thesis attempt, Page accused the examiners of having an anti-Russian and anti-American bias, and a different pair of academics finally passed his thesis in 2011.

Ed Cox, chair of the New York Republican State Committee at the time (and husband to Tricia Nixon, the late President Nixon's daughter), had introduced Page to Trump campaign officials in January 2016. Page said that he wanted to help Trump improve relations with Russia, and he sent emails to campaign officials touting his Russian connections and including Russia-related talking points, briefing memos, and a proposal.

"I spent the past week in Europe and have been in discussions with some individuals with close ties to the Kremlin," Page wrote in a January 30, 2016, email to senior Trump campaign officials. He said these Russian individuals recognized that Trump could have a "game-changing effect...in bringing the end of the new Cold War.... Through my discussions with these high level contacts, I believe a direct meeting in Moscow between Mr. Trump and Putin could be arranged." He ended the email by criticizing US sanctions against Russia.

After Trump named him as a foreign policy advisor, Page did policy-related work for the campaign over the next several months. Senior Trump officials seemed pleased with Page's contributions. While forwarding some of Page's notes to then–Trump campaign manager Corey Lewandowski, chief campaign policy advisor Sam Clovis wrote, "I wanted to let you know the type of work some of our advisors are capable of." Page also offered feedback on the outline of a foreign policy speech that Trump gave at the Mayflower Hotel in April 2016, and he prepared his own outline of an energy policy speech that Trump delivered in Bismarck, North Dakota, in May 2016. Page traveled to be there.

Page's appointment to the Trump foreign policy team made him a magnet for Russian attention. In late April, Page was invited to be the commencement speaker at the New Economic School (NES) in Moscow in July. That ceremony usually featured high-profile speakers, such as Barack Obama in 2009, and NES officials said later that they had invited Page based solely on his status as the Trump campaign's Russia expert.

Given how much interest in Moscow Trump's run for the White House was generating, the NES top brass thought bringing a member of the campaign to the school would be a shrewd move.

Eager to accept the invitation, Page asked Trump campaign officials for permission to make the trip. He also emailed Clovis, Trump campaign national security director J. D. Gordon, and advisor Walid Phares on May 16 suggesting that Trump give the commencement speech instead of him. Page followed up with another email on June 19 again seeking approval to deliver this speech but also to reiterate that the NES "would love to have Mr. Trump speak at this annual celebration" instead of him.

"If you want to do this, it would be out side [*sic*] of your role with the DJT for President campaign," Lewandowski responded the same day. "I am certain Mr. Trump will not be able to attend."

So Page traveled to Russia in early July 2016 to participate in the NES ceremony. Some prominent Russians took note.

"Page is Trump's adviser on foreign policy," NES employee Denis Klimentov emailed to Maria Zakharova, director of the Russian Ministry of Foreign Affairs' Information and Press Department. "He is a known businessman; he used to work in Russia.... If you have any questions, I will be happy to help contact him."

Dmitri Klimentov, a New York–based public relations consultant who was cc'd by his brother Denis in the email, contacted Russian press secretary Dmitry Peskov to see whether Peskov wanted to introduce Page to any Russian government officials.

"I have read about him," Peskov replied. "Specialists say that he is far from being the main one. So I better not initiate a meeting in the Kremlin."

In the first of two NES speeches that he delivered, on July 7, Page criticized US foreign policy toward Russia. "Washington and other Western Capitals have impeded potential progress through their often hypocritical focus on ideas such as democratization, inequality, corruption and regime change," he said. The next day Page pursued similar themes in his

NES commencement address, with Russian deputy prime minister Arkady Dvorkovich speaking afterward to say that US sanctions on Russia had hurt the NES. Page and Dvorkovich shook hands at the ceremony, and Dvorkovich suggested they work together in the future.

During the Moscow trip, Page contacted some of his old Russian colleagues and acquaintances, including a former Gazprom employee who learned of Page's Trump connection and suggested selling Page a stake in his current Russian energy company. Individuals from another Russian energy company, Tatneft, proposed possibly bringing on Page as a consultant.

Although he was not in Russia on official campaign business, Page emailed several Trump campaign officials from Moscow on the day of his commencement speech, saying he would send them "a readout soon regarding some incredible insights and outreach I've received from a few Russian legislators and senior members of the Presidential Administration here."

Page followed up the next day with an email to Clovis, which stated in part,

Russian Deputy Prime minister and NES board member Arkady Dvorkovich also spoke before the event. In a private conversation, Dvorkovich expressed strong support for Mr. Trump and a desire to work together toward devising better solutions in response to the vast range of current international problems. Based on feedback from a diverse array of other sources close to the Presidential Administration, it was readily apparent that this sentiment is widely held at all levels of government.

When our office investigated Page's Russian connections and this trip to Moscow, we could not obtain additional evidence regarding with whom Page met or communicated in Moscow. So his activities in Russia, as described in his emails to campaign officials, were not fully explained.

After returning to the United States, Page attended the Republican

National Convention, which began on July 18 in Cleveland. There he met with Russian ambassador Sergey Kislyak and later emailed campaign officials that Kislyak was very worried about Hillary Clinton's international views.

A few weeks later, the press began to report about Page's activities and statements. An August 5 *Washington Post* story began,

> *In early June, a little-known adviser to Donald Trump stunned a gathering of high-powered Washington foreign policy experts meeting with the visiting prime minister of India, going off topic with effusive praise for Russian President Vladimir Putin and Trump.*
>
> *The adviser, Carter Page, hailed Putin as stronger and more reliable than President Obama, according to three people who were present at the closed-door meeting at Blair House — and then touted the positive effect a Trump presidency would have on U.S.-Russia relations.*
>
> *A month later, Page dumbfounded foreign policy experts again by giving another speech harshly critical of U.S. policy — this time in Moscow.*

The *Post* story also noted,

> *Since being named to the Republican nominee's team in March, his stature within the foreign policy world has grown considerably, drawing alarm from more-established foreign policy experts who view him as having little real understanding about U.S.-Russia relations. Many also say that Page's views may be compromised by his investment in Russian energy giant Gazprom.*

The Trump team distanced itself from Page; campaign spokesperson Hope Hicks said in the *Post* story that Page was an "informal foreign policy adviser" who "does not speak for Mr. Trump or the campaign." The story's authors then felt compelled to point out that "Trump first named Page as one of a handful of his foreign policy advisers during a meeting at the *Washington Post*."

Yahoo News's Michael Isikoff turned up the heat with a September 23 story reporting that US intelligence officials were investigating whether Page had created a private back channel with Russian officials to discuss the possibility of Trump lifting economic sanctions if he became president. The story stated,

> *The activities of Trump adviser Carter Page, who has extensive business interests in Russia, have been discussed with senior members of Congress during recent briefings about suspected efforts by Moscow to influence the presidential election, the sources said. After one of those briefings, Senate minority leader Harry Reid wrote FBI Director James Comey, citing reports of meetings between a Trump adviser (a reference to Page) and "high ranking sanctioned individuals" in Moscow over the summer as evidence of "significant and disturbing ties" between the Trump campaign and the Kremlin that needed to be investigated by the bureau.*

Trump campaign spokesperson Jason Miller told Yahoo News that Page "has no role" on the campaign, adding, "We are not aware of any of his activities, past or present." Isikoff then noted, "Miller did not respond when asked why Trump had previously described Page as one of his advisers."

Page was formally removed from the campaign on September 24. The *Washington Post* later reported that the FBI and Justice Department obtained a secret FISA warrant the following month to wiretap Page after they convinced a Foreign Intelligence Surveillance Court judge they had probable cause that Page was acting as an agent of a foreign power, Russia. The ninety-day warrant was renewed three times.

13

"A new beginning with Russia"

We have covered many names already, with more to come, but given that this one appears more than a hundred times in our report, we ought to mention Dimitri Simes. He is someone whom author Malcolm Gladwell might term a connector. He had made many introductions over the years, including members of the Trump campaign to people associated with Russia.

Simes was born in the former Soviet Union in 1947 and emigrated to the United States in 1973. He maintained contacts with many current and former Russian government officials as he pursued an academic career in the United States, with teaching stints at the University of California at Berkeley and Columbia University before becoming president and chief executive officer of the Center for the National Interest (CNI).

Former president Richard Nixon established the CNI in 1994 as the Nixon Center for Peace and Freedom before the name was changed to the Nixon Center and, in 2011, the Center for the National Interest. A Washington, DC–based think tank that touts its "unparalleled access to Russian officials and politicians," the center has arranged for US delegations to visit Russia and for Russian delegations to visit the United States as part of "Track II" diplomatic efforts. Simes, who advised Nixon on foreign policy and accompanied him on trips to Russia and other former Soviet states, was Nixon's choice to lead the center from the beginning.

Simes also is publisher and chief executive officer of the CNI's bimonthly foreign policy magazine, the *National Interest*.

The Trump campaign had been under scrutiny for its apparent lack of an experienced foreign policy team in March 2016. Jeff Sessions was serving on CNI's advisory council when he became the first US senator to endorse Trump on February 28, and Trump named him to lead his national security advisory committee three days later. Then, on March 14, Jared Kushner attended a CNI luncheon honoring Henry Kissinger in New York's Time Warner Building with the intention of soliciting Simes to help bolster the campaign's foreign policy credentials.

A week later, Trump unveiled his foreign policy team in his meeting with the *Washington Post* editorial board, and Kushner and Simes spoke on the phone three days after that, followed by a one-on-one meeting in Kushner's office on March 31. At that meeting, Simes suggested that the campaign should organize an advisory group of experts to meet with Trump to develop a foreign policy approach compatible with his voice. Simes and Kushner also explored the possibility of CNI hosting a foreign policy speech that Trump would deliver.

Simes was in contact with other Trump campaign members as well, sending J. D. Gordon, who managed Sessions's National Security Advisory Committee for the campaign, a June 17 email that included a memo to be shared with Sessions. It proposed assembling "a small and carefully selected group of experts" to help Sessions's foreign policy campaign work because "Hillary Clinton is very vulnerable on national security and foreign policy issues." Included in the memo's outline of key campaign issues was a call for "a new beginning with Russia."

The Trump campaign liked the idea of a CNI-hosted Trump speech, and plans progressed. The two parties agreed that CNI officials would coordinate the event's logistics with Sessions and his staff, including Sessions's chief of staff, Rick Dearborn, while CNI offered input on the speech itself. Kushner connected Simes with Trump senior policy advisor Stephen Miller in April 2016 and sent Simes an outline of the speech that Miller had prepared. Simes responded with bullet-point suggestions that he had drafted with two other CNI officials. Miller sent him further outlines, and Simes and CNI's executive director spoke with Miller on the phone about substantive changes that Miller made to the speech.

After some CNI board members told Simes they feared that hosting this speech could be perceived as an endorsement of Trump, the organization shifted the hosting duties to the *National Interest* magazine it owned, moving the event to the National Press Club and later, at Kushner's request, to the Mayflower Hotel. CNI booked the Mayflower to host the speech as well as a VIP reception where invited guests could meet Trump. CNI's guest list for the VIP reception included Sessions and Russian ambassador Kislyak; Simes had told Kislyak that he would have an opportunity to meet Trump.

The event took place on April 27, with Sessions standing next to Trump during the prespeech receiving line until Simes took his place to introduce the candidate to CNI's invited guests, including Kislyak. Trump and Kislyak had what was termed a positive, friendly exchange, and Kislyak also met Kushner, the two of them shaking hands and chatting.

"We like what your candidate is saying," the Russian ambassador told Trump's son-in-law. "It's refreshing."

Kislyak also was reported to have talked with Sessions, though Sessions later told investigators that he did not remember any such conversation.

Kushner remained in contact with Simes after the Mayflower Hotel speech, meeting with him in person and talking with him on the phone to discuss the campaign's handling of Russia-related issues and the assembly of a foreign policy advisory group. Simes counseled Kushner on matters such as the bad optics that would result if the campaign developed hidden Russian contacts, and he suggested that the campaign not highlight Russia as an issue.

Meanwhile, Dearborn emailed Kushner on May 17 about a request that a high-level campaign official meet with a Russian state-owned bank official "to discuss an offer [that the official] claims to be carrying from President Putin to meet with" Trump.

"Pass on this," Kushner responded, cc'ing Manafort and Gates. "A lot of people come claiming to carry messages. Very few are able to verify. For now I think we decline such meetings. Most likely these people go back home and claim they have special access to gain importance for themselves. Be careful."

Months later, on August 17, after both Trump and Clinton had been confirmed as their parties' nominees, Simes requested that Kushner meet with him in Kushner's New York office to address Hillary Clinton's Russia-related attacks against Trump. Before they met, Simes sent Kushner a "Russia Policy Memo" suggesting "what Mr. Trump may want to say about Russia." The memo recommended "downplaying Russia as a U.S. foreign policy priority at this time," noted that "some tend to exaggerate Putin's flaws," suggested exploring "how to work with Russia to advance important U.S. national interests…and not go abroad in search of monsters to destroy," and addressed questions about Russia's invasion and annexation of Crimea.

In the accompanying email, Simes also mentioned that he had "a well-documented story of highly questionable connections between Bill Clinton" and the Russian government, some of which had been "discussed with the CIA and the FBI in the late 1990s and shared with the [independent counsel] at the end of the Clinton presidency."

Kushner forwarded the email to Miller, Manafort, and Gates with the note "suggestion only." Manafort forwarded the email to his assistant and scheduled a meeting with Simes, but as Manafort was about to leave the campaign, only Kushner and Simes met. At their meeting, Simes relayed to Kushner the information about Clinton, saying that he had received it from a former Central Intelligence Agency (CIA) and Reagan White House official, not Russian sources. Simes also presented this information at a small meeting of foreign policy experts with Sessions.

Kushner later denied receiving information from Simes that could be "operationalized" by the Trump campaign.

14

"Kostya, the guy from the GRU"

Speaking of working with Russian agents...

Paul Manafort, Trump's campaign chair from mid-June through mid-August 2016, and his deputy, Rick Gates, shared internal campaign polling data with a man considered by the FBI to have ties to Russian intelligence. Why would they do this? Why would the Trump campaign share its data with a possible Russian spy?

Let's back up.

Paul Manafort was about to turn sixty-seven when he joined the Trump campaign in March 2016, at which point he had known the candidate for more than two decades. He had been a Republican political consultant who advised the presidential campaigns of Gerald Ford, Ronald Reagan, George H. W. Bush, and Bob Dole, and in 1980, he cofounded the Washington, DC–based lobbying firm Black, Manafort & Stone with Charles R. Black Jr. and future Trump advisor Roger Stone. Trump hired the firm to support his business efforts in 1982, and Manafort saw Trump over the years at political and social events in New York City, as well as at Stone's wedding. At the 1988 and 1996 Republican National Conventions, where Manafort worked for presidential nominees George H. W. Bush and Bob Dole, respectively, Trump requested VIP status.

Among Manafort's lobbying clients were Ferdinand Marcos of the Philippines, former Zaire dictator Mobutu Sese Seko, and Viktor Yanukovych, the pro-Russia president of Ukraine who was overthrown in

February 2014. By the time he joined the Trump campaign, Manafort had spent much time working in Russia and forging connections there.

Those Russian ties date back to his consulting work for Russian oligarch Oleg Deripaska, who was closely aligned with Vladimir Putin, from 2005 through 2009. Dole, who had lobbied for Deripaska in the United States, connected Manafort to him. Deripaska, whose global empire included aluminum and power companies and who, as an oligarch, met with Putin regularly, used Manafort to ensure the presence of friendly political officials in countries where he did business, often the post-Soviet republics. Future Manafort campaign deputy Rick Gates, who interned at Manafort's DC-based lobbying firm and eventually moved to the Kiev office of a spin-off Manafort consulting firm, described Manafort's work for Deripaska as "political risk insurance." A 2005 memo referred to the benefits of Manafort's work to "the Putin Government" and the need to brief the Kremlin. Manafort's company earned tens of millions of dollars from Deripaska, who also loaned it millions of dollars.

Through Deripaska, Manafort met Ukrainian oligarch Rinat Akhmetov, who hired him to do political work for the Russia-aligned Party of Regions in Ukraine after its presidential candidate, Viktor Yanukovych, had seen his victory overturned in late 2004. Manafort became close to Yanukovych and helped engineer the Party of Regions' rebound and Yanukovych's ascent to the Ukrainian presidency in 2010, despite the US government's opposition to his candidacy because of his perceived connection to Putin. Yanukovych remained in power until his overthrow in February 2014.

During this extended stretch, Konstantin Kilimnik, a Russian national who spoke Russian and Ukrainian, worked for Manafort in Kiev. He had direct access to Yanukovych and his senior entourage and facilitated many of Manafort's communications with Deripaska and Ukrainian oligarchs. Kilimnik also had an ongoing relationship with Deripaska's deputy, Victor Boyarkin. Although Manafort would tell the special counsel's office that he did not think Kilimnik was a Russian "spy," the FBI concluded that he was tied to Russian intelligence.

Born on April 27, 1970, Kilimnik attended school at the Military Institute of the Ministry of Defense in Moscow, which trains interpreters for the Russian military intelligence agency known as the GRU, the wing that hacked Hillary Clinton and Democratic officials. Kilimnik became a translator for the Russian army, and US government visa records showed that he obtained a visa to travel to the United States with a Russian diplomatic passport in 1997.

He did translation work for the International Republican Institute's (IRI) Moscow office from 1998 to 2005. Writing about Kilimnik in August 2016, Politico spoke with five people who worked with the institute who said that Kilimnik was known to have been in the intelligence service and said he learned such fluent English from "Russian military intelligence."

"It was like 'Kostya, the guy from the GRU' — that's how we talked about him," one political operative said in Politico.

A former Kilimnik associate at IRI told the FBI that Kilimnik was fired from his post because his links to Russian intelligence were too strong.

Public relations consultant Jonathan Hawker, a British national who worked with Manafort's consulting firm, DMI, on a public relations campaign for Yanukovych, said that after that work ended, Kilimnik asked him to help a Russian government entity to promote, in Western and Ukrainian media, Russia's position on its 2014 invasion of Crimea. Gates suspected that Kilimnik was a spy and shared that view with Manafort, Hawker, and Alexander van der Zwaan, a lawyer who had worked with DMI on a report for the Ukrainian Ministry of Foreign Affairs.

Meanwhile, Manafort's relationship with Deripaska had deteriorated over some financial dealings. Deripaska became the sole investor in Pericles Emerging Market Partners LP, a Cayman Islands–based fund created in 2007 by Manafort and his former business partner Richard Davis to pursue investments in Eastern Europe. In court filings years later,

Deripaska would accuse Manafort and Gates of defrauding him of $18.9 million, the amount that his firm, Surf Horizon, had invested in Pericles (plus $7.35 million in management fees), for what was supposed to be a $200 million fund to make private equity deals, primarily in Russia and Ukraine.

Deripaska's January 2018 New York State Court lawsuit, which followed a similar one filed in 2014 in the Cayman Islands, said that the fund's only investment was a Ukrainian cable TV station, accused Manafort and Gates of overstating the station's cost, and claimed that Manafort and Gates "siphoned for themselves millions of dollars." Deripaska complained that when he asked for his money back during the 2008 credit crunch, he received nothing.

By 2009, Manafort's business relationship with Deripaska had, in Gates's words, "dried up." But years later, Manafort saw an opportunity to revive this relationship and to resolve the financial conflict.

He would join the Trump campaign.

15

"The guy who gave you your biggest black caviar jar"

Roger Stone, who had been Manafort's longtime consulting-firm partner, recommended that Trump add Manafort to the campaign team. So
did Thomas Barrack, a Trump friend and advisor who had known
Manafort for decades and who told the *Washington Post* that he had
loaned Manafort $1.5 million to refinance a home in the Hamptons and
was paid back in fourteen months. Barrack suggested that given
Manafort's prior experience in this area, he should manage the Republican National Convention for Trump.

When Manafort met Trump at his Mar-a-Lago estate in Florida in
March 2016, the candidate hired him. Manafort agreed to work on the
campaign for no pay, even though he had no meaningful income at that
point.

Manafort saw other ways in which he would be compensated.

For one, resuscitating his political campaign career could be financially beneficial. If Trump became president, Manafort told associates he
planned to remain outside the government so that he could monetize his
relationship with the new administration. Manafort also had made much
money in Russia and Ukraine and saw an opportunity to renew those
relationships as well as to resolve conflicts in which he was said to owe
millions of dollars.

Right after joining the campaign, Manafort instructed Gates to prepare separate memos to Deripaska and to three Ukrainian oligarchs who

were senior officials with the Opposition Bloc, the successor to the pro-Russian Party of Regions. The memos discussed Manafort's position with the Trump campaign and his availability to consult on Ukrainian politics. Gates emailed the memoranda and an announcement of Manafort's Trump campaign appointment to Kilimnik on March 30 so that this Russian colleague could translate and distribute the messages. Manafort followed up on April 11 with an email to Kilimnik asking whether Kilimnik had shown "our friends" the media coverage of his new position.

"Absolutely," Kilimnik replied. "Every article."

"How do we use [this] to get whole?" Manafort asked. "Has Ovd [Oleg Vladimirovich Deripaska] operation seen [it]?"

"Yes," Kilimnik wrote back the same day. "I have been sending everything to Victor [Boyarkin, Deripaska's deputy], who has been forwarding the coverage directly to OVD."

Manafort told Gates that being hired on the campaign was "good for business" and would boost Manafort's chances of getting paid the $2 million or so he felt he was owed for previous political consulting work in Ukraine. Gates also later explained to our office that Manafort thought his role on the campaign could help "confirm" that Deripaska had dropped the Pericles lawsuit. Plus, Deripaska wanted a visa to the United States, so having Manafort inside the campaign — and later, perhaps, the administration — might be helpful to him.

In April or early May, Manafort directed Gates to send the Trump campaign's internal polling data and other updates to Kilimnik so that Kilimnik, in turn, could share it with the three Ukrainian oligarchs mentioned above and with Deripaska. Gates told our office that he didn't know why Manafort wanted him to pass along the polling information. Maybe, Gates thought, Manafort wished to showcase his work to elicit job offers after the campaign was over. Gates also believed that Manafort sent polling data to Deripaska so that Deripaska would not pursue his lawsuit against Manafort.

Of course, Kilimnik had worked with the GRU, and Deripaska was close to Putin, who was assumed to be pushing the Russian efforts to boost the Trump campaign through social media and other means.

Manafort carried on these actions after Trump named him to replace Corey Lewandowski as campaign manager on June 20. Manafort directed Gates to send the Russians internal polling data prepared for the campaign by pollster Tony Fabrizio, a longtime Manafort colleague whom Manafort brought into the campaign. Following Manafort's instructions, Gates would send Kilimnik polling data via WhatsApp and then delete the communications every day. Even after Manafort left the campaign in mid-August, Gates continued sending Kilimnik polling data, although with less frequency and including less internal and more publicly available data.

There is evidence that Manafort was motivated to share the polling data with Deripaska to help resolve his financial conflict with the Russian oligarch. After receiving an email from a Ukrainian reporter on July 7 asking about Manafort's failed investment that Deripaska backed, Manafort asked Kilimnik whether there had been any movement on "this issue with our friend," referring to Deripaska. When Kilimnik's reply referred to "the issue" and "our biggest interest," he was speaking of a resolution of the Deripaska-Pericles conflict:

I am carefully optimistic on the question of our biggest interest.

Our friend [Boyarkin, Deripaska's deputy] said there is lately significantly more attention to the campaign in his boss' mind, and he will be most likely looking for ways to reach out to you pretty soon, understanding all the time sensitivity. I am more than sure that it will be resolved and we will get back to the original relationship with V.'s boss [Deripaska].

Manafort replied eight minutes later that Kilimnik should tell Deripaska "that if he needs private briefings, we can accommodate."

While working on the campaign, Manafort met twice in person with Kilimnik, the first time on May 7 in New York City. Before the meeting,

Kilimnik had been collecting information about the political situation in Ukraine, including what he had learned from a recent Moscow trip that a former Party of Regions official had taken, presumably to meet with high-ranking Russian officials. Kilimnik traveled to Washington, DC, around May 5 and had prearranged meetings with State Department employees.

Late on May 6, Gates arranged for Kilimnik to take a 3:00 a.m. train from Washington to meet Manafort in New York for breakfast. At their meeting, Manafort and Kilimnik discussed Ukraine and the Trump campaign, and Manafort expected Kilimnik to pass the information back to individuals in Ukraine and elsewhere. Opposition Bloc members saw Manafort's position on the campaign as an opportunity for their pro-Russia party, but Manafort told investigators that Kilimnik did not ask for anything. Instead, he said that Kilimnik spoke about a plan to boost election participation in the Opposition Bloc–strong eastern zone of Ukraine. After their breakfast, Kilimnik returned to Washington, DC.

The two met again on the evening of August 2 at the Grand Havana Club in New York City, after using code words to set the whole thing up. Kilimnik flew from Kiev to Moscow on July 28, and the next day, in an email to Manafort with the subject line "Black Caviar," Kilimnik requested they meet, writing,

> I met today with the guy who gave you your biggest black caviar jar several years ago. We spent about 5 hours talking about his story, and I have several important messages from him to you. He asked me to go and brief you on our conversation. I said I have to run it by you first, but in principle I am prepared to do it. . . . It has to do about the future of his country, and is quite interesting.

Manafort later explained that "the guy who gave you your biggest black caviar jar" was Yanukovych, who in 2010 had given Manafort a large jar of caviar worth about $30,000 to $40,000 to celebrate his victorious presidential election. When Kilimnik visited Moscow before this trip to the United States, Yanukovych was living there.

Kilimnik flew back from Moscow to Kiev on July 31 and wrote to Manafort that he needed "about 2 hours" for their meeting "because it is a long caviar story to tell." Kilimnik would land at JFK Airport at 7:30 p.m. on August 2, and then he and Manafort, joined by Gates, would have a late dinner. As it happened, Deripaska's private plane flew to Teterboro Airport in New Jersey on the evening of August 2. Customs and Border Protection records show that the only passengers on the plane were Deripaska's wife, daughter, mother, and father-in-law, while Kilimnik was confirmed to have flown to New York on a commercial flight.

Here is what interviews and other evidence suggest Manafort, Kilimnik, and Gates discussed at their dinner meeting:

1. **A plan to resolve Ukraine's ongoing political problems by creating an autonomous republic in its eastern region of Donbas.** Supported by the Russian military, pro-Russian Ukrainian militia forces had occupied the region since 2014, the year President Yanukovych was ousted. Under this plan, Russia would assist in withdrawing the military, and Donbas would become an autonomous region within Ukraine with its own prime minister: Yanukovych.

Manafort later admitted the plan was a "backdoor" way for Russia to control eastern Ukraine, and he told our office that he advised Kilimnik that the plan was crazy. If he had not cut off discussion with Kilimnik, Manafort said, Kilimnik would have pressed him to convince Trump to support the plan publicly, and Yanukovych would have expected Manafort to tap his European and Ukrainian connections to bolster it. Yet despite Manafort's contention that he shot down this plan, the discussion didn't end there. Kilimnik emailed Manafort about the peace plan again on December 8 and discussed it with him in meetings in January and February 2017.

2. **The Trump campaign and its strategies.** Manafort briefed Kilimnik on the campaign's messaging and shared its internal polling

data, with a focus on the "battleground" states of Michigan, Wisconsin, Pennsylvania, and Minnesota. All of those states but Minnesota wound up going to Trump by small margins, swinging the election his way.

3. **How Manafort might resolve his two financial disputes related to his Russia/Ukraine work.** This topic covered Deripaska's action against Manafort to regain his sizable Pericles investment and the money Manafort said the Opposition Bloc owed him for earlier political consulting work.

When they finished their dinner meeting, Gates and Manafort left separately from Kilimnik. By then, the media was tracking Manafort's Russia connections, so they wished to avoid him being publicly linked with a man whom US intelligence considered to be a Russian spy.

16

"Appropriate assistance"

Paul Manafort was put in charge of the Republican National Convention in large part because of his experience in wrangling and managing delegates during the previous conventions on which he had worked. That aspect of the 2016 convention, which occurred July 18–21 in Cleveland, went smoothly and was considered a success for the candidate and the party. But there was a lingering area of contention as well, one that related to questions about Ukrainian autonomy that Manafort had been addressing in his pro-Russia consulting work.

When the Trump campaign's foreign advisors reviewed the 2012 Republican convention's foreign policy platform items, they identified changes they might want to make on behalf of their candidate. Given that Trump and his team had been advocating for better US-Russia relations, they proposed toning down the 2012 language that named Russia as the top US threat. At the same time, the Trump team was mindful of not appearing to overrule the party's wishes regarding the platform discussion.

Trump campaign members attended platform committee meetings knowing that while they could request changes, only delegates could participate in formal discussions and vote on the platform. The first meeting to propose amendments took place on July 11, and Diana Denman, a Ted Cruz–supporting Republican delegate from the San Antonio, Texas, area, submitted an amendment that referred to Russia's "ongoing military aggression" in Ukraine and advocated "maintaining (and, if warranted, increasing) sanctions against Russia until Ukraine's sovereignty and territorial integrity are fully restored." It also called for "providing lethal defensive weapons to Ukraine's armed forces and greater coordination with NATO on defense planning."

Senior Trump campaign advisor J. D. Gordon flagged this amendment as contradicting what he contended was Trump's stated position on Ukraine: Europeans should be responsible for any assistance to Ukraine while the United States worked toward better relations with Russia. Gordon then moved to dilute the proposed platform change. When Denman offered her amendment at the meeting of the National Security and Defense Platform Subcommittee, Gordon and fellow campaign staff Matt Miller asked a committee cochair to table it to allow for more discussion. Gordon objected to the phrase "providing lethal defense weapons to Ukraine," but Denman refused to strike that language.

Denman said later that Gordon spoke with her while, he said, he was on the phone with Trump, but she was skeptical. Gordon later denied telling her that he had Trump on the line, and his phone records did not reveal calls to any known Trump numbers. But Gordon did call Jeff Sessions, who oversaw national security issues for the campaign, in Washington, DC, that afternoon.

Gordon consulted with two more campaign advisors and discussed changing the amendment's wording from providing "lethal defense weapons" to "appropriate assistance." One of those two advisors, campaign policy director John Mashburn, had been suggesting that the campaign take a hands-off approach at the platform meetings. He told Gordon that Trump had not taken a stance on this issue, so the campaign should not intervene in the proposed amendment.

Nonetheless, when the platform subcommittee addressed the amendment again, it replaced "lethal defense weapons" with "appropriate assistance" before approving the amendment as a whole. Sam Clovis, the campaign's national cochair and chief policy advisor, said later that he was surprised by the wording change and did not think it reflected Trump's position. Upon seeing "appropriate assistance," Mashburn concluded that Gordon had violated his directive not to intervene.

As the Republican National Convention got under way, Jeff Sessions and Gordon spoke at the Global Partners in Diplomacy conference in Cleveland. About eighty foreign ambassadors to the United States, including Russian ambassador Kislyak, were invited to this event, which was cosponsored by the State Department and the Heritage Foundation, a conservative think tank. Gordon's speech on July 20 asserted that the United States should maintain better relations with Russia. Sessions, who spoke the same day, took questions from the audience, including one supposedly asked by Kislyak.

After the speeches, several ambassadors greeted Gordon and Sessions. Shaking hands with Kislyak, Gordon told the Russian ambassador that he meant what he said about improving US-Russia relations. Sessions also spoke with Kislyak and other ambassadors, although he later told our office that he had no recollection of what he and the Russian ambassador discussed.

Gordon and Kislyak ate together at a conference reception later that evening and were joined at the table by the ambassadors from Azerbaijan and Kazakhstan, as well as Russia-centric Trump advisor Carter Page. Gordon again brought up the need for improved US-Russia relations.

The interactions between the Russian ambassador and Gordon and Sessions continued past the convention. On August 3, a Russian embassy official wrote to Gordon "on behalf of" Kislyak and invited Gordon "to have breakfast/tea with the Ambassador at his residence" in Washington, DC, the following week.

"These days are not optimal for us, as we are busily knocking down a constant stream of false media stories while also preparing for the first debate with HRC," Gordon responded by email five days later. "Hope to take a raincheck for another time when things quiet down a bit. Please pass along my regards to the Ambassador."

A Russian embassy representative also reached out to Sessions at his Senate office to try to set up a meeting with Kislyak. As a member of the Senate Foreign Relations Committee, Sessions would meet routinely with foreign officials, but such requests increased dramatically in 2016, given Sessions's prominent involvement in the Trump campaign and speculation that he would be under serious consideration for a Trump administration cabinet-level position.

Saying later that he thought he was helping the campaign by meeting with such foreign ambassadors, Sessions spoke with Kislyak in his Senate office on September 8. With at least two of his Senate staff present, Sessions communicated his concern about Russia's sale of a missile-defense system to Iran, Russian planes' buzzing of US military in the Middle East, and Russian aggression in Ukraine and Moldova. Kislyak presented Russia's point of view on those issues and complained about NATO land forces' presence in former Soviet-bloc countries bordering Russia. They also spoke of the presidential race, with Kislyak calling it "an interesting campaign." No one present later recalled any discussion of Russian election interference or a request for Sessions to pass along any information from the Russian government to the Trump campaign.

Before the meeting ended, Kislyak invited Sessions to another discussion of US-Russia relations over a meal at the ambassador's residence. Sessions was noncommittal, and after the Russian ambassador had left, Sandra Luff, Sessions's legislative director, warned the senator against a one-on-one meeting with an "old school KGB guy" such as Kislyak.

Our investigation discovered no evidence that they met again. But the meetings they did have would become relevant months later when during his confirmation hearings to become Trump's attorney general, Sessions would be asked whether anyone associated with the campaign had communicated with representatives of the Russian government.

17

"Russia, if you're listening..."

After WikiLeaks posted thousands of hacked DNC documents on July 22, 2016, there was increased public questioning of the Russian government's actions and its possible efforts to influence the presidential election. The *New York Times* reported on July 26 that US intelligence agencies had "told the White House they now have 'high confidence' that the Russian government was behind the theft of emails and documents from the Democratic National Committee."

Robby Mook, Hillary Clinton's campaign manager, made a similar point on ABC News's *This Week with George Stephanopoulos*. "Experts are telling us that Russian state actors broke into the DNC, took all these emails and now are leaking them out through these websites," Mook said. "It's troubling that some experts are now telling us that this was done by the Russians for the purpose of helping Donald Trump."

The Trump campaign was not troubled. On the contrary, its officials were enthusiastic about the releases, and Trump, who had been anointed the Republican presidential nominee the previous week in Cleveland, expressed eagerness among his team over the prospect of more such leaks. In public, though, Trump dismissed the suggestion that Russia was in any way trying to help him.

"In order to try and deflect the horror and stupidity of the Wikileakes [*sic*] disaster, the Dems said maybe it is Russia dealing with Trump. Crazy!" he tweeted on July 26. Three minutes later, he tweeted, "For the record, I have ZERO investments in Russia."

This was the same day in which the Australian government quietly alerted the FBI about Russia's collecting "dirt" about Hillary Clinton. The following day, July 27, was day three of the four-day Democratic National Convention in Philadelphia. President Barack Obama would deliver a rousing endorsement of Hillary Clinton that night from the convention floor before Clinton accepted the nomination the following evening.

But on that morning, Trump held a news conference on his golf course in Doral, Florida, and declared "this whole thing with Russia" to be "a total deflection," as well as "farfetched" and "ridiculous."

Yet he added, "Russia, if you're listening, I hope you're able to find the thirty thousand emails that are missing. I think you will probably be rewarded mightily by our press. Let's see if that happens. That'll be next. Yes, sir."

Trump was referring to emails that had been stored on Hillary Clinton's personal server during her tenure as secretary of state. The Federal Bureau of Investigation had been investigating Clinton's use of a personal server for official government business, and there were reports that as her staff sorted through professional and personal emails, some thirty thousand (or thirty-three thousand) of the latter had been deleted.

Following up on Trump's Russia request, NBC reporter Katy Tur asked whether he had any qualms about suggesting that a foreign government "hack into a system of anybody's in this country, let alone your rival?"

"No, it gives me no pause," Trump responded. "If they have them, they have them. We might as well — hey, you know what gives me more pause? That a person in our government, crooked Hillary Clinton — here's what gives me pause. Be quiet. I know you want to save her. That a person in our government, Katy, would delete or get rid of 33,000 emails. That gives me a big problem. After she gets a subpoena! She gets subpoenaed, and she gets rid of 33,000 emails? That gives me a problem. Now, if Russia or China or any other country has those emails, I mean, to be honest with you, I'd love to see them."

During the Doral news conference, Trump said, "I have nothing to do with Russia," five times. He also stressed his desire to "have Russia friendly" and floated the idea of recognizing Crimea as a Russian territory and lifting US sanctions against Russia. "We'll be looking at that. Yeah, we'll be looking."

He denied any recent business dealings with Russia, saying that after the 2013 Miss Universe pageant in Moscow, he had spoken with Russian companies that wanted to develop Trump-branded properties, but "it never worked out.... We decided not to do it."

Reporting on the news conference in the *New York Times*, Ashley Parker and David E. Sanger wrote,

> *If Mr. Trump is serious in his call for Russian hacking or exposing Mrs. Clinton's emails, he would be urging a power often hostile to the United States to violate American law by breaking into a private computer network. He would also be contradicting the Republican platform, adopted last week in Cleveland, saying that cyberespionage "will not be tolerated," and promising to "respond in kind and in greater magnitude" to all Chinese and Russian cyberattacks.*

Michael Cohen, Donald Trump's personal counsel, had a different concern. He knew that the Trump Organization had been actively involved in talks to develop Trump Tower Moscow from September 2015 through June 2016, because as vice president of the organization, he had represented the Trump side for many of these negotiations. He also had updated his boss regularly about the project's progress, or lack thereof, and explored potential trips to Moscow for both him and Trump to promote and to finalize the deal.

So when Cohen heard Trump telling reporters that he had no business dealings with Russia, Cohen thought, *That isn't true.*

After the news conference, the lawyer expressed his misgivings to Trump, who replied that Trump Tower Moscow was not actually a deal yet. "Why mention it if it's not a deal?" Trump asked.

The Trump campaign was not going to modify its message. It would dig in and stick to this party line: Donald Trump has no business or connections with Russia.

Yet he had just asked Russia to find Hillary Clinton's emails.

Was Russia listening?

Within five hours of Trump's request, the Russian GRU military wing hacked Hillary Clinton's personal office for the first time. GRU's Unit 26165, which specialized in hacking efforts, created and sent malicious links to fifteen private email accounts associated with Clinton's office. It also hacked a DNC cloud-based account and eventually stole about three hundred gigabytes of data from it.

18

"Assange has kryptonite on Hillary"

WikiLeaks' massive dump of hacked materials had grabbed the Trump campaign's attention, and Trump and his team were eager to see what Julian Assange's organization would release next. They wanted to take advantage of it. The Trump team even worked up a press and communications strategy to be executed the moment that WikiLeaks released Hillary Clinton's missing emails.

The Trump camp's efforts to obtain information harmful to the Clinton campaign—and to gain insights as to when WikiLeaks might be releasing more such materials—became an all-hands-on-deck affair. Michael Cohen and Paul Manafort, Trump's campaign chair at the time, kept tabs on WikiLeaks' activities on their boss's behalf, and Trump stayed involved in these discussions. While en route to New York's LaGuardia Airport one day, the candidate received a call, apparently from advisor Roger Stone, after which he told Rick Gates, Manafort's campaign deputy, that more damaging-to-Clinton releases were on their way.

Stone, a longtime political operative who had an up-and-down relationship with Trump over many years, was a key player in the efforts to keep tabs on WikiLeaks. Described as a "dirty trickster" going back to his days working for President Nixon's reelection campaign in 1972, Stone lobbied on behalf of Trump's airline in the 1980s and casino business in the 1990s and advised Trump during his abortive 2000 presidential run. By 2008, when *The New Yorker* profiled Stone, he had drawn the future president's ire.

"Roger is a stone-cold loser," Trump said in Jeffrey Toobin's article. "He always tries taking credit for things he never did."

Trump took issue with Stone's role in bringing down New York governor Eliot Spitzer in a prostitution scandal and allegedly leaving a phone message for the governor's eighty-three-year-old father, Bernard Spitzer, in which Stone said that the father might be investigated for loans to his son's campaigns. The message went, "If you resist this subpoena, you will be arrested and brought to Albany. And there is not a goddam thing your phony, psycho, piece-of-shit son can do about it." Although it sounded like his voice on the call, which came from his wife's phone, Stone denied it was him, and Trump had a problem with Stone not telling the truth.

"They caught Roger red-handed lying," Trump was quoted in *The New Yorker*. "What he did was ridiculous and stupid. I lost respect for Eliot Spitzer when he didn't sue Roger Stone for doing that to his father, who is a wonderful man."

But by the time he was in his midsixties, Stone was back on Trump's team as an early supporter of his 2016 presidential campaign. Then the two allegedly sparred over Trump's performance at a Republican candidates' debate, and Trump fired Stone from the campaign in August 2015.

"I terminated Roger Stone last night because he no longer serves a useful function for my campaign," Trump was quoted in the *Washington Post* on August 8, 2015, adding, "I really don't want publicity seekers who want to be on magazines or who are out for themselves. This campaign is not about them. It's about victory and making America great again… I'm going to surround myself only with the best and most serious people. We want top of the line professionals."

Stone responded on Twitter, "I fired Trump."

Still, Stone remained involved in the campaign informally and was back in Trump's good graces by the time the candidate appeared on conspiracy theorist Alex Jones's radio show in December 2015. "Roger's a good guy," Trump told Jones. "He's been so loyal and so wonderful."

One of Stone's services to the Trump campaign was to appear in a March 2016 *National Enquirer* story that alleged that Republican primary rival Ted Cruz had carried on secret affairs with five women. "These stories have been swirling about Cruz for some time," Stone was quoted as saying. "I believe where there is smoke there is fire. I have to believe this will hurt him with his evangelical Christian supporters."

Calling the story "garbage" and "complete and utter lies," Cruz accused Stone of having smeared him. "Mr. Stone is a man who has 50 years of dirty tricks behind him," Cruz said.

As Trump sought more information on WikiLeaks' plans, Stone took charge of making contact with Assange, directly or indirectly. Stone enlisted Jerome Corsi, who attacked previous Democratic presidential candidates with his books *Unfit for Command: Swift Boat Veterans Speak Out Against John Kerry* (2004) and *The Obama Nation: Leftist Politics and the Cult of Personality* (2008), to serve as a liaison between him and WikiLeaks.

"Get to [Assange] at Ecuadorian Embassy in London and get the pending [WikiLeaks] emails," Stone emailed Corsi on July 25, the first day of the Democratic National Convention. "They deal with [the Clinton] Foundation, allegedly."

Corsi forwarded this request to Ted Malloch, an American Trump supporter living in Britain who was close to British politician and Brexit champion Nigel Farage. Stone emailed Corsi again on July 31 to say that Malloch should see Assange. Malloch later told investigators he never communicated directly with Assange, although he and Corsi had numerous FaceTime discussions about WikiLeaks starting in August 2016.

Corsi wrote back to Stone on August 2 suggesting how the campaign might exploit the next WikiLeaks releases of hacked materials:

Word is friend in embassy [Assange] plans 2 more dumps. One shortly after I'm back. 2nd in Oct. Impact planned to be very damaging.... Time to let more than Podesta to be exposed as in bed w enemy if they are not ready to drop HRC [Hillary Rodham Clinton]. That appears to be the game hackers are now about. Would not hurt to start suggesting HRC old, memory bad, has stroke — neither

he nor she well. I expect that much of next dump focus, setting stage
for Foundation debacle.

As it happened, the day after Clinton was videotaped almost fainting on September 10 from what later was diagnosed to be pneumonia, WikiLeaks posted a Twitter poll:

Hillary Clinton's collapse on Saturday, prior coughing fits and
unusual body movements are best explained by:
- *Allergies & personality*
- *Parkinsons*
- *MS*
- *Head injury complications*

WikiLeaks deleted the poll that night, noting that it was "too speculative."

By the time Corsi and Stone were inquiring about WikiLeaks' future releases, Assange's organization had obtained a motherlode of documents that would prove damaging to the Clinton campaign: campaign chair John Podesta's emails, which Russia's GRU wing had stolen in the spring. After WikiLeaks' first releases of Russian-hacked materials, the GRU-operated DCLeaks and WikiLeaks continued to communicate and to coordinate their efforts. They were in touch in September, and a metadata analysis suggested that the GRU prepared Podesta's emails for transfer to WikiLeaks on September 19, with documents attached to the emails separately on October 2. The stolen documents also might have been transferred to WikiLeaks via intermediaries that summer.

Corsi informed Malloch that Podesta's emails would be coming from WikiLeaks, at which point he said that "we" would be in the driver's seat. Roger Stone began making public references about WikiLeaks and Podesta's emails.

"I actually have communicated with Assange," Stone told a Florida audience on August 8. "I believe the next tranche of his documents pertain to the Clinton Foundation, but there's no telling what the October surprise may be." Stone also said in an August 12 interview that he had been "in communication with" Assange but was "not at liberty to discuss what I have."

In an interview on August 16, Stone mentioned having "had some back-channel communication with WikiLeaks and Assange." He said in another interview that day that he had communicated with Assange and they had "a mutual acquaintance who is a fine gentleman." Two days later, he said in a television interview that he had been communicating with Assange through an "intermediary, somebody who is a mutual friend."

On August 21, Stone tweeted, "Trust me, it will soon the Podesta's time in the barrel. #CrookedHillary."

New York radio host Randy Credico asked Stone on August 23, "You've been in touch indirectly with Assange.... Can you give us any kind of insight? Is there an October surprise happening?"

"Well, first of all, I don't want to intimate in any way that I control or having influence with Assange because I do not," Stone said on the air. "We have a mutual friend, somebody we both trust, and therefore I am a recipient of pretty good information."

Although Credico was interviewing Stone about his communications with Assange, the radio host soon was facilitating them, as the two of them continued to communicate through text messages and emails about WikiLeaks and its plans. Credico texted Stone that on August 25, he was going to have Assange on his show. The day after that appearance, Credico texted Stone that Assange had talked about him.

What did Assange say?

"He didn't say anything bad," Credico said. "We were talking about how the press is trying to make it look like you and he are in cahoots."

The next day Credico texted Stone, "Assange has kryptonite on Hillary."

In September, Stone was using Credico as a go-between with Assange.

"I am emailing u a request to pass on to Assange," Stone texted the radio host on September 18.

"OK," Credico replied, later adding, "Just remember do not name me as your connection to Assange[;] you had one before that you referred to."

Stone then emailed Credico an article making allegations against Hillary Clinton involving her years as secretary of state. "Please ask Assange for any State or HRC e-mail from August 10 to August 30 — particularly on August 20, 2011 that mention [the article's subject] or confirm this narrative."

Stone followed up the next day, instructing Credico to "pass my message" to Assange.

"I did," Credico replied.

On September 30, Credico texted Stone a photo of himself standing outside the London Ecuadorian embassy, where Assange was staying. Around this time, the press had been reporting that Assange planned to make a public announcement on or around Tuesday, October 4, WikiLeaks' ten-year anniversary. Credico sent Stone a text on Saturday, October 1 saying, "big news Wednesday...now pretend u don't know me."

"U died five years ago," Stone replied.

"Great," Credico wrote. "Hillary's campaign will die this week."

Roger Stone was not the only Trump campaign associate who was in contact with WikiLeaks around this time. Donald Trump Jr. also corresponded with Assange's organization after it reached out to him.

On September 20, 2016, someone named Jason Fishbein, who was not a Trump supporter, sent WikiLeaks the password for a yet-to-be-launched website that highlighted candidate Trump's "unprecedented and dangerous" ties to Russia. WikiLeaks then gave Trump Jr. a heads-up about this site via a direct Twitter message: "A PAC run anti-Trump site putintrump .org is about to launch. The PAC is a recycled pro-Iraq war PAC. We have guessed the password. It is 'putintrump.' See 'About' for who is behind it. Any comments?"

Later that day, Trump Jr. emailed his father's campaign's senior staff:

Guys I got a weird Twitter DM from wikileaks. See below. I tried the password and it works and the about section they reference contains the next pic in terms of who is behind it. Not sure if this is anything but it seems like it's really wikileaks asking me as I follow them and it is a DM. Do you know the people mentioned and what the conspiracy they are looking for could be? These are just screen shots but it's a fully built out page claiming to be a PAC let me know your thoughts and if we want to look into it.

The anti-Trump site went public the next day, and Trump Jr. sent a direct message back to WikiLeaks: "Off the record, I don't know who that is but I'll ask around. Thanks."

WikiLeaks sent another direct message to Trump Jr. on October 3, asking "you guys" to publicize a link to a piece claiming that Hillary Clinton had advocated using a drone to target Julian Assange.

"I've already done so," Trump Jr. replied. "What's behind this Wednesday leak I keep reading about?"

WikiLeaks did not respond, though the organization would be back in touch with the candidate's son soon enough. Stone also was anticipating something significant that Wednesday. As he tweeted on Sunday, October 2, "Wednesday @HillaryClinton is done."

The following day, he tweeted, "I have total confidence that @wikileaks and my hero Julian Assange will educate the American people soon. #LockHerUp."

Assange's address marking WikiLeaks' tenth anniversary was scheduled for Tuesday, October 4, and two days beforehand, Stone was disappointed to read that WikiLeaks was canceling its "highly anticipated Tuesday announcement due to security concerns."

Stone emailed the story to Credico along with a note: "WTF?"

"head fake," Credico responded.

"Did Assange back off?"

"I can't tal[k] about it," Credico replied, although he later said, "I think it[']s on for tomorrow.... Off the record Hillary and her people are doing a full-court press they keep Assange from making the next dump..... That's all I can tell you on this line.... Please leave my name out of it."

Stone relayed this information to others inside and outside the Trump campaign.

"Spoke to my friend in London last night," he wrote on October 3 to a Trump supporter working on the campaign. "The payload is still coming."

That same day a journalist, revealed by the *New York Times* to be Breitbart Washington editor Matthew Boyle, emailed Stone: "Assange — what's he got? Hope it's good."

"It is," Stone responded.

Assange held a news conference on October 4 but did not release any new documents related to Hillary Clinton or her campaign. Trump campaign chair Steve Bannon, whom Stone had been trying to engage about the WikiLeaks releases, was puzzled.

"What was that this morning???" Bannon, identified in this exchange by the *New York Times*, emailed Stone after Assange's news conference.

"Fear," Stone replied. "Serious security concern. He thinks they are going to kill him and the London police are standing done [*sic*]. However — a load [of releases] every week going forward."

The aforementioned Trump supporter texted Stone that day as well to ask, "Heard anymore from London?"

"Yes," Stone replied, "want to talk on a secure line — got Whatsapp?" He went on to tell the supporter that more material was coming that would be damaging to the Clinton campaign.

On October 6, Stone tweeted, "Julian Assange will deliver a devastating expose on Hillary at a time of his choosing. I stand by my prediction."

His prediction came true the following day, although the circumstances would prove to be more dramatic than anyone on either campaign might have predicted.

19

"Grab 'em by the pussy"

On October 7, two days before the second scheduled debate between Trump and Clinton, the *Washington Post* published a video and accompanying story of Trump and *Access Hollywood* host Billy Bush having an on-mic conversation while en route to a September 2005 taping of a segment for that entertainment show. In the first part of the video, Trump discusses how he had tried to seduce Bush's then-cohost, Nancy O'Dell:

> *I moved on her, and I failed. I'll admit it. I did try and fuck her. She was married. And I moved on her very heavily.... I moved on her like a bitch. But I couldn't get there.*

In another passage, Trump anticipated his and Bush's imminent on-camera meeting with actress-model Arianne Zucker:

> *I better use some Tic Tacs just in case I start kissing her. You know I'm automatically attracted to beautiful — I just start kissing them. It's like a magnet. Just kiss. I don't even wait. And when you're a star, they let you do it. You can do anything. Grab 'em by the pussy. You can do anything.*

The fallout from Trump's comments was immediate, not only from his political opponents ("This is horrific. We cannot allow this man to become president," Hillary Clinton tweeted) but also Republicans such as speaker of the house Paul Ryan, who disinvited Trump from a campaign rally and announced he would no longer support his presidential campaign (at least at that particular moment); previous presidential nominee Mitt Romney ("Hitting on married women? Condoning assault? Such vile degradations demean our wives and daughters and corrupt America's face to the world"); former California governor Arnold Schwarzenegger ("For the first time since I became a citizen in 1983, I will not vote for the Republican candidate for president"); Arizona senator John McCain (one of several Republicans who rescinded their endorsement of Trump); and others who called for Mike Pence to replace Trump at the top of the ticket.

Trump issued a statement that day offering a conditional apology that roped in his opponent's husband:

This was locker room banter, a private conversation that took place many years ago. Bill Clinton has said far worse to me on the golf course — not even close. I apologise if anyone was offended.

Amid this uproar came serious speculation, among politicians as well as press observers, that Trump's campaign might not survive. But thirty minutes after the *Washington Post* posted the *Access Hollywood* tapes, WikiLeaks began publishing the Russia-hacked emails from Clinton campaign chair John Podesta, providing a counternarrative to the campaign coverage.

Assange's organization released 2,050 emails that first day, more than 50,000 in all, many parceled out day by day over the next month leading up to Election Day. The most recent of the published emails was dated March 21, 2016, two days after the GRU sent Podesta a spear phishing email. Included were texts from private Clinton speeches, internal communications between Podesta and other senior Clinton campaign workers, and correspondences related to the Clinton Foundation. Many of these documents reflected poorly on the Clinton campaign, such as excerpts from high-priced speeches Hillary Clinton had delivered to investment banks (reinforcing Bernie Sanders's accusation that she was too close to Wall Street) and the revelation that she may have received debate questions in advance from CNN's Donna Brazile.

Undaunted that they were dealing with stolen private materials being released with hostile political intent, mainstream news outlets pored through the releases to produce a series of attention-grabbing headlines. "Leaked Speech Excerpts Show a Hillary Clinton at Ease With Wall Street" was the *New York Times*'s headline on an October 7 story that began,

> *In lucrative paid speeches that Hillary Clinton delivered to elite financial firms but refused to disclose to the public, she displayed an easy comfort with titans of business, embraced unfettered international trade and praised a budget-balancing plan that would have required cuts to Social Security, according to documents posted online Friday by WikiLeaks.*

Three days later the *Times* published "Highlights from the Clinton Campaign Emails: How to Deal With Sanders and Biden." They included the following:

- "Emails reveal the care advisers took with every part of the campaign — right down to a single Twitter post."
- "Clinton allies expressed concern in 2015 about a possible Biden run."
- "The Clinton camp seemed unprepared for the insurgent campaign of Bernie Sanders."
- "But the campaign did get a heads-up later from a D.N.C. official about some of Sanders's efforts."
- "Clinton's team was keenly aware of how vulnerable her Wall Street ties made her appear next to Sanders."

In all, WikiLeaks released thirty-three tranches of stolen Podesta emails between October 7 and November 7, the day before the presidential election, ensuring a stream of media reports that portrayed the Clinton campaign in a bad light.

With so much happening on October 7, it might have been easy to overlook the statement issued that day by the Department of Homeland Security and Office of the Director of National Intelligence on Election Security. It began,

> *The U.S. Intelligence Community (USIC) is confident that the Russian Government directed the recent compromises of e-mails from US persons and institutions, including from US political organizations. The recent disclosures of alleged hacked e-mails on sites like DCLeaks.com and WikiLeaks and by the Guccifer 2.0 online persona are consistent with the methods and motivations of Russian-directed efforts. These thefts and disclosures are intended to interfere with the US election process. Such activity is not new to Moscow — the Russians have used similar tactics and techniques across Europe and Eurasia, for example, to influence public opinion there. We believe, based on the scope and sensitivity of these efforts, that only Russia's senior-most officials could have authorized these activities.*

But the Trump campaign and Roger Stone weren't fretting about this statement. In conversations with senior Trump officials, Stone took credit for correctly predicting the big WikiLeaks dump. An associate of one high-ranking Trump official sent him a simple text: "well done."

Clinton campaign chair John Podesta was less sanguine, telling reporters on October 11,

> *Stone pointed his finger at me and said that I could expect some treatment that would expose me and ultimately sent out a tweet that said it would be my time in the barrel. So I think it's a reasonable assumption to — or at least a reasonable conclusion — that Mr. Stone had advance warning and the Trump campaign had advance warning about what Assange was going to do.*

Podesta also disclosed that the FBI had been in touch with him and was "investigating a criminal hack of my email," with the focus on "Russian intelligence."

Trump struck back that night at a campaign appearance in Florida, contending that the leaked emails — and the press's connecting them to his campaign — proved that he was the true victim. "WikiLeaks also shows something I've been warning everybody about for a long time," the Republican candidate said. "The media is simply an extension of Hillary Clinton's campaign. It's just one more way that the system is rigged."

The next day, October 12, WikiLeaks sent another message to Donald Trump Jr.: "Great to see you and your dad talking about our publications. Strongly suggest your dad tweets this link if he mentions us wlsearch.tk." The link, the message said, would help Trump in "digging through" leaked emails. It added, "We just released Podesta emails Part 4."

Trump Jr. tweeted the wlsearch.tk link two days later.

Also on October 14, a Fox News anchor asked vice presidential candidate Mike Pence whether the Trump campaign was "in cahoots" with WikiLeaks over the hacked email releases.

Replied Pence, "Nothing could be further from the truth."

20

"Why are you so interested in Seth Rich's killer?"

Here's a slice of tragedy that should have nothing to do with our story but does.

Twenty-seven-year-old Seth Rich was walking home from his favorite Washington, DC, bar in the residential Bloomingdale neighborhood in the early morning hours of July 10 when he was approached by one or more assailants. There was some sort of struggle, Rich's watchband was torn, and when the confrontation was over, the young man lay on the ground with two bullet wounds in his back while his attackers fled the scene.

About an hour and a half later, Rich was pronounced dead in the hospital. Police investigators concluded that his death was the result of a botched robbery. The killers remained at large.

That, aside from the family's grief and the hunt for the assailants, might have been the end of the story. But it was not.

Conspiracy theorists had been targeting Bill and Hillary Clinton for years, with Alex Jones's InfoWars site keeping a tally of an alleged Clinton body count. To people promoting such stories, Rich's murder presented another opportunity.

Rich had been a Democratic National Committee junior staffer in charge of voter expansion data. Two days after his death, on the same day that Bernie Sanders endorsed Hillary Clinton, came this tweet from the account @Luma923: "RIP Seth Conrad Rich who was set 2 testify in the California election fraud case. Investigate Clintons @TheDemocrats." That posting, which had no basis in fact, gained very little social media attention.

But, as reported by Michael Isikoff of Yahoo News and sourced to a US federal prosecutor, Russia's foreign intelligence service, the SVR, released a fake "bulletin" on July 13 alleging that Rich was about to tell the FBI about Hillary Clinton's corruption when the candidate's hit squad gunned him down. The website whatdoesitmean.com repeated those details the same day, and tweets linked to that and other conspiracy sites over the next few days bearing such messages as "CLINTON HIT TEAM STRIKES AGAIN. SETH RICH, RECENTLY MURDERED BY CIA TEAM. HAD FOUND CONNECTION PAY2PLAY C.F. COMEY!"; "Seth Rich killed, FBI Captures Clinton's 'Hit Team after gun battle near White House?'"; and "Seth Rich (Democrat Party Official) was murdered. He knew too much. Is it the Clinton Hit Team?"

But the Seth Rich conspiracy theories didn't gain significant traction until the following month, when Julian Assange got involved. By then, there was much public speculation that Russian hackers were the source of the stolen documents released by WikiLeaks, which was true. WikiLeaks wrote to the GRU's Guccifer 2.0 account on July 6 asking for Clinton-related materials before the Democratic National Convention, Guccifer 2.0 sent WikiLeaks its "big archive" on July 14, and WikiLeaks dumped its stash of twenty thousand stolen Democratic emails on July 22.

But on August 9, Assange and his organization began promoting an alternate explanation, one that implied that the late DNC worker was involved in the leaks and paid the ultimate price.

"ANNOUNCE: WikiLeaks has decided to issue a US$20k reward for information leading to conviction for the murder of DNC staffer Seth Rich," the @WikiLeaks Twitter account posted that day.

That same day a Dutch TV interviewer asked Assange, "Why are you so interested in Seth Rich's killer?"

"We are very interested in anything that might be a threat to alleged WikiLeaks sources," the WikiLeaks founder replied.

"I know you don't want to reveal your source, but it certainly sounds like you're suggesting a man who leaked information to WikiLeaks was then murdered," the interviewer said.

"If there's someone who's potentially connected to our publication and that person has been murdered in suspicious circumstances, it doesn't necessarily mean that the two are connected," Assange said. "But it is a very serious matter. . . . That type of allegation is very serious, as it's taken very seriously by us."

That got the ball rolling. On the day of Assange's interview, Roger Stone tweeted a photo of Rich, referred to him as "another dead body in the Clinton's wake" and also wrote, "Coincidence? I think not." InfoWars followed with conspiracy-implying pieces on August 11 and August 18, the former amplifying an August 11 WikiLeaks tweet about the Rich family's "spokesman" by saying, "The very fact that Wikileaks is still talking about Seth Rich's murder and his family's representation by a Democratic Party operative clearly suggests that the whistle-blower organization thinks there may be a cover-up taking place." The August 18 InfoWars story, which offered unsubstantiated claims about Rich having gone missing for hours before his shooting, was shared on Twitter by @TEN_GOP, which, you may recall, was the Russia-created Twitter account pretending to represent Tennessee's Republican Party.

The fake social media accounts controlled by Russia's Internet Research Agency tweeted and retweeted about Rich more than two thousand times, pushing the premise that the young man had been murdered by Hillary Clinton's assassins. These efforts continued even after the election. Chief White House strategist Steve Bannon texted a *60 Minutes* producer about Rich in March 2017, "Huge story . . . he was a Bernie guy . . . it was a contract kill, obviously," as Yahoo News reported.

Fox News ran a story on May 16, 2017, claiming, with no basis in fact, that the FBI had found evidence that Rich was in contact with WikiLeaks before his murder. Fox News commentator Sean Hannity took to the air to proclaim that this story "might expose the single biggest fraud, lies, perpetrated on the American people by the media and the Democrats in our history."

The victim's parents, Mary Rich and Joel Rich, had had enough. They demanded a retraction from Fox News and sent a cease-and-desist letter to a private investigator who had been contributing to Fox News. They also wrote about "our family's nightmare" in a May 23, 2017, column for the *Washington Post*:

> *Seth's death has been turned into a political football. Every day we wake up to new headlines, new lies, new factual errors, new people approaching us to take advantage of us and Seth's legacy. It just won't stop. The amount of pain and anguish this has caused us is unbearable. With every conspiratorial flare-up, we are forced to relive Seth's murder and a small piece of us dies as more of Seth's memory is torn away from us.*

Fox retracted the entire story.

Yet the following March 1, the conservative-leaning *Washington Times* regurgitated previously refuted points with a column titled "More Cover-Up Questions," in which author and retired navy admiral James A. Lyons asserted, "Interestingly, it is well known in the intelligence circles that Seth Rich and his brother, Aaron Rich, downloaded the DNC emails and was paid by Wikileaks for that information." The writer also implied that Aaron Rich had avoided being interviewed by investigators.

Jerome Corsi — who had contact with WikiLeaks as Roger Stone's liaison with the organization and who, in an August 2, 2016, email to Stone, had credited "hackers" with supplying WikiLeaks' materials — pushed the same conspiracy theory four days later. In a March 5, 2018, piece for InfoWars, Corsi called Seth Rich the "likely perpetrator" of the leak and said the young man was murdered for breaching the Democrats' email systems and delivering the materials to Assange's organization.

After the Rich family demanded and did not get a retraction from the *Washington Times*, it sued the paper and others — including Matt Couch, who had been advancing Rich-related conspiracy claims through his America First Media company — for making false and defamatory statements. The *Washington Times* settled the suit six months later and offered a full retraction and apology on September 30, 2018:

> *The Column included statements about Aaron Rich, the brother of former Democratic National Committee staffer Seth Rich, that we now believe to be false… The Washington Times understands that law enforcement officials have interviewed Mr. Rich and that he has cooperated with their investigation. The Washington Times did not intend to imply that Mr. Rich has obstructed justice in any way, and The Washington Times retracts and disavows any such implication. The Washington Times apologizes to Mr. Rich and his family.*

Corsi issued his own apology/retraction on the InfoWars site on March 4, 2019. He attributed his false assertions to the *Washington Times* column that had been retracted six months earlier:

> *Dr. Corsi acknowledges that his allegations were not based upon any independent factual knowledge regarding Seth or Aaron Rich.… It was not Dr. Corsi's intent to rely upon inaccurate information, or to cause any suffering to Mr. Rich's family. To that end, Dr. Corsi retracts the article and apologizes to the Rich family.*

Corsi also tweeted that day,

> *I'm not being threatened. My retracted article in error relied on a retracted Wash Times article retracted for making false statements. As Christians [sic] gentleman, I have sympathy for the suffering the Seth Rich family has gone through. I hope all will understand that. God Bless.*

You might think that would be the last word on this subject from Corsi, but no. CNN media reporter Oliver Darcy tweeted later that day, "Just spoke to Corsi. He told me he retracted this specific story because it relied on info that was retracted by the Washington Times. However, he said that he continues to believe it's possible DNC leak was inside job & that ppl should look into whether Seth Rich played a role."

So although InfoWars took down Corsi's March 5, 2018, piece, two earlier Corsi-written articles published on May 30, 2017 — with the head-lines "NEW EVIDENCE SUGGESTS SETH RICH WAS DNC LEAKER" and "SETH RICH MYSTERY: DNC LEAKS CAME FROM INSIDE, NOT RUSSIAN HACKERS" — remained up on the site.

On August 25, 2019, America First Media's Matt Couch tweeted again about the Seth Rich conspiracy theory, and Rudy Giuliani, President Trump's lawyer, promoted the tweet. When the Daily Beast called out Giuliani for going along with a long-refuted conspiracy theory, he texted the news site, "Either you haven't been trained in proper seductive [sic] reasoning or the most truthful explanation is irrelevant."

21

"It would be catastrophic to the Clinton campaign"

Donald Trump still wanted those Hillary Clinton emails that he had asked Russia to find, so he put his campaign staff on the case. Trump's future short-tenured national security advisor Michael Flynn became his point person whom he requested repeatedly to try to track down the emails.

Flynn cast a wide net, sending two colleagues on a quest that would take an ultimately dark turn. Flynn reached out to Barbara Ledeen, a Republican Senate staffer who worked for Senate Judiciary Committee chair Chuck Grassley. Flynn was well acquainted with Ledeen's husband, Michael Ledeen, having coauthored with him the 2016 book *The Field of Fight: How We Can Win the Global War Against Radical Islam and Its Allies*. Back in 1980, Michael Ledeen also wrote the "Billygate" articles that linked Jimmy Carter's brother Billy with Libyan leader Muammar Al Gaddafi and Palestinian Liberation Organization leader Yasser Arafat. (A *Wall Street Journal* investigation later indicated that Ledeen's Billy Carter work was part of a disinformation campaign intended to influence the 1980 presidential election.)

Flynn also contacted Peter Smith, a Republican investment banker who, in the early days of Bill Clinton's presidency, helped bankroll the "Troopergate" investigation into the former Arkansas governor's sexual activities. Not only did Smith and Barbara Ledeen know each other, but Ledeen had already attempted to obtain Hillary Clinton's missing emails with Smith's help. She sent him an email on December 3, 2015, proposing that they contact a certain person who "can get the emails which 1. Were classified and 2. Were purloined by our enemies. That would demonstrate what needs to be demonstrated."

At that time, Ledeen wrote a twenty-five-page proposal stating that Clinton's email server "was, in all likelihood, breached long ago" and that Chinese, Russian, and Iranian intelligence could "re-assemble the server's email content." She made clear the political stakes of this exercise: "Even if a single email was recovered and the providence [sic] of that email was a foreign service, it would be catastrophic to the Clinton campaign."

Smith declined Ledeen's "initiative" on December 16, deeming it not viable. But when Trump put out the call for Clinton's emails the following summer, Smith got to work on his own. On August 28, 2016, he used an encrypted account to send an email to undisclosed recipients, including then–Trump campaign cochair Sam Clovis, with the subject "Sec. Clinton's unsecured private email server":

> *Just finishing two days of sensitive meetings here in DC with involved groups to poke and probe on the above. It is clear that the Clinton's home-based, unprotected server was hacked with ease by both State-related players and private mercenaries. Parties with varying interests are circling to release ahead of the election.*

Smith set up a new company, KLS Research LLC, to facilitate the email search and to raise funds for the effort. The company collected more than $30,000 during the presidential campaign, although Smith said he raised even more than that. He also hired security personnel to seek out and to authenticate the emails.

In early September 2016, Smith distributed a document saying that these efforts were being done "in coordination" with the Trump campaign "to the extent permitted as an independent expenditure organization." In actuality, the Federal Election Commission states that an independent expenditure "is not made in coordination with any candidate or his or her campaign or political party," so if Smith was coordinating this project with the Trump campaign, he was violating the law. Smith's document named Flynn, Clovis, Bannon, and Kellyanne Conway among the Trump campaign officials he was keeping in the loop.

Smith and Ledeen reconvened in September 2016, and Ledeen said that she had obtained from the "dark web" a stash of what she thought were Clinton's deleted emails, but she needed funding to pay for their authentication. Enter Erik Prince, the billionaire founder of the private security company Blackwater and younger brother of future Trump education secretary Betsy DeVos. Prince underwrote the hiring of a tech advisor who, Prince said later, deemed the emails not to be authentic.

Smith continued sending emails about Clinton's deleted emails to that undisclosed recipient list including Clovis, writing on October 28 about a "tug of war going on within WikiLeaks over its planned releases in the new few days" and saying that Wikileaks "has maintained that it will save its best revelations for last under the theory that this allows little time for response prior to the U.S. Election November 8." An attachment to this email noted that WikiLeaks would release "All 33k deleted Emails" by November 1.

But neither WikiLeaks nor anyone else wound up releasing the thirty thousand–plus emails from Clinton's server before the election.

In his email drafts, Smith discussed having made contact with Russian hackers. In August 2016, he wrote that KLS Research had organized meetings with people "with ties and affiliations to Russia" who had access to the deleted Clinton emails. Our investigation could not independently confirm that such meetings actually took place; that Smith was in contact with Russian hackers; or that he, Ledeen, or anyone else in touch with the Trump campaign obtained Clinton's deleted emails.

So, you would think, we can close the book on this part of the story.

But six months after the election, in an interview he conducted with the *Wall Street Journal* on May 4, 2017, Smith discussed his efforts to obtain Clinton's deleted emails from Russian hackers with the help of

Michael Flynn. "We knew the people who had these [emails] were probably around the Russian government," he told the *Journal*.

This was the last interview the eighty-one-year-old Smith would ever
give. The next day, well before the *Journal* story had run, he checked into
the Aspen Suites Hotel in Rochester, Minnesota, and on May 14, his dead
body was found in his room with a bag over his head attached to a helium
tank. The reported cause of death was "asphyxiation due to displacement
of oxygen in confined space with helium."

A note left in the room proclaimed there was "NO FOUL PLAY
WHATSOEVER — ALL SELF-INFLICTED," "NO PARTY ASSISTED OR
HAD KNOWLEDGE AS AN ACCOMPLICE BEFORE THE FACT," and
he was taking his life due to a "RECENT BAD TURN IN HEALTH SINCE
JANUARY, 2017...LIFE INSURANCE OF $5 MILLION EXPIRING."

Rochester police deemed the death a suicide and used "normal protocol" to handle it.

22

"My father just didn't want to have that the distraction"

August 2016 was a turbulent month for the Trump campaign. As it began, Trump was under fire for clashing with a Gold Star family whose son, an American Muslim, had been killed in Iraq while trying to save his fellow US Army troops. Soon Trump was fending off criticism for his comments that "Second Amendment people" might take action against Hillary Clinton if she became president and got to choose a Supreme Court justice, and he also was taking heat for calling Obama and Hillary Clinton, respectively, "the founder of ISIS" and "the co-founder."

He was infuriated by an August 13 *New York Times* story with the headline "Inside the Failing Mission to Tame Donald Trump's Tongue," but the increased scrutiny he faced was not only for his behavior and management style but also for his campaign's ties to Russia. Manafort, whose second meeting with Kilimnik had taken place on August 2, found himself in the spotlight's harsh glare as stories addressed his political consulting work for — and the money he had collected from — Ukraine's pro-Russia Party of Regions.

The *New York Times* reported on August 14 that government investigators were trying

to untangle a corrupt network they say was used to loot Ukrainian assets and influence elections during the administration of Mr. Manafort's main client, former President Viktor F. Yanukovych.

Handwritten ledgers show $12.7 million in undisclosed cash pay-
ments designated for Mr. Manafort from Mr. Yanukovych's pro-
Russian political party from 2007 to 2012, according to Ukraine's
newly formed National Anti-Corruption Bureau. Investigators assert
that the disbursements were part of an illegal off-the-books system
whose recipients also included election officials.

The *Times* story also discussed "murky transactions" such as the Pericles investment, described as an "$18 million deal to sell Ukrainian cable
television assets to a partnership put together by Mr. Manafort and a
Russian oligarch, Oleg Deripaska, a close ally of President Vladimir V.
Putin."

Other reports suggested that Jared Kushner, the president's son-in-law
and advisor who had backed Manafort over Lewandowski, had soured
on the campaign manager amid the reports of his Russian entanglements
at a time when Trump's team was trying to downplay such connections.
The *Times* reported that Trump had turned on Manafort too, calling him
"low energy" (a phrase the candidate had previously used against primary rival Jeb Bush) and blaming him for the *Times* story about taming
his tongue.

On August 19, Trump announced his campaign manager's "resignation" with a statement:

This morning Paul Manafort offered, and I accepted, his resignation
from the campaign. I am very appreciative for his great work in help-
ing to get us where we are today, and in particular his work guiding
us through the delegate and convention process. Paul is a true profes-
sional and I wish him the greatest success.

Eric Trump's subsequent comments to Fox News's *Sunday Morning
Futures* made clear that Manafort's departure was the choice of the candidate, not the campaign manager: "I think my father didn't want to be,
you know, distracted by, you know, whatever things Paul was dealing

with.... My father just didn't want to have that the distraction looming over the campaign."

Kellyanne Conway, a pollster then serving as an unpaid advisor, became the new campaign manager, and Steve Bannon, chair of the right-wing Breitbart News site, moved up to be the campaign's chief executive.

But after leaving his post, Manafort kept in touch with the campaign through the election, telling Gates that he still spoke with Kushner, Bannon, and Trump himself. Manafort emailed Kushner a strategy memo on October 21 that proposed that the campaign paint Clinton "as the failed and corrupt champion of the establishment" and that "Wikileaks provides the Trump campaign the ability to make the case in a very credible way—by using the words of Clinton, its campaign officials and DNC members."

In a November 5 email titled "Securing the Victory," Manafort wrote to Kushner, "I'm really feeling good about our prospects on Tuesday and focusing on preserving the victory." He then expressed concern that if Clinton lost, her campaign might "move immediately to discredit the [Trump] victory and claim voter fraud and cyber-fraud, including the claim that the Russians have hacked into the voting machines and tampered with the results."

Manafort was looking forward to a Trump presidency in which he could follow through on his plan to monetize his relationship with the administration while continuing to generate business in Ukraine, Russia, and other countries. Such a scenario had long seemed a long shot, but Election Day was approaching, and Trump, Manafort, and the Russians would soon learn whether their work had paid off.

Part Two

AFTER THE ELECTION

23

"Don't want to blow off Putin!"

After all the ballots had been tallied, Donald Trump had 304 electoral votes, and Hillary Clinton had 227. Clinton had led in almost every pre-election poll, and almost three million more individuals voted for her than Trump, the largest-ever margin for a presidential candidate who didn't win. Trump triumphed in the key swing states — with less-than-1-percent victory margins in Michigan, Pennsylvania, and Wisconsin — to put him over the top in the Electoral College.

Donald J. Trump would become the forty-fifth president of the United States, making him, at age seventy, the oldest person to begin his first term in that office and the only elected president with no prior experience in public service or the military.

As Trump was celebrating his victory, Kirill Dmitriev, a Russian businessman who referred to Vladimir Putin as his "boss," received a simple three-word message: "Putin has won."

Who, you might ask, sent that message? When you look for that information in our report, you encounter a big black box. It is redacted. Sorry, I cannot get into that because of other ongoing legal proceedings. But it would be logical to conclude that this message was sent from someone not unfamiliar with Dmitriev and Russian government leadership and its actions.

At about 2:40 a.m. on November 9, 2016, Hillary Clinton phoned Donald Trump to concede the election.

At 3:00 a.m., Trump campaign press secretary Hope Hicks's personal cell phone rang. The number that came up had a DC area code, but the caller spoke with a foreign accent. Hicks could not understand what he was saying except for the words "Putin call."

"Please send me an email," she finally said.

Sergey Kuznetsov, an official at the Russian embassy to the United States, emailed Hicks from his Gmail address the next morning with the subject line "Message from Putin." Attached was what the subject line promised — a note from the Russian president in both English and Russian, along with a message from Kuznetsov asking Hicks to relay Putin's words to the new president-elect.

"I look forward to working with you on leading Russian-American relations out of crisis," Putin wrote to Trump, congratulating him on his electoral victory.

Hicks forwarded the email to Kushner.

"Can you look into this?" Hicks asked. "Don't want to get duped but don't want to blow off Putin!"

As Kushner later testified before Congress, he thought he could verify the email's authenticity through the Russian ambassador, whom Kushner had met in April 2016 at Trump's Mayflower Hotel speech. But Kushner could not remember his name, so he emailed Dimitri Simes, the Center for the National Interest president who had hosted that speech and had introduced him and Trump to the Russian ambassador.

"What is the name of the Russian ambassador?" Kushner asked.

"Sergey Kislyak," Simes replied.

Kushner forwarded Simes's response to Hicks.

(Brief aside: our office did not determine why Kushner would not have used Google.)

Hicks forwarded Putin's letter to Trump's transition officials, and five days later, on November 14, Putin spoke by phone with Trump. Transition team members, including incoming national security advisor Michael Flynn, were at Trump's side during this conversation.

Trump's victory spurred an influx of calls not just from Russian government officials but also from prominent Russian businesspeople trying to make inroads into the new administration, often on behalf of the Russian hierarchy. This flurry of activity involved official contacts through the Russian embassy plus Russian individuals who had been encouraged at the highest levels of the Russian power structure to reach out.

This brings us to Petr Aven, a Russian national who heads Russia's largest commercial bank, Alfa-Bank. He was one of about fifty wealthy Russian businessmen — a.k.a. the oligarchs — who would meet regularly with Putin in the Kremlin. Aven also had one-on-one meetings with Putin each quarter, typically preceded by a preparatory meeting with Putin's chief of staff, Anton Vaino. Aven knew that he was expected to take any of Putin's suggestions or critiques as implicit directives, and if he did not follow through, he would suffer the consequences.

When Aven met with Putin not long after the US presidential election, the Russian president suggested that the United States might impose additional sanctions on Russian interests, including against Aven and Alfa-Bank, so Aven needed to take steps to protect himself and his bank. Putin also mentioned that the Russian government was having difficulty getting in touch with the incoming Trump administration. Putin did not know the people around the new president-elect or to whom he should be directing formal communications, as Aven told our office.

Aven assured Putin that he would take steps to protect himself and Alfa-Bank's shareholders, in part by trying to establish a line of communication with the incoming Trump administration. Putin was skeptical that Aven would succeed and did not expressly direct Aven to reach out to Trump's transition team. But Putin did expect Aven to respond to the issues he had raised.

In the months following the election, Aven was not the only Putin-connected businessman who set out to connect with incoming Trump administration officials. Kirill Dmitriev, who had received the "Putin has won" message, also got to work.

Dmitriev was a Russian national who headed that country's sovereign wealth fund, the Russian Direct Investment Fund (RDIF), and reported directly to Putin, calling him his "boss." Putin had assigned Dmitriev to oversee the financial and political relationships between Russia and the Gulf states, in part because Dmitriev had been educated in the West and spoke fluent English. Dmitriev interacted often with George Nader, a senior advisor to United Arab Emirates' (UAE) Crown Prince Mohammed bin Zayed, about his fund's dealings with that Middle Eastern country. Nader considered Dmitriev to be Putin's middleman in the Gulf region and would relay Dmitriev's views directly to Crown Prince Mohammed.

Nader developed contacts with Trump's and Clinton's campaigns during the 2016 election and kept Dmitriev apprised of his efforts. Dmitriev told Nader that he and the Russian government wanted Trump to win, and he asked Nader to help him meet members of the Trump campaign.

Nader apparently did not connect Dmitriev with anyone associated with the Trump campaign before the election, but Dmitriev, acting on Putin's wishes, stepped up his interest afterward and asked Nader to introduce him to Trump's transition officials. Nader turned to Erik Prince, the billionaire Blackwater founder and Trump supporter who had underwritten efforts to authenticate Hillary Clinton's emails.

Although Prince lacked a formal role in the Trump campaign, he maintained close relationships with various officials and advisors, including Steve Bannon, Donald Trump Jr., and Roger Stone. Prince had offered to host a Trump fund-raiser and would send Bannon unsolicited policy papers covering such issues as foreign policy, trade, and Russian election interference. After the election, Prince often visited the transition offices in Trump Tower, usually to meet with Bannon and sometimes to touch base with Michael Flynn and others. When Prince and Bannon met, they discussed foreign policy issues, and Prince made recommendations about whom Trump should appoint to key national security positions. So even though Prince was not officially part of the transition, Nader was assured that the incoming administration considered him a trusted associate.

On the morning after Election Day, Dmitriev texted Nader, who was in New York.

"Great results," Dmitriev wrote, and he requested a meeting with the "key people" in the incoming administration. "We want to start rebuilding the relationship in whatever is a comfortable pace for them. We understand all of the sensitivities and are not in a rush."

Dmitriev also told Nader that he would ask Putin for permission to travel to the United States so that he could speak with media outlets about the positive impact of Trump's election and the need for reconciliation between the United States and Russia.

Later that day, Dmitriev flew to New York, where Russian Federation press secretary Dmitry Peskov was attending the World Chess Championship. Dmitriev invited Nader to the tournament's opening, noting, "If there's a chance to see anyone key from Trump camp, I would love to start building for the future."

Such connections at the chess championship apparently did not get made, but Dmitriev kept pushing Nader to arrange a meeting with transition officials, preferably Kushner or Donald Trump Jr. Dmitriev told Nader that Putin would be very grateful for such a meeting. It would make history.

24

"This guy is designated by Steve
to meet you!"

George Nader did not introduce Kirill Dmitriev to anyone from the incoming Trump administration on that post–Election Day trip to New York, and Dmitriev remained anxious to make these contacts, telling Nader he would seek out other routes in addition to going through him. In early December, Dmitriev suggested to Nader that the two of them might meet with Trump officials in January or February. He included a list of positive, public quotes that he had made about Trump "in case they are helpful."

Nader discussed Dmitriev with Erik Prince over lunch and dinner meetings on January 3 in New York. Nader told Prince that the Russians were looking to build a link with the incoming administration, so Dmitriev had been pushing to be connected with someone on the Trump team. Given Prince's close relationship with transition team officials, Nader suggested that Prince might meet with Dmitriev so that they could discuss mutual interests. Prince said he would think about it and check with the transition team.

After their dinner meeting, Nader sent Prince a link to a Wikipedia entry about Dmitriev. He also texted Dmitriev that he had just met "with some key people within the family and inner circle" and had praised Dmitriev at length to them. Nader told Dmitriev that the people he met had asked for Dmitriev's bio, and Dmitriev responded by sending Nader a two-page biography and a list of his positive quotes about Trump.

The next morning, Nader forwarded Dmitriev's message and attachments to Prince, noting that these documents were "to be used with some additional details for" the incoming administration members. Prince opened the attachments at the Trump Tower transition offices within an hour of receiving them, and during the three hours in which he was there that day, he spoke with Kellyanne Conway, Wilbur Ross, Steve Mnuchin, and others while waiting to see Bannon. Prince later told investigators that he could not recall whether, during those three hours, he had met with Bannon and discussed Dmitriev with him.

Nader texted Dmitriev the next day to say he had a "pleasant surprise" for him: an arrangement for him to meet "a Special Guest" from "the New Team." Could Dmitriev travel to the Seychelles for a January 12 meeting?

Yes, he could.

Prince booked a ticket to the Seychelles on January 7.

But Dmitriev was not enthusiastic about meeting with Prince and texted Nader seeking assurance that this Seychelles meeting would be worthwhile.

"This guy is designated by Steve [Bannon] to meet you!" Nader wrote. "I know him and he is very very well connected and trusted by the New Team. His sister [Betsy DeVos] is now a Minister of Education."

Prince had led Nader to believe that Bannon was aware of Prince's upcoming meeting with Dmitriev, and Prince acknowledged that it was reasonable for Nader to conclude that Prince would pass along information to the transition team. Bannon, however, later told our office that Prince did not tell him in advance about his Dmitriev meeting. (You may notice that Bannon's memories about these events often are not in sync with those of the other participants.)

On January 11, Dmitriev and his wife arrived in the Seychelles and checked into the Four Seasons Resort, where Crown Prince Mohammed and Nader were staying. Prince arrived that day as well, and he and Dmitriev met for the first time for about thirty to forty-five minutes that afternoon in Nader's villa, with Nader present. Prince made critical comments about the Obama administration's eight-year reign and said that he looked forward to a new era of cooperation and conflict resolution.

Prince also told Dmitriev that Bannon was effective if not conventional and that Prince often provided policy papers to him. The topic of Russian interference in the 2016 election supposedly did not come up.

When Prince returned to his room, he learned that a Russian aircraft carrier had sailed to Libya. He called Nader to ask him to set up another meeting with Dmitriev, because he had checked with his associates back home and needed to tell Dmitriev that Libya was "off the table."

Nader texted Dmitriev that Prince had "received an urgent message that he needs to convey to you immediately" and arranged for him, Dmitriev, and Prince to meet at a restaurant on the Four Seasons property. At this second meeting, Prince told Dmitriev that the United States could not accept Russian involvement in Libya because it would dramatically worsen the situation.

It must be noted that at this time President Trump and his administration had yet to take office, and President Obama remained in charge of US foreign policy. Prince later told our office that he made these remarks to Dmitriev not in an official capacity for Trump's transition team but based on his experience as a former naval officer.

After that brief second meeting had ended, Dmitriev told Nader that he was disappointed in his discussions with Prince for two reasons:

1. He believed the Russians needed to communicate with someone with more authority than Prince within the incoming administration.
2. He had hoped for a more substantive conversation that included outlining a strategic road map for both countries to follow. Dmitriev also found some of Prince's comments to be insulting.

Hours after the second meeting, Prince sent two text messages to Bannon from the Seychelles. Investigators were not able to obtain the content of these or other messages between Prince and Bannon, and the special counsel's probe also did not identify evidence of any further communication between Prince and Dmitriev after their Seychelles meetings.

Prince told Nader that he would inform Bannon about his discussion with Dmitriev and would communicate that someone representing the Russian power structure was seeking better relations with the incoming administration. Prince met Bannon at Bannon's home in mid-January and briefed him about his meeting with Dmitriev and other topics. Prince explained that Dmitriev led a Russian sovereign wealth fund and sought improved relations between the United States and Russia. Prince showed Bannon a cell phone screenshot of Dmitriev's Wikipedia page, dated January 16, 2017, and gave him Dmitriev's contact information. Bannon told him not to follow up with Dmitriev, perhaps because Bannon did not consider the issue a priority. Bannon did not appear angry, just relatively uninterested. That is Prince's version.

Bannon told our office that he never had any discussion with Prince about Dmitriev, RDIF, or meetings with Russians who were associated with Putin. If Prince had mentioned such a meeting, Bannon said, he would have remembered it and would have objected to the meeting having taken place.

That these two accounts are wildly in conflict makes it tough to determine the truth. The special counsel's investigation could not resolve the incongruities because neither Prince nor Bannon was able to produce any of the messages they exchanged in the time period surrounding the Seychelles meeting. Prince's phone contained zero text messages prior to March 2017, although his provider's records indicate that he and Bannon exchanged dozens of messages. Prince denied deleting any messages and claimed he had no idea why his device contained no messages from before March 2017.

Bannon's devices also contained zero messages from the relevant time period. He too said he did not know why. Bannon told our office that during the months before and after the Seychelles meeting, he regularly used his personal BlackBerry and personal email for work-related communications, including those with Prince, and he took no steps to preserve these work communications.

Missing messages...personal email used for work-related communications...this sounded familiar.

25

"They took it seriously!"

When Dmitriev told Nader that he would not rely solely on him to reach out to the incoming Trump administration, he meant it. In late November 2016, the United Arab Emirates' national security advisor introduced Dmitriev to Rick Gerson, a Jared Kushner friend who ran a hedge fund in New York. Although Gerson had no formal role in the transition or official involvement in the Trump campaign other than occasional casual discussions with Kushner, he did work to assist with the transition, such as arranging meetings for Trump officials with former UK prime minister Tony Blair and a UAE delegation led by Crown Prince Mohammed.

When Dmitriev and Gerson met, they discussed possible joint ventures between Gerson's hedge fund and Dmitriev's wealth fund. Stating his desire for improved economic cooperation between the United States and Russia, Dmitriev asked Gerson with whom he might meet in the incoming administration to pursue this matter further. Gerson replied that he would look into making appropriate introductions, but confidentiality would be required because of the sensitivity of holding such meetings before the new administration took office and before the Senate had confirmed cabinet nominees. Gerson said that he would ask Kushner and Michael Flynn for the "key person or people" for addressing reconciliation with Russia, joint security concerns, and economic matters.

Dmitriev told Gerson that Putin had tasked him with developing and executing a reconciliation plan between the United States and Russia. If Russia was "approached with respect and willingness to understand our position," Dmitriev texted, "we can have Major Breakthroughs quickly."

In December 2016, Gerson and Dmitriev exchanged ideas about what such a reconciliation plan might include. Gerson later told investigators that Trump's transition team had not asked him to discuss these issues with Dmitriev; he was doing so on his own initiative as a private citizen.

On January 9, 2017, the same day in which Dmitriev expressed concerns to Nader about meeting with Prince, Dmitriev sent his biography to Gerson with a request that he "share it with Jared (or somebody else very senior in the team) — so that they know that we are focused from our side on improving the relationship and my boss asked me to play a key role in that."

Dmitriev also asked Gerson whether he knew Prince and whether Prince was somebody important or worth spending time with. After his trip to the Seychelles, Dmitriev told Gerson that Bannon had asked Prince to meet with Dmitriev and that the two had enjoyed a positive meeting.

Following up on his discussions with Gerson about US-Russia reconciliation, Dmitriev created a two-page document on January 16 that laid out the key points:

1. Jointly fighting terrorism
2. Jointly engaging in efforts to curb weapons of mass destruction
3. Developing "win-win" economic and investment initiatives
4. Maintaining an honest, open, and continual dialogue regarding issues of disagreement
5. Ensuring proper communication and trust by "key people" from each country

Gerson gave a copy of the document to Kushner on January 18, explaining that Dmitriev was the well-connected head of RDIF. Kushner told Gerson that he would get the document to the right people and eventually gave one copy to Bannon and another to Rex Tillerson, soon to be confirmed as secretary of state. Kushner later said that neither of them followed up with him about it.

On January 19, Dmitriev sent the two-page document to Nader as well, telling him it was "a view from our side that I discussed in my meeting on the islands and with you and with our friends. Please share with them — we believe this is a good foundation to start from."

Dmitriev followed up with Gerson on January 26, writing that his "boss," Putin, was asking whether he had received any feedback on the proposal.

"We do not want to rush things and move at a comfortable speed," Dmitriev said. "At the same time, my boss asked me to try to have the key US meetings in the next two weeks if possible."

Dmitriev also informed Gerson that Putin and President Trump would speak by phone that Saturday. He noted that this information was "very confidential."

On the same day, Dmitriev texted Nader that he had seen his "boss" again yesterday. "He emphasized that this is a great priority for us and that we need to build this communication channel to avoid bureaucracy," Dmitriev reported.

Dmitriev sent another text to Nader on January 28 "to see if I can confirm to my boss that your friends may use some of the ideas from the 2 pager I sent you in the telephone call that will happen at 12 EST" — the time of the scheduled call between Putin and Trump.

"Definitely," Nader replied, "paper was so submitted to Team by Rick and me. They took it seriously!"

After the call between Trump and Putin, Dmitriev followed up by text with Nader.

"The call went very well," Dmitriev wrote. "My boss wants me to continue making some public statements that us [sic] Russia cooperation is good and important."

Gerson also texted Dmitriev to say that the call had been a success. Dmitriev responded that the document they had drafted together "played an important role."

26

"A very positive response!"

While the Russians were seeking contact with members of the incoming Trump administration, Trump's inner circle was trying to set up its own communication channels with the Russians in the two-plus months before the president-elect actually took office. Jared Kushner, Trump's son-in-law and one of his closest advisors, was especially keen to determine the best contacts for dealing with issues related to Russia, and so he saw an opportunity when Russian ambassador Sergey Kislyak contacted Kushner's executive assistant, Catherine Vargas, on November 16, 2016, asking for a meeting with Kushner.

After receiving Kislyak's request, Vargas sent Kushner an email with the subject "MISSED CALL: Russian Ambassador to the US, Sergey Ivanovich Kislyak…" and the text, "RE: setting up a time to meet w/you on 12/1. LMK how to proceed."

"I think I do this one — confirm with Dimitri [Simes of CNI] that this is the right guy," Kushner responded, once again using CNI's president and chief executive officer for reference on Russian matters.

Vargas reached out to one of Simes's colleagues at CNI and reported back to Kushner that Kislyak was "the best go-to guy for routine matters in the US," while Yuri Ushakov, a Russian foreign policy advisor, was the better contact for "more direct/substantial matters."

Incoming national security advisor Michael Flynn was on a similar quest as he tried to determine a Russian-contacts pecking order while at an early December meeting in New York with his designated deputy, K.

T. McFarland, and Robert Foresman, the New York–based investment banker who previously had tried inviting Trump to speak at the St. Petersburg International Economic Forum. Toward the end of the meeting, Flynn asked Foresman for his thoughts on Kislyak, and Foresman replied that although he had not met Kislyak, he thought the ambassador was an important person but did not have a direct line to Putin.

Foresman then went to great lengths to chase down a more complete answer for Flynn. He traveled to Moscow and spoke with a source he believed to be close to Putin, who told him that Flynn should use Ushakov as his official channel for dealing with Russia. When our office later asked Foresman about this trip, he said that he took it on his own initiative, without having been asked by Flynn, because he felt obligated to collect and report the information back to the incoming national security advisor.

Foresman then set up a face-to-face meeting with Flynn in January 2017 to communicate the intelligence he had gathered. Emails indicate that this meeting took place, although Flynn later said he had no recollection of that meeting or the earlier one in December when Foresman said they had discussed Kislyak.

In the meantime, despite concluding that Kislyak probably was not the right Russian point of contact for him, Kushner went ahead with the meeting that Kislyak had requested on November 16. It took place at Trump Tower on November 30, and Kushner invited Flynn and Bannon to attend. Flynn was there; Bannon was not.

At the half-hour-long meeting, Kushner said the incoming Trump administration desired a fresh start to US-Russian relations, and he asked Kislyak whether the ambassador or someone else would be the best person for future discussions on these matters. Kushner said he wished to be in touch with someone who had regular contact with Putin and could speak for the Russian leader.

The three men also discussed US policy toward Syria, and Kislyak suggested that Russian generals might brief the transition team on this topic via a secure communications line. After Flynn explained that the transition team offices lacked a secure line, Kushner suggested that they might communicate using secure facilities at the Russian embassy. Kislyak shot down that idea.

In the aftermath of this Trump Tower meeting, the Russian embassy contacted Kushner's assistant on December 6 to set up a follow-up between Kislyak and Kushner. Kushner declined several proposed dates, but Kislyak was insistent with Kushner's assistant about pinning down a second meeting. Because Kushner had decided that the ambassador was not the right channel for him to use to communicate with Russia, Kushner arranged to have one of his assistants, Avi Berkowitz, meet with Kislyak instead.

Kislyak was not satisfied with this arrangement, so Russian embassy official Sergey Kuznetsov wrote to Berkowitz to say that Kislyak considered it "important" that he "continue the conversation with Mr. Kushner in person." Soon it became apparent that Kushner would not take that meeting, so Kislyak agreed to meet with Berkowitz. At that meeting, which lasted only a few minutes, Kislyak suggested that Kushner meet with someone who had a direct line to Putin: Sergey Gorkov, the head of the Russian government-owned bank Vnesheconombank (VEB).

Kushner did agree to take that meeting, and it happened quickly. Kushner and Gorkov met one-on-one the next day, December 13, at the Colony Capital building in Manhattan, a common meeting place for Kushner. Kushner said later that he did not prepare for the meeting and no one on the transition team even googled Gorkov's name. Berkowitz told investigators that he did google Gorkov's name and then told Kushner that Gorkov appeared to be a banker.

If they had done a full search on Gorkov, they would have learned that the United States and European Union had imposed economic sanctions on Gorkov's bank in response to Russia's annexation of Crimea. Also, as the *New York Times* reported in a May 2017 story about Kushner's meeting with Gorkov,

> His bank is controlled by members of Mr. Putin's government, including Prime Minister Dmitri A. Medvedev. It also has long been

intertwined with Mr. Putin's inner circle: It has been used by the Russian government to bail out oligarchs close to Mr. Putin, and has helped fund the Russian president's pet projects, such as the Winter Olympics in Sochi in 2014.

Vnesheconombank has also been used by Russian intelligence to plant spies in the United States. In March 2016, an agent of Russia's foreign intelligence service, known as the S.V.R., who was caught posing as an employee of the bank in New York, pleaded guilty to spying against the United States.

That spy was Evgeny Buryakov, a Vnesheconombank employee who, as noted earlier, was recorded speaking with fellow indictee Victor Podobnyy about recruiting Trump campaign associate Carter Page (a.k.a. Male-1) as a foreign source.

The *Times* story also noted,

Mr. Gorkov is a graduate of the academy of the Federal Security Service of Russia, a training ground for Russian spies. Though current and former Americans said it was unlikely that Mr. Gorkov is an active member of Russian intelligence, they said his past ties to the security services in Moscow were a reason he was put in charge of the bank.

At the top of their one-on-one meeting, Gorkov presented Kushner with two gifts: a painting and a bag of dirt from the Belarus town where Kushner's family originated.

When asked about this meeting after the fact, Kushner and Gorkov characterized it in very different ways. Kushner said it was strictly diplomatic, a conversation in which Gorkov expressed disappointment about US-Russia relations under President Obama and hoped for an improvement with Trump. Kushner told investigators that he did not recall any discussion with Gorkov about the sanctions against VEB or sanctions in general. He did remember that Gorkov talked a bit about his bank and the Russian economy, but they did not discuss Kushner's companies or any private business dealings.

Why might they have discussed Kushner's business? At the time, Kushner Companies had a large debt coming due on its 666 Fifth Avenue building, and the *Wall Street Journal* had recently reported on Kushner's efforts to secure lending on the property amid possible conflicts of interest arising out of his company's borrowing from foreign sources. As Peter Grant wrote in a November 29, 2016, *Journal* story,

> *The real-estate company controlled by Jared Kushner, President-elect Donald Trump's son-in-law, has hundreds of millions of dollars in loans outstanding from domestic and foreign financial institutions, markets condominiums to wealthy U.S. and foreign buyers and has obtained development financing through a controversial U.S. program that sells green cards.*
>
> *Those and other business activities could raise conflict-of-interest issues if Mr. Kushner is named to a staff position in the Trump administration.*

Yet Gorkov denied that his meeting with Kushner had anything to do with diplomacy. Instead, he said, it was strictly business. His bank issued this statement about it to ABC News the following June:

> *During 2016, when preparing the new Vnesheconombank's Strategy, the Bank's CEOs repeatedly met with representatives of the leading global financial institutions in Europe, Asia and America. In the course of negotiations the parties discussed the business practices applied by foreign development banks, as well as most promising business lines and sectors. The roadshow meetings devoted to Vnesheconombank's Strategy 2021 were held with representatives of major US banks and business circles, including the CEO of Kushner Companies Mr. Jared Kushner.*

At the time of the Kushner-Gorkov meeting, ABC News noted, "Kushner Companies, the family's real estate firm, was in the midst of what it has described in public statements as 'active, advanced negotiations… with a number of potential investors' about the redevelopment of the financially troubled skyscraper it owns at 666 Fifth Avenue in New York City."

It turned out that Foresman, the New York–based investment bank executive with Kremlin connections, met with Gorkov and VEB deputy chair Nikolay Tsekhomsky in Moscow just before Gorkov left for New York to meet Kushner. According to Foresman, Gorkov and Tsekhomsky told him that they were traveling to New York to discuss postelection issues with US financial institutions, that Putin had sanctioned their trip, and that they would be reporting back to the Russian president upon their return.

Our investigation could not conclude whether Gorkov's meeting with Kushner was diplomatic, was focused on business, or landed somewhere in between. But we did learn the following.

A few days afterward, Gorkov's assistant texted Kushner's assistant to pass along this message from Russia: "Hi, please inform your side that the information about the meeting had a very positive response!"

27

"We ought to get on with our lives"

The transition period between two presidential administrations can be a tricky one. The outgoing administration has lame duck status but is still responsible for running the country, no small task. That entails dealing with foreign policy crises and other urgent situations that arise. The incoming administration, in the meantime, wants to lay the groundwork for the policies it wishes to pursue, but it cannot—or at least should not—get in the way of the leaders still in power.

Working in opposition to the current administration's policies is not the norm and, in some cases, may be illegal. A US federal law called the Logan Act makes it a crime for unauthorized persons to engage in negotiations with a foreign power that is in conflict with the United States.

Please keep all of that in mind.

Now let's discuss Michael Flynn.

You have encountered him previously in this narrative as one of candidate Trump's advisors. He spearheaded the quest to find Hillary Clinton's emails and retweeted some of the Russian-created social media propaganda targeting Clinton and trumpeting Trump. You also may remember him as the speaker at the Republican National Convention who led the "Lock her up!" chants directed at Hillary Clinton.

After the election, Trump named Lieutenant General Flynn, US Army (retired), to be his incoming national security advisor and set him to work addressing policy matters, sometimes sensitive, with foreign governmental officials. Flynn, who was fifty-eight at the time, had numerous connections with Russia by then. President Obama had named him director of the Defense Intelligence Agency in April 2012, and the following year, Flynn had become the first US officer allowed inside GRU headquarters — that is, the home of Russia's military intelligence wing.

The Obama administration removed him from the post in mid-2014, and a *Washington Post* story at the time cited his "chaotic" management style and "significant turbulence" during his tenure. In September 2016, BuzzFeed News got hold of emails from Colin Powell that had been stolen and released by Russia's DCLeaks.com site, and in one to his son Michael, the former secretary of state said that when he spoke at DIA that summer, "I asked why Flynn got fired. Abusive with staff, didn't listen, worked against policy, bad management, etc. He has been and was right-wing nutty every [*sic*] since."

After his retirement from the military in 2014, Flynn did consulting work, much of it for Russia-related companies. This work was reportedly lucrative, and his stature in Russia was such that he appeared as a regular analyst for the Russian government-controlled TV network RT (originally Russia Today), which was often characterized in the West as a propaganda arm for the Kremlin. Not only was Flynn paid a reported $45,000 to appear at a December 2015 gala for the network, but also he was seated next to Vladimir Putin, an unusual arrangement for a US military figure at a time of pronounced tensions between the two countries. Flynn's ties to Russia were widely reported during the campaign.

Flynn did not view Russia as the United States' primary adversary. He had long been advocating a worldview that the United States — and, really, the rest of the civilized world — was at war with Islamic militants; hence, his 2016 book (written with Michael Ledeen), *The Field of Fight: How We Can Win the Global War Against Radical Islam and Its Allies*. Putin, in Flynn's view, was an ally to be enlisted in this fight.

"I am pleased that Lieutenant General Michael Flynn will be by my side as we work to defeat radical Islamic terrorism, navigate geopolitical challenges and keep Americans safe at home and abroad," Trump said in a statement upon appointing Flynn as his national security advisor. "General

Flynn is one of the country's foremost experts on military and intelligence matters, and he will be an invaluable asset to me and my administration."

Flynn was active as a Trump transition team member in advance of officially joining the Trump administration. Despite Jared Kushner's conclusion that Russian ambassador Sergey Kislyak did not wield influence inside the Russian government, the Trump team tasked Flynn with dealing with the ambassador on two fraught issues during the transition. The first was an Israel-related United Nations Security Council vote that the Trump administration wished to quash.

On December 21, 2016, Egypt submitted a resolution to the UN Security Council calling on Israel to quit building settlements in Palestinian territory. The Security Council, which includes Russia, was scheduled to vote on the resolution the following day, and some press reports were speculating that the Obama administration would not oppose it.

Seeing this vote as significant, the Trump team wanted to support Israel by blocking the resolution. Multiple transition officials and President-Elect Trump himself communicated with foreign government officials on December 22 to gauge their views on this looming issue and to try to persuade them to delay the vote or to shoot down the resolution. Kushner led this effort, and Flynn was given the responsibility of dealing with the Russian government.

Flynn spoke on the phone with Kushner early in the morning of December 22 and called Kislyak minutes later. Flynn later told investigators that he informed Kislyak of the transition team's opposition to the resolution, and he asked that Russia either vote against it or move to delay it. Trump spoke with Egyptian president Abdel Fattah al-Sisi about the vote later in the day, and Egypt postponed the vote.

But Malaysia, New Zealand, Senegal, and Venezuela resubmitted the resolution the next day, and Trump team officials continued to reach out to foreign leaders, Flynn again communicating with Kislyak. The Russian ambassador told Flynn that if the resolution came to a vote, Russia would not vote against it. The resolution later passed 14–0, with the United States abstaining.

Meanwhile, more and more reports, sourced to American and foreign intelligence officers, were concluding that Russian president Vladimir Putin had personally directed Russian hacking and other methods of interference in the 2016 presidential election. By December 28, there was much media speculation that the Obama administration was about to take retaliatory measures against Russia for its alleged attacks on the democratic process.

Asked that morning about the prospect of US sanctions against Russia, President-Elect Trump, who already had been publicly disputing US intelligence findings that Russian hackers had helped him win the election, told reporters, "I think we ought to get on with our lives. I think that computers have complicated lives very greatly. The whole age of computer has made it where nobody knows exactly what's going on."

Later that day, President Obama signed Executive Order 13757, which took effect at 12:01 a.m. the following day and imposed sanctions on nine Russian individuals and entities. These sanctions were not announced publicly until the morning of December 29, when the Obama administration also expelled thirty-five Russian government officials and closed two Russian government-owned compounds in the United States. The president released a statement that read, in part,

> Today, I have ordered a number of actions in response to the Russian government's aggressive harassment of U.S. officials and cyber operations aimed at the U.S. election. These actions follow repeated private and public warnings that we have issued to the Russian government, and are a necessary and appropriate response to efforts to harm U.S. interests in violation of established international norms of behavior.
>
> All Americans should be alarmed by Russia's actions. In October, my Administration publicized our assessment that Russia took actions intended to interfere with the U.S. election process. These data theft and disclosure activities could only have been directed by the highest levels of the Russian government. Moreover, our diplomats

have experienced an unacceptable level of harassment in Moscow by Russian security services and police over the last year. Such activities have consequences....

In addition to holding Russia accountable for what it has done, the United States and friends and allies around the world must work together to oppose Russia's efforts to undermine established international norms of behavior, and interfere with democratic governance.

If anything, the predominant criticism from Republican leaders in the Senate was that Obama had taken too long to respond to Russia's actions. "The retaliatory measures announced by the Obama administration today are long overdue," read a joint statement from Arizona senator John McCain and South Carolina senator Lindsey Graham. "But ultimately, they are a small price for Russia to pay for its brazen attack on American democracy. We intend to lead the effort in the new Congress to impose stronger sanctions on Russia."

Senate majority leader Mitch McConnell also presented himself as a hard-liner against Russian cyberattacks on US targets. "The Russians are not our friends," McConnell said. "And clearly the Obama administration has not yet dissuaded them from attempting to breach our cybersecurity systems or harass our diplomats in Moscow."

The Trump team had a different take.

28

"Tit for tat w Russia not good"

When President Obama announced the sanctions against Russia for 2016 election interference, President-Elect Trump and multiple senior members of his team were staying at his Mar-a-Lago club in Palm Beach, Florida. These officials included campaign chief executive Steve Bannon, Republican National Committee chair and incoming White House chief of staff Reince Priebus, and K. T. McFarland, who had been tapped to be deputy national security advisor under Flynn.

McFarland was working as a Fox News national security commentator — and had not been in government in the thirty years since she was a deputy assistant secretary in the Department of Defense's public affairs office — when Trump named her to the position in late November. She was sixty-five at the time. Among McFarland's work for Fox News was a September 2013 commentary with the headline "Putin Is the One Who Really Deserves That Nobel Peace Prize."

"I am proud that KT has once again decided to serve our country and join my national security team," Trump said in a statement announcing her appointment. "She has tremendous experience and innate talent that will complement the fantastic team we are assembling, which is crucial because nothing is more important than keeping our people safe."

Down at Mar-a-Lago, the Trump team was concerned that the new sanctions would damage the United States' relationship with Russia, so the president-elect and his officials designated Flynn to speak with the

Russian government. Flynn was on vacation in the Dominican Republic at the time but remained in contact with McFarland.

Kislyak was the first to make contact with Flynn, texting him on the evening of December 28, "can you kindly call me back at your convenience." Flynn did not respond that night, and a Russian embassy representative called Flynn the next day at 10:38 a.m., although they did not talk then either.

At 1:53 p.m. on December 29, the day that President Obama announced the sanctions, McFarland began exchanging emails with multiple transition team members and advisors about the sanctions' potential impact on the incoming administration. At 2:07 p.m., a transition team member texted Flynn a link to a *New York Times* article about the sanctions. McFarland called Flynn at 2:29 p.m., and although they did not talk at that time, McFarland soon was discussing the sanctions with Bannon, who said that Obama's action would damage the Trump administration's ability to have good relations with Russia and that the inevitable Russian escalation in response to the sanctions would make the situation more difficult. McFarland told Bannon that Flynn was scheduled to talk to Kislyak later that night, and she said the same to Priebus when they discussed the sanctions.

"Time for a call???" Flynn texted a transition team member who was assisting McFarland.

The transition team member replied that McFarland was on the phone with Tom Bossert, a transition team senior official who would become Trump's homeland security advisor.

"Tit for tat w Russia not good," Flynn responded. "Russian AMBO reaching out to me today."

McFarland echoed this sentiment in an email exchange with Bossert, which the *New York Times* reprinted almost a year later. McFarland wrote that Obama's sanctions were meant to "box Trump in diplomatically with Russia" and to "lure Trump in trap of saying something" and were aimed at "discrediting Trump's victory by saying it was due to Russian interference."

She added, "If there is a tit-for-tat escalation Trump will have difficulty improving relations with Russia, which has just thrown U.S.A. election to him."

McFarland had just drawn a direct line between Russia's actions and Trump's victory.

Bossert responded that Trump's top advisors should "defend election legitimacy now." He also forwarded this email exchange to six high-ranking Trump officials, including Flynn, Bannon, Priebus, and Sean Spicer, Trump's incoming communications director.

McFarland made multiple transition team members aware that Flynn would be speaking with Kislyak that evening. In addition to her conversations with Bannon and Reince Priebus, McFarland emailed Trump officials about the sanctions at 4:43 p.m., informing the group, "Gen [F]lynn is talking to russian ambassador this evening."

Less than an hour later, McFarland met in person with Trump and his senior officials and briefed them on possible Russian responses to the sanctions. Trump characterized the sanctions as Obama's attempt to embarrass him by delegitimizing his election. The president-elect also asked McFarland whether the Russians did "it" — that is, take actions to influence the presidential election.

Yes, McFarland said, they did.

Trump said that he doubted it was the Russians.

McFarland also speculated on potential Russian responses to the sanctions, saying their reaction would signal what the country wanted going forward. Trump said he thought the sanctions gave him leverage with the Russians. McFarland suggested that this situation with Russia might be "cooled down" instead of escalated.

McFarland thought that toward the end of the meeting, she may have mentioned to Trump that Flynn was scheduled to speak with the Russian ambassador that evening. But when asked about it later, neither she nor anyone else could remember Trump's possible response.

Flynn would tell investigators that he did not communicate with Kislyak about the sanctions until he had heard back from the Trump team at

Mar-a-Lago. The incoming national security advisor first spoke for twenty minutes with his *Field of Fight* coauthor, Michael Ledeen, a transition team member who advised on foreign policy and national security matters and whose wife, Barbara, had searched for Hillary Clinton's emails. Flynn then talked with McFarland for almost twenty minutes to figure out what to communicate to Kislyak about the sanctions. They discussed the sanctions' potential impact on Trump's foreign policy goals as well as the transition team members' desire that Russia not escalate the conflict. Flynn and McFarland agreed that Flynn would relay a message to Kislyak to try to contain the situation.

After finishing his call with McFarland, Flynn phoned Kislyak. The two of them discussed Russia's views about the Middle East, an upcoming terrorism conference, and the scheduling of a video teleconference between Trump and Putin. But the most pressing matter was the Obama administration's sanctions against Russia. Flynn requested that Russia not escalate the situation, not get into a "tit for tat," and instead respond to the sanctions only in a reciprocal manner. The call ended cordially. Kislyak apparently had been listening.

Afterward, Flynn and McFarland spoke again, and Flynn recounted the substance of his conversation with Kislyak about the sanctions and other matters. The Russians would not escalate the situation, Flynn told McFarland, because they wanted a good relationship with the incoming administration.

The next day, December 30, Russian foreign minister Sergey Lavrov sounded a more discordant note, saying publicly that Russia would respond in kind to the sanctions and suggesting that the Russian government expel thirty-one US diplomats from Moscow and four from St. Petersburg as well as shut down a wooded picnic spot outside Moscow that was popular among diplomats.

"We, of course, cannot leave these tricks unanswered," Lavrov said in televised remarks. "Reciprocity is the law of diplomacy and foreign relations."

But two hours later, Putin took a different tack and released a statement that Russia would not retaliate in response to the sanctions at that time.

"While we reserve the right to take reciprocal measures, we're not going to downgrade ourselves to the level of irresponsible 'kitchen' diplomacy," Putin said. "In our future steps on the way toward the restoration of Russia-United States relations, we will proceed from the policy pursued by the [Trump] administration."

The Russian president said he would even leave the picnic area open so as not to deprive the diplomats' children of a beloved place.

Hours later, President-Elect Trump tweeted, "Great move on delay (by V. Putin) — I always knew he was very smart!"

Soon after Putin's response, Flynn texted McFarland in order to document his call with Kislyak from the previous day, and she forwarded Flynn's message via email to Kushner, Bannon, Priebus, and other transition team members. But neither Flynn's text message nor McFarland's email mentioned the discussion of sanctions with Kislyak. Flynn later told our office that he chose not to make an official note of this topic out of concern of being perceived as interfering with Obama's foreign policy.

On December 31, the day after Putin's response, Kislyak called Flynn to say that his request had been received at the Russian government's highest levels and that Russia had chosen not to retaliate to the sanctions because of it. Two hours later, Flynn told McFarland about his latest conversation with Kislyak, and he noted that the relationship with the Russians was back on track. Flynn also said that he believed his phone call with Kislyak had made a difference. McFarland congratulated him.

Flynn spoke with other transition team members that day but later could not recall whether they discussed the sanctions. Flynn did remember discussing the sanctions with Bannon the next day, and he got the impression that Bannon already knew about Flynn's conversation with Kislyak. The two of them agreed that they had "stopped the train on Russia's response."

Bannon later told our office that yes, he remembered meeting with

Flynn that day but no, he had no recollection of discussing sanctions with him.

Flynn discussed the Russian reaction in a meeting with Trump on January 3 as well, although Flynn said later that he did not recall telling the president-elect the specifics of his calls with the Russian ambassador.

Meanwhile in the intelligence community, there was surprise that Russia had not retaliated to the sanctions, as would have been standard practice. As the intelligence professionals analyzed Russia's response, they became aware of Flynn's sanctions discussion with Kislyak. The FBI already had been investigating Flynn's relationship with the Russian government but had yet to find evidence of crimes, and as FBI director James Comey would later testify, the bureau was preparing to shut down this investigation in December 2016.

But Flynn's contacts with Kislyak offered the FBI new avenues to pursue, so the investigation remained open. Soon actual charges against Flynn, ones with serious implications for the incoming administration, would be under consideration.

29

"A very minor 'wink' (or slight push) from DT"

The plan was working out for Paul Manafort. Sure, he had been forced to resign as Trump's campaign manager, but he continued advising Jared Kushner and others on the team while maintaining his business activities overseas.

And the long shot had paid off. Trump had won. Now many new opportunities were presenting themselves.

Manafort had told associates he would not vie for a position in the Trump administration because he preferred to stay outside government and monetize his relationship with the administration. Officials in Cuba, South Korea, China, Middle Eastern countries, and elsewhere wanted to know what to expect from a Trump presidency, so Manafort traveled to these places, offered an explanation, and was compensated for his efforts.

Manafort also remained involved with Ukraine and Russia, and some of his early 2017 meetings related to them. In January, he ventured to Madrid, where he met with former Russian embassy worker Georgiy Oganov, a senior executive at a Deripaska company who was said to report directly to Deripaska. When our office asked Manafort about this meeting, he denied it at first. Then he acknowledged he was there at the behest of his lawyers, who, Manafort said, had arranged the meeting to deal solely with the Pericles lawsuit. But text messages to Manafort from a number associated with Konstantin Kilimnik, Manafort's longtime Russian associate and a suspected Russian intelligence agent, indicate that it was Kilimnik and Victor Boyarkin, Deripaska's deputy — and not Manafort's lawyers — who set up Manafort's meeting with Oganov.

Kilimnik's message to Manafort said the meeting was meant to be "not about money or Pericles" but instead "about recreating [the] old friendship" between Manafort and Deripaska "and talking about global politics."

"I need this finished before Jan. 20," Manafort texted back, indicating that he wanted to resolve the dispute before Trump's inauguration date.

On January 15, three days after returning from Madrid, Manafort emailed K. T. McFarland, who would soon be sworn in as Trump's deputy national security advisor. "I have some important information I want to share that I picked up on my travels over the last month," Manafort said. Our office later asked Manafort about this, and he said his email referred to Cuba, not Russia or Ukraine.

McFarland's boss, Michael Flynn, instructed her not to respond. Apparently she did not.

Manafort participated in another Russia/Ukraine-related meeting around the time of Trump's inauguration, getting together with Kilimnik and Ukrainian oligarch Serhiy Lyovochkin at the Westin hotel in Alexandria, Virginia. Kilimnik pitched the Ukrainian peace plan that he had brought up at the August 2 meeting and raised again in a detailed December 8 email to Manafort. This was the proposal in which ousted Ukraine president Victor Yanukovych would become prime minister of a newly carved-out autonomous eastern Ukraine republic in Donbas.

"All that is required to start the process is a very minor 'wink' (or slight push) from DT," Kilimnik wrote in the December 8 email, using the president-elect's initials, "and a decision to authorize you to be a 'special representative' and manage this process."

With that authority, Kilimnik continued, Manafort "could start the process and within 10 days visit Russia. [Yanukovych] guarantees your reception at the very top level.... DT could have peace in Ukraine basically within a few months after inauguration."

In interviews with our office, Manafort continued to deny that he supported this plan.

Kilimnik flew from Moscow to Madrid to meet with Manafort on February 26, 2017. Manafort initially denied to our office that he had met Kilimnik on his Madrid trip, but after being confronted with evidence that Kilimnik was in Madrid at the same time, he acknowledged the meeting. Manafort said that Kilimnik had updated him on a criminal investigation into "black ledger" payments to Manafort that was being conducted by Ukraine's National Anti-Corruption Bureau. (As the US district court later considered whether Manafort had breached his cooperation plea agreement by lying to the special counsel's office, it determined that he lied about, among other things, his contacts with Kilimnik regarding the Ukraine peace plan, including the meeting in Madrid.)

Manafort kept in contact with Kilimnik throughout 2017 and into the spring of 2018, as they addressed such matters as the Ukraine peace plan and the criminal charges brought against Manafort by our office, but we'll get to those later. In early 2018, Manafort had his longtime polling firm craft a draft poll in Ukraine, sent the pollsters a three-page primer on Kilimnik's plan, and worked with Kilimnik to formulate the polling questions. This primer specifically called for the United States and President Trump to support the Autonomous Republic of Donbas with Yanukovych as prime minister, the plan that Manafort kept denying that he supported. A series of questions also sought opinions on Yanukovych's role in resolving the conflict in Donbas.

Our office did not uncover evidence showing that Manafort communicated the Ukraine peace plan to the Trump campaign or administration, although Kilimnik continued to promote it to members of the US State Department into the summer of 2018. We kept ourselves busy with other matters related to Manafort.

30

"It could blow up"

Donald Trump Jr. and Jared Kushner maintained that it was inconsequential, yet their June 9, 2016, Trump Tower meeting with Russian representatives, who claimed to have damaging information about Hillary Clinton but also were lobbying against US sanctions, continued to have consequences.

After the US presidential election, Natalia Veselnitskaya, the lawyer who had been representing individuals exposed in the fraud that led to the Magnitsky Act, and Moscow-based real estate magnate Aras Agalarov pressed again for meetings with Trump representatives. They still wished to pursue action against investor Bill Browder, who had run afoul of the Russian government as an ally of whistle-blowing accountant Magnitsky, and to push for an end to the Magnitsky Act. Ike Kaveladze, who worked for Agalarov, emailed Goldstone, the British publicist go-between, on November 23 asking him to set up another meeting "with T people." He attached a document containing allegations about Browder.

"Aras Agalarov has asked me to pass on this document in the hope it can be passed on to the appropriate team," Goldstone wrote as he forwarded Kaveladze's email to Rhona Graff, Trump's personal secretary. "If needed, a lawyer representing the case is in New York currently and happy to meet with any member of his transition team."

Kaveladze asked again in January 2017 about setting up another meeting, but Goldstone did not pass along that request. Our investigation did not determine whether transition team members followed up.

By early June 2017, the Trump Organization had grown concerned about the implications of the June 9, 2016, Trump Tower meeting and began contacting those who were there. They reached out to Goldstone, and he identified Veselnitskaya as "the woman who was the attorney who spoke at the meeting from Moscow." On June 27, 2017, Goldstone, in turn, emailed Emin Agalarov, Agas Agalarov's son who had spoken with Trump Jr. while setting up the June 9 meeting, to say that Trump attorneys had interviewed him about the meeting because they were "concerned because it links Don Jr. to officials from Russia—which he has always denied meeting.... I did say at the time this was an awful idea and terrible meeting." Emin Agalarov sent a screenshot of Goldstone's email to Kaveladze.

On July 8, 2017, the *New York Times* published its first story about the June 9, 2016, meeting. Goldstone texted Emin Agalarov the next day.

"I made sure I kept you and your father out of this story," Goldstone wrote. "If contacted I can do a dance and keep you out of it. FBI investigating.... I hope this favor was worth [it] for your dad—it could blow up."

On July 12, Emin Agalarov texted to Kaveladze that his father, Aras, "never listens" to him and that their relationship with "mr T has been thrown down the drain."

The next month found Goldstone complaining to Emin Agalarov about the negative publicity generated by the June 9 gathering in Trump Tower: "My reputation is basically destroyed by this dumb meeting which your father insisted on even though Ike and Me told him would be bad news and not to do so. I am not able to respond out of courtesy to you and your father. So am painted as some mysterious link to Putin."

After the press began to write about the June 9 meeting, Trump Organization representatives again reached out to participants. On July 10, a Trump counsel emailed Goldstone to propose that he issue this statement:

As the person who arranged the meeting, I can definitively state that the statements I have read by Donald Trump Jr. are 100% accurate.

The meeting was a complete waste of time and Don was never told Ms. Veselnitskaya's name prior to the meeting. Ms. Veselnitskaya mostly talked about the Magnitsky Act and Russian adoption laws and the meeting lasted 20 to 30 minutes at most. There was never any follow up and nothing ever came of the meeting.

Goldstone proposed that he instead state that he had been asked "by my client in Moscow — Emin Agalarov — to facilitate a meeting between a Russian attorney (Natalia Veselnitzkaya [sic]) and Donald Trump Jr. The lawyer had apparently stated that she had some information regarding funding to the DNC from Russia, which she believed Mr. Trump Jr. might find interesting."

Goldstone never released either statement.

The Russians involved in the meeting also communicated about what its participants should say. Veselnitskaya and the owner of Prevezon, the real estate company exposed by Magnitsky's antifraud whistle-blowing, controlled a group opposing the Magnitsky Act that had hired Anatoli Samochornov, the Russian translator and lobbyist who was at the Trump Tower meeting. The company offered to pay $90,000 of Samochornov's legal fees and, at Veselnitskaya's request, sent Samochornov a transcript of a Veselnitskaya press interview for his inspection.

As Samochornov interpreted the message, the organization would pay his legal fees only if he made statements consistent with Veselnitskaya's. He declined, not wanting to perjure himself.

31

"Project A was too explosive to discuss"

All this time, Vladimir Putin still had Russian business leaders working to establish communication channels with the incoming Trump administration. Petr Aven, the head of Russia's Alfa-Bank, was determined to advance Putin's interests with the Americans.

Weeks after their one-on-one meeting in which the Russian president advised Aven to protect his bank's interests from possible US sanctions, Aven attended a December 2016 "all-hands" meeting of the oligarchs with Putin. Among this collection of Russia's most prominent businessmen, Putin again raised the prospect of forthcoming US sanctions and suggested taking action to deal with them.

After this meeting, Aven sought help from one of his associates, Richard Burt, who was on the board of directors for Letter One (L1), another of Aven's companies, and had done work for Alfa-Bank. With Alfa-Bank and L1, Burt had facilitated introductions to business contacts in the United States and other Western countries. He also previously served as US ambassador to Germany and assistant secretary of state for European and Canadian affairs.

At an L1 board meeting in Luxembourg in late December, Aven pulled Burt aside and told him that he had spoken to someone high in the Russian government who sought to establish a communications channel between the Kremlin and Trump's transition team. Aven asked Burt to help make contact with Trump officials, a request that Burt found unusual despite his having helped Aven forge connections in the past. This scenario was outside the normal realm of their dealings.

Burt was also a CNI board member, so he turned to that organization's president, Dimitri Simes, for help. At that time, Burt already had Simes lobbying the Trump transition team to appoint Burt the US ambassador to Russia.

Burt asked Simes whether he could arrange a meeting with Kushner to discuss setting up a high-level communications channel between Putin and the incoming administration. Simes responded that given the media spotlight on Russian influence in the US presidential election, setting up such a channel was not a good idea at that point. Simes expressed concern that Trump's business connections could be exploited by Russia, and he did not want CNI to be seen as an intermediary between the Russian government and the Trump administration or to have any involvement in facilitating some secret connection.

Burt emailed Aven on December 22 to recount this conversation with Simes, using cryptic language:

> Through a trusted third party, I have reached out to the very influential person I mentioned in Luxembourg concerning Project A. There is an interest and an understanding for the need to establish such a channel. But the individual emphasized that at this moment, with so much intense interest in the Congress and the media over the question of cyber-hacking (and who ordered what), Project A was too explosive to discuss. The individual agreed to discuss it again after the New Year. I trust the individual's instincts on this.
>
> If this is unclear or you would like to discuss, don't hesitate to call.

Burt later confirmed that the "very influential person" was Simes and the "trusted third party" was a fabrication, since none existed. In light of the sensitivities surrounding Aven's request amid attention on Russia's influence in the US presidential election, Burt had come up with Project

A to represent Aven's effort to establish a communications channel between Russia and the Trump team. Burt also said he may have added "hype" to his email to reflect that the transition team was more interested in a secret communications channel than it actually was.

"Thank you," Aven emailed back that same day. "All clear."

Aven later explained to our office that his email was meant to indicate that he did not wish the outreach to continue. Yet when Burt spoke to Aven some time later, they continued discussing his attempts to contact the Trump team. Burt told Aven that the environment surrounding Trump, the election, and possible Russia connections made such efforts impossible.

Aven met again with Putin and other Russian officials in the first quarter of 2017, and Putin asked about Aven's attempt to build relations with the Trump administration. Aven recounted his lack of success, and Putin raised the subject again in subsequent quarterly meetings.

When the FBI eventually subpoenaed Aven, he told Putin's chief of staff that the bureau had asked him whether he had worked to create a back channel between the Russian government and the Trump administration. Aven took note that Putin's chief of staff appeared indifferent to this information.

32

"They don't know, and I don't know"

Let's pause and take stock of where we are regarding Donald Trump's and his team's relationship to Russia.

By early 2016, Trump was advocating for closer ties with Russia, saying he would get along well with "strong leader" Putin and questioning the continued existence of the NATO alliance. From February 2016 through that summer, the press reported on several Trump advisors' ties to Russia, including Michael Flynn and that December 2015 Russian TV gala where he was seated next to Putin and paid a reported $45,000. Also, Trump foreign policy advisor Carter Page had been publicly tied to a Russian state-run gas company (Gazprom), and reports had revealed Trump campaign chair Paul Manafort's lobbyist work for the Russia-backed former Ukrainian president Viktor Yanukovych. After the Republican National Convention in July 2016, reporters questioned Trump's involvement in changing the Republican platform so that it would no longer support giving arms to Ukraine in its fight against Russia-backed rebel forces.

Did these pieces fit together to create a greater picture, one that depicted Donald Trump and his officials in sync with Vladimir Putin despite the Russian leader's involvement in attacks on US institutions? An increasing number of commentators and observers were saying so.

Trump adamantly denied such connections, even as he was asking Russia to find Hillary Clinton's missing emails (which he later said was a joke) and deputizing officials to learn when WikiLeaks might release more documents to embarrass the Clinton campaign. In public, the Trump campaign distanced itself from Russian contacts, so when, as previously mentioned, Russian ambassador Sergey Kislyak invited Trump foreign policy advisor J. D. Gordon to his residence after their interactions during the Republican National Convention, Gordon declined, calling the timing "not optimal." As reports spread of Paul Manafort's links to Russian business and a pro-Russia political party in Ukraine, the campaign pushed him to resign as its chair on August 19. After the press dug into Carter Page's Russian connections, Trump terminated the aide's association with the campaign in late September, and Trump officials told reporters that Page had played "no role" in the campaign.

October 7 proved to be another significant day; WikiLeaks released its first set of Russia-hacked emails from Clinton campaign chair John Podesta just a half hour after the *Washington Post*'s publication of the *Access Hollywood* tapes in which Donald Trump bragged about kissing and groping women. Also that day, the Department of Homeland Security and Office of the Director of National Intelligence on Election Security stated they were "confident that the Russian Government directed the recent compromises of e-mails from US persons and institutions, including from US political organizations."

Two days after Trump was elected president, Russian officials told reporters that their government had maintained contact with Trump's "immediate entourage" during the campaign.

"We are not aware of any campaign representatives that were in touch with any foreign entities before yesterday, when Mr. Trump spoke with many world leaders," Trump campaign spokesperson Hope Hicks responded. Specifically addressing possible contact between the campaign and Russian officials, Hicks added in a statement, "It never happened. There was no communication between the campaign and any foreign entity during the campaign."

After making that statement, Hicks recalled later, she checked its accuracy with campaign advisors Kellyanne Conway, Stephen Miller,

Jason Miller, and probably Kushner and Bannon. None of them raised any objections.

On December 10, 2016, the *Washington Post*, *New York Times*, and Reuters reported that US intelligence agencies had concluded with "high confidence" that Russia had interfered in the election through hacked emails provided to WikiLeaks and other means in order to help Trump win the White House.

The Trump team rejected these findings and immediately issued this statement: "These are the same people that said Saddam Hussein had weapons of mass destruction." In an interview with Fox News's Chris Wallace the following day, Trump said of the Russian interference scenario, "I think it's ridiculous. I think it's just another excuse. I don't believe it."

He added, "They have no idea if it's Russia or China or somebody. It could be somebody sitting in a bed some place. I mean, they have no idea.... I think the Democrats are putting it out because they suffered one of the greatest defeats in the history of politics in this country. And, frankly, I think they're putting it out. It's ridiculous.... Personally, it could be Russia. It — I don't really think it is. But who knows? I don't know either. They don't know, and I don't know."

Podesta told the press on December 18 that the election had been "distorted by the Russian intervention," and he questioned whether Trump campaign officials had been "in touch with the Russians." Appearing on Fox News that day, incoming chief of staff Reince Priebus declined to say whether Trump accepted the intelligence communities' conclusions, and he denied any campaign contact or coordination with the Russians.

"Even this question is insane," Priebus said. "Of course we didn't interface with the Russians.... This whole thing is a spin job." He asked why the Democrats were "doing everything they can to delegitimize the outcome of the election."

The Obama administration announced on December 29 that it was imposing sanctions on Russian individuals and entities in response to its cyberoperations that targeted the election, prompting Trump's response: "I think we ought to get on with our lives."

Later Trump put out a statement:

It's time for our country to move on to bigger and better things. Nevertheless, in the interest of our country and its great people, I will meet with leaders of the intelligence community next week in order to be updated on the facts of this situation.

That briefing and its aftermath would make for an eventful week.

33

"Stopped flow of tapes from Russia"

Trump's intelligence briefing about Russian election interference took place on January 6, 2017. As the intelligence agencies announced to the public afterward, they had concluded with a high degree of confidence that Russia had used a variety of means to harm Clinton's chances in the election, with Putin and the Russian government showing a clear preference for Trump.

After the briefing ended, FBI director James Comey stuck around to speak with Trump. Before Comey brought up the topic he wished to discuss, Trump complimented the FBI director for conducting himself honorably over the past year and having a great reputation. (These details are reflected in a memo about the conversation that Comey began drafting immediately afterward.)

Comey had drawn attention to himself over that past year with some controversial decisions made during the campaign. In July 2015, the FBI opened a criminal investigation into Hillary Clinton's use of a private email server during her secretary of state tenure, and a year later, on July 5, 2016, Comey hosted a news conference in which he announced the FBI's recommendation that the Department of Justice not press charges against Clinton, even as he called her behavior "extremely careless." There was no known precedent for the FBI to make public its prosecutorial recommendation to the Department of Justice.

Then on October 26, 2016, less than two weeks before the election, the FBI discovered emails between Hillary Clinton and her campaign vice chair, Huma Abedin, during an unrelated investigation of Abedin's husband, former congressman Anthony Weiner. Two days later, Comey defied a reported recommendation by senior Justice Department officials and wrote a letter to Congress explaining that the FBI had reopened its Clinton email investigation to review more emails. Comey's letter went public almost immediately, and the FBI director received widespread criticism for revealing such information so close to the election. On November 6, two days before the election, Comey sent another letter to Congress saying essentially that Clinton had been cleared again.

"Based on our review, we have not changed our conclusions that we expressed in July," Comey wrote.

People on both sides of the political aisle objected to Comey's handling of the investigation. Some thought his late-October letter to Congress deterred potential Clinton voters, and Clinton agreed, saying on CNN in May 2017, "I was on the way to winning until a combination of Jim Comey's letter on October 28 and Russian WikiLeaks raised doubts in the minds of people who were inclined to vote for me and got scared off." Some Republicans, meanwhile, accused Comey of bias against Trump in his public exoneration of Clinton.

Now Trump was saying that he thought highly of Comey, looked forward to working with him, and hoped he would stay on in his job. Comey said that he planned to continue serving as FBI director. Then he briefed Trump on the matter at hand.

His office had obtained some unverified, potentially embarrassing allegations about Trump compiled by former British intelligence officer Christopher Steele. Included in Steele's dossier was a report of an unverified allegation that Russia possessed compromising tapes of Trump from his 2013 trip to Moscow for the Miss Universe pageant.

This was not the first time that these tapes had been brought to the Trump team's attention. Michael Cohen received a text on October 30, 2016, nine days before the election, from Russian businessman Giorgi Rtskhiladze, who back in September 2015 had pitched Cohen on a New

York meeting about Trump Tower Moscow between Trump's people and "the highest level of the Russian Government." Rtskhiladze's October 30 text to Cohen read, "Stopped flow of tapes from Russia but not sure if there's anything else. Just so you know."

Rtskhiladze later told our office that he was referring to compromising tapes of Trump rumored to be held by people associated with the Crocus Group, Aras Agalarov's company that helped host the 2013 Miss Universe pageant and had negotiated with the Trump Organization about a potential Trump Tower Moscow from late 2013 till November 2014. More recently Agalarov had pushed for the June 9 Trump Tower meeting and continued working for a meeting to turn the Trump team against the Magnitsky Act. In our interview, Rtskhiladze said he had been told that the supposedly incriminating Trump tapes were fake, but he did not communicate that point to Cohen. For his part, Cohen said that after Rtskhiladze texted, he discussed the matter with Trump.

As Comey revealed the contents of the Steele dossier to Trump, he noticed the president-elect growing defensive, so the FBI director assured him that the FBI was not investigating him personally.

Comey's briefing of Trump became the subject of media reports on January 10. That same day BuzzFeed News published the entire Steele dossier, with the headline "These Reports Allege Trump Has Deep Ties to Russia." Its introduction read,

A dossier making explosive — but unverified — allegations that the Russian government has been "cultivating, supporting and assisting" President-elect Donald Trump for years and gained compromising information about him has been circulating among elected officials, intelligence agents, and journalists for weeks.

The dossier, which is a collection of memos written over a period of months, includes specific, unverified, and potentially unverifiable allegations of contact between Trump aides and Russian operatives, and graphic claims of sexual acts documented by the Russians.

In a press conference the next day, Trump called the BuzzFeed release "an absolute disgrace" and reiterated, "I have no dealings with Russia.... We could make deals in Russia very easily if we wanted to. I just don't want to because I think that would be a conflict." Trump complained to intelligence leaders about the leak and asked them to make public statements refuting the Steele dossier allegations. They did not.

The president-elect viewed these stories linking him to Russia and its election inference as a threat to his victory's legitimacy — and thus his presidency. Hicks called the intelligence community's assessment of Russian interference Trump's "Achilles' heel," because if people thought that Russia had helped him win, his accomplishment would be diminished. Sean Spicer, Trump's first communications director, Gates, and Priebus agreed with this assessment of Trump's attitude.

Over the next few weeks, three congressional committees — the Senate Select Committee on Intelligence, the House Permanent Select Committee on Intelligence (HPSCI), and the Senate Judiciary Committee — opened investigations into Russia's interference in the election and possible Trump cooperation with Putin's government.

That Achilles' heel would be growing larger.

34

"What the hell is this about?"

Michael Flynn had yet to take office as national security advisor, yet his work was already attracting attention — not the kind that Donald Trump or his team desired. In a January 12 *Washington Post* column, David Ignatius reported on the Flynn-Kislyak conversation that took place following the Obama administration's announcement of Russian sanctions earlier that day. The columnist wondered whether Flynn's side of the discussion had "undercut the U.S. sanctions" and violated the letter or spirit of the Logan Act, which makes it a crime for a US citizen to become involved in unauthorized negotiations with representatives of a foreign government in dispute with the United States.

When Trump saw the column, he was not happy.

"What the hell is this about?" Trump asked Priebus.

Priebus called Flynn to tell him that the president-elect was angry about this report that recounted his conversations with Kislyak. The incoming chief of staff directed Flynn, "Kill the story."

Flynn tried to do that, instructing McFarland to call Ignatius at the *Post*. McFarland knew that such a call would involve passing on false information — because she could not convince Ignatius to retract the story unless he thought it was inaccurate, which it was not. But the deputy national security advisor made the call anyway, and Ignatius and the *Washington Post* added a note to the bottom of the column:

UPDATE: The Trump transition team did not respond Thursday night to a request for comment. But two team members called with information Friday morning. A first Trump official confirmed that Flynn had spoken with Kislyak by phone, but said the calls were before sanctions were announced and didn't cover that topic. This official later added that Flynn's initial call was to express condolences to Kislyak after the terrorist killing of the Russian ambassador to Ankara Dec. 19, and that Flynn made a second call Dec. 28 to express condolences for the shoot-down of a Russian plane carrying a choir to Syria. In that second call, Flynn also discussed plans for a Trump-Putin conversation sometime after the inauguration. In addition, a second Trump official said the Dec. 28 call included an invitation from Kislyak for a Trump administration official to visit Kazakhstan for a conference in late January.

The identity of the second Trump official mentioned here is unknown. According to his December 2017 Statement of Offense, Flynn subsequently told Priebus and other incoming Trump administration officials who asked about the *Post* column that he and Kislyak had not discussed sanctions. He supposedly said the same to Vice President–Elect Mike Pence and incoming press secretary Sean Spicer. Priebus, Pence, and Spicer went on to deny in media interviews that Flynn and Kislyak had discussed sanctions.

When senior Department of Justice officials heard these incoming Trump administration officials making public statements that denied that Flynn and Kislyak had discussed sanctions, they became alarmed. FBI agent Andrew McCabe, whom Comey would name deputy director on January 29, 2016, told my office that Justice Department officials were "really freaked out about it." These statements were untrue, as the officials knew, and if Flynn had lied to his colleagues, who then had misled the American public, then the Russian government could have leverage over him because it could prove that he lied. FBI investigators also viewed Flynn's calls with Kislyak as potential Logan Act violations that were relevant to the agency's broader Russian probe.

President Trump was inaugurated on January 20, and Flynn was sworn in as national security advisor. Three days later, in his first press briefing, Spicer said that he had spoken to Flynn the previous night and the new national security advisor had confirmed that his calls with Kislyak were not related to sanctions. Hearing Spicer make these statements, DOJ officials became even more concerned that Russia could use its knowledge of Flynn's lies to compromise him.

Flynn agreed to be interviewed by FBI agents on January 24, and as they spoke in the White House, Flynn lied that he did not ask Kislyak to refrain from escalating the situation in response to the Obama administration's sanctions. He also said, falsely, that he did not remember a follow-up call in which Kislyak said Russia had moderated its reaction to the sanctions due to Flynn's request.

Two days later, Acting Attorney General Sally Yates told the White House counsel, Don McGahn, that she needed to meet with him in person to discuss a sensitive situation. Trump had named McGahn to his post after the former Federal Election Commission member had successfully managed Trump-related litigation, including ballot challenges, during the 2016 campaign. (McGahn joined the White House from the Washington, DC–based law firm Jones Day, which did work for Russia's Alfa-Bank as well as such Russian oligarchs as Oleg Deripaska and Viktor Vekselberg.) Later that day, Yates and Mary McCord, a senior national security official at the Department of Justice, met with McGahn and White House counsel's office attorney James Burnham at the White House. Yates told them that the vice president's statements denying that Flynn and Kislyak had discussed sanctions were untrue and made Flynn vulnerable to compromise because the Russians would know that he lied. She also revealed that the FBI had interviewed Flynn, and his statements to the agency were similar to those he had given to Pence and Spicer in denying the discussion of sanctions.

That afternoon McGahn told the president about Yates's visit and described what she had said. McGahn said that although Flynn did not tell the FBI that he had discussed sanctions with Kislyak, that did not mean he necessarily had violated 18 U.S. Code § 1001, a law that prohibits, among other offenses, knowingly making "false, fictitious or fraudulent statements... within the jurisdiction of the executive, legislative, or judicial branch of the Government of the United States." McGahn explained the law, as well as the Logan Act, to the president, who instructed McGahn to work out the situation with Priebus and Bannon and not to discuss it with anyone else.

By this time, as Hicks observed, Flynn already was "on thin ice" with Trump. President Obama had warned Trump against hiring him shortly after the election, and, Priebus said, even before the Kislyak story broke, Trump had grown so unhappy with Flynn that he would not look at him during intelligence briefings. Trump also didn't think Flynn showed good judgment in his tweets. Not that these were specified by Trump, but days before the election, Flynn tweeted, falsely, a story that the New York police had found evidence on Anthony Weiner's laptop "to put Hillary and her crew away for life." The previous July, he accused Clinton of "showing disrespect for American Values and Principles" as he linked to a tweet that claimed she was "wearing hijab in solidarity with islamic terrorists." The photo actually came from her 2009 trip to Pakistan as secretary of state when she wore a head covering out of respect while entering a mosque. More inflammatory tweets from Flynn's son, Michael Flynn Jr., also may not have helped.

When Priebus spoke with the president about Yates's White House visit, Trump directed his anger at Flynn.

"Not again, this guy, this stuff," Trump said.

35

"Like gum on the bottom of your shoe"

Over dinner on the night of Sally Yates's visit to the White House, Trump asked his senior advisors what they thought of James Comey. None of them said Trump should fire him, but not everyone was enthusiastic about the FBI director either. The national intelligence director, Daniel Coats, suggested that Trump spend more time with Comey before deciding his fate.

Trump called Comey the next day, January 27, and invited him for dinner that night. Comey accepted.

McGahn already had advised the president not to communicate directly with the Department of Justice to avoid any perception that he might be interfering in law enforcement. Before the dinner, Priebus reinforced this point.

"Don't talk about Russia, whatever you do," Priebus told Trump.

The president promised he would not.

Bannon suggested that he or Priebus join Trump and Comey at the dinner, but Trump insisted that he wished to dine alone with the FBI director.

When Comey arrived at the White House, he was surprised, as well as concerned, that no one but the president was present at dinner. Trump picked up this conversation where he had left off the previous one, repeatedly discussing Comey's future and probing whether Comey wished to remain FBI director. Given that Trump previously had told Comey he wanted him to stay, the FBI director sensed that the president was trying to create a patronage relationship by prompting him to ask for his job.

Trump told Comey that he was considering ordering the FBI to investigate the Steele allegations to prove they were false. Comey cautioned Trump about taking such an action because it could give the impression that the FBI was investigating him personally, which was not the case.

As the dinner continued, Trump brought up Michael Flynn.

"The guy has some serious judgment issues," the president said.

Comey did not respond, and Trump did not mention any FBI interest in or contact with Flynn. But at some point, Trump made a dramatic declaration.

"I need loyalty. I expect loyalty."

Comey let that comment pass, and the conversation continued down other paths. But the president once again raised the point at the end of dinner, returning to the subject of Comey's tenure as FBI director and repeating, "I need loyalty."

"You will always get honesty from me," Comey responded.

"That's what I want, honest loyalty," Trump said.

"You will get that from me," Comey said.

(This account stems from Comey's contemporaneous memo, his interview with my office, and his congressional testimony. Although the president and his advisors disputed some aspects of the account after it was made public—such as Trump claiming that Comey had asked for the dinner to keep his job—much evidence corroborates Comey's account, including the president's daily diary noting that he invited Comey to dinner that night. Also, senior FBI officials recalled Comey's telling them about the loyalty request at the time, and Comey recounted this moment while under oath with Congress and under penalty for lying in his interview with investigators.)

On the same day that Comey dined with Trump, McGahn and National Security Council legal advisor John Eisenberg were discussing whether Michael Flynn may have violated the Espionage Act, the Logan Act, or 18 U.S.C. § 1001, a law prohibiting making false statements to someone in the government. Eisenberg, who had been researching this matter, said he thought Flynn might have violated the Logan Act and 18 U.S.C. § 1001, although he noted that no one in the United States had ever been successfully prosecuted for a Logan Act violation.

McGahn invited Yates back to the White House later that day and told her that the White House did not want to do anything to interfere with an ongoing investigation of Flynn. Yates said the Justice Department had notified the White House so that it could take action based on the information it had collected. The meeting ended with McGahn asking Yates for the DOJ's underlying information regarding Flynn's conversations with Kislyak. Eisenberg reviewed this material on February 2 and discussed with McGahn that although a Logan Act prosecution of Flynn was unlikely, they could not assess his chances of being prosecuted for violating 18 USC § 1001.

Flynn and the president had a one-on-one conversation in the Oval Office the week of February 6. Upset about the negative media coverage generated by his national security advisor, Trump pressed Flynn for details about his conversations with Kislyak. When Flynn listed the dates on which he remembered speaking with the Russian ambassador, Trump corrected him on one of them. Flynn said Trump also asked him what he and Kislyak discussed, and Flynn said he might have brought up the sanctions.

The *Washington Post* reported on February 7 that Flynn had discussed sanctions with Kislyak while Obama was still in office. After that story was published, Vice President Pence was told of the Department of Justice's notification to the White House about Flynn's calls, and he and others in the administration read the underlying information that had been collected. McGahn and Priebus spoke with Flynn, who also had told White House officials that the FBI was closing its investigation of him, and recommended to the president that he be fired.

As they flew back on Air Force One from Mar-a-Lago to Washington, DC, on February 12, the president asked Flynn whether he had lied to the vice president. Flynn said he may have forgotten details but hadn't lied.

"OK, that's fine," Trump said. "I got it."

The next day Priebus instructed Flynn to resign. Flynn asked to say goodbye to the president, so Priebus took him to the Oval Office. Trump gave his now-former national security advisor a hug and shook his hand.

"We'll give you a good recommendation," the president said. "You're a good guy. We'll take care of you."

The White House counsel's office distributed talking points to the communications team stating that while McGahn had advised Trump that Flynn was not likely to be prosecuted, the president's issue was trust. So Spicer told the press the following day, February 14, that Flynn was forced to resign "not based on a legal issue but based on a trust issue. A level of trust between the president and General Flynn had eroded to the point where [the president] felt he had to make a change."

That same day, New Jersey governor Chris Christie, who had run against Trump in the Republican primaries and had been named to lead Trump's transition team before he was pushed out in favor of Pence, joined the president for lunch in the White House, with Kushner at the table as well.

"Now that we fired Flynn, the Russia thing is over," Trump said.

"No way," Christie responded with a laugh. "This Russia thing is far from over. We'll be here on Valentine's Day 2018 talking about this."

"What do you mean?" the president asked. "Flynn met with the Russians. That was the problem. I fired Flynn. It's over."

Christie said that based on his experience as a prosecutor as well as the subject of an investigation, firing Flynn would not end the probe. "There's no way to make an investigation shorter," Christie said, "but there are a lot of ways to make it longer."

"What do you mean?"

"Look, don't talk about the investigation even if you get frustrated," Christie advised. "Flynn is going to be like gum on the bottom of your shoe, tough to get rid of."

At some point during the lunch, Kushner received a call from Flynn, who was complaining about what Spicer had said about him during that day's press briefing.

"You know the president respects you," Kushner told him over the phone. "The president cares about you. I'll get the president to send out a positive tweet about you later."

Hearing this, the president nodded at his son-in-law. No such tweet apparently followed, although Trump did tell reporters the following day, "General Flynn is a wonderful man. I think he's been treated very, very unfairly by the media."

As the lunch neared its end, Trump asked Christie whether he was still friendly with Comey. Christie said he was.

"Call him and tell him that I really like him," Trump said. "Tell him he's part of the team."

Trump repeated the request before they parted ways, but Christie had no intention of complying, considering the request "nonsensical." Christie wasn't about to put Comey in the position of receiving such a call, and the governor wouldn't have been comfortable passing along that message.

Comey, Sessions, and other officials joined the president for a homeland security briefing that afternoon. When it ended, Trump dismissed everyone but Comey, to whom he said he wanted to speak alone. Sessions and Jared Kushner remained in the Oval Office anyway, but the president insisted they leave so that he could speak solely with Comey. After the others had departed, Priebus opened the door, but Trump sent him away too.

"I want to talk about Mike Flynn," Trump said once he and Comey were alone. The president explained that Flynn hadn't done anything wrong in speaking to the Russians, but he had to go because he misled the vice president.

The president and FBI director discussed leaks of classified information before Trump brought the conversation back to Flynn.

"He's a good guy and has been through a lot," Trump said. "I hope you can see your way clear to letting this go, to letting Flynn go. He is a good guy. I hope you can let this go."

Comey agreed only with the part about Flynn being "a good guy." The FBI director did not commit to ending the investigation about him. But Comey, as he would testify under oath, felt that Trump was giving him "a direction," given the president's position and the meeting's one-on-one nature.

Afterward, Comey began to write a memo to document this conversation, and he discussed the president's request with his leadership team. They decided not to share the president's words with the FBI officials working on the Flynn case to prevent them from being influenced by the request.

Comey also set up a meeting with Sessions, where he made one particular point:

"Do not leave me alone with the president again."

36

"I didn't direct him, but I would have directed him"

As Christie predicted, Flynn's forced resignation did not close the book on questions about Russia and the Trump campaign. At the White House daily briefing the day after the firing, White House press secretary Sean Spicer engaged in this exchange with a reporter:

ABC White House correspondent Jonathan Karl: "Back in January, the President said that nobody in his campaign had been in touch with the Russians. Now, today, can you still say definitively that nobody on the Trump campaign, not even General Flynn, had any contact with the Russians before the election?"

Spicer: "My understanding is that what General Flynn has now expressed is that during the transition period — well, we were very clear that during the transition period, he did speak with the ambassador —"

Karl: "I'm talking about during the campaign."

Spicer: "I don't have any — there's nothing that would conclude me — that anything different has changed with respect to that time period."

Karl: "And why would the President — if he was notified 17 days ago that Flynn had misled the vice president [and] other officials here and that he was a potential threat to blackmail by the Russians, why would he be kept on for almost three weeks?"

Spicer: "Well, that's not — that assumes a lot of things that are not true. The president was informed of this. He asked the White House Counsel to review the situation. The first matter was whether there was a legal issue. We had to review whether there was a legal issue, which the White House Counsel concluded there was not, as I stated in my comments. This was an act of trust. Whether or not he actually misled the Vice President was the issue, and that was ultimately what led to the President asking for and accepting the resignation of General Flynn. That's it, pure and simple. It was a matter of trust."

Another reporter asked Spicer, "Did the president instruct [Flynn] to talk about sanctions with the Russian ambassador?"

"No, absolutely not," Spicer responded. "No, no, no."

Trump held a news conference two days later in which he said that he let Flynn go because Flynn "didn't tell the vice president of the United States the facts, and then he didn't remember. And that just wasn't acceptable to me." Yet the president also said that "what [Flynn] did wasn't wrong, what he did in terms of the information he saw. What was wrong was the way that other people, including yourselves in this room, were given that information, because that was classified information that was given illegally. That's the real problem. And you can talk all you want about Russia, which was all a fake news, fabricated deal to try and make up for the loss of the Democrats, and the press plays right into it.... It's all fake news. It's all fake news."

Asked whether he directed Flynn to discuss sanctions with Kislyak, Trump said, "No, I didn't," but he soon added, "It certainly would have been okay with me if he did it. I would have directed him to do it if I thought he wasn't doing it. I didn't direct him, but I would have directed him because that's his job."

Trump also denied having "any deals with Russia" and said that he had "nothing to do with" Russia or WikiLeaks.

The next shoe to drop was Deputy National Security Advisor

McFarland. Priebus and Bannon told her on February 22 that the president wanted her to resign. But they also dangled the opportunity of the US ambassadorship to Singapore. First, though, the president would have a request.

Trump asked Priebus the next day to have McFarland write an internal email confirming that the president did not direct Flynn to call Kislyak about sanctions. The chief of staff told Trump that he would tell McFarland to draft such a note only if she were comfortable doing so.

Priebus called McFarland into his office to pass along the president's request that she memorialize in writing that he did not direct Flynn to discuss sanctions with the Russian ambassador. McFarland responded that she did not know whether or not the president had directed Flynn to talk with Kislyak, and she didn't give Priebus a yes or no. Priebus was left with the impression that she was not comfortable with Trump's request, and he suggested she speak with attorneys in the White House counsel's office.

McFarland informed National Security Council legal advisor Eisenberg that she had been fired as deputy national security advisor and offered the ambassadorship to Singapore, but first the president and chief of staff wanted her to write a letter denying that Trump had directed Flynn to discuss sanctions with Kislyak. McFarland wrote in a contemporaneous Memorandum for the Record that Eisenberg told her that writing such an email would be "a bad idea — from my side because the email would be awkward. Why would I be emailing Priebus to make a statement for the record? But it would also be a bad idea for the President because it looked as if my ambassadorial appointment was in some way a quid pro quo."

Priebus visited McFarland's office later that evening and told her not to write the email and to forget he even mentioned it.

It wasn't until April 9 that reports were made public that McFarland was being removed as deputy national security advisor to become the US ambassador to Singapore. She remained in her job for weeks longer, and in December 2017, the Senate Foreign Relations Committee placed a formal hold on her confirmation as ambassador amid widespread reports about her role in the Flynn matter. The Senate eventually sent her nomination back to the White House. The administration renominated her in January 2018, but she withdrew herself from consideration the following month.

Back around the time that Priebus was asking McFarland to write that email, the president asked Priebus to reach out to Flynn to let him know that Trump still cared about him. Priebus, who thought the president was concerned that Flynn might speak badly of him, called Flynn and told him he was an American hero.

Weeks later, Flynn agreed to testify before the FBI and congressional investigators in exchange for immunity. "Mike Flynn should ask for immunity," Trump tweeted on March 31, 2017, "in that this is a witch hunt (excuse for big election loss), by media & Dems, of historic proportion!"

Trump also asked McFarland to pass a message from him to Flynn saying that the president felt bad for him and that he should stay strong.

37

"I have decided to recuse myself"

Back in February 28, 2016, Donald Trump had "a little surprise" for his supporters who had come out for a rally in Madison, Alabama, just two days before the Super Tuesday primaries, including the one in that state.

"I have a man who is respected by everybody here, greatly respected," Trump teased the stadium crowd. "He's really the expert as far as I'm concerned on borders, on so many things....When I talk about immigration and when I talk about illegal immigration and everything else, I think about a great man. Who am I talking about? Nobody knows because we've kept it a surprise."

And out came Alabama senator Jeff Sessions.

Sessions's endorsement was indeed unexpected at the time. Embraced by Tea Party Republicans, evangelicals, and others who appreciated his hard line on immigration, Sessions was presumed by some to be a natural fit for Trump primary rival Ted Cruz's campaign. But the Alabama senator went all in for Trump, telling the crowd, "I told Donald Trump this isn't a campaign, this is a movement. Look at what's happening. The American people are not happy with their government....At this time, in my best judgment, at this time in America's history, we need to make America great again."

Onto his head went a red cap bearing Trump's campaign slogan.

Sessions became one of the Trump campaign's major policy advisors, particularly on the topics of immigration and national security. Trump had him on his short list of potential running mates before opting for

Mike Pence. But Sessions's consolation prize was a big — some, including the president, would say the biggest — position in Trump's cabinet. On November 18, 2016, the president-elect announced Jeff Sessions's appointment as attorney general.

The process of confirming Sessions would have major implications not only for Sessions but also for the entire Trump presidency.

During Sessions's confirmation hearings in January 2017, Democratic Minnesota senator Al Franken mentioned a CNN report about an intelligence-community document alleging "a continuing exchange of information during the campaign between Trump's surrogates and intermediaries for the Russian government." Then Franken asked Sessions, "If there is any evidence that anyone affiliated with the Trump campaign communicated with the Russian government in the course of this campaign, what will you do?"

"Senator Franken," Sessions responded, "I'm not aware of any of those activities. I have been called a surrogate at a time or two in that campaign, and I didn't have — did not have communications with the Russians, and I'm unable to comment on it."

Also that month, Democratic Vermont senator Patrick J. Leahy submitted this written question to Sessions: "Several of the President-elect's nominees or senior advisers have Russian ties. Have you been in contact with anyone connected to any part of the Russian government about the 2016 election, either before or after election day?"

"No," Sessions responded.

Yet by March 1, 2017, there were reports that Sessions had met twice with Russian ambassador Kislyak during the campaign, and some senators and representatives, including Franken and Republican senator Lindsey Graham, were calling on Sessions to recuse himself from any role in investigations of Russia's connections with the Trump campaign.

"If there's something there that the FBI thinks is criminal in nature, then for sure you need a special prosecutor," Graham said at a CNN town hall.

But one person in particular did not want Sessions to recuse himself from the Russia investigation: Donald Trump.

On the morning of March 2, the day after the *Washington Post* ran a story with the headline "Sessions Met with Russian Envoy Twice Last Year, Encounters He Later Did Not Disclose," the president called White House counsel McGahn and urged him to tell Sessions not to recuse himself. McGahn understood Trump's concern that a recusal would make Sessions look guilty for omitting details in the confirmation hearing and that the president would be left unprotected from an investigation that could thwart his policy objectives and presidency itself. McGahn contacted the attorney general and related the president's unhappiness about the possibility of recusal. Sessions replied that his intention was to follow the rules.

When McGahn relayed this conversation to the president, Trump reiterated his point: he did not want Sessions to recuse himself. McGahn stepped up his efforts that day, reaching out to Sessions's personal counsel and chief of staff as well as the Senate majority leader, Mitch McConnell. He also contacted Sessions another two times that day, and other White House advisors called the attorney general as well. They were all pushing the case against recusal.

That afternoon, Sessions made an announcement:

> *During the course of the confirmation proceedings on my nomination to be Attorney General, I advised the Senate Judiciary Committee that "if a specific matter arose where I believed my impartiality might reasonably be questioned, I would consult with Department ethics officials regarding the most appropriate way to proceed."*
>
> *During the course of the last several weeks, I have met with the relevant senior career Department officials to discuss whether I should recuse myself from any matters arising from the campaigns for President of the United States.*
>
> *Having concluded those meetings today, I have decided to recuse myself from any existing or future investigations of any matters related in any way to the campaigns for President of the United States.*

I have taken no actions regarding any such matters, to the extent they exist.

This announcement should not be interpreted as confirmation of the existence of any investigation or suggestive of the scope of any such investigation.

Consistent with the succession order for the Department of Justice, Acting Deputy Attorney General and U.S. Attorney for the Eastern District of Virginia Dana Boente shall act as and perform the functions of the Attorney General with respect to any matters from which I have recused myself to the extent they exist.

To Sessions, the recusal question was not a close call, when he considered the language in the Code of Federal Regulations, which states that "no employee shall participate in a criminal investigation or prosecution if he has a personal or political relationship with . . . any person or organization substantially involved in the conduct that is the subject of the investigation or prosecution." But he knew that the president was upset with him and did not think he had done his duty.

The White House counsel's office distributed an internal communication on March 2 directing officials not to contact Sessions about his recusal because of "serious concerns about obstruction." Whether the president was aware of this directive is unclear, especially in light of his actions.

The following day, Trump called McGahn into the Oval Office, where other advisors, including Priebus and Bannon, were present.

"I don't have a lawyer," the president declared, directing his anger at McGahn. He said he wished that the late Roy Cohn, most famous for being Senator Joseph McCarthy's aggressive chief counsel during the senator's anti-communism crusade of the early 1950s — and Trump's lawyer in the 1970s — were his attorney because he would have fought for the president, whereas his current counsel did not.

The president told McGahn to talk to Sessions about his recusal, but McGahn noted that the Department of Justice's ethics officials had supported the attorney general's decision. Trump asserted that Robert Kennedy, attorney general under President John F. Kennedy, and Eric Holder, President Obama's attorney general, had protected their president.

"You're telling me that Bobby and Jack didn't talk about investigations?" Trump raged. "Or Obama didn't tell Eric Holder who to investigate?"

As he screamed at McGahn about how weak Sessions was, Trump was as angry as Bannon had ever seen him. Before the inauguration, Bannon had told the president that Sessions would have to recuse himself from any campaign-related investigations because of his work on the Trump campaign, so the attorney general's decision should not have come as a surprise. Yet President Trump would not abide it.

Sessions and McGahn flew down to Mar-a-Lago that weekend, and President Trump got Sessions alone to tell him he should "unrecuse" from the Russia investigation and to develop strategies to help his president, as Robert Kennedy and Eric Holder had done.

Sessions declined.

38

"What can be done to lift the cloud?"

I am not in this story yet. I thought I would mention that at this point of the narrative. The FBI, under James Comey's leadership, was investigating Russian interference into the presidential election, and Dana Boente was serving as acting attorney general on this matter due to Jeff Sessions's recusal. The fact gathering and investigating were proceeding pretty much by the book. The process was moving forward at its own deliberate pace. That is how the wheels of justice roll.

But President Trump was agitated. He could not tolerate this situation. He could not stand the idea that people might think he was being investigated for wrongdoing involving the election and the Russians. And if people thought that he somehow hadn't completely earned his presidential victory, that was unacceptable.

Trusted advisors, such as Chris Christie and Reince Priebus, had told him to pull back and to let the investigation take its course. But pulling back and waiting was not Donald Trump's style.

So the president told his advisors on March 6 that he wanted to call Dana Boente to learn whether he or the White House was being investigated. Other information about the investigation would soon be coming from other officials.

Comey briefed the group of congressional leaders dubbed the "Gang of Eight" on March 9, and he identified the principal US suspects of the bureau's Russian interference investigation. White House counsel Don McGahn's chief of staff, Annie Donaldson, recorded the president's reaction in her notes: "POTUS in panic/chaos. Need binders to put in front of POTUS. (1) All things related to Russia."

Senate Select Committee on Intelligence chair Senator Richard Burr also gave a briefing to the White House counsel's office, and he noted the existence of four to five investigative targets, which Donaldson also documented in her notes: "Flynn (FBI was in — wrapping up)→DOJ looking for phone records"; "Comey→Manafort (Ukr + Russia, not campaign)"; "Carter Page ($ game)"; "Greek Guy" and one other name redacted from public record. "Greek Guy" could refer to Papadopoulos, who was later charged with lying to the FBI. I cannot comment on the redacted name but will note that Roger Stone also was under investigation.

Comey was scheduled to testify before the House Permanent Select Committee on Intelligence on March 20, and congressional officials made clear that they expected to receive information about the FBI investigation. Boente authorized Comey to confirm the investigation's existence at the hearing, but the acting attorney general and FBI director agreed that Comey would decline comment about whether any individuals, including the president, were being investigated.

"The FBI, as part of [its] counterintelligence mission, is investigating the Russian government's efforts to interfere in the 2016 presidential election, and that includes investigating the nature of any links between individuals associated with the Trump campaign and the Russian government and whether there was any coordination between the campaign and Russia's efforts," Comey said in his opening remarks, which had been drafted in consultation with the Department of Justice. "As with any counterintelligence investigation, this will also include an assessment of whether any crimes were committed."

Was President Trump "under investigation during the campaign" or "under investigation now"? Comey declined to answer. He also would not say whether the FBI was investigating the content of the Steele dossier.

President Trump already had been expressing frustration about Comey to his aides, complaining that the FBI director made too many headlines and didn't attend enough White House intelligence briefings. This hearing made matters worse. Comey, the president said, was acting like "his own branch of government." More to the point, the press now was concluding from Comey's testimony that the president *was* under investigation. Trump was "beside himself," according to Donaldson's March 21 notes, saying the "Comey bombshell...made me look like a fool."

As Trump grew "hotter and hotter," he called McGahn multiple times that day, telling him to step in with the Department of Justice. Officials in the White House counsel's office grew so concerned that Trump would fire Comey that they began drafting a memo examining whether the president needed cause for such an action.

McGahn followed his president's orders, contacting Boente several times on March 21 to enlist him in persuading Comey or the Department of Justice to publicly correct the misperception that the president was under investigation. McGahn also asked whether there was a way to speed up or to end the Russia investigation as quickly as possible. The president was under a cloud, he said, and that made it hard for him to govern.

Echoing Christie's lunchtime conversation with the president, Boente said that there was no good way to shorten the investigation and that trying to do so could undermine its credibility. McGahn agreed and dropped the issue. Boente also told McGahn that he did not want to speak directly with President Trump about this request, as the president had desired.

But the president would not drop his push to be cleared in the Russia investigation. He asked Director of National Intelligence Daniel Coats and the director of the CIA, Michael Pompeo, to remain in the Oval Office after the March 22 presidential daily briefing so that he could request that they state publicly that there was no link between him and Russia. Coats said that as his office had nothing to do with the investigation, making a public statement about it was beyond the bounds of his job. Pompeo also would not perform this deed, and he observed the president regularly urging other officials to come out and say he had done nothing wrong involving Russia.

Several of Coats's office staffers recalled the national intelligence director saying after this meeting that the president also had asked him to contact Comey to see whether there was any way to get past or to end this investigation (though Coats later would deny Trump made such a request). Coats was said to have told the president that he would not intervene in an ongoing FBI investigation, and he was upset at being asked to contact Comey.

Three days later, Trump called Coats again.

"I can't do anything with Russia. There's things I'd like to do with Russia, with trade, with ISIS, they're all over me with this," the president said, adding of the investigation, "What can you do to help get it done?"

"The best way to get it done," Coats responded, "is to let the investigation run its course."

The next day, March 27, President Trump called the National Security Agency's director, Admiral Michael Rogers, to complain that the Russia investigation was hindering his work and that the stories linking him to Russia were untrue, so he wanted Rogers to refute them. Richard Ledgett, the National Security Agency's deputy director who was present for the call, said that he had never witnessed a more unusual request in his forty years of government service. After the call ended, Ledgett drafted a memo documenting the conversation and President Trump's request, he and Rogers signed it, and they stashed it in a safe.

The president kept venting. He began at least two of his presidential daily briefings by stating there was no collusion with Russia and a press statement should be issued to say that. He complained to Pompeo that there was no evidence against him, yet no one would publicly defend him.

"The Russia thing has got to go away," he told Rogers, saying he had done nothing wrong.

Trump also continued raising the Russia probe with Coats until the national intelligence director told Trump that his job was to provide intelligence, not to get involved in investigations.

At 8:14 a.m. on March 30, Trump finally called Comey directly about the Russia investigation. The president said the cloud of this Russia situation was making it hard for him to run the country.

"What can be done to lift the cloud?" the president asked.

"We're running it down as quickly as possible, and there will be a great benefit, if we don't find anything, to having our Good Housekeeping seal of approval," Comey replied. "But we have to do our work." Comey also said that congressional leaders were aware the president was not being investigated personally.

"We need to get that fact out," Trump said, and he repeated this point several times throughout the conversation. "I hope you'll find a way to get out that you aren't investigating me."

Afterward, Comey called Acting Attorney General Boente, asking for guidance on how to respond to the president because he was uncomfortable with this direct contact about the investigation.

President Trump called Comey again on the morning of April 11, saying he was "following up to see if you did what I asked last time: getting out that I'm not personally under investigation."

Comey told the president that he had relayed his request to Boente and had not heard back. But the traditional channel through which to raise such matters was for the president to direct the White House counsel to contact Department of Justice leadership.

President Trump said he would do that and added, "Because I have been very loyal to you, very loyal. We had that thing, you know."

Maria Bartiromo of Fox Business Network taped an interview with the president later that afternoon and asked whether it was too late for him to ask Comey to step down.

"No, it's not too late, but you know, I have confidence in him," Trump said. "We'll see what happens. You know, it's going to be interesting."

Director of Strategic Communications Hicks was watching this taping, and after it was finished, she suggested to the president that his comment about Comey should be removed from the interview's broadcast. But Trump wanted to keep it in, which puzzled her.

That day, President Trump told McGahn, Priebus, and other senior advisors that he had contacted Comey twice in recent weeks, even as he acknowledged that Priebus had advised him not to reach out to Comey in order to avoid being perceived as interfering in the investigation.

"I know you told me not to, but I called Comey anyway," the president said.

Trump said that Comey told him that if the Department of Justice approved, the FBI could make a public statement that he was not being investigated. McGahn followed up on this point with Boente, who told the White House counsel that although Comey had told him there was nothing obstructive about the president's calls, they made the FBI director uncomfortable. Boente also did not want to announce that the president was not under investigation due to possible political ramifications, and he did not want to order Comey to issue such a statement because doing so could spur the appointment of a special counsel.

The president did not want me in this story, did he?

39

"Don't talk me out of this"

Donald Trump decided that James Comey was down to his last straw. As the FBI director prepared to testify at a Senate Judiciary Committee FBI oversight hearing, the president told his advisors that Comey had better reveal publicly that the president was not under investigation...or else.

But when the hearing took place on May 3, 2017, Comey declined to answer questions about the Russia investigation except to say, "The Department of Justice has authorized me to confirm that it exists. We're not going to say another word about it until we're done."

"And you have not, to my knowledge, ruled out anyone in the Trump campaign as potentially a target of that criminal investigation, correct?" Democratic senator Richard Blumenthal of Connecticut asked.

"Well, I haven't said anything publicly about who we've opened investigations on," Comey said. "I briefed the chair and ranking on who those people are. And so I can't — I can't go beyond that in this setting."

"Have you ruled out anyone in the campaign that you can disclose?" Blumenthal asked.

"I don't feel comfortable answering that, senator, because I think it puts me on a slope to talking about who we're investigating," Comey replied.

"Have you ruled out the President of the United States?"

"I don't want people to over-interpret this answer," Comey said. "I'm not going to comment on anyone in particular, because...if I say no to that, then I have to answer succeeding questions. So what we've done is brief the chair and ranking on who the U.S. persons are that we've opened investigations on. And that's — that's as far as we're going to go, at this point."

Democratic senators also asked Comey about his decision to announce eleven days before the election that the FBI was investigating a fresh batch of Hillary Clinton emails. "It makes me mildly nauseous to think that we might have had some impact on the election," Comey said. "But honestly, it wouldn't change the decision." He reiterated later in the hearing, "I've gotten all kinds of rocks thrown at me, and this has been really hard, but I think I've done the right thing at each turn."

That afternoon Trump met with McGahn, Sessions, and Sessions's chief of staff, Jody Hunt, and the president asked McGahn how Comey had done at the hearing. When McGahn mentioned that Comey wouldn't answer whether the president was under investigation, Trump grew angry and directed his ire at Sessions.

"This is terrible, Jeff," the president said. "It's all because you recused. AG is supposed to be the most important appointment. Kennedy appointed his brother. Obama appointed Holder. I appointed you, and you recused yourself. You left me on an island. I can't do anything."

"I had no choice," Sessions responded. "This was a mandatory rather than discretionary decision."

The attorney general then pivoted. Perhaps the FBI needed a new start, so the president should consider replacing Comey.

The FBI director remained on Trump's mind, and the president brought him up to Bannon at least eight times on May 3 and 4, saying the same thing each time: "He told me three times I'm not under investigation. He's a showboater. I don't know any Russians. There was no collusion."

Bannon told President Trump that he could not fire Comey. "That ship has sailed," the White House strategist said, adding that even if Trump fired Comey, he could not fire the FBI. The investigation would continue no matter what.

Trump spent the weekend at his Bedminster, New Jersey, resort, and over dinner on Friday, May 5, he told Jared Kushner, senior advisor Stephen Miller, and other advisors and family members that he intended to fire Comey. He already had ideas for what to put in the letter that announced the FBI director's departure. The president dictated his arguments and specific language while Miller took notes.

Trump said the letter should begin,

> *While I greatly appreciate you informing me that I am not under investigation concerning what I have often stated is a fabricated story on a Trump-Russia relationship pertaining to the 2016 presidential election, please be informed that I, and I believe the American public — including Ds and Rs — have lost faith in you as director of the FBI.*

Using these notes and adding his own research to support the president's points, Miller worked on a termination letter and communicated back and forth with Trump about edits over the weekend. The president made clear to Miller that he wanted the letter to open with a reference to his not being under investigation. Trump also sought to establish that Comey had been working under a "review period" with no assurances from the president that he could keep his job.

The termination letter's final version did not vary greatly from what the president had dictated over dinner:

> *Dear Director Comey:*
>
> *While I greatly appreciate your informing me, on three separate occasions, that I am not under investigation concerning the fabricated and politically motivated allegations of a Trump-Russia relationship with respect to the 2016 Presidential Election, please be informed that I, along with members of both political parties and, most importantly, the American Public, have lost faith in you as Director of the FBI, and you are hereby terminated.*

The four-page letter criticized Comey's judgment and conduct, his May 3 Judiciary Committee testimony, his handling of the Clinton email investigation, and his failure to hold leakers accountable. It also brought up the FBI director's one-on-one dinner with the president, claiming that Comey "asked me at dinner shortly after inauguration to let you stay on in the Director's role, and I said that I would consider it.... [But] I concluded that I have no alternative but to find new leadership for the Bureau — a leader that restores confidence and trust."

On the morning of Monday, May 8, the president gathered in the Oval Office with his senior advisors — including McGahn, Priebus, and Miller — and told them he was firing Comey.

"Don't talk me out of this," Trump said. "I've made my decision."

He read aloud the first paragraphs of the termination letter he had crafted with Miller, and he told the group that Miller had researched the matter and concluded that the president had the authority to terminate the FBI director without cause.

Wanting to pump the brakes, McGahn told the president that the Department of Justice leadership already had been discussing Comey's status, so the White House counsel's office attorneys should speak first with Sessions and Rod Rosenstein. Fifty-two at the time, Rosenstein was bookish and thin with frameless glasses, a long-serving George W. Bush–appointed US attorney for the District of Maryland who had specialized in prosecuting police corruption cases. Trump had nominated him to serve as deputy attorney general on February 1, and the Senate confirmed him on April 25 by a 94–6 vote, meaning he had been in his position for thirteen days at this point. He had replaced Boente as the Department of Justice acting attorney general on the Russian interference investigation. McGahn already had a meeting scheduled with Sessions and Rosenstein that day, so he could consult with them about Comey then.

When McGahn, Sessions, and Rosenstein gathered in a noon White House meeting that also included Jody Hunt and White House counsel's office attorney Uttam Dhillon, McGahn revealed that the president had decided to fire Comey and asked for their views. Neither Sessions nor

Rosenstein objected to this action, so McGahn and Dhillon felt more confident that firing Comey would not be considered an attempt to obstruct justice.

Sessions and Rosenstein met with the president and White House officials at 5:00 p.m. that day. Trump told them that he could tell from the May 3 hearing that something was "not right" with Comey, so he had to go. Sessions reminded Trump of previously recommending that the FBI director be replaced, and McGahn and Dhillon criticized Comey's handling of the Clinton email investigation. Trump passed out copies of his termination letter, and the group discussed how the firing should be handled. McGahn and Dhillon favored letting Comey resign, but the president insisted he should be fired.

Someone suggested that perhaps Rosenstein and Sessions could recommend in writing that Comey be terminated. The president thought this was a good idea and instructed Rosenstein to draft a memo for him to see the first thing the next morning. Trump told Rosenstein to make sure to mention that Comey had refused to confirm that the president was not personally under investigation.

"Put the Russia stuff in the memo," Trump said.

Rosenstein replied that since the Russia investigation was not the basis of his firing recommendation, he did not think it should be included.

"I would appreciate if you put it in there anyway," the president said.

Sessions's letter and Rosenstein's memo, titled "Restoring Public Confidence in the FBI," were delivered to the White House the next day, May 9. Sessions's letter stated, "Based on my evaluation, and for the reasons expressed by the Deputy Attorney General in the attached memorandum, I have concluded that a fresh start is needed at the leadership of the FBI."

Rosenstein's memo concluded,

The way the Director handled the conclusion of the email investigation was wrong. As a result, the FBI is unlikely to regain public and congressional trust until it has a Director who understands the gravity of the mistakes and pledges never to repeat them. Having refused to admit his errors, the Director cannot be expected to implement the necessary corrective actions.

Rosenstein's memo did not mention Russia.

The president nonetheless was pleased and agreed to write a new cover letter to accept the recommendations to dismiss Comey, and he tabled his original termination letter. Trump asked Miller to draft this new cover letter and to make sure to include that Comey had informed the president three times that he was not under investigation. McGahn, Priebus, and Dhillon countered that such language should not be included, but the president apparently considered that to be the most important part of the letter. Dhillon suggested one more time that Comey be allowed to resign. Trump refused.

Later that afternoon the White House issued the following statement:

Today, President Donald J. Trump informed FBI Director James Comey that he has been terminated and removed from office. President Trump acted based on the clear recommendations of both Deputy Attorney General Rod Rosenstein and Attorney General Jeff Sessions.

Trump's termination letter, which was attached to Sessions's and Rosenstein's recommendations, read,

Dear Director Comey:

I have received the attached letters from the Attorney General and Deputy Attorney General of the United States recommending your dismissal as the Director of the Federal Bureau of Investigation. I have accepted their recommendation and you are hereby terminated and removed from office, effective immediately.

While I greatly appreciate you informing me, on three separate occasions, that I am not under investigation, I nevertheless concur

*with the judgment of the Department of Justice that you are not able
to effectively lead the Bureau.*

*It is essential that we find new leadership that restores public trust
and confidence in its vital law enforcement mission.*

I wish you the best of luck in your future endeavors.

[Signed] Donald J. Trump

Comey was speaking to FBI agents in the Los Angeles field office when
he learned about his termination as a TV screen flashed the news. He flew
back to Washington, DC, immediately, and the president became angry
that Comey was allowed to travel on an FBI jet after he had been fired.

President Trump summoned FBI deputy director Andrew McCabe to
the Oval Office that night and told him that he had fired Comey because
of his decisions regarding the Clinton email investigation and other reasons. He then made the forty-eight-year-old McCabe the acting FBI
director. He asked McCabe whether he was aware that Comey had told
him three times that he was not under investigation, whether many people in the FBI disliked Comey, and whether McCabe was part of the
"resistance" that disagreed with Comey's decisions regarding Clinton's
emails. McCabe replied that he knew Comey had told the president he
was not personally under investigation, that Comey was well liked at the
FBI, and that he had worked "very closely" with Comey and was involved
in the director's decisions regarding the email investigation.

As the president monitored the press coverage of Comey's termination, he was not pleased. He ordered his communications team that night
to go out and defend him. He also called Chris Christie to complain that
he was getting "killed" in the press over the firing.

"What should I do?" Trump asked.

"Did you fire him because of what Rod wrote in the memo?" Christie
asked.

"Yes."

"Well, then, get Rod out there and have him defend the decision."

"Good idea," the president said.

The White House press office called the Department of Justice that night to say that the White House wished to issue a statement saying that firing Comey was Rosenstein's idea. Rosenstein told Department of Justice officials that he would not participate in putting out a "false story." Enthusiastic about the coverage on Fox News, Trump then called Rosenstein directly and suggested that Rosenstein conduct a news conference.

Rosenstein demurred, explaining that if asked, he would tell the truth — that firing Comey was not his idea. Sessions told the White House counsel's office that Rosenstein was upset that his memo was being cited as the reason behind Comey's termination.

Meanwhile, White House press secretary Sean Spicer was finishing a nighttime interview outside the White House with Fox Business. Upon seeing a cluster of reporters who were no doubt seeking answers about Comey's firing waiting in the area between him and his office, he hid behind some bushes. After several minutes, Janet Montesi, a press office executive assistant, told reporters that Spicer would answer some questions as long as the cameras and lights remained off.

During the ensuing impromptu press conference in the dark, Spicer pinned the decision to terminate Comey on Rosenstein.

"It was all him," Spicer said. "That's correct.... No one from the White House. That was a DOJ decision."

40

"He was crazy, a real nut job"

The morning after firing his FBI director in part for not publicly stating that he was not being investigated for ties to the Russians, President Trump was telling Russian officials in the Oval Office about the move.

"I just fired the head of the FBI," the president told Russian foreign minister Sergey Lavrov and Russian ambassador Sergey Kislyak on May 10, 2017. "He was crazy, a real nut job. I faced great pressure because of Russia. That's taken off...I'm not under investigation."

That same morning President Trump asked FBI acting director McCabe to visit the White House so that they could discuss whether the president should make a speech to personnel at FBI headquarters. During that call to McCabe, Trump claimed he had received "hundreds" of emails from FBI employees backing the decision to fire Comey. Trump said that not only should the newly fired FBI director not have been allowed to fly back to Washington, DC, on the FBI plane but that he was barred from setting foot "in the building again," even to collect his possessions. When McCabe met with the president that afternoon, Trump said without prompting that FBI employees loved him and at least 80 percent had voted for him.

"Who did you vote for?" the president asked McCabe.

McCabe declined to answer.

White House deputy press secretary Sarah Sanders spoke to the president that afternoon about Comey's firing before she faced reporters in the White House's daily press briefing.

"The president, over the last several months, lost confidence in Director Comey," Sanders said in her opening remarks. "The DOJ lost confidence in Director Comey. Bipartisan members of Congress made it clear that they had lost confidence in Director Comey. And most importantly, the rank and file of the FBI had lost confidence in their director. Accordingly, the president accepted the recommendation of his deputy attorney general to remove James Comey from his position."

"Yes or no, did the president direct Rod Rosenstein to write this memo on James Comey?" one reporter asked.

"No," Sanders responded.

"So it's the White House's assertion that Rod Rosenstein decided on his own, after being confirmed, to review Comey's performance?" the reporter followed up.

"Absolutely," Sanders said. She reiterated later that Rosenstein "came to [Trump] on his own."

"Sarah, isn't it true that the president had already decided to fire James Comey, and he asked the Justice Department to put together the rationale for that firing?" another reporter asked.

"No," Sanders said.

"What gives you such confidence that the rank and file within the Bureau lost faith in the FBI Director?" one reporter asked later. "There's a special agent who is inside who wrote us who said: 'The vast majority of the Bureau is in favor of Director Comey. This is a total shock. This is not supposed to happen. The real losers here are twenty thousand front-line people in the organization because they lost the only guy working here in the past fifteen years who actually cared about them.' So what's your response to these rank-and-file FBI agents who disagree with your contention that they lost faith in Director Comey?"

"Look, we've heard from countless members of the FBI that say very different things," Sanders said.

After the news conference ended, the president praised Sanders for her performance and did not point out any inaccuracies. More than a year later, she told our office that her reference to hearing "from countless members" of the FBI was "a slip of the tongue" that was not true and her assertion that the FBI's rank and file had lost confidence in Comey had no basis in fact and was made "in the heat of the moment" (despite it being part of her opening statement).

That same day, Sessions and Rosenstein each communicated their concern to McGahn that the White House was crafting a narrative in which Rosenstein had initiated the decision to fire Comey. McGahn agreed with them that saying the Department of Justice had initiated Comey's termination was factually wrong, so he asked attorneys in the White House counsel's office to work with the press office to correct this misrepresentation.

Another person did not think everyone was getting the story right: President Trump. But his reasons were different. On the following day, May 11, he sat down for an interview with NBC's Lester Holt, and early in their conversation, the president admitted that he had decided to fire Comey before he met with Sessions and Rosenstein.

"Oh, I was gonna fire regardless of [their] recommendation," the president said, later adding, "Regardless of recommendation I was going to fire Comey knowing there was no good time to do it. And in fact when I decided to just do it, I said to myself, I said, you know, this Russia thing with Trump and Russia is a made-up story. It's an excuse by the Democrats for having lost an election they should have won."

Trump also said of Comey, "Look, he's a showboat. He's a grandstander. The FBI has been in turmoil. You know that. I know that. Everybody knows that. You take a look at the FBI a year ago, it was in virtual turmoil.... It hasn't recovered from that."

When Holt pressed about the Russia investigation, Trump said, "I want that thing to be absolutely done properly. When I did this [firing] now, I said I probably, maybe will confuse people. Maybe I'll expand that, you know, lengthen the time [of the investigation] because it should be over with, in my opinion, should have been over with a long time ago. 'Cause all it is is an excuse, but I said to myself I might even lengthen out the investigation, but I have to do the right thing for the American people. He's the wrong man for that position."

"Did you ever ask him to drop the investigation?" Holt asked.

"No. Never," Trump responded.

"Did anyone from the White House?"

"No, in fact I want the investigation speeded up."

Following the Lester Holt interview, Trump tweeted that evening, "Russia must be laughing up their sleeves watching as the U.S. tears itself apart over a Democrat EXCUSE for losing the election."

That same day the *New York Times* reported that Trump had asked Comey to pledge his loyalty in their private dinner soon after the inauguration. The president tweeted the next morning, "James Comey better hope that there are no 'tapes' of our conversations before he starts leaking to the press!" He also tweeted, "When [former director of national intelligence] James Clapper himself, and virtually everyone else with knowledge of the witch hunt, says there is no collusion, when does it end?"

Clapper himself weighed in on Comey's firing on two Sunday-morning political talk shows on May 14, calling it "another victory on the scoreboard" for the Russian government and an indication that "our institutions are under assault, both externally . . . [and] internally."

"Internally from the president?" CNN *State of the Union* anchor Jake Tapper asked.

"Exactly," Clapper said.

On May 19, the *New York Times* reported on the president's remarks to Russia's foreign minister and ambassador during their Oval Office visit nine days earlier. The headline: "Trump Told Russians That Firing 'Nut Job' Comey Eased Pressure from Investigation."

After the story's publication, the president did not deny his remarks or seem concerned about their being made public.

"He *is* crazy," Trump told Hicks when she asked him about the report.

McGahn also inquired about the president's comments to Lavrov and Kislyak, prompting Trump to respond that firing Comey was helpful because it made clear that he was not under investigation, which relieved pressure and allowed him to get more work done.

The White House issued a statement that day:

By grandstanding and politicizing the investigation into Russia's actions, James Comey created unnecessary pressure on our ability to engage and negotiate with Russia. The investigation would have always continued, and obviously, the termination of Comey would not have ended it. Once again the real story is that our national security has been undermined by the leaking of private and highly classified information.

But by that point another story had come to dominate the headlines and the president's psyche.

It had to do with me.

41

"I'm fucked"

Jeff Sessions's phone rang as he, President Trump, White House counsel McGahn, and Sessions's chief of staff Hunt sat in the Oval Office on May 17 to consider candidates to replace James Comey, the FBI director whom the president had fired eight days earlier. The call was from Rod Rosenstein, the acting attorney general overseeing the Russia investigation in light of Sessions's recusal. Sessions stepped out of the Oval Office to take it.

"What is it?" the president asked upon Sessions's return.

"Rosenstein has appointed a special counsel to investigate Russian interference in the election," Sessions replied.

"Oh my God, this is terrible," Trump declared, slumping back in his chair. "This is the end of my presidency. I'm fucked."

Sessions, McCann, and Hunt looked around awkwardly—because what else can you do when the president is dropping an F-bomb to announce that an investigation will force him from office?

Here is the order that Rosenstein, the man whom the White House inaccurately had credited with initiating the move to fire Comey, issued that day:

By virtue of the authority vested in me as Acting Attorney General, including 28 U.S.C. §§ 509, 510, and 515, in order to discharge my responsibility to provide supervision and management of the Department of Justice, and to ensure a full and thorough investigation of the

Russian government's efforts to interfere in the 2016 presidential election, I hereby order as follows:

> *(a) Robert S. Mueller III is appointed to serve as Special Counsel for the United States Department of Justice.*
>
> *(b) The Special Counsel is authorized to conduct the investigation confirmed by then-FBI Director James B. Comey in testimony before the House Permanent Select Committee on Intelligence on March 20, 2017, including:*
>
>> *(i) any links and/or coordination between the Russian government and individuals associated with the campaign of President Donald Trump; and*
>>
>> *(ii) any matters that arose or may arise directly from the investigation; and*
>>
>> *(iii) any other matters within the scope of 28 C.F.R. § 600.4(a).*
>
> *(c) If the Special Counsel believes it is necessary and appropriate, the Special Counsel is authorized to prosecute federal crimes arising from the investigation of these matters.*
>
> *(d) Sections 600.4 through 600.10 of Title 28 of the Code of Federal Regulations are applicable to the Special Counsel.*

As his initial sense of resignation gave way to anger, Trump's face turned red, and he homed in on Sessions. "You *had* to recuse yourself. How could you let this happen, Jeff?"

Sessions said nothing. The president was just getting started, once again asserting that the position of attorney general was his most important appointment and that previous occupants of the office, such as Eric Holder and Robert Kennedy, had served their presidents in a way that "weak" Sessions had failed. "You let me down. You were supposed to protect me."

Sessions kept his mouth shut, his jaw clenched.

"Everyone tells me if you get one of these independent counsels, it ruins your presidency," Trump moaned, slumping back again. "It takes years and years, and I won't be able to do anything. This is the worst thing that ever happened to me."

He leaned toward Sessions with one final glare.

"You should resign," he ordered.

"I will submit my resignation," Sessions replied and left the office.

When Hope Hicks entered the Oval Office a bit later, the president was still raging about the special counsel's appointment. She flashed back to the only previous time she had seen him this upset: the day the *Access Hollywood* recordings were released revealing Trump's "grab 'em by the pussy" comments.

Trump, as usual, did not keep his anger to himself. "This is the single greatest witch hunt of a politician in American history!" he tweeted early the next morning.

That day, May 18, the political stakes continued to rise. FBI agents delivered a letter to McGahn ordering that the White House preserve all documents relevant to Comey's firing because the agency was investigating his termination. When McGahn received the preservation notice, he issued a document hold to the White House staff, instructing them not to send out any burn bags over the weekend while he clarified these matters.

Also that day, Sessions finalized his resignation letter. He kept it simple: "Pursuant to our conversation of yesterday, and at your request, I hereby offer my resignation."

With Hunt in tow, Sessions took the letter to the White House and handed it to the president. Trump pocketed it and asked Sessions multiple times whether he wished to continue serving as attorney general.

"I would like to stay," Sessions said, "but that is up to you, Mr. President."

"I would like you to stay," the president said finally and shook Sessions's hand.

But as Sessions left, the resignation letter remained in the president's pocket.

Afterward, Sessions told Priebus and Bannon about the meeting, and they expressed worry that the president had held on to his resignation letter.

"That's not good," Priebus said, noting that Trump could use the letter as a "shock collar" against the Department of Justice whenever he wanted. "He's got the DOJ by the throat."

Priebus and Bannon said they would try to retrieve the letter from Trump along with a notation that he was not accepting the attorney general's resignation.

President Trump took off for the Middle East the next day, Sessions's resignation letter still in his pocket. En route from Saudi Arabia to Tel Aviv, he pulled out the letter and asked a group of senior advisors what he should do with it. During the trip, Priebus asked the president about the letter and suggested he return it to Sessions, but Trump told him it was somewhere back in his White House residence.

After the president returned from the Middle East on May 27, Priebus asked him for the letter again, and Trump slapped the desk and said he had forgotten it at the hotel. But when White House staff secretary Rob Porter was in the Oval Office, Trump pulled out the letter and showed it to him.

Finally, on May 30, Trump finally handed the letter back to his still-employed attorney general. On it was a notation:

"Not accepted."

42

"Trump is definitely considering it"

I am in the story at last. President Trump did not want me here and attempted to move me out of the picture. That, of course, became part of the story as well.

Trump grew consumed with finding a way to disqualify me as special counsel. In the wake of my appointment, the president repeatedly told his advisors, including Priebus, Bannon, and McGahn, that I had conflicts of interest that should bar me from holding this position. They were the following:

1. I had interviewed, unsuccessfully, to become FBI director not long before being appointed special counsel.
2. I had worked for a law firm that represented people affiliated with the president.
3. I had disputed certain fees when I was a member of a Trump golf course in Northern Virginia.

The president's advisors rejected these arguments, saying that such matters did not rise to the level of actual conflicts of interest. Bannon even called Trump's claims "ridiculous" and said none of them was real or came close to justifying my disqualification as special counsel. Bannon pointed out that the White House had invited me to offer insights about the FBI as an institution, not to interview for the director's job. Trump even considered asking me to serve as FBI director for a second time, but I did not come seeking the job. I had previously run the bureau for twelve years and now was seventy-two years old. This was not a job interview.

Bannon also said that no one in the legal community would view my law firm position as a conflict in any way. Representing people affiliated with a presidential administration was far from unusual in Washington, DC. As for the so-called golf club dispute, Bannon said pressing this claim would make the president come across as "ridiculous and petty."

Here is the background on that. We had a family membership in Trump National Golf Club in Sterling, Virginia, more than twenty-five miles from our Washington, DC, home, and we were not using the club enough to justify the cost. These things happen. So I resigned from the club in October 2011 with a letter that noted, "We live in the District and find that we are unable to make full use of the Club." I also asked "whether we would be entitled to a refund of a portion of our initial membership fee" from 1994. About two weeks later, the club's controller responded that our resignation would become effective October 31, 2011, and that I would be "placed on a waitlist to be refunded on a first resigned/first refunded basis," as dictated by the club's legal policy. That was our final interaction with the club.

Dramatic, right?

When Bannon pushed back on these stated conflicts of interest, the president declined to respond. But that did not mean he was relenting.

On May 23, six days after my appointment, the Department of Justice announced that ethics officials had concluded that my prior law firm position did not impede my ability to serve. Media reports followed that I had been cleared to take office. Yet Trump continued to complain about the "conflicts" and prodded McGahn to contact Rosenstein about the issue. McGahn responded that he could not make such a call because this was not a White House matter; the president was free to consult his personal lawyer if he wished to pursue it further. But McGahn recommended that Trump not call Rosenstein or try to get his personal attorney involved.

"It would look like you're still trying to meddle in the investigation,"

McGahn told the president. "Knocking out Mueller would be another fact used to claim obstruction of justice against you. Your biggest exposure was not the act of firing Comey but your other contacts and calls, such as your asks about Flynn."

In the meantime, the press continued to report on the president's requests for Comey's loyalty and his asking the former FBI director to consider "letting Flynn go," both of which Trump denied. But the president did not deny the continued reports of his telling the Russian foreign minister and ambassador that firing Comey had relieved "great pressure."

Comey testified before the Senate Select Intelligence Committee on June 8 about his interactions with the president, including the requests for loyalty and "letting Flynn go," as well as for Comey to "lift the cloud" of the ongoing investigation. The former FBI director also admitted that after Trump tweeted on May 12, "James Comey better hope that there are no 'tapes' of our conversations before he starts leaking to the press!" Comey allowed his memo documenting his February 14 meeting with the president — the one in which the president said, "I hope you can see your way clear to letting this go, to letting Flynn go" — to be leaked to the *New York Times*.

Comey's testimony prompted more press accounts and legal analysts to conclude that the president may have obstructed justice. The day after the hearing, our office informed the White House counsel's office that we planned to interview intelligence community officials whom the president may have asked to push back against the Russia investigation.

The president was still pushing. When Christopher Ruddy, a longtime Trump friend and chief executive of the conservative media company Newsmax, met with Priebus and Bannon at the White House on June 12, the two officials told him that the president was strongly considering firing me as special counsel and would do so without consulting with administration officials. Ruddy asked Priebus whether he could speak publicly about this conversation, and Priebus gave permission, saying he wished to avoid another media blowup like the one that followed Comey's firing.

Later that day Ruddy said in an interview on PBS's *NewsHour* that the president was "considering perhaps terminating the special counsel" based on supposed conflicts of interest. "I think he's weighing that option."

White House press secretary Sean Spicer issued a statement hours later: "Mr. Ruddy never spoke to the president regarding this issue. With respect to this subject, only the president or his attorneys are authorized to comment."

Ruddy responded by texting ABC News the next day: "Spicer issued a bizarre late night press release that a) doesn't deny my claim the president is considering firing Mueller and b) says I didn't speak to the president about the matter — when I never claimed to have done so."

Ruddy stood by his comments about my possible firing. "Trump is definitely considering it," he told ABC News. "It's not something that's being dismissed."

Mutual friends told Ruddy that Trump was upset with him, and Sarah Sanders asked the president how she should respond to the many press inquiries about the prospect of the special counsel's termination. Trump dictated the answer that Sanders delivered to reporters on Air Force One late on June 13: "While the president has every right to [fire the special counsel], he has no intention to do so."

Nonetheless, the president, ignoring McGahn's advice, directed his personal counsel to contact the special counsel's office that same day to raise concerns about my possible conflicts, which once again included my previous law firm position, my supposed interview to become FBI director, and now my personal relationship with James Comey, who had succeeded me in that job in 2013. Also that day, Rosenstein testified before Congress that he saw no reason to remove me as special counsel.

Two days later, our office relayed the president's counsel's concerns to Rosenstein's office, then informed the president's counsel that the Department of Justice could take whatever action it deemed appropriate. In the meantime, we had work to do.

The president had gone on the offensive in his fight to shoot down my appointment. He was about to be back on defense.

43

"Mueller has to go"

The first public word that our office was investigating President Trump for possible obstruction of justice came in a June 14, 2017, *Washington Post* story. It reported that our investigators were interviewing intelligence community officers, including Director of National Intelligence Daniel Coats and National Security Agency director Admiral Michael Rogers, about what the president had asked them to do following Comey's March 20 congressional testimony in which he confirmed the Russia probe's existence. As the story stated,

> *The move by special counsel Robert S. Mueller III to investigate Trump's conduct marks a major turning point in the nearly year-old FBI investigation, which until recently focused on Russian meddling during the presidential campaign and on whether there was any coordination between the Trump campaign and the Kremlin. Investigators have also been looking for any evidence of possible financial crimes among Trump associates, officials said.*
>
> *Trump had received private assurances from then-FBI Director James B. Comey starting in January that he was not personally under investigation. Officials say that changed shortly after Comey's firing.*

Other media outlets immediately picked up on the story. A CNN chyron read, "WASH POST: MUELLER INVESTIGATING TRUMP FOR OBSTRUCTION OF JUSTICE."

With this burst of negative coverage on his mind, the president called Don McGahn on the White House counsel's personal cell phone at about 10:30 that night. Early the next morning, Trump took to Twitter for a series of posts:

They made up a phony collusion with the Russians story, found zero proof, so now they go for obstruction of justice on the phone story. Nice.

You are witnessing the single greatest WITCH HUNT in American political history — led by some very bad and conflicted people!

Crooked H destroyed phones w/ hammer, "bleached" emails, & had husband meet w/AG days before she was cleared — &they talk about obstruction?

More tweets followed the next day:

After 7 months of investigations & committee hearings about my "collusion with the Russians," nobody has been able to show any proof. Sad!

I am being investigated for firing the FBI Director by the man who told me to fire the FBI Director! Witch Hunt.

President Trump was at Camp David on Saturday, June 17 when he called McGahn at home and issued this order: get Mueller removed as special counsel.

McGahn received two such calls from the president, both instructing him to call Rosenstein and say that my conflicts disqualified me from serving as special counsel.

"You gotta do this," President Trump told McGahn. "You gotta call Rod."

"I'll see what I can do," McGahn replied.

But McGahn had no intention of following through. He and other advisors already had told the president that these supposed conflicts were "silly" and "not real," and Rosenstein had disregarded the claims. Getting the White House counsel's office involved in pressing such "conflicts" would only make matters worse. McGahn recalled Richard Nixon's "Saturday Night Massacre" during the Watergate scandal, in which Solicitor General Robert Bork fired special prosecutor Archibald Cox on October 20, 1973, after Attorney General Elliot Richardson and Deputy Attorney General William Ruckelshaus had refused to do so and resigned instead. McGahn wanted to be remembered as a distinguished judge, as he felt Bork had become, and not as a hatchet man, as had been Bork's 1970s reputation. The White House counsel also wished to stave off the president's urge to remove the special counsel, which he considered an inflection point with possibly dire consequences.

President Trump floated the idea of firing me to his confidant, New Jersey governor Chris Christie, as well. In their phone conversation, Christie responded that this was a bad idea because the president had no substantive basis to terminate the special counsel, and he risked losing the support of congressional Republicans.

But Trump was not to be deterred.

"Call Rod," the president ordered McGahn on another phone call. "Tell Rod that Mueller has conflicts and can't be the special counsel. Mueller has to go. Call me back when you do it."

The president was wearing McGahn down. The White House counsel had refuted the notion of my conflicts and told the president he didn't want to call Rosenstein. But Trump kept pushing. McGahn finally gave President Trump the impression that he would call the acting attorney general in the investigation. By that point, he just wanted to get off the phone.

McGahn felt trapped. He wasn't going to follow the president's orders, but he also didn't know what he would say the next time that Trump called. He finally reached a decision.

He had to resign.

McGahn called his personal lawyer and his chief of staff, Annie Donaldson, to inform them of his decision, although he didn't tell Donaldson the specifics of the president's request other than to say Trump had called back to ask, "Have you done it?" Donaldson, who assumed that her boss was withholding information to shield her from being dragged into an investigation, prepared for her own resignation as well. McGahn drove to his office with the intention of picking up his belongings and submitting his resignation letter, but before turning in the letter, he called Priebus and Bannon.

"The president asked me to do some crazy shit," McGahn told Priebus, although he didn't share details with him or Bannon about what Trump had ordered, presumably to protect them as well.

Both White House officials urged McGahn not to quit. The White House counsel relented.

So McGahn arrived at work as usual on Monday. He did not tell the president he had intended to resign. And when they next saw each other, the president did not ask McGahn whether he had followed through on his request to call Rosenstein.

The inflection point apparently had passed.

44

"It's extremely unfair, and that's a mild word"

As focused as President Trump had been on removing me as special counsel, he had other ways in which he was trying to affect the Russia investigation. On June 19, two days after telling McGahn to have me terminated, the president conducted a one-on-one Oval Office meeting with Corey Lewandowski, his former campaign manager. Although Lewandowski had parted ways with the Trump campaign in June 2016 in what was widely reported as a firing—his replacement, Paul Manafort, the victor in an apparent power struggle—the president had remained close to him. One aide described Lewandowski as a "comfort to the president."

During Trump's chat with his former campaign manager, he criticized Sessions for recusing himself from the Russia investigation, called him weak, and said he would not have appointed Sessions had he anticipated his recusal.

The president then instructed Lewandowski, "Write this down," and for the first time in their relationship, Trump began to dictate to him. This, Trump said, was a speech that he wanted his attorney general to deliver in public:

> *I know that I recused myself from certain things having to do with specific areas. But our POTUS...is being treated very unfairly. He shouldn't have a Special Prosecutor/Counsel b/c he hasn't done*

anything wrong. I was on the campaign w/ him for nine months, there were no Russians involved with him. I know it for a fact b/c I was there. He didn't do anything wrong except he ran the greatest campaign in American history. . . .

Now a group of people want to subvert the Constitution of the United States. I am going to meet with the Special Prosecutor to explain this is very unfair and let the Special Prosecutor move forward with investigating election meddling for future elections so that nothing can happen in future elections.

In other words, Trump wanted Sessions to announce that he would be limiting the special counsel's jurisdiction to future elections rather than allowing him to examine the election that already had occurred.

"If Sessions delivers that statement," Trump told Lewandowski, "he'll be the most popular guy in the country."

Lewandowski responded that he understood what the president wanted from Sessions, and he set about to arrange a meeting with the attorney general. Lewandowski wanted to do this in person rather than over the phone, but he didn't want to meet at the Department of Justice because there would be a public log of the visit and he felt like he would put Sessions at an advantage if the meeting took place on his turf. So when Lewandowski called Sessions, he managed to schedule their meeting for the following evening in Lewandowski's office. But Sessions canceled due to a last-minute conflict, and soon Lewandowski was leaving Washington, DC, without having conveyed the president's message. The former campaign manager stashed the notes in a safe at home, which he called standard procedure for sensitive materials.

Eventually, Lewandowski asked senior White House official Rick Dearborn whether he could pass a message to Sessions. Dearborn said he would, though he didn't know the message's content. Lewandowski helped arrange for Dearborn to have dinner with Sessions in late July, at which point Dearborn would deliver the message. Although the president had asked Lewandowski to deliver the message because he trusted him, Lewandowski decided that Dearborn would be a better messenger because of his longstanding relationship with the attorney general and because, unlike Lewandowski, he remained in the government.

The president met with Lewandowski alone in the Oval Office again on July 19, a time when details about the June 9, 2016, Trump Tower meeting between Russian officials and Donald Trump Jr., Jared Kushner, and Paul Manafort had recently been made public. Trump asked whether Lewandowski had spoken with Sessions as requested, and Lewandowski said the message was being delivered soon. The president told him that if Sessions failed to meet with Lewandowski, then Lewandowski should inform Sessions that he was fired.

As Lewandowski exited the Oval Office, he saw Dearborn in the anteroom and gave him a copy of the speech that the president had dictated to be delivered by Sessions (and that Lewandowski had just enlisted Hope Hicks to type up). Lewandowski explained to Dearborn that this was the message they had discussed to be delivered to Sessions, and Dearborn raised an eyebrow but decided not to ask where it came from or to think more about actually doing anything with it. Dearborn was uncomfortable with Lewandowski's making him the messenger, and although he later told Lewandowski he had taken care of the matter, he never actually followed through on delivering the message to Sessions and did not keep a copy of the typewritten notes that Lewandowski had handed him.

The president revived his theme about Sessions's recusal in a previously unplanned Oval Office interview with three *New York Times* reporters on July 19, the same day he met with Lewandowski in the Oval Office.

"Sessions should have never recused himself," the president told the reporters, "and if he was going to recuse himself, he should have told me before he took the job, and I would have picked somebody else."

"He gave you no heads up at all, in any sense?" *Times* reporter Maggie Haberman asked.

"Zero," Trump said. "So Jeff Sessions takes the job, gets into the job, recuses himself... which, frankly, I think is very unfair to the president.

How do you take a job and then recuse yourself? If he would have recused himself before the job, I would have said, 'Thanks, Jeff, but I can't, you know, I'm not going to take you.' It's extremely unfair, and that's a mild word, to the president. So he recuses himself. I then end up with a second man, who's a deputy."

"Rosenstein," Haberman said.

"Who is he?" Trump asked. "And Jeff hardly knew. He's from Baltimore."

Hicks, who was present for the interview, grew concerned about how it was going and tried to get between the reporters and president at various times. But Trump loved how it was going.

Later that day, Lewandowski and Hicks met and discussed Trump's *New York Times* interview. Lewandowski mentioned the president's request to him about Sessions and the speech, and he joked at the prospect that he, a private citizen, could fire Sessions if the attorney general did not meet with him. As they talked, the president called Hicks to say how happy he was about the coverage of his criticism of Sessions in the *Times* interview.

The *Washington Post* reported two days later, on July 21, that contrary to Sessions's public statements, US intelligence intercepts showed that he had discussed campaign-related matters with Russian ambassador Kislyak. Anticipating the president's reaction to this report, Priebus called Jody Hunt, Sessions's chief of staff, to whom he spoke when tensions arose between Trump and Sessions. That had been happening with increased frequency. Priebus raised with Hunt the possibility that the attorney general might be fired or resign. Hunt said if the president wanted Sessions out, he would have to fire him, because there was no way Sessions planned to resign.

"What would firing him accomplish anyway?" Hunt asked Priebus. "There was an investigation before, and there will be an investigation after."

The president took to Twitter the following morning to react to the *Washington Post*'s report: "A new INTELLIGENCE LEAK from the

Amazon Washington Post, this time against A.G. Sessions. These illegal leaks, like Comey's, must stop!"

(If I may note here, our office did not leak. And the press, despite the president's frequent attacks, provided much information that proved useful to our and others' investigations, in part because these reports would prompt reactions from the participants, thus leading to further developments.)

He tweeted again about an hour later, "So many people are asking why isn't the A.G. or Special Council [sic] looking at the many Hillary Clinton or Comey crimes. 33,000 emails deleted?"

Later that morning of July 22, while aboard Marine One en route to Norfolk, Virginia, Trump told Priebus to get Sessions to resign immediately. The country had lost confidence in him, the president said, and he couldn't tolerate the negative press.

"I need a letter of resignation on my desk immediately," Trump said. "He has no choice. He must immediately resign."

"If we fire Sessions, we'll never get a new attorney general confirmed," Priebus responded. "And the Department of Justice and Congress will turn their backs on you."

"I'll make a recess appointment," Trump said.

Still, Priebus did not want to pull the trigger on this request.

"It's all wrong," he told McGahn when he called the White House counsel for advice. Although the president had attributed his order to Sessions's congressional testimony and bad publicity, Trump had been consumed with the attorney general's recusal from the Russia investigation, and that, Priebus believed, was at the root of this latest attempt to oust him.

"Don't do it," McGahn said. "We should talk to our personal counsel. Attorney-client privilege will protect us.... We may both have to resign rather than carry this out."

The president followed up with Priebus that afternoon. "Did you get it?" Trump asked. "Are you working on it?"

"I will get him to resign," Priebus responded, even though he had no intention of executing the president's directive and felt like his job was on the line.

Priebus called the president back later in the day and told him that terminating Sessions would have disastrous consequences: Rosenstein and Associate Attorney General Rachel Brand also likely would resign, and then the president wouldn't be able to get any of their replacements confirmed.

The president agreed to wait on ousting Sessions until after the next day's Sunday-morning political talk shows, because if he fired him beforehand, that's all they would talk about. When the weekend had ended, the president agreed not to demand Sessions's resignation. Instead, on the following morning, he expressed himself on Twitter:

"So why aren't the Committees and investigators, and of course our beleaguered A.G., looking into Crooked Hillarys crimes & Russia relations?" he tweeted on Monday, July 24.

"Attorney General Jeff Sessions has taken a VERY weak position on Hillary Clinton crimes (where are E-mails & DNC server) & Intel leakers!" he tweeted the next day.

"Why didn't A.G. Sessions replace Acting FBI Director Andrew McCabe, a Comey friend who was in charge of Clinton investigation but got…" he tweeted in two installments on July 26, "…big dollars ($700,000) for his wife's political run from Hillary Clinton and her representatives. Drain the swamp!"

Amid this constant stream of attacks, Sessions wrote another resignation letter. He would carry it in his pocket every time he visited the White House for the rest of the year.

45

"A program about the adoption of Russian children"

Many issues were coming to a head for the president over that summer of 2017. He was unhappy about my appointment and was trying to get me removed — and then he had to deal with the fact that our office was investigating him for obstruction of justice in addition to our probe into Russian election interference. He remained infuriated at his attorney general for recusing himself from the Russia investigation and now saw Sessions generating negative headlines for his undisclosed contacts with Russian ambassador Kislyak. Investigations continued to target such former Trump officials as Paul Manafort, Michael Flynn, Roger Stone, and George Papadopoulos.

And that June 9, 2016, Trump Tower meeting was a fire that would not be extinguished.

It was in the middle of June 2017 that some senior administration officials became aware of the emails exchanged to set up the June 9 meeting that involved Donald Trump Jr., Paul Manafort, Jared Kushner, and a Russian entourage led by lawyer Natalia Veselnitskaya. The emails included Rob Goldstone's relaying to Donald Trump Jr. that "the Crown prosecutor of Russia" had offered "to provide the Trump campaign with some official documents and information that would incriminate Hillary and her dealings with Russia and would be very useful to your father. This is obviously very high level and sensitive information but is part of Russia and its government's support of Mr. Trump."

Then there was Trump Jr.'s reply, which included, "If it's what you say I love it."

The president would not sit for any interviews with our office, although we considered them essential to our investigation. Instead he offered written answers to at least some of our questions and, in this case, claimed to have no memory of learning of this meeting and no knowledge of the emails that set it up. He also declined to answer questions about his knowledge of the meeting itself.

On May 17, 2017, the Senate Select Committee on Intelligence requested documents and associated records from the Trump campaign, including a "list and a description of all meetings" between any "individual affiliated with the Trump campaign" and "any individual formally or informally affiliated with the Russian government or Russian business interests which took place between June 16, 2015 and 12 p.m. on Jan. 20, 2017," the day of Trump's inauguration.

In the first week of June 2017, Trump Organization attorneys began interviewing participants in the meeting and provided to the president's personal counsel the emails leading up to it. By the end of the month, Trump advisors were getting media calls relating to the Trump Tower meeting.

As the president's senior staff learned about the emails and meeting, they tried to devise the best damage control strategy. Communications advisors Hope Hicks and Josh Raffel told Jared Kushner and Ivanka Trump that given the inevitability that these emails would be leaked, the administration should be proactive and release them to the press. At a June 22 meeting in the White House residence with President Trump, Ivanka Trump, and Hicks, Kushner said that he wanted to fill in the president about something relating to a meeting involving him, Manafort, and Trump Jr. — presumably the June 9 Trump Tower one. Kushner had brought with him a folder of documents that he had to provide to congressional committees, but as he tried to pull out the relevant ones, the president halted him.

"I don't want to know about it," Trump said, shutting down the conversation.

Hicks finally got a firsthand look at the emails at Kushner's attorney's office on June 28, and she was shocked. They looked damaging. She communicated her concern privately to the president the next day, in part because they soon would be shared with Congress. Too many people knew about the emails, an upset president responded, so only one lawyer should be dealing with the matter. He didn't think the emails would leak unless everyone had access to them.

Later that day, Hicks returned to the president with Kushner and Ivanka Trump. Kushner said the June 9 meeting was about Russian adoption and no big deal, but there were emails that had set up the meeting. Hicks suggested they get in front of the story by having Trump Jr. release the emails during an interview in which he was fed "softball questions." But the president said he didn't want to know about it and didn't want to go to the press.

"The emails are really bad," Hicks responded, "and the story will be massive when it breaks."

"I don't want to talk about it, and I don't want details," President Trump insisted.

Then the president asked his son-in-law when he was due to produce the requested documents. Kushner said it would be a couple of weeks.

"Then leave it alone," Trump said.

He didn't want the group to be proactive about the emails, because he was confident the emails wouldn't leak.

The president left for the G20 summit in Hamburg, Germany, the next week, with Hicks, Raffel, Kushner, and Ivanka Trump among those accompanying him. While there, on July 7, Hicks and Raffel received word that the *New York Times* was working on a story related to the June 9 meeting. When she told the president about it the next day, he instructed her not to comment, which Hicks considered unusual, given that he generally considered not responding to the press to be the ultimate sin. The story came up in another conversation between them later that day, and Trump asked Hicks what the meeting had been about. She said she was told it was about Russian adoption.

"Then just say that," the president directed.

While flying home from Hamburg on July 8, Hicks received and brought to the president a draft statement about the June 9 meeting for Trump Jr. to release.

"I was asked to have a meeting by an acquaintance I knew from the 2013 Miss Universe pageant with an individual who I was told might have information helpful to the campaign," it began.

Hicks again said that she favored revealing the whole story at once, but the president said this statement should not be issued because it disclosed too much. He told Hicks the statement should say only that Trump Jr. took a brief meeting, and it was about Russian adoption. Hicks subsequently texted Trump Jr. a revised statement about the June 9 meeting:

> It was a short meeting. I asked Jared and Paul to stop by. We discussed a program about the adoption of Russian children that was active and popular with American families years ago and was since ended by the Russian government, but it was not a campaign issue at that time and there was no follow up.

Hicks asked at the end of the text, "Are you ok with this? Attributed to you."

Trump Jr. texted back that he wanted to add the word "primarily" before "discussed," so that it would read, "We *primarily* discussed a program about the adoption of Russian children." He explained, also via text, "They started with some Hillary thing which was bs and some other nonsense we shot down fast."

"I think that's right too but boss man worried it invites a lot of questions," Hicks replied. "Ultimately defer to you and [your attorney] on that word Bc I know it's important and I think the mention of a campaign issue adds something to it in case we have to go further."

"If I don't have it in there," Trump Jr. wrote, "it appears as though I'm lying later when they inevitably leak something."

With the word "primarily" added and some other tweaks made, Trump Jr.'s statement was sent to the *New York Times*, reading in full,

> *It was a short introductory meeting. I asked Jared and Paul to stop by. We primarily discussed a program about the adoption of Russian children that was active and popular with American families years ago and was since ended by the Russian government, but it was not a campaign issue at the time and there was no follow up. I was asked to attend the meeting by an acquaintance, but was not told the name of the person I would be meeting with beforehand.*

The meeting's actual primary subjects — the relaying of damaging information related to Hillary Clinton and the Russian lobbying against the Magnitsky Act and US sanctions — went unmentioned.

While still aboard Air Force One, Hicks learned that Priebus knew about the emails; he'd said he recalled hearing about the June 9 meeting from Fox News host Sean Hannity in late June 2017. Hicks returned to the president, again making the case that if so many people already knew about the emails, they were that much more likely to leak, so the White House would be better off getting in front of the story and being transparent about the June 9 meeting.

"No," President Trump responded. "You've given a statement. We're done."

Later during the flight, Hicks went back to the president's cabin while he was on the phone with one of his personal attorneys. President Trump handed the phone to Hicks, and the attorney told her that he had been working with Circa News, an online news service owned by the conservative Sinclair Broadcast Group, on a separate story, so she should not speak to the *New York Times*.

Before the flight had touched down, the *New York Times* had published its story about the June 9 meeting with the headline "Trump Team Met with Lawyer Linked to Kremlin During Campaign." It included

Trump Jr.'s statement and identified Veselnitskaya as being "best known for mounting a multipronged attack against the Magnitsky Act."

The story also spoke to and included a statement from Mark Corallo, who had been hired as spokesperson for Trump's personal legal team, implying that the meeting was a setup to damage the Trump campaign. This was because Veselnitskaya employed a private investigator who worked for the firm Fusion GPS, which produced the Steele dossier after being hired to do opposition research on Trump by Republican clients during the Republican primaries and then by a law firm representing the Clinton campaign and DNC. (A Fusion GPS statement asserted no prior knowledge of the meeting.) Corallo also participated in the Circa News story, published an hour later, that speculated that Democratic operatives might have arranged the June 9 meeting to make Trump family members appear to have improper connections with Russia.

Upset about Corallo's public statement, Hicks called him that evening to say the president had not approved what he said. The president joined her in a call to Corallo the next day, July 9, so that Trump could criticize his statement. Corallo replied that his statement had been authorized, while Trump Jr.'s was inaccurate and that a document existed that would contradict it. (Corallo used the word "document" to mean emails because he didn't know whether Trump was aware of the emails.)

"It will never get out," Hicks said in reference to this "document," although she had been telling the president that the emails were destined to leak.

On the morning of July 11, after being told that the *New York Times* was about to publish a story about the emails, Trump Jr. tweeted redacted images of them along with a photo of this statement:

To everyone, in order to be totally transparent, I am releasing the entire email chain of my emails with Rob Goldstone about the meeting on June 9, 2016. The first email on June 3, 2016 was from Rob, who was relating a request from Emin, a person I knew from the 2013 Ms. [sic] Universe Pageant near Moscow. Emin and his father have a very highly respected company in Moscow. The information they suggested they had about Hillary Clinton I thought was Political Opposition Research. I first wanted to just have a phone call but when they didn't work out, they said the woman would be in New York and asked if I would meet. I decided to take the meeting. The woman, as she has said publicly, was not a government official. And, as we have said, she had no information to provide and wanted to talk about adoption policy and the Magnitsky Act. To put this in context, this occurred before the current Russian fever was in vogue. As Rob Goldstone said just today in the press, the entire meeting was "the most inane nonsense I ever heard. And I was actually agitated by it."

The *Times* story — with the headline "Russian Dirt on Clinton? 'I Love It,' Donald Trump Jr. Said" — laid out the email sequence in which Trump Jr. was offered documents that "would incriminate Hillary and her dealings with Russia and would be very useful to your father."

"If the future president's eldest son was surprised or disturbed by the provenance of the promised material — or the notion that it was part of a continuing effort by the Russian government to aid his father's campaign — he gave no indication," *Times* reporters Jo Becker, Adam Goldman, and Matt Apuzzo wrote. They then included Trump Jr.'s money quote: "If it's what you say I love it especially later in the summer."

The *Times* published another piece on July 11 that discussed the president's involvement in crafting Donald Trump Jr.'s statement about the June 9 meeting — the one in which they "primarily" discussed adoption — that he had provided to the *Times* three days earlier.

As Air Force One jetted back from Europe on Saturday, a small cadre of Mr. Trump's advisers huddled in a cabin helping to craft a statement for the president's eldest son, Donald Trump Jr., to give to The New York Times explaining why he met last summer with a lawyer connected to the Russian government. Participants on the plane and back in the United States debated how transparent to be in the statement, according to people familiar with the discussions.

Ultimately, the people said, the president signed off on a statement from Donald Trump Jr. for The Times that was so incomplete that it required day after day of follow-up statements, each more revealing than the last. It culminated on Tuesday with a release of emails making clear that Mr. Trump's son believed the Russian lawyer was seeking to meet with him to provide incriminating information about Hillary Clinton as "part of Russia and its government's support for Mr. Trump."

Over the next several days, the president's personal counsel, Jay Sekulow, repeatedly and falsely told media outlets that the president had played no role in drafting Trump Jr.'s statement.

"I wasn't involved in the statement drafting at all, nor was the president," Sekulow told CNN's *New Day* on July 12. "I'm assuming that was between Mr. Donald Trump Jr. and his lawyers. I'm sure his lawyer was involved; that's how you do it. To put this on the president, I think, is absolutely incorrect."

On that same day, Sekulow said on *Good Morning America*, "The president didn't sign off on anything.... The president wasn't involved in that." And he doubled down on *Meet the Press* on July 16: "I do want to be clear: The president was not involved in the drafting of the statement."

Aaron Blake took stock of Sekulow's media rounds in a July 31 *Washington Post* news analysis with the headline "Trump's Lawyer Repeatedly Denied Trump Was Involved in Trump Jr.'s Russia Statement. But He Was." Blake wrote,

Individuals say White House advisers had decided to be transparent about the meeting, but the president changed the game plan at the last minute to misleadingly suggest that the meeting was about adoption. The full truth soon came out that the meeting was arranged

to discuss compromising information, supposedly from the Russian government, about Hillary Clinton.

The problem for Sekulow? He denied at least twice, pretty unequivocally, that the president played any role in the drafting of that statement....

What's remarkable is that...the New York Times *had reported at the time, on July 11, that the president himself approved the statement.... So it's difficult to believe Sekulow didn't have an opportunity to verify that information.*

The White House refined its message again on August 1, as press secretary Sarah Sanders, after consulting with the president, told the White House daily briefing crowd, "Look, the statement that Don Jr. issued is true. There's no inaccuracy in the statement. The President weighed in as any father would, based on the limited information that he had."

"Can you clarify the degree to which the President weighed in?" a reporter asked.

"He certainly didn't dictate," Sanders said, "but he—like I said, he weighed in, offered suggestions like any father would do."

In other words, the president's lawyer had not been telling the truth, and Trump Jr.'s meeting *was* primarily about Russian adoption, as that initial statement has claimed.

Months later, Trump's personal counsel sent our office a private communication crediting the president with writing Trump Jr.'s statement after all: "The president dictated a short but accurate response to the *New York Times* article on behalf of his son, Donald Trump Jr."

By a June 15, 2018, press gaggle, the president was singing yet another tune as he implied that a different set of rules apply to issuing statements to the *New York Times*:

Reporter: Did you dictate the statement about Donald Trump Jr.?
Trump: Let's not talk about it. You know what that is?
Reporter: But can you tell us?

Trump: It's irrelevant. It's a statement to the *New York Times*—the phony, failing *New York Times*.

Reporter: Well, just to clear it up. To clear it up.

Trump: Just wait a minute. Wait a minute. That's not a statement to a high tribunal of judges.

Reporter: Understood.

Trump: That's a statement to the phony *New York Times*.

Yet the president had spoken to three *New York Times* reporters in the Oval Office on July 19, and he discussed with them Donald Trump Jr.'s June 9 meeting with the Russians—and not just in the context of adoptions.

"As I've said—most other people, you know, when they call up and say, 'By the way, we have information on your opponent,' I think most politicians—I was just with a lot of people, they said... 'Who wouldn't have taken a meeting like that?'"

46

"Come on Jeff, you can do it"

The president *still* wanted Attorney General Sessions to "unrecuse" from overseeing the Russia investigation. He called Sessions at home some time after my appointment as special counsel on May 17, 2017, to ask him to reverse his recusal so that he could direct the Department of Justice to investigate and prosecute Hillary Clinton. Trump wanted Sessions to unrecuse from "all of it." Sessions made no commitment and did not wind up reversing his recusal or ordering a Clinton investigation.

President Trump explored other options. He asked White House staff secretary Rob Porter in early July for his opinion of Associate Attorney General Rachel Brand, whom Porter knew. Was she good? Tough? "On the team?" Did Porter think Brand would like to be responsible for the special counsel's investigation and to be attorney general someday? The president asked Porter to feel her out about overseeing the investigation and taking Sessions's job.

"Keep in touch with your friend," Trump instructed.

The president followed up with Porter a few times, asking in passing whether he had spoken with Brand. Porter had not. He was uncomfortable with the request, because he understood that the president wished to find someone to end the Russia investigation and to fire the special counsel, even if Trump did not use those exact words. Porter did not want to become a link in a chain of events leading to the investigation's shuttering and my termination, so he did not contact Brand.

The president kept circling back to McGahn as well. Over the summer of 2017, Trump told the White House counsel that if Sessions were out of the picture, then the special counsel would report directly to a nonrecused attorney general. McGahn responded that a new attorney general would not necessarily have an impact on the investigation, but President Trump kept voicing his displeasure with Sessions throughout July. Sessions's recusal from the Russia investigation, Trump argued, was an act of disloyalty. The president complained to McGahn and Hicks about other aspects of Sessions's job performance as well. He was not letting this issue go.

Such conversations continued into the fall. President Trump met privately with Sessions on October 16 and complained that the Department of Justice was not investigating whom and what he thought it should be investigating. For instance, Hillary Clinton and her emails.

"Don't have to tell us," the president said. "Just take a look."

It must be noted that it is not the norm for the president to direct the Department of Justice to investigate political opponents. Sessions offered no assurances that the department would follow the president's suggestions. So Trump applied pressure from other angles.

"Wow, FBI confirms report that James Comey drafted letter exonerating Crooked Hillary Clinton long before investigation was complete," Trump tweeted on October 18, 2017. "Many people not interviewed, including Clinton herself. Comey stated under oath that he didn't do this — obviously a fix? Where is Justice Dept?"

On October 29, the president wrote a series of tweets about "Republican ANGER & UNITY . . . concerning the lack of investigation on Clinton" as well as "the Comey fix. . . . Instead they look at phony Trump/Russia 'collusion,' which doesn't exist. . . . DO SOMETHING!"

After an Oval Office cabinet meeting on December 6, the president again asked Sessions to "unrecuse." Porter was present for this conversation and documented the conversation in his notes:

Trump: I don't know if you could un-recuse yourself. You'd be a hero. Not telling you to do anything. Dershowitz says POTUS can get involved. Can order AG to investigate. I don't want to get involved. I'm not going to get involved. I'm not going to do anything or direct you to do anything. I just want to be treated fairly.

Sessions: We are taking steps; whole new leadership team. Professionals; will operate according to the law.

Sessions also told the president, "I never saw anything that was improper," presumably in reference to the Trump campaign's actions regarding Russia. Porter thought Sessions was reassuring the president that he was on his team.

In a December 28 *New York Times* story, Trump said it was "too bad" that Sessions had recused himself from the Russia investigation. Asked whether Eric Holder had been a more loyal attorney general to President Obama than Sessions had been to him, the president said, "I don't want to get into loyalty, but I will tell you that, I will say this: Holder protected President Obama. Totally protected him. When you look at the things that they did, and Holder protected the president. And I have great respect for that, I'll be honest."

Trump again raised the prospect of replacing Sessions in January 2018, telling Porter he wanted to "clean house" at the Department of Justice. Porter was at a meeting in the White House residence on January 27 in which the president touted the impressive win records of his former attorneys such as Roy Cohn and Jay Goldberg. One of his biggest failings as president, Trump continued, was that he had not surrounded himself with good attorneys. Jeff Sessions, for instance. Again Trump brought up Sessions's recusal and criticized the special counsel's investigation.

Throughout 2018, Trump continued to complain about Sessions on Twitter, including entreaties for him to take action on the Russia investigation despite his recusal.

February 28, 2018: "Why is A.G. Jeff Sessions asking the Inspector General to investigate potentially massive FISA [Foreign Intelligence Surveillance Act] abuse. Will take forever, has no prosecutorial power and already late with reports on Comey etc. Isn't the I.G. an Obama guy? Why not use Justice Department lawyers? DISGRACEFUL!"

April 7, 2018: "Lawmakers of the House Judiciary Committee are angrily accusing the Department of Justice of missing the Thursday Deadline for turning over UNREDACTED Documents relating to FISA abuse, FBI, Comey, Lynch, McCabe, Clinton Emails and much more. Slow walking — what is going on? BAD!"

April 22, 2018: " 'GOP Lawmakers asking Sessions to Investigate Comey and Hillary Clinton.' @FoxNews Good luck with that request!"

June 5, 2018: "The Russian Witch Hunt Hoax continues, all because Jeff Sessions didn't tell me he was going to recuse himself.... I would have quickly picked someone else. So much time and money wasted, so many lives ruined...and Sessions knew better than most that there was No Collusion!"

August 1, 2018: "Attorney General Jeff Sessions should stop this Rigged Witch Hunt right now."

December 16, 2018: "Jeff Sessions should be ashamed of himself for allowing this total HOAX to get started in the first place!"

President Trump also took his grievances to television, telling the Fox News show *Fox & Friends* on August 23, 2018, that the Department of Justice was pursuing politically motivated prosecutions, as shown by the fact that Paul Manafort had been charged but Democrats had not. The reason? "I put in an Attorney General that never took control of the Justice Department, Jeff Sessions," Trump bemoaned.

"I took control of the Department of Justice the day I was sworn in," Sessions volleyed back in a press statement later that day. "While I am Attorney General, the actions of the Department of Justice will not be improperly influenced by political considerations."

The president responded to Sessions on Twitter the next day:

"Department of Justice will not be improperly influenced by political considerations." Jeff, this is GREAT, what everyone wants, so look into all of the corruption on the "other side" including deleted Emails,

Comey lies & leaks, Mueller conflicts, McCabe, Strzok, Page, Ohr, FISA abuse, Christopher Steele & his phony and corrupt Dossier, the Clinton Foundation, illegal surveillance of Trump campaign, Russian collusion by Dems — and so much more. Open up the papers & documents without redaction? Come on Jeff, you can do it, the country is waiting!

The midterm elections took place on November 6, 2018. The Republicans expanded their Senate majority by two seats, but Democrats took control of the House with a gain of forty-one seats. The following day, the president had one final request from Sessions as his attorney general.

His resignation.

Sessions delivered his letter to the then–White House chief of staff, John Kelly. It was undated and began,

Dear Mr. President,

At your request, I am submitting my resignation.

For his new acting attorney general, the president selected Sessions's chief of staff, Matthew Whitaker. Multiple lawsuits questioned the constitutionality of Whitaker's appointment because he had not been confirmed by the Senate and a succession statute dictated that Deputy Attorney General Rod Rosenstein should have been next in line to serve as acting attorney general. Critics of the move also wondered whether the president had considered Whitaker's August 7, 2017, CNN commentary to be a qualification. Its headline: "Mueller's Investigation of Trump Is Going Too Far."

Whitaker would not keep that position for long, however, as President Trump nominated William Barr to the post in December 2018. Barr, who had previously served as attorney general for two years under President George H. W. Bush, had publicly supported Trump's firing of FBI director James Comey and had told the *New York Times* in November 2017, in reference to the president's having asked the Department of Justice to investigate Hillary Clinton, "There is nothing inherently wrong about a president calling for an investigation."

Barr was now overseeing our investigation and would determine the Department of Justice's actions to be taken with regard to our final report.

47

"Lawyers don't take notes"

White House counsel Don McGahn thought that he was protecting himself and the president when, in June 2017, he declined to follow through on Trump's order to call the then-acting attorney general, Rod Rosenstein, to have me removed as special counsel. If the president was being investigated for obstruction of justice, after all, moving to thwart this investigation could be considered another count of obstruction all by itself. It might even be allotted its own section in the special counsel's final report.

But people talk, reporters do their jobs, and soon the president was having uncomfortable discussions about those previous uncomfortable discussions.

"Trump Ordered Mueller Fired, but Backed Off When White House Counsel Threatened to Quit" was the headline of a January 25, 2018, *New York Times* story about President Trump's impasse with McGahn.

Citing four anonymous sources with knowledge of the matter, the story's authors, Michael S. Schmidt and Maggie Haberman, wrote,

Amid the first wave of news media reports that Mr. Mueller was examining a possible obstruction case, the president began to argue that Mr. Mueller had three conflicts of interest that disqualified him from overseeing the investigation.... After receiving the president's order to fire Mr. Mueller, the White House counsel, Donald F.

McGahn II, refused to ask the Justice Department to dismiss the spe-
cial counsel, saying he would quit instead....

Mr. McGahn disagreed with the president's case and told senior
White House officials that firing Mr. Mueller would have a cata-
strophic effect on Mr. Trump's presidency. Mr. McGahn also told
White House officials that Mr. Trump would not follow through on
the dismissal on his own. The president then backed off.

The *Washington Post* published a mild corrective the next day, reporting that McGahn had not actually told the president he would resign in
lieu of carrying out Trump's order to have Mueller removed. "McGahn
did not deliver his resignation threat directly to Trump but was serious
about his threat to leave," the *Post* reported, adding later in the story,
"Despite internal objections, Trump decided to assert that Mueller had
unacceptable conflicts of interest and moved to remove him from his
position, according to the people familiar with the discussions. In
response, McGahn said he would not remain at the White House if
Trump went through with the move, according to a senior administration official. The president, in turn, backed off."

Asked about the *Times* story while in Davos, Switzerland, for the
World Economic Forum, Trump responded, "Fake news, folks. Fake
news. A typical *New York Times* fake story."

Despite calling the story fake in public, the president acted as if the
threat were real. His personal counsel called McGahn's attorney on January 26 to say that the president wanted McGahn to issue a statement
denying he had been asked to fire the special counsel and had threatened
to resign in protest. McGahn's attorney spoke with McGahn and then
called the president's counsel back. No, the attorney said, McGahn would
not make such a statement because the *Times* story, although inaccurate
in parts, correctly reported that the president had pushed to have Mueller
fired.

That same day President Trump asked White House press secretary
Sarah Sanders to contact McGahn about the story. When she did,

McGahn told her that some of it was accurate and there was no need to respond.

Appearing on *Meet the Press* on February 4, former White House chief of staff Priebus said that he had not heard Trump say he wanted the special counsel fired. The president was happy with Priebus's appearance, called him to say he did a great job and added that he "never said any of those things" about the special counsel.

Trump told staff secretary Rob Porter the next day that the *Times* article was "bullshit," and he had not sought the special counsel's removal. Instead, McGahn had leaked the story to make himself look good. The president instructed Porter to tell McGahn to create a record that would show that Trump never directed him to fire the special counsel. Porter thought this was a matter for the White House communications office, not him, but Trump insisted, saying he wanted McGahn to write a letter "for our records" that would go beyond a press statement deeming the reporting inaccurate.

"He's a lying bastard," Trump said of McGahn, "and I want a record from him. If he doesn't write a letter, then maybe I'll have to get rid of him."

Porter delivered the president's message to McGahn later in the day, telling the White House counsel he was required to write a letter denying that Trump ever ordered him to have the special counsel terminated.

"But the reports are true," McGahn said, shrugging off the request. "The president was insistent on firing the special counsel, and I had planned to resign rather than carry out the order. I just hadn't personally told him the last part."

"The president said you'll be fired if you don't write the letter," Porter said.

"The optics would be terrible if he followed through with firing me on that basis," McGahn returned. "I will not write the letter the president requested."

As far as Porter knew, the letter never came up again with the president.

But the next day, February 6, Chief of Staff John Kelly scheduled an Oval Office meeting with Trump and McGahn to discuss the *Times* story. The president's personal counsel called McGahn's attorney that morning to say that no matter what happened in the meeting, McGahn could not resign.

Once they were together in the Oval Office, the president told McGahn, "I never said to fire Mueller. I never said 'fire.' This story doesn't look good. You need to correct this. You're the White House counsel."

"It's true that I did not tell you directly that I was planning to resign, but otherwise the story is true," McGahn returned.

"Did I say the word 'fire'?" Trump asked.

"What you said is 'Call Rod [Rosenstein]. Tell Rod that Mueller has conflicts and can't be the special counsel.'"

"I never said that," Trump said. He explained that he merely wanted McGahn to raise the conflicts issue with Rosenstein and to let the acting attorney general decide what to do.

"I did not understand the conversation that way," McGahn said. "I heard, 'Call Rod. There are conflicts. Mueller has to go.'"

The president asked McGahn to "do a correction" nonetheless.

McGahn said no. He thought the president was testing his mettle.

"Why did you tell the special counsel's office investigators that I told you to have Mueller removed?" the president asked.

"I had to," McGahn replied. "Our conversations are not protected by attorney-client privilege."

"What about those notes?" Trump asked. "Why do you take notes? Lawyers don't take notes. I never had a lawyer who took notes."

"I keep notes because I'm a real lawyer," McGahn shot back. "Notes create a record, and that's not a bad thing."

"I've had a lot of great lawyers, like Roy Cohn," Trump said. "He did not take notes."

After the meeting ended, McGahn told Kelly that he and the president "did have that conversation" about firing Mueller. Kelly subsequently pointed out to the president that McGahn had not backed down and would not budge.

Not long afterward, the president's personal counsel called the White House counsel's attorney again, this time to say that the president was "fine" with McGahn.

48

"They destroyed his life"

On January 24, 2017, four days after he had taken office as national security advisor, Michael Flynn sat down for an interview with the FBI and did not tell the truth. Asked about his December 29, 2016, conversation with Russian ambassador Sergey Kislyak, Flynn denied requesting Russia not to escalate the situation in response to the Obama administration's just-announced sanctions related to Russian election interference. Flynn also falsely told agents that he could not recall his follow-up conversation on December 31 in which Kislyak told him that his request had convinced Russia to moderate its reaction.

Flynn also lied about his calls related to the December 21, 2016, Egypt-proposed United Nations resolution that directed Israel to quit building settlements in Palestinian territory. Flynn told investigators that he had asked about how certain countries would vote but did not request for them to take any particular action when, in fact, he had been pushing for opposition to the resolution or a delay in the vote. He presented false information about his December 22 call to Kislyak in which he informed the Russian ambassador of the incoming Trump administration's opposition to the resolution and asked that Russia vote against or delay it. He also claimed, falsely, that Kislyak never got back to him with Russia's response to that request, when Kislyak, in fact, had told Flynn on December 23 that Russia would not oppose the resolution if a vote came up.

Given the negative impact that Flynn's false statements and omissions had on the FBI's investigation into Russian interference in the 2016 presidential election — as well as separate falsehoods he subsequently presented to the Department of Justice in relation to the Foreign Agents Registration Act regarding his lobbying work for Turkey — our office charged him with making false statements to the FBI, in violation of 18 U.S.C. § 1001(a). This was the scenario that White House counsel Don McGahn and National Security Council legal advisor John Eisenberg had envisioned after Acting Attorney General Sally Yates visited the White House a couple of days following Flynn's FBI interview to discuss his false statements.

President Trump had asked for Michael Flynn's resignation as national security advisor on February 13, 2017, a mere three and a half weeks after the inauguration, but praised him in public as a "wonderful man," "a fine person," and a "very good person." He also prompted advisors to pass along private messages to Flynn reassuring him of the president's affection and support.

Flynn began to cooperate with our office in November 2017, and on November 22, he withdrew from a joint defense agreement he had with the president. Flynn's counsel informed the president's personal counsel and the White House counsel that his client no longer could maintain confidential communications with the president or the White House.

That night, the president's personal counsel left a voice mail for Flynn's counsel:

> I understand your situation, but let me see if I can't state it in starker terms....It wouldn't surprise me if you've gone on to make a deal with...the government....If...there's information that implicates the President, then we've got a national security issue,...so, you know,... we need some kind of heads up. Um, just for the sake of protecting all our interests if we can....Remember what we've always said about the President and his feelings toward Flynn and, that still remains.

Flynn's attorneys called the president's personal counsel back the next day and reiterated that they no longer could share information under any sort of privilege. The president's personal counsel disagreed with this point and became indignant, concluding that Flynn must be hostile toward the president. The counsel said he would report that last point back to the president. Flynn's attorneys felt like the president's counsel was pressing them to reconsider their position because the counsel assumed Flynn would not want the president to be told that his former national security advisor was hostile toward him.

On December 1, as part of a cooperation agreement, Flynn pleaded guilty to making false statements to the FBI and also admitted his falsehoods submitted to the Department of Justice. Trump told a group of reporters outside the White House the next day that he was unconcerned about what Flynn might tell our office.

"Do you stand behind Michael Flynn?" one reporter called out.

"We'll see what happens," Trump responded.

That evening Trump posted a sympathetic tweet about Flynn: "So General Flynn lies to the FBI and his life is destroyed, while Crooked Hillary Clinton, on that now famous FBI holiday 'interrogation' with no swearing in and no recording, lies many times . . . and nothing happens to her? Rigged system, or just a double standard?"

Before taking off for Salt Lake City on December 4, Trump expanded on that sentiment. "I feel badly for General Flynn," he told reporters. "I feel very badly. He's led a very strong life. And I feel very badly. I will say this: Hillary Clinton lied many times to the FBI and nothing happened to her. Flynn lied and they destroyed his life."

On December 15 outside the White House, a reporter asked President Trump, "Would you consider a pardon for Michael Flynn?"

"I don't want to talk about pardons for Michael Flynn yet," the president said. "We'll see what happens. Let's see. I can say this: When you look at what's gone on with the FBI and with the Justice Department, people are very, very angry."

49

" 'Hi, how are you?' That's it."

Flynn's was far from the only indictment that our office's investigation produced. Three days after the FBI interviewed Michael Flynn, its agents spoke with former Trump campaign foreign policy advisor George Papadopoulos. He did not tell the truth either.

During the January 27, 2017, interview, Papadopoulos acknowledged that he had met Joseph Mifsud and that the Russia-connected, London-based professor had told him the Russians had "dirt" on Clinton in the form of "thousands of emails." But Papadopoulos repeatedly said that the two of them had these conversations prior to his joining the Trump campaign and that it was a "very strange coincidence" to be told of such "dirt" before he was working for the candidate. In fact, this "dirt" conversation took place more than a month after Trump had announced Papadopoulos as a campaign advisor.

Papadopoulos also minimized how seriously he took his interactions with Mifsud, calling him "a nothing" and "just a guy talk[ing] up connections or something" whom Papadopoulos thought was "BS'ing, to be completely honest with you." Actually, Papadopoulos had told the campaign about Mifsud's high-level Russian government connections, saying the London professor had consulted with important officials in Moscow before revealing the existence of "dirt" about Clinton. The former Trump advisor also had communicated for months with Mifsud about foreign policy issues and spent much time and effort trying to arrange a meeting between top Trump campaign officials and Russian government representatives.

In addition, when investigators asked whether Papadopoulos had met with Russian nationals or anyone "with a Russian accent" during the campaign, he said no. He did not mention that Mifsud had introduced him to Ivan Timofeev, the Russian national whom Papadopoulos understood to be connected to the Russian Ministry of Foreign Affairs and with whom he had multiple exchanges to try to lay the "groundwork" for a possible meeting between Trump campaign and Russian government officials.

Papadopoulos made more false statements related to Olga Polonskaya, whom, he told the FBI, he had met before he joined the campaign and with whom he claimed he had "no" relationship. He told investigators the two of them merely exchanged emails: "Just, 'Hi, how are you?' That's it." Papadopoulos actually met Polonskaya after he had joined the campaign and thought she had high-level Russian government connections, at first mistakenly believing she was Putin's niece. During the campaign, he emailed and spoke via Skype with her multiple times while trying to arrange a campaign foreign policy trip to Russia.

As Flynn's lies had done, Papadopoulos's false statements to the FBI impeded the agency's investigation into Russian election interference. They also had a negative impact on FBI investigators' questioning of Mifsud in a Washington, DC, hotel lobby on February 10, 2017. During that interview, Mifsud admitted to knowing Papadopoulos and introducing him to Polonskaya and Timofeev but denied any knowledge of Russia possessing emails damaging to Hillary Clinton. Mifsud said that Papadopoulos must have misunderstood their conversation, which he said had been about cybersecurity and hacking in general.

Mifsud also claimed, falsely, that he had not seen Papadopoulos since the meeting in which Mifsud introduced him to Polonskaya, even though emails, text messages, and other information showed that Mifsud met with Papadopoulos at least two more times. Mifsud also failed to acknowledge that he had drafted — or perhaps edited — Polonskaya's follow-up message to Papadopoulos following their initial meeting and that Mifsud may have been involved in a personal relationship with Polonskaya at the time. (He had written to her, "Baby, thank you!") If Papadopoulos had not lied in his FBI interview, investigators would have been better able to respond to Mifsud's inaccurate statements.

As Papadopoulos stepped off a flight from Munich, Germany, to Dulles Airport outside Washington, DC, on the evening of July 27, 2017, he was met by FBI agents and taken into custody. A booking photo of him was shot in an Alexandria, Virginia, detention center early the next morning, although his arrest drew no publicity. Our office had charged him with making false statements to the FBI in violation of 18 U.S.C. § 1001(a), the same offense for which Flynn had been booked.

Papadopoulos pleaded guilty to that charge pursuant to a plea agreement on October 7, 2017. Almost a year later, on September 7, 2018, he received a sentence of fourteen days in prison, a $9,500 fine, and two hundred hours of community service. He wound up serving twelve days at a medium-security prison in Wisconsin, entering on November 26, 2018, and being released on December 7.

A few weeks after Papadopoulos's plea deal was made public, President Trump referred to him on Twitter as a "young, low level volunteer named George, who has already proven to be a liar." Papadopoulos later alleged that his meetings with Mifsud were part of an entrapment scheme conducted by the FBI to justify their surveillance of Trump's campaign. The president eventually signed on to this conspiracy theory, dubbing it "Spygate" in May 2018 and claiming, without evidence, that the Obama administration had placed a spy in his campaign.

50

"Wow, what a tough sentence"

On October 27, 2017, a grand jury in the District of Columbia indicted former Trump campaign manager Paul Manafort and former deputy campaign manager Rick Gates on multiple felony counts. An Eastern District of Virginia grand jury delivered more felony charges on February 22, 2018. Manafort's alleged criminal conduct began as early as 2005 and lasted through 2018. As a Superseding Criminal Information filing from September 2018 would sum up, Manafort collected more than $60 million through lobbying for the Ukraine and its political parties and officials, and, with the help of Gates and Konstantin Kilimnik (who also was indicted), he concealed the payments.

Manafort also "used his hidden overseas wealth to enjoy a lavish lifestyle in the United States, without paying taxes on that income," did not report to the United States his lobbying work for a foreign country as the law required, gave "a series of false and misleading statements" to the Department of Justice when asked about these activities in 2016, and "laundered more than $30 million to buy property, goods, and services in the United States, income that he concealed from the United States Treasury, the Department of Justice and others. Manafort cheated the United States out of over $15 million in taxes."

Manafort and Gates remained in touch, and in January 2018, Manafort told him that he had spoken with the president's personal counsel.

"They're going to take care of us," Manafort said, noting that it would be stupid to make a plea deal given his conversation with the president's counsel. "We should sit tight. We'll be taken care of."

"Has anyone mentioned pardons?" Gates asked.

"No one used that word," Manafort responded.

As Manafort's cases progressed, President Trump told Rob Porter he had never liked his former campaign chair, who, Trump said, didn't know what he was doing while he worked on the campaign. The president wondered aloud to aides whether and how Manafort might be cooperating with the special counsel's investigation and whether Manafort had information that could hurt him.

But as he had with Flynn, in public, Trump questioned how Manafort and others under investigation were being treated. "Like Manafort has nothing to do with our campaign, but I feel so — I tell you, I feel a little badly about it," Trump said in a White House press gaggle on June 15, 2018, before that day's court hearing to determine whether Manafort's bail should be revoked due to new witness-tampering charges. "They went back twelve years to get things that he did twelve years ago?...I feel badly for some people, because they've gone back twelve years to find things about somebody, and I don't think it's right."

A reporter followed up: "Is there any consideration at any point of a pardon for any of the people that you —"

"I don't want to talk about that," Trump interjected. "No, I don't want to talk about that...But look, I do want to see people treated fairly. That's what it's all about."

At Manafort's hearing, US District Court judge Amy Berman Jackson ordered that he be jailed for allegedly working to shape the accounts of two men who worked with him on a Ukraine public relations campaign. "I am concerned you seem to treat these proceedings as just another marketing exercise," the judge told the sixty-nine-year-old defendant before announcing that she was revoking his house arrest, which had been in effect since the previous October. "You have abused the trust the court placed in you six months ago."

The president commented publicly, and negatively, about the judge's ruling. "Wow, what a tough sentence for Paul Manafort, who has represented Ronald Reagan, Bob Dole and many other top political people and campaigns," he tweeted that day. "Didn't know Manafort was the head of the Mob. What about Comey and Crooked Hillary and all the others? Very unfair!"

Manafort had not actually received a sentence at this hearing.

Soon Rudy Giuliani, the president's personal lawyer, was raising the prospect of a Manafort pardon in interviews. "When the whole thing is over, things might get cleaned up with some presidential pardons," the former New York mayor told the *New York Daily News* on the day Manafort was sent to jail. He told the *New York Times* that same day that although the president should not pardon anyone during the special counsel's probe, "when the investigation is concluded, he's kind of on his own, right?"

Talking to CNN two days later, Giuliani returned to this point: "I guess I should clarify this once and for all.... The president has issued no pardons in this investigation. The president is not going to issue pardons in this investigation.... When it's over, hey, he's the president of the United States. He retains his pardon power. Nobody is taking that away from him."

When asked whether this statement might imply that defendants need not cooperate in a criminal prosecution because presidential pardons could rescue them, Giuliani said his comments were "certainly not intended that way" but were meant to acknowledge that someone involved in the investigation would not be "excluded from [a pardon], if in fact the president and his advisors...come to the conclusion that you have been treated unfairly." Pardons are not unusual in political investigations, Giuliani said. "That doesn't mean they're going to happen here. Doesn't mean that anybody should rely on it.... Big signal is, nobody has been pardoned yet."

Manafort's criminal trial in the Eastern District of Virginia began on July 31, 2018, and drew much press coverage — and inspired more presidential tweets the next day:

"This is a terrible situation and Attorney General Jeff Sessions should stop this Rigged Witch Hunt right now, before it continues to stain our country any further. Bob Mueller is totally conflicted, and his 17 Angry Democrats that are doing his dirty work are a disgrace to USA!" Trump tweeted at 9:24 a.m.

"Paul Manafort worked for Ronald Reagan, Bob Dole and many other highly prominent and respected political leaders. He worked for me for a very short time. Why didn't government tell me that he was under investigation. These old charges have nothing to do with Collusion — a Hoax!" he tweeted at 9:34 a.m.

"Looking back on history, who was treated worse, Alfonse Capone, legendary mob boss, killer and 'Public Enemy Number One,' or Paul Manafort, political operative & Reagan/Dole darling, now serving solitary confinement — although convicted of nothing? Where is the Russian Collusion?" he tweeted at 11:35 a.m.

When White House press secretary Sarah Sanders met with reporters later that day, she was asked about the tweets, which had drawn much attention. Responding to a question about the president's comment that "Attorney General Jeff Sessions should stop this Rigged Witch Hunt right now," Sanders said, "It's not an order. It's the president's opinion." She also commented on Trump's tweets about Manafort: "Certainly, the president's been clear. He thinks Paul Manafort's been treated unfairly."

On August 15, the day before the Manafort case went to the jury for deliberations, Giuliani called me out to Bloomberg News reporters, saying my investigation needed to get wrapped up. "If he doesn't get it done in the next two or three weeks, we will just unload on him like a ton of bricks," Giuliani said, claiming that continuing the investigation into the sixty-day window before the midterm elections would be "a very, very serious violation of the Justice Department rules."

There actually is no such rule. The informal Justice Department custom is to avoid doing anything that could have an overt impact on the election. So our investigation continued, with media stories speculating that a Manafort acquittal could amplify criticism of our office's probe while a conviction could justify extending the investigation.

In an impromptu exchange with reporters on the White House South Lawn on August 17, while Manafort's unsequestered jury was in the midst of deliberations, the president twice called our investigation a "rigged witch hunt," characterized the case against Manafort in a negative way, and again declined to comment on whether he would pardon Manafort if his former aide were convicted. "I don't talk about that now. I don't talk about that. I think the whole Manafort trial is very sad when you look at what's going on there. I think it's a very sad day for our country. He worked for me for a very short period of time. But you know what, he happens to be a very good person. And I think it's very sad what they've done to Paul Manafort."

"Mr. Manafort really appreciates the support of President Trump," Manafort's attorney, Kevin Downing, told reporters outside the courtroom in response to Trump's comments.

The jury returned on August 21 and apparently was not swayed by the president's words. It pronounced Manafort guilty on eight felony counts, although a mistrial was declared on the other ten counts due to one juror's reported holdout.

"I must tell you that Paul Manafort is a good man," President Trump said after stepping off a plane in West Virginia for a rally that evening. "He was with Ronald Reagan. He was with a lot of different people over the years. And I feel very sad about that. It doesn't involve me, but I still feel — you know, it's a very sad thing that happened. This has nothing to do with Russian collusion. This started as Russian collusion. This has absolutely nothing to do — this is a witch hunt, and it's a disgrace."

Ainsley Earhardt of *Fox & Friends* asked the president the next day, "Are you considering pardoning Paul Manafort?"

"I have great respect for what he's done, in terms of what he's gone through," Trump responded. "He worked for many, many people many, many years, and I would say what he did, some of the charges they threw against him, every consultant, every lobbyist in Washington probably does."

Giuliani subsequently told reporters that Trump "really thinks Manafort has been horribly treated" but after seeking legal advice about possible pardons for him and others, the president was following their advice that he not consider pardons until the Russia investigation had ended.

Before a second trial on seven more criminal counts, Manafort pleaded guilty on September 14 to two of those counts: conspiracy to defraud the United States and conspiracy to obstruct justice due to attempts to tamper with witnesses. He signed a plea deal in which he admitted guilt to seven counts that had been hung up in the previous trial, and he agreed to cooperate with investigators. Yet Giuliani told Reuters for an October 22 story that Manafort remained in a joint defense agreement with the president, meaning that lawyers representing both clients could share information without violating attorney-client privilege. The legal community considered such an arrangement, in which one party in the defense agreement has pleaded guilty and agreed to cooperate with prosecutors, to be unusual, but Giuliani, representing Trump in the Russia investigation, said he was regularly speaking to and exchanging information with Manafort's lawyers.

He revealed more in a November 27 *New York Times* story, which reported that Manafort's lawyer was regularly briefing President Trump's lawyers about Manafort's discussions with our investigators. The *Times* wrote,

The arrangement was highly unusual and inflamed tensions with the special counsel's office when prosecutors discovered it after Mr. Manafort began cooperating two months ago, the people [familiar with the conversations] said. Some legal experts speculated that it was a bid by Mr. Manafort for a presidential pardon even as he worked with the special counsel, Robert S. Mueller III, in hopes of a lighter sentence.

Rudolph W. Giuliani, one of the president's personal lawyers, acknowledged the arrangement on Tuesday and defended it as a source of valuable insights into the special counsel's inquiry and where it was headed.

So the president's team was using Manafort to learn more about where our investigation was going. For example, the story stated that Manafort's lawyer had told Giuliani that investigators were pressing Manafort about whether Trump knew in advance about Donald Trump Jr.'s June 9, 2016, Trump Tower meeting to get damaging information about Hillary Clinton. Referring to me, Giuliani said in the story, "He wants Manafort to incriminate Trump."

The day before that story was published, our office disclosed in a public court filing that Manafort had lied repeatedly to federal investigators about "a variety of subject matters," thus breaching his plea agreement, though he could not withdraw his guilty plea. Giuliani said that the president had been "upset for weeks" about "the un-American, horrible treatment of Manafort" while Trump, in a November 28 interview with the *New York Post*, commended Manafort for not "flipping."

"If you told the truth, you go to jail," Trump said. "You know this flipping stuff is terrible. You flip, and you lie, and you get — the prosecutors will tell you 99 percent of the time they can get people to flip." But, Trump said, he "had three people" — Manafort, former advisor Roger Stone, and Jerome Corsi, Stone's go-between with WikiLeaks — who turned down deals to flip.

"It's actually very brave," the president said.

As for a potential pardon of Manafort, Trump said, "It was never discussed, but I wouldn't take it off the table. Why would I take it off the table?"

51

"If you stay on message, he has your back"

Michael Cohen, who had recently turned fifty when his boss was elected president, had long been seen as Donald Trump's loyal soldier and enforcer, the man who did damage control and had his back at all times. A 2011 ABC News profile called him Trump's "pit bull" and noted, "Some have even nicknamed him 'Tom,' a reference to Tom Hagen, the consigliore to Vito Corleone in the *Godfather* movies." Cohen told the ABC interviewer, "It means that if somebody does something Mr. Trump doesn't like, I do everything in my power to resolve it to Mr. Trump's benefit. If you do something wrong, I'm going to come at you, grab you by the neck and I'm not going to let you go until I'm finished."

Cohen's skill set and tenaciousness came into great demand before and during Trump's campaign for president, and now as the investigations threatened to overwhelm his presidency.

Let's recap some of the issues that required Cohen's deep involvement.

As Trump Organization executive vice president and Donald Trump's personal counsel, Cohen served as point person for negotiations for a Trump Tower Moscow project. Cohen received permission from Trump in September 2015 to negotiate on behalf of the Trump Organization for a Russian corporation to build a Moscow tower that would license Trump's name and brand. Cohen spoke about the project multiple times with Trump, who requested that Cohen provide regular updates on developments and circled back with the lawyer if he had not heard anything recently. Cohen also kept Donald Trump Jr. and Ivanka Trump in the loop.

Trump signed a letter of intent for the project in the fall of 2015, with the Trump Organization receiving highly lucrative terms. Felix Sater, the colorful real estate advisor (and US intelligence informant) who represented the Russian corporation in negotiations, asked Cohen for copies of his and Trump's passports in December 2015 so that the pair could travel to Russia for meetings with government officials and potential financing partners. Cohen discussed the trip with Trump and obtained the passport copy from Rhona Graff, Trump's personal secretary.

But when Sater had not set up any meetings with Russian government officials by January 2016, an impatient Cohen emailed the office of Dmitry Peskov, Putin's deputy chief of staff and press secretary. Cohen wound up speaking with Peskov's personal assistant, Elena Poliakova, about pushing the Trump Tower Moscow project forward. Cohen told Trump about the call afterward, referring to the woman as "someone from the Kremlin" who was so professional and asked such detailed questions that he wished the Trump Organization's assistants were that competent.

Cohen's phone call apparently got the ball rolling again, Sater texting him the next day, "It's about Putin they called today."

The Russian government liked the project, Sater told Cohen, and on January 25, Sater sent an invitation for Cohen to make "a working visit" to Moscow. Cohen relayed to Trump that he was awaiting word about the project moving forward.

Such conversations with Sater and Trump continued into the next few months, with Trump never discouraging Cohen from pursuing the project even as the candidate entered the thick of primary season. In March or April 2016, Trump asked Cohen what was going on with Trump Tower Moscow, and that spring, Cohen also spoke with Donald Trump Jr. about the deal, because it was potentially worth $1 billion. Meanwhile, Sater was texting Cohen to invite him and Trump to be Russian press secretary Peskov's guests at the St. Petersburg International Economic Forum. Cohen read the text to Trump, and they discussed the invitation, Cohen mentioning that Putin or Russian prime minister Dmitry Medvedev might be there. Trump said that he would agree to travel to Russia if Cohen could "lock and load" on the deal.

But in June, Cohen decided not to attend the St. Petersburg forum because Sater had yet to arrange a formal invitation for him from Peskov. Cohen had a brief conversation with Trump at that time but did not declare the project finished as he did not want his boss to complain that the deal was on-again, off-again as long as it might be revived.

That summer of 2016, Trump publicly declared he had nothing to do with Russia. Soon afterward, he again was asking Cohen about progress on the Trump Tower Moscow.

Cohen thought this: *Interesting…*

Eventually he told Trump that the Moscow tower project was hitting a dead end because the Russian corporation had not lined up a piece of property for it.

"That's too bad," Trump said, and the two apparently did not discuss it again.

For the record, though, Cohen was clear on this point. At no time during the campaign did Trump tell him not to pursue the project or to abandon it.

Yet given all of the questions that had arisen during the campaign, the "party line" was that Trump had no personal, financial, or business connections to Russia.

After Trump was elected president, sometime in January, Cohen fielded press inquiries about Trump Tower Moscow, which was on a list of deals that the Trump Organization wanted to close out before the inauguration. Cohen spoke to Trump about these questions because he was concerned that truthful answers about Trump Tower Moscow would contradict the "message" that the president-elect had no relationship with Russia.

Cohen subsequently stuck with the talking points that Trump and others developed with him in order to "stay on message," even though he knew they were untrue — and he knew that Trump knew this too. Cohen told a *New York Times* reporter that the Trump Tower Moscow deal was deemed unfeasible and had been scuttled in January 2016, before the Iowa Republican caucuses kicked off the primary season. That story, published on February 19, repeated Cohen's altered timetable and "message":

> *[Sater] said he had been working on a plan for a Trump Tower in Moscow with a Russian real estate developer as recently as the fall of 2015, one that he said had come to a halt because of Mr. Trump's presidential campaign. (Mr. Cohen said the Trump Organization had received a letter of intent for a project in Moscow from a Russian real estate developer at that time but determined that the project was not feasible.)*

To Cohen it felt important to say that the deal had fallen through by January 2016 rather than to admit that talks continued through May and June; this would avoid Trump appearing to have had a relationship with Russia after he had nailed down the Republican nomination.

As part of its investigations into Russian election interference, Congress requested Cohen's testimony and related documents in early May 2017. Cohen believed the House committee wanted to focus on a supposed meeting between Cohen and Russian officials in Prague, as noted in the Steele dossier. But, Cohen maintained, he had never been to Prague, so he was unconcerned about that allegation. He met with the president on May 18 to discuss Congress's request, and Trump said he should cooperate, given the lack of any substance there.

Cohen entered into a joint defense agreement with the president and other subjects of the Russia investigation and spoke frequently with the president's counsel throughout the months preceding his congressional testimony. The president's counsel assured Cohen that if they all stayed on message, the investigations would end soon, likely by the summer or fall of 2017. The Trump Organization was covering Cohen's legal bills, and the president's counsel told Cohen that he remained protected by the joint defense agreement unless he "went rogue."

"The president loves you," the counsel said. "If you stay on message, he has your back."

When Cohen drafted a statement about the Trump Tower Moscow project to submit to Congress, he included several statements that he knew to be false:

1. *"The proposal was under consideration at the Trump Organization from September 2015 until the end of January 2016. By the end of January 2016, I determined that the proposal was not feasible for a variety of business reasons and should not be pursued further. Based on my business determinations, the Trump Organization abandoned the proposal."*

Actually, the Trump Organization remained in talks about the project through at least June 2016 and never abandoned it.

2. *"Despite overtures by Mr. Sater, I never considered asking Mr. Trump to travel to Russia in connection with this proposal. I told Mr. Sater that Mr. Trump would not travel to Russia unless there was a definitive agreement in place."*

Actually, Cohen and Trump did discuss travel to Russia and even sent along copies of their passports.

3. *"Mr. Trump was never in contact with anyone about this proposal other than me on three occasions, including signing a non-binding letter of intent in 2015."*

Actually, Cohen and Trump spoke often about the project, with Trump desiring frequent updates on its status.

4. Cohen did *"not recall any response to my email [to Peskov], nor any other contacts by me with Mr. Peskov or other Russian government officials about the proposal."*

Actually, Cohen's January 2016 email to Peskov led to a lengthy phone conversation with a Kremlin representative.

Members of the joint defense agreement vetted and edited Cohen's statement before it was submitted. Cohen had written, "The building project led me to make limited contacts with Russian government officials." The joint defense agreement deleted that sentence from the final draft, and Cohen did not object, telling the president's counsel he would not buck the agreement's decisions.

While drafting his statement, Cohen also spoke with the president's personal counsel about his efforts to set up a meeting between Trump and Putin at the 2015 United Nations General Assembly, another link between the candidate and Russia. Cohen had suggested the meeting to Trump in September 2015, and Trump had instructed him to contact Putin's office to try to set it up. While Cohen was speaking and emailing with a Russian official, Trump asked multiple times for updates on this proposed Putin meeting. The Russian official wound up telling Cohen that such a meeting would not follow proper protocol for Putin, and Cohen passed along this information to Trump.

Having discussed this meeting on Sean Hannity's radio show, Cohen now feared he might be asked about it. He told the president's counsel the "whole story," and the two of them considered ways to keep Trump out of the narrative. The president's counsel concluded that the story was not relevant, so Cohen should omit it from his statement to Congress.

In making false statements to Congress regarding Trump Tower Moscow, Cohen's "agenda" was to minimize the links between Trump and the project and to protect the president by not contradicting anything he had said, particularly about there having been no connections between him and Russia while he was a candidate. The fact that the deal never happened made it easier for Cohen to rationalize his false testimony, and given that everyone involved was sticking to the party line, he had no fear that his statements would be contradicted. Cohen wanted the president's continued support and felt like staying on message would help squelch the special counsel's and congressional investigations.

Cohen spoke with the president's personal counsel almost daily between August 18 and August 28 as his statement moved from its initial draft to its submission to Congress. On August 27, the day before he submitted it, Cohen had multiple phone conversations with the president's counsel and told him that his statement was omitting numerous communications with Russia and with Trump. The counsel responded that those details were not necessary to include because the project didn't happen, and Cohen should keep his statement short and "tight." Then the investigation would soon come to an end. Cohen also told the counsel about his conversation with the woman from the Kremlin.

"So what?" the counsel replied. "The deal never happened."

The counsel said his "client," Trump, appreciated Cohen and wanted him to stay on message and not to contradict the president or otherwise muddy the waters. It was time to move on.

Cohen agreed, as he was expected to do.

Later, the president's personal counsel refused our office's request for an interview about these conversations.

Cohen was a source for a *Washington Post* story published on August 27 that reported that the Trump Organization was "pursuing a plan to develop a massive Trump Tower in Moscow" while Trump was "running for president in late 2015 and early 2016." Cohen stayed on message regarding the time line, and the story followed his lead, noting that "the project was abandoned at the end of January 2016, just before the presidential primaries began, several people familiar with the proposal said."

Cohen submitted his statement to Congress on August 28 and assured the president that he would stay on message in his testimony. The president's personal counsel had told Cohen that the president liked it when Jared Kushner previously had released a statement in advance of his congressional testimony. Cohen followed suit, releasing his opening remarks on September 19 to shape the narrative and to alert other potential witnesses about what he would be saying so that they could conform to this message. Cohen's remarks criticized the Steele allegations and claimed that the Trump Tower Moscow project "was terminated in January of 2016; which occurred before the Iowa caucus and months before the very first primary." After the press reported on Cohen's opening remarks, Trump's personal counsel told Cohen that the president was pleased.

Cohen repeated his false statements in his testimony before the House Permanent Select Committee on Intelligence on October 24 and 25. He spoke with the president's counsel before and after his testimony on both days.

As he told *Vanity Fair* for an article in its September 2017 issue, "I'm the guy who protects the president and the family. I'm the guy who would take a bullet for the president."

52

"Sorry, I don't see Michael doing that"

Michael Cohen's duties for Trump extended to Stephanie Clifford, a.k.a. adult film actress Stormy Daniels, who claimed to have had a sexual encounter with Donald Trump before he ran for office (and while his third wife, Melania Trump, was pregnant with their son, Barron). Cohen's $130,000 payment to Clifford ostensibly had nothing to do with our investigation into Russian inference in the 2016 election, yet it wound up having a major impact on the probe as well as on the president's relationship with his tenacious advocate.

News outlets reported on Cohen's payment in January 2018, alleging that it was meant to keep Clifford from discussing her affair with Trump. Cohen released a statement to the *New York Times* on February 13 that explained,

> *In a private transaction in 2016, I used my own personal funds to facilitate a payment of $130,000 to Ms. Stephanie Clifford....Neither the Trump Organization nor the Trump campaign was a party to the transaction with Ms. Clifford, and neither reimbursed me for the payment, either directly or indirectly. The payment to Ms. Clifford was lawful, and was not a campaign contribution or a campaign expenditure by anyone.*

Denying that the payment confirmed the validity of any claim, Cohen also noted, "Just because something isn't true doesn't mean that it can't cause you harm or damage. I will always protect Mr. Trump."

On February 19, the day after a lengthy *New York Times* story called Cohen the president's "fixer," Trump's personal counsel texted Cohen, "Client says thank you for what you do."

Cohen testified before the House Oversight and Reform Committee on February 27 that he had discussed with the president what to say about the payment and that the president had him say that Trump "was not knowledgeable... of [Cohen's] actions."

About six weeks later, the other shoe dropped.

In conjunction with the US Attorney's Office for the Southern District of New York, FBI agents raided Cohen's home, his suite at the Regency Hotel on Manhattan's Upper East Side (where he reportedly was staying while his home was being renovated), and his office in Rockefeller Center on April 9. Without giving Cohen advance notice, the agents executed a search warrant to remove business records, emails, and documents related to the payment to Clifford and other matters.

The raid angered President Trump, who opened a White House press opportunity that evening by saying,

> So I just heard that they broke into the office of one of my personal attorneys — a good man. And it's a disgraceful situation. It's a total witch hunt. I've been saying it for a long time. I've wanted to keep it down. We've given, I believe, over a million pages' worth of documents to the Special Counsel....
>
> And it's a disgrace. It's, frankly, a real disgrace. It's an attack on our country, in a true sense. It's an attack on what we all stand for. So when I saw this and when I heard it — I heard it like you did — I said, that is really now on a whole new level of unfairness.

Cohen, meanwhile, was feeling vulnerable. The searches had made him "an open book," and he knew he could be harmed if information came out about payments to Daniels and another woman (*Playboy* model Karen McDougal, who also alleged an affair with Trump) and his false statements to Congress.

The president called him a few days after the raid to "check in" and to ask whether Cohen was OK. "Hang in there," Trump said. "Stay strong."

Other Trump friends also touched base with Cohen to pass along the president's support.

"I'm with the boss at Mar-a-Lago," one friend told him, "and he says he loves you and don't worry."

"The boss loves you," a Trump Organization official told him.

"Everyone knows the boss has your back," another Trump friend said.

On April 17, Cohen began speaking with attorney Robert Costello, who was close to Trump's personal lawyer, Rudy Giuliani. Costello told Cohen that he had a "back channel of communication" to the president's lawyer that Giuliani said was "crucial" and "must be maintained."

The *New York Times* published a story three days later with the headline "Michael Cohen Has Said He Would Take a Bullet for Trump. Maybe Not Anymore." It reported,

> *For years Mr. Trump treated Mr. Cohen poorly, with gratuitous insults, dismissive statements and, at least twice, threats of being fired, according to interviews with a half-dozen people familiar with their relationship.*
>
> *"Donald goes out of his way to treat him like garbage," said Roger J. Stone Jr., Mr. Trump's informal and longest-serving political adviser.*

The story added that Trump and Cohen had dined together at Mar-a-Lago a few weeks earlier, "but since the raid Mr. Cohen has told associates he feels isolated. Mr. Trump has long felt he had leverage over Mr. Cohen, but people who have worked for the president said the raid has changed all that."

The president responded to the story with a string of tweets the following morning:

> *The New York Times and a third rate reporter...are going out of their way to destroy Michael Cohen and his relationship with me in*

the hope that he will "flip." They use non existent "sources" and a drunk/drugged up loser who hates Michael, a fine person with a wonderful family. Michael is a businessman for his own account/ lawyer who I have always liked & respected. Most people will flip if the Government lets them out of trouble, even if it means lying or making up stories. Sorry, I don't see Michael doing that despite the horrible Witch Hunt and the dishonest media!

That same day Costello sent an email to Cohen saying he'd had a "Very Very Positive" conversation with Giuliani. "You are 'loved,'" Costello assured Cohen. "They are in our corner. Sleep well tonight. You have friends in high places."

Cohen, who appreciated that the Trump Organization continued to pay his legal fees, felt like he still had the White House's support as long as he stuck with the party line. He wanted Trump's power on his side. So he would stay on message, defend the president, and remain on the team.

Amid media reports of discussions of pardons at the White House, Cohen asked Trump's personal counsel about the possibility that he might receive one. The FBI raids had put him in an uncomfortable position. What was in it for him?

Stay on message, the counsel responded. The investigation was a witch hunt, and everything would be fine.

Cohen continued to believe that as long as he stuck to the team's talking points, the president would take care of him, either through a pardon or shuttering the investigation.

"It was noticed by some that you didn't close the door one way or the other on the President pardoning Michael Cohen," a reporter inquired of White House press secretary Sarah Sanders at the April 23 White House daily briefing. "What is your read on that right now?"

"It's hard to close a door on something that hasn't taken place," Sanders responded. "I don't like to discuss or comment on hypothetical situations that may or may not ever happen. I would refer you to personal attorneys to comment on anything specific regarding that case, but we don't have anything at this point."

The following morning, a reporter asked Trump, "Are you considering a pardon for Michael Cohen?"

"Stupid. Stupid question," the president responded.

Asked again about the possibility of pardons for Manafort or Cohen on June 8, Trump said, "I haven't even thought about it.... It certainly is far too early to be thinking about that.... They haven't been convicted of anything. There's nothing to pardon."

During a press gaggle on the White House's North Lawn a week later, the president said he felt "badly" about the treatment of Manafort, Flynn, and Cohen.

"I think a lot of it is very unfair."

53

"I will not be a punching bag"

Finally, it was Michael Cohen's turn to drop a bomb on Twitter.

"Spent Saturday afternoon with @GStephanopoulos @abc (not on camera) interview for Monday's @GMA. My silence is broken!" the president's former counsel tweeted on the evening of July 1, 2018.

Early the next morning, ABC News's George Stephanopoulos posted an online story in advance of his segment on *Good Morning America*. "In his first in-depth interview since the FBI raided his office and homes in April, Cohen strongly signaled his willingness to cooperate with special counsel Robert Mueller and federal prosecutors in the Southern District of New York — even if that puts President Trump in jeopardy," the story stated and then quoted Cohen: "My wife, my daughter and my son have my first loyalty and always will. I put family and country first."

Cohen was willing to take a bullet for Trump no more.

In the interview, the president's former lawyer and fixer said that he disagreed with "those who demonize or vilify the FBI," and he declined to criticize our investigation, saying, "I don't like the term 'witch hunt.'... As an American, I repudiate Russia's or any other foreign government's attempt to interfere or meddle in our democratic process, and I would call on all Americans to do the same."

Cohen also revealed that he had a new lead counsel, former federal prosecutor Guy Petrillo, and the story noted that Cohen would be pulling out of his joint defense agreement with the president. "At that point," Stephanopoulos wrote, "the legal interests of the president of the United

States and his longtime personal attorney could quickly become adversarial."

Asked how he might respond if the president or his legal team came after him, Cohen, Stephanopoulos wrote, "sat up straight. His voice gained strength. 'I will not be a punching bag as part of anyone's defense strategy,' he said emphatically. 'I am not a villain of this story, and I will not allow others to try to depict me that way.'"

Cohen had gone off script.

A couple of days later, the press reported that Lanny Davis, Bill Clinton's special counsel and legal spokesperson during his impeachment trial, was joining Cohen's legal team. On July 20, the *New York Times* broke the story—and the *Washington Post* and other outlets quickly followed—that two months before the election, Cohen had secretly taped a conversation with Trump in which they discussed paying off a *Playboy* model who said she'd had an affair with Trump. The FBI had taken possession of this recording during its raids on Cohen.

"Inconceivable that the government would break into a lawyer's office (early in the morning) — almost unheard of," the president responded on Twitter the next morning. "Even more inconceivable that a lawyer would tape a client — totally unheard of & perhaps illegal. The good news is that your favorite president did nothing wrong!"

Soon came reports that Cohen was willing to tell investigators that Donald Trump Jr. had told his father about the June 9, 2016, Trump Tower meeting to get information to hurt Hillary Clinton's campaign. Early in the morning of July 27, the president responded again on Twitter, "And so the Fake News doesn't waste my time with dumb questions, NO, I did NOT know of the meeting with my son, Don jr. Sounds to me like someone is trying to make up stories in order to get himself out of an unrelated jam (Taxi cabs maybe?). He even retained Bill and Crooked Hillary's lawyer. Gee, I wonder if they helped him make the choice!" (The taxi cab comment referred to reports that investigators were looking into Cohen's financial interests in taxi medallions.)

On the same day that a federal jury found Manafort guilty on eight felony counts, Cohen pleaded guilty August 21 to eight felony charges in the Southern District of New York. These included two counts of campaign-finance violations based on the payments he had made during the final weeks of the campaign to women who said they'd had affairs with Trump. During the plea hearing, Cohen said that one campaign-finance violation occurred "in coordination with, and at the direction of, a candidate for federal office" — that is, Donald Trump.

The next morning, the president compared Cohen unfavorably to Manafort on Twitter: "I feel very badly for Paul Manafort and his wonderful family. 'Justice' took a 12 year old tax case, among other things, applied tremendous pressure on him and, unlike Michael Cohen, he refused to 'break' — make up stories in order to get a deal. Such respect for a brave man!"

When he spoke with Ainsley Earhardt of *Fox & Friends* on August 22, President Trump floated the idea of making it illegal for defendants to cooperate in criminal cases.

"[Cohen] makes a better deal when he uses me," Trump said and went on to praise Manafort again for not "flipping." "For thirty, forty years I've been watching flippers. Everything's wonderful, and then they get ten years in jail, and they — they flip on whoever the next highest one is, or as high as you can go. It almost ought to be outlawed. It's not fair."

The special counsel's office submitted written questions to the president on September 17 addressing the Trump Tower Moscow project; we attached Cohen's written statement to Congress and the letter of intent signed by Trump. We asked the president to describe the timing and substance of his discussions with Cohen about the project, whether the two of them discussed a potential trip to Russia, and whether the president "at any time direct[ed] or suggest[ed] that discussions about the Trump Moscow project should cease" or whether he was "informed at any time that the project had been abandoned."

President Trump submitted written responses on November 20, but he did not answer those questions about Trump Tower Moscow directly or provide any information about the timing of his conversations with

Cohen about the project. Nor did he say whether he participated in any discussions about abandoning or no longer pursuing the project. What he wrote was this:

I had few conversations with Mr. Cohen on this subject. As I recall, they were brief, and they were not memorable. I was not enthused about the proposal, and I do not recall any discussion of travel to Russia in connection with it. I do not remember discussing it with anyone else at the Trump Organization, although it is possible. I do not recall being aware at the time of any communications between Mr. Cohen and Felix Sater and any Russian government official regarding the Letter of Intent.

Cohen pleaded guilty on November 29 to making false statements to Congress. In his plea agreement with our office, he agreed to "provide truthful information regarding any and all matters as to which this Office deems relevant." After Cohen's guilty plea became public that day, the president spoke to reporters about the Trump Tower Moscow project.

"I decided not to do the project," Trump said. "So I didn't do it. So we're not talking about doing a project; we're talking about not doing a project."

He went on to call Cohen "a weak person. And by being weak, unlike other people that you watch — he is a weak person. And what he's trying to do is get a reduced sentence. So he's lying about a project that everybody knew about....I decided ultimately not to do it. There would have been nothing wrong if I did do it. If I did do it, there would have been nothing wrong. That was my business."

"When did you decide not to do the project?" a reporter asked.

"I don't know when I decided, but somewhere during the period of time," the president said. "I was never very enthused. Somewhere during the period — because I was running for president. My focus was running for president. But I — when I run for president, that doesn't mean I'm not allowed to do business. I was doing a lot of different things when I was running."

"But, Mr. President, you said you had no deals with Russia."

"Well, this was a deal that didn't happen. That was no deal.... I decided not to do it. The primary reason — there could have been other reasons. But the primary reason, it was very simple: I was focused on running for president. There would be nothing wrong if I did do it. I was running my business while I was campaigning. There was a good chance that I wouldn't have won, in which case I would have gotten back into the business. And why should I lose lots of opportunities?

"So here's the story: go back and look at the paper that Michael Cohen wrote before he testified in the House and/or Senate. It talked about his position."

In Cohen's statement to Congress, he wrote that he, not the president, "decided to abandon the proposal" in January 2016; that he, Cohen, "did not ask or brief Mr. Trump...before I made the decision to terminate further work on the proposal"; and that this decision was "unrelated" to the campaign.

Trump added of Cohen, "He's got himself a big prison sentence, and he's trying to get a much lesser prison sentence by making up a story. Now here's the thing: Even if he was right, it doesn't matter because I was allowed to do whatever I wanted during the campaign."

Taking note of the president's public statements about how he "decided not to do the project," our office again submitted questions to him asking whether he participated in any discussions about the project being abandoned or no longer pursued, including when he "decided not to do the project." We also asked with whom he spoke about that decision, what motivated the decision, and in "what period of the campaign" he was involved in discussions about the project.

"The president has fully answered the questions at issue," the president's personal counsel responded — and declined to provide further information.

Over the ensuing weeks, the president repeatedly attacked Cohen and implied that his family members were guilty of crimes. After Cohen filed his sentencing memorandum on December 3, the president tweeted, "'Michael Cohen asks judge for no Prison Time.' You mean he can do all of the TERRIBLE, unrelated to Trump, things having to do with fraud, big loans, Taxis, etc., and not serve a long prison term? He makes up stories to get a GREAT & ALREADY reduced deal for himself, and get his wife and father-in-law (who has the money?) off Scott Free. He lied for this outcome and should, in my opinion, serve a full and complete sentence."

Minutes later Trump followed up with this tweet about his former advisor Roger Stone, also under investigation at that time:

"I will never testify against Trump." This statement was recently made by Roger Stone, essentially stating that he will not be forced by a rogue and out of control prosecutor to make up lies and stories about "President Trump." Nice to know that some people still have "guts!"

Cohen was sentenced on December 12, 2018, to three years' imprisonment. The president sent more tweets the next day: "I never directed Michael Cohen to break the law.... Those charges were just agreed to by him in order to embarrass the president and get a much reduced prison sentence, which he did — including the fact that his family was temporarily let off the hook. As a lawyer, Michael has great liability to me!"

President Trump tweeted again on December 16, "Remember, Michael Cohen only became a 'Rat' after the FBI did something which was absolutely unthinkable & unheard of until the Witch Hunt was illegally started. They BROKE INTO AN ATTORNEY'S OFFICE! Why didn't they break into the DNC to get the Server, or Crooked's office?"

Amid reports in January 2019 that Cohen would testify publicly in a congressional hearing, the president continued to suggest that Cohen's family members had committed crimes. When Fox News's Jeanine Perro asked Trump on January 12 whether he was worried about Cohen's testimony, he responded,

> *In order to get his sentence reduced, [Cohen] says, "I have an idea, I'll ah, tell — I'll give you some information on the president." Well, there is no information. But he should give information maybe on his father-in-law because that's the one that people want to look at because where does that money — that's the money in the family. And I guess he didn't want to talk about his father-in-law, he's trying to get his sentence reduced. So it's ah, pretty sad. You know, it's weak and it's very sad to watch a thing like that.*

The president also tweeted on January 18, "Kevin Corke, @FoxNews 'Don't forget, Michael Cohen has already been convicted of perjury and fraud, and as recently as this week, the Wall Street Journal has suggested that he may have stolen tens of thousands of dollars....' Lying to reduce his jail time! Watch father-in-law!"

Citing threats against his family, Cohen postponed his congressional testimony on January 23. The president tweeted the next day, "So interesting that bad lawyer Michael Cohen, who sadly will not be testifying before Congress, is using the lawyer of Crooked Hillary Clinton to represent him — Gee, how did that happen?"

Meanwhile, Trump's own lawyer was giving press interviews in January 2019 that supported Cohen's account of the Trump Tower Moscow time line. Giuliani acknowledged that the Trump Organization pursued the Trump Tower Moscow project well past January 2016.

"It's our understanding that [discussions about the Trump Moscow project] went on throughout 2016," Giuliani told *Meet the Press* on January 20. "Weren't a lot of them, but there were conversations. Can't be sure of the exact date. But the president can remember having conversations with him about it.... The president also remembers — yeah, probably up — could be up to as far as October, November."

Speaking to the *New York Times* for a story published that same day, Giuliani quoted the president saying that discussions about the Trump Moscow project were "going on from the day I announced to the day I won."

The next day Giuliani issued a public corrective: "My recent statements about discussions during the 2016 campaign between Michael Cohen and candidate Donald Trump about a potential Trump Moscow 'project' were hypothetical and not based on conversations I had with the president."

54

"Prepare to die cock sucker"

Just before dawn on January 25, 2019, with CNN cameras there to capture the action, a dozen FBI agents in combat gear approached the front door of Roger Stone's South Florida home, pounded on it four times, and one of them shouted, "FBI, open the door!"

More pounding. "FBI warrant!"

Within a few hours, Stone was being arraigned in federal court in Ft. Lauderdale facing one count of obstruction of justice, five counts of making false statements, and one count of witness tampering. Our office had obtained these indictments from a grand jury the previous day.

At the courthouse, Stone, characteristically, was not backing down.

"This morning at the crack of dawn, 29 FBI agents arrived at my home with 17 vehicles with their lights flashing, when they could simply have contacted my attorneys and I would have been more than willing to surrender voluntarily," he told reporters. "They terrorized my wife, my dogs."

Stone also said, "I will plead not guilty to these charges. I will defeat them in court. As I have said previously, there is no circumstance whatsoever under which I will bear false witness against the president; nor will I make up lies to ease the pressure on myself. I look forward to being fully and completely vindicated."

President Trump tweeted, "Greatest Witch Hunt in the History of our Country! NO COLLUSION! Border Coyotes, Drug Dealers and Human Traffickers are treated better. Who alerted CNN to be there?"

The cable news network's communications Twitter account, @CNNPR, responded, "CNN's ability to capture the arrest of Roger Stone was the result of determined reporting and interpreting clues revealed in the course of events. That's called journalism."

The charges stemmed from Stone's responses to investigations related to Russian election interference conducted by the House of Representatives Permanent Select Committee on Intelligence, the Senate Select Committee on Intelligence, and the FBI, all of which were under way in early 2017. The HPSCI sent Stone a letter in May 2017 asking him to appear before the committee and to produce "any documents, records, electronically stored information including e-mail, communication, recordings, data and tangible things (including, but not limited to, graphs, charts, photographs, images and other documents) regardless of form, other than those widely available (e.g., newspaper articles) that reasonably could lead to the discovery of any facts within the investigation's publicly-announced parameters."

Stone's response followed on May 22:

Mr. Stone has no documents, records, or electronically stored information, regardless of form, other than those widely available that reasonably could lead to the discovery of any facts within the investigation's publicly-announced parameters.

Stone testified before the House committee on September 26, 2017, saying in his prepared opening remarks,

I am most interested in correcting a number of falsehoods, misstatements, and misimpressions regarding allegations of collusion between Donald Trump, Trump associates, The Trump Campaign and the Russian state. I view this as a political proceeding because a number of members of this Committee have made irresponsible, indisputably, and provably false statements in order to create the impression

*of collusion with the Russian state without any evidence that would
hold up in a U.S. court of law or the court of public opinion....*

*These hearings are largely based on a yet unproven allegation that
the Russian state is responsible for the hacking of the DNC and
John Podesta and the transfer of that information to WikiLeaks. No
member of this Committee or intelligence agency can prove this
assertion....*

*Members of this Committee have made three basic assertions
against me which must be rebutted here today. The charge that I
knew in advance about, and predicted, the hacking of Clinton campaign chairman John Podesta's email, that I had advanced knowledge of the source or actual content of the WikiLeaks disclosures
regarding Hillary Clinton or that, my now public exchange with a
persona that our intelligence agencies claim, but cannot prove, is a
Russian asset, is anything but innocuous and are entirely false.
Again, such assertions are conjecture, supposition, projection, and
allegations but none of them are facts.*

During his HPSCI testimony, Stone was asked, did he truly not have
any emails, texts, or other documents that concerned "the allegations of
hacked documents" or discussed Assange?

"That is correct," Stone replied. "Not to my knowledge."

In fact, Stone had sent and received many emails and text messages
during the campaign in which WikiLeaks, Assange, and their possession
of hacked emails were discussed. Stone remained in possession of many
of these emails and texts at the time of his testimony. His false claims that
he had no such emails or texts denied HPSCI a basis "to subpoena records
in his possession that could have shown that other aspects of his testimony were false and misleading."

Stone also took steps to obstruct the investigations into his contacts
with WikiLeaks, including making "multiple false statements to HPSCI
about his interactions" with Assange's organization and falsely denying
that he possessed "records that contained evidence of these interactions."

He also attempted "to persuade a witness to provide false testimony to and withhold pertinent information from the investigations."

Asked to explain his statements in early August 2016 that he "actually ha[d] communicated with Assange" and that he was "in communication with" Assange but was "not at liberty to discuss what I have," Stone said he was referring only to being in contact with a journalist who served as "go-between, as an intermediary, as a mutual friend" of Assange. He later confirmed that this "Person 2" was radio host Randy Credico. But Credico didn't interview Assange until August 25, after Stone's public statements about being in touch with Assange.

Stone never identified "Person 1," Jerome Corsi, whom Stone had instructed to contact Assange and who reported back that their "friend in embassy plans 2 more dumps," including one in October. Stone also did not disclose his exchanges with Jerome Corsi before those August statements about Assange. In addition, Stone falsely denied asking the intermediaries to communicate anything else to Assange when he had asked both Corsi and Credico to pass along his requests for emails dealing with the Clinton Foundation.

Asked how he communicated with his intermediary — whom he had identified as Credico — Stone said it was exclusively "over the phone."

Q: Never emailed him or texted him?
A: He's not an email guy.
Q: So all your conversations with him were in person or over the phone.
A: Correct.

Yet Stone and Credico — and Corsi — communicated often by text and email regarding WikiLeaks. In fact, on the day of Stone's HPSCI testimony, he and Credico exchanged more than thirty text messages.

Stone also lied in response to this question: "Did you discuss your conversations with the intermediary with anyone involved in the Trump campaign?"

"I did not," he said. Yet he had spoken with multiple Trump campaign members about what he said he learned regarding WikiLeaks' plans.

After his testimony, on October 19, Stone sent Credico the excerpt of his letter that identified him as "Person 2" and asked him to back up his testimony. Credico told Stone multiple times that he should correct his false testimony instead. But Stone would not do this and kept trying to prevent Credico from contradicting his false statements. In November 2017, Credico received a request to testify voluntarily before HPSCI, and in a series of conversations and text exchanges, Stone tried to convince Credico to testify falsely either that he was the identified intermediary or that Credico could not remember what he had told Stone. Stone also suggested that Credico invoke his Fifth Amendment right against self-incrimination.

"'Stonewall it. Plead the fifth. Anything to save the plan'...Richard Nixon," went one Stone text from November 19, 2017.

Corsi informed HPSCI the following day that he was declining the committee's request for a voluntary interview. The next day, November 21, Credico texted Stone, "I was told that the house committee lawyer told my lawyer that I will be getting a subpoena."

"That was the point at which your lawyers should have told them you would assert your 5th Amendment rights if compelled to appear," Stone replied.

Credico received a subpoena November 28 compelling his testimony before HPSCI. Two days later, Stone asked Corsi to write publicly about Credico.

"Are you sure you want to make something out of this now?" Corsi responded. "Why not wait to see what [he] does. You may be defending yourself too much — raising new questions that will fuel new inquiries. This may be a time to say less, not more."

Stone wrote back that Credico "will take the 5th — but let's hold a day."

On December 1, Stone suggested that Credico do a "Frank Pentangeli" before the committee, referring to a *The Godfather Part II* character who gives congressional testimony claiming not to know critical information that he actually does. "And if you turned over anything to the FBI you're a fool," Stone texted Credico.

"You need to amend your testimony before I testify on the 15th," Credico texted back to Stone later that day.

"If you testify you're a fool," Stone replied. "Because of tromp [sic] I could never get away with a certain [sic] my Fifth Amendment rights but you can. I guarantee you you are the one who gets indicted for perjury if you're stupid enough to testify."

Credico informed HPSCI on December 12 that he would assert his Fifth Amendment privilege against self-incrimination if required to appear by subpoena — in part because he wished to avoid providing evidence that would demonstrate that Stone's testimony to Congress had been false.

Stone and Credico continued to communicate about the various investigations into Russian election interference, and Stone repeatedly tried to convince Credico not to talk to investigators.

"I met Assange for f[i]rst time this yea[r] sept 7...docs prove that," Credico texted Stone on December 24. "You should be honest w fbi...there was no back channel...be honest."

"I'm not talking to the FBI and if your smart you won't either," Stone replied two minutes later.

Their relationship apparently had gone south by the time Stone emailed Credico on April 9, 2018, "You are a rat. A stoolie. You backstab your friends — run your mouth my lawyers are dying Rip you to shreds." Stone also said that he would "take that dog away from you," referring to Credico's actual pet, and texted, "I am so ready. Let's get it on. Prepare to die cock sucker."

Credico shared these texts with the progressive magazine *Mother Jones* and said he interpreted this last message as a threat. Contacted by *Mother Jones*, Stone did not deny sending the message but explained via text: "He told me he had terminal prostate cancer. It was sent in response to that. We talked about it too. He was depressed about it. Or he was lying?"

The article then noted, "Credico says he does not have prostate cancer and did not have such a discussion with Stone."

Credico emailed Stone again on May 21 to say, "You should have just been honest with the house Intel committee... you've opened yourself up to perjury charges like an idiot."

"You are so full of shit," Stone responded. "You got nothing. Keep running your mouth and I'll file a bar complaint against your friend."

On February 18, 2019, in the month following his arrest, Stone posted on Instagram a photo of the judge in his case, with a crosshairs target symbol next to her forehead and the caption "Through legal trickery Deep State hitman Robert Mueller has guaranteed that my upcoming show trial is before Judge Amy Berman Jackson, an Obama appointed Judge who dismissed the Benghazi charges again [sic] Hillary Clinton and incarcerated Paul Manafort prior to his conviction for any crime #fixisin." A plea for contributions to his defense fund followed.

Later that day, Stone took down the post and filed a notice of apology with the court. Three days later, the judge nonetheless imposed a full gag order on him, saying that without it, she believed he would "pose a danger" to others.

55

"I have no recollection..."

We tried to speak with President Trump. He had commented publicly on our investigation so many times that one might think he would have appreciated the opportunity to tell us exactly what he thought — how there was "no collusion, no obstruction," as he asserted so often. In December 2017, we began trying for more than a year to interview the president about Russian election interference and obstruction of justice. We asked politely, respectfully. We advised his counsel that the president was an investigation "subject," as defined in the Justice Manual as "a person whose conduct is within the scope of the grand jury's investigation."

"An interview with the President is vital to our investigation," we told the counsel. We also noted that the counsel had presented no arguments, constitutional or otherwise, that gave us "reason to forgo seeking an interview."

"It is in the interest of the Presidency and the public for an interview to take place," we told him.

We offered "numerous accommodations to aid the President's preparation and avoid surprise." After much negotiation, we agreed that we would submit only written questions to the president addressing certain Russia-related topics, with nothing about obstruction.

We submitted questions to the president. We received his written responses in late November 2018.

"I was asked a series of questions. I've answered them very easily. Very easily," he told reporters on November 16 before returning the answers to us. He added, "You have to always be careful when you answer questions with people that probably have bad intentions."

The previous day he had tweeted,

> The inner workings of the Mueller investigation are a total mess. They have found no collusion and have gone absolutely nuts. They are screaming and shouting at people, horribly threatening them to come up with the answers they want. They are a disgrace to our Nation and don't…
>
> …care how many lives the ruin. These are Angry People, including the highly conflicted Bob Mueller, who worked for Obama for 8 years. They won't even look at all of the bad acts and crimes on the other side. A TOTAL WITCH HUNT LIKE NO OTHER IN AMERICAN HISTORY!

The following month we informed the president's counsel that Trump's responses were insufficient in many ways. We noted that President Trump said more than thirty times that he "does not 'recall' or 'remember' or have an 'independent recollection'" of information we asked about.

For example:

> I have no recollection of being told that WikiLeaks possessed or might possess emails related to John Podesta before the release of Mr. Podesta's emails was reported by the media. Likewise, I have no recollection of being told that Roger Stone, anyone acting as an intermediary for Roger Stone, or anyone associated with my campaign had communicated with WikiLeaks on October 7, 2016.
>
> I do not recall being told during the campaign that Roger Stone or anyone associated with my campaign had discussions with any of the entities named in the question regarding the content or timing of release of hacked emails.

I spoke by telephone with Roger Stone from time to time during the campaign. I have no recollection of the specifics of any conversations I had with Mr. Stone between June 1, 2016 and November 8, 2016. I do not recall discussing WikiLeaks with him, nor do I recall being aware of Mr. Stone having discussed WikiLeaks with individuals associated with my campaign, although I was aware that WikiLeaks was the subject of media reporting and campaign-related discussion at the time.

And:

I had no knowledge of Mr. Manafort offering briefings on the progress of my campaign to an individual named Oleg Deripaska, nor do I remember being aware of Mr. Manafort or anyone else associated with my campaign sending or directing others to send internal Trump Campaign information to anyone I knew to be in Ukraine or Russia at the time or to anyone I understood to be a Ukrainian or Russian government employee or official. I do not remember Mr. Manafort communicating to me any particular positions Ukraine or Russia would want the United States to support.

And:

I have no recollection of the details of what, when, or from what source I first learned about the change to the [Republican convention] platform amendment regarding arming Ukraine, but I generally recall learning of the issue as part of media reporting. I do not recall being involved in changing the language to the amendment.

We deemed other answers to be "incomplete or imprecise." We told his counsel that the president's responses "demonstrate the inadequacy of the written format, as we have had no opportunity to ask follow up questions that would ensure complete answers and potentially refresh your client's recollection or clarify the extent or nature of his lack of recollection." We again requested an in-person interview, one that we would agree to limit to certain topics.

"This is the President's opportunity to voluntarily provide us with information for us to evaluate in the context of all of the evidence we have gathered," we told the president's counsel.

The president declined.

Given that he would not agree to a voluntary interview and we considered his written answers inadequate, we considered issuing a subpoena to compel President Trump's testimony. But at that point, we had interviewed many other people, gathered much evidence, and made significant progress in our investigation. Did we wish to delay its completion to engage in potentially lengthy constitutional litigation over the president's testimony? Or had we collected enough information from other sources that we could draw relevant factual conclusions about his intent and credibility? We determined that we had done the latter. As you have read throughout this account, Donald Trump's intentions are often not opaque.

In the end, our office did not produce any indictments against President Trump. You no doubt know this already. I have stated the reasons for this multiple times, but given how many people, willfully or not, have misstated this point, it bears repeating.

In our investigation of coordination between the Russian government and the Trump campaign regarding interference in the 2016 presidential election, we did not find the critical mass of evidence needed to prove that Trump and his team were actively, consciously, cooperating in the Russians' efforts to damage Hillary Clinton's campaign and to benefit Trump's. This is not to say that the Trump campaign did not welcome the Russians' actions or that we felt confident that we had uncovered all of the relevant information. Messages were encrypted. Tracks were covered. But we are professional lawyers, the kind who take notes, and we will move forward only on the cases we can prove. This was not such a case.

Our investigation into obstruction of justice was a different matter. The Office of Legal Counsel, which is part of the Department of Justice, issued a memo in 1973 and reaffirmed it on October 16, 2000, that states, "The indictment or criminal prosecution of a sitting President would unconstitutionally undermine the capacity of the executive branch to perform its constitutionally assigned functions."

Our office felt compelled to adhere to that Department of Justice guideline, so we removed from the table the prospect of indicting the president. We still, however, felt it was our duty to complete our investigation, to do our work while memories remained fresh and documentary evidence was still available. You have read what we learned, at least if you reached these words without skipping.

As we put it in our official report,

> *If we had confidence after a thorough investigation of the facts that the President clearly did not commit obstruction of justice, we would so state. Based on the facts and the applicable legal standards, however, we are unable to reach that judgment. The evidence we obtained about the President's actions and intent presents difficult issues that prevent us from conclusively determining that no criminal conduct occurred. Accordingly, while this report does not conclude that the President committed a crime, it also does not exonerate him.*

That is pretty clear, no? You do not require further explanation to explain this explanation, do you? I have repeated this point out loud a few times too, just in case.

President Trump, of course, was free to interpret our findings in any way he saw fit.

"I'm having a good day," the president said on the day of our report's release. "It was called no collusion, no obstruction.... This hoax — it should never happen to another president again."

President Trump sounded a similar note after I completed my two sessions of Capitol Hill testimony on July 24, 2019. "This was a very big day for our country," he told reporters. "This was a very big day for the Republican Party. And you could say it was a great day for me, but I don't even like to say that. It's great."

He said our investigation was "a phony cloud, that's all it was." He also called it, not for the first time, "a hoax" and a "witch hunt."

"I think Robert Mueller did a horrible job, both today and with respect to the investigation," Trump said. "Obviously he did very poorly today. I don't think there's anybody — even among the fakers — I don't think there's anybody that would say he did well."

Well, I never was much for performing. My talent always has had more to do with uncovering the truth — bringing it from the darkest corners into the light of day. Some corners are indeed very dark right now, and it's tough to shine a light into every single one. There is yet more truth to be illuminated.

But now that you see what has been exposed, in our investigation and the dedicated efforts of so many others, you have pathways to explore further. My work here is done. You now are in possession of the torch.

Keep it lit and move forward.

Epilogue

Here are updates about some of the key players in the investigation into Russian election interference.

Michael Cohen: On February 27, 2019, Donald Trump's former lawyer testified before the House Committee on Oversight and Reform. Cohen's key points included the following:

- Trump knew in advance about the June 9, 2016, Trump Tower meeting aimed at getting information to damage Hillary Clinton's campaign.
- Trump knew in advance that WikiLeaks was going to release thousands of emails stolen from Democrats. When told by Roger Stone about this "massive dump of emails that would damage Hillary Clinton's campaign," Cohen said Trump responded, "Wouldn't that be great."
- Trump remained involved in discussions to build a Trump Tower Moscow while running for president. "To be clear, Mr. Trump knew of and directed the Trump Moscow negotiations through the campaign and lied about it," Cohen said.
- Trump directed Cohen to lie about Trump's knowledge of the payment to adult film actress Stephanie Clifford, a.k.a. Stormy Daniels.

In his closing statement, Cohen said, "My loyalty to Mr. Trump has cost me everything: my family's happiness, friendships, my law license, my company, my livelihood, my honor, my reputation, and soon my freedom. And I will not sit back, say nothing, and allow him to do the same to the country. Indeed, given my experience working for Mr. Trump, I fear that if he loses the election in 2020, there will never be a peaceful transition of power, and this is why I agreed to appear before you today."

Cohen entered prison on May 6, 2019, to begin a three-year sentence for false testimony and tax fraud. CNN reported on September 11, 2019, that Cohen was cooperating with a New York district attorney's office investigation into whether the Trump Organization violated New York State law by falsifying records of reimbursement payments to Cohen regarding hush money paid to conceal Donald Trump's affairs.

James Comey: The fired FBI director's memoir, *A Higher Loyalty: Truth, Lies and Leadership*, was released in April 2018 and became an instant best seller. In the book, on the lecture circuit, in television appearances, and in op-ed columns, he was an outspoken opponent of President Trump. Although a registered Republican for most of his life, a few months before the 2018 midterm elections, Comey tweeted: "All who believe in this country's values must vote for Democrats this fall. Policy differences don't matter right now. History has its eyes on us."

A Justice Department inspector general report released on August 29, 2019, criticized Comey for providing his lawyers with government memos, including a document that he allowed to be leaked to the *New York Times.* Comey has said one reason he did so was to prompt the appointment of a special counsel. The document was determined not to be classified.

"Comey violated F.B.I. policy and the requirements of his F.B.I. employment agreement when he chose this path," the report said, accusing him of setting "a dangerous example."

Noting that the report did not find he had broken any laws, Comey responded on Twitter:

> DOJ IG *"found no evidence that Comey or his attorneys released any of the classified information contained in any of the memos to members of the media."* I don't need a public apology from those who defamed me, but a quick message with a "sorry we lied about you"

would be nice…And to all those who've spent two years talking
about me "going to jail" or being a "liar and a leaker"—ask your-
selves why you still trust people who gave you bad info for so long,
including the president.

Jerome Corsi: Roger Stone's first go-between with WikiLeaks did his
own leaking when, in November 2018, he released a plea agreement
drafted by our office in which he would have admitted to lying to investigators. But after having announced that he was discussing such a deal
with our prosecutors, he told interviewers that he would not sign the
agreement after all. Our office did not charge him.

Michael Flynn: Trump's former national security advisor was scheduled
to be sentenced on December 18, 2019, a little more than two years after he
pleaded guilty to lying to the FBI about his meetings with Russian ambassador Sergey Kislyak and exactly a year after his original sentencing hearing, during which Judge Emmet Sullivan rebuked him and warned him of
possible prison time if the sentencing went forward that day.

"Arguably, you sold your country out," the judge told Flynn on December 18, 2018. "I'm not hiding my disgust, my disdain for this criminal
offense." Sullivan also asked prosecutors whether they had considered
charging Flynn with treason. (The answer was no.)

Flynn agreed to delay his sentencing at that time so he could demonstrate his cooperation with the government. But over the summer of
2019, he hired new lawyers who sought to have the case dismissed on the
basis of our investigation being tainted and biased while the prosecutors
had engaged in "malevolent conduct."

Hope Hicks: The White House communications director told a congressional committee on February 27, 2018, that she had told "white lies" for
Trump. She submitted her resignation the following day. On October 8,
2018, Fox Corporation announced her appointment as an executive vice
president and chief communications officer.

Konstantin Kilimnik: Indicted in conjunction with Paul Manafort on obstruction of justice charges, this Russian citizen and suspected intelligence operative lives in Moscow, far away from US courtrooms.

Jared Kushner: Interviewed onstage at the Time 100 Summit in April 2019 after the release of our report, the president's son-in-law and senior advisor said, "You look at what Russia did, you know, buying some Facebook ads to try and sow dissent and do it, it's a terrible thing. But I think the investigations and all of the speculation that's happened for the last two years has had a much harsher impact on our democracy than a couple Facebook ads."

Kushner initially had been denied top-secret security clearance, but it was then granted in May 2018. President Trump told the *New York Times* in January 2019 that he had nothing to do with Kushner's receiving such clearance, but the following month the paper revealed memos from then–chief of staff John Kelly and White House counsel Don McGahn showing their objections to this move, with Kelly noting that he had been "ordered" to give Kushner top-secret clearance.

Paul Manafort: In June 2018 Trump's former campaign chairman began serving seven and a half years in prison, stemming from two federal cases and a variety of charges, after a judge revoked his bail over witness-tampering allegations. A New York State court brought sixteen more fraud-related charges against Manafort in March 2019, and these charges, unlike the federal ones, could not be undone by a presidential pardon. Manafort, who turned seventy on April 1, 2019, pleaded not guilty in June, and his lawyers filed a motion complaining that the overlap between some of the state and federal charges amounted to double jeopardy.

K. T. McFarland: After she withdrew herself from consideration for the post of US ambassador to Singapore in February 2018, amid reports of discrepancies in her statements about Michael Flynn's interactions with Russian ambassador Sergey Kislyak, the former deputy national security advisor clarified her account with our office and was not charged with a crime. By the fall of 2019, she was appearing frequently on the network where she had served as a commentator before her White House stint: Fox News.

Don McGahn: Eleven days after the *New York Times* reported that the White House counsel had "cooperated extensively" with our office's investigation, President Trump announced McGahn's resignation on August 29, 2018. McGahn departed on October 17. Weighing whether to pursue articles of impeachment against the president, the House Judiciary Committee subpoenaed McGahn to testify. But on May 7, 2019, the White House instructed him not to comply, and McGahn defied the subpoena on May 21. The committee filed suit against McGahn on August 7, 2019, to compel him to testify.

"McGahn is the Judiciary Committee's most important fact witness in its consideration of whether to recommend articles of impeachment and its related investigation of misconduct by the president, including acts of obstruction of justice described in the special counsel's report," the fifty-four-page filing states.

As of October 2019, the case remained pending.

Carter Page: After the election, Page — who had been let go from the campaign due to negative attention regarding his Russia connections — sought a position in the Trump administration. In his November 14 application, he claimed that as a Trump campaign foreign policy advisor, he had met with "top world leaders" and "effectively responded to diplomatic outreach efforts from senior government officials in Asia, Europe, the Middle East, Africa, [and] the Americas." The transition team apparently did not respond to his application.

In December 2016, Page was back in Moscow, pursuing business opportunities and touting his links to the incoming Trump administration. Konstantin Kilimnik, who long worked for Paul Manafort in Russia, said Page gave individuals in Russia the impression that he had maintained his connections to the president-elect.

"Carter Page is in Moscow today, sending messages he is authorized to talk to Russia on behalf of DT on a range of issues of mutual interest, including Ukraine," Kilimnik emailed Manafort on December 8.

The next day Page had dinner with NES employees Shlomo Weber and Andrej Krickovic. Weber had alerted Russian deputy prime minister Arkady Dvorkovich that Page was in town and invited Dvorkovich to stop by the dinner. Dvorkovich did, meeting with Page at the restaurant for a few minutes. He suggested that he and Page might work together by forming an academic partnership. Dvorkovich also congratulated Page on Trump's election, expressed interest in starting a dialogue between the United States and Russia, and asked Page whether he could connect Dvorkovich with individuals involved in the transition so they could discuss future cooperation.

We have no record of Page's response.

Our office ultimately did not charge Page with any crime; we lacked evidence to prove beyond a reasonable doubt that he had acted as an agent of the Russian government. On four occasions, the Foreign Intelligence Surveillance Court (FISC) had issued warrants tied to finding probable cause to believe that Page was acting as an agent of a foreign power. Trump's allies on Capitol Hill and in the media argued that these warrants had been illegally obtained.

George Papadopoulos: After completing a twelve-day prison term at the end of 2018 following his guilty plea for lying to the FBI, this young former Trump advisor set about reshaping his story as one in which he was entrapped by US and foreign intelligence agencies attempting to justify the FBI's surveillance of the Trump campaign. He presented this alternative narrative in his 2019 book, *Deep State Target*, and became a fixture on Fox News. In August 2019, an announcement named him as a guest of the Digital Soldiers Conference, scheduled for September 14 in Atlanta and presented by supporters of the QAnon conspiracy theory. This involves a "deep state" plot against Trump in which Democrats are involved in a child-trafficking ring and in which I am actually a Trump ally secretly investigating the Democrats after Trump pretended to collude with the Russians. The conference was intended to support Michael

Flynn's legal defense fund, but after *Mother Jones* reported on its QAnon ties, Flynn pulled out, and the event was canceled.

Rob Porter: The White House staff secretary announced his resignation on February 7, 2018, after his two ex-wives publicly alleged that he had physically abused them. During his White House tenure, he reportedly had been dating White House communications director Hope Hicks.

Yevgeniy Prigozhin: Although under indictment in the United States along with his company, Concord, on multiple felony counts (including conspiracy to defraud the United States and conspiracy to commit wire fraud and bank fraud), the man known as Putin's chef continues his work in Russia supporting his president. He has been reported to be a funder of the Wagner group, a private military contractor that has clashed with US troops in Syria and fought in Ukraine. Prigozhin has denied any involvement in the Wagner group or troll farms and showed little concern about my office's indictments, saying, "I am not at all disappointed that I appear in this list. If they want to see the devil, let them."

Vladimir Putin: On June 28, 2019, President Trump met with the Russian president for the first time since the release of our report at the G20 summit in Osaka, Japan. As they sat next to each other before a room full of press, one reporter asked, "Mr. President, will you tell Russia not to meddle in the 2020 presidential election?"

"Yes, of course, I will," Trump responded. Then he turned to his geopolitical rival and deadpanned, "Don't meddle in the election, president." Trump repeated himself with a smirk and mock finger wag: "Don't meddle in the election." Putin chuckled.

Sarah Sanders: Sean Spicer's successor as White House press secretary held the job from July 21, 2017, until June 30, 2019. Her new position as a Fox News contributor was announced the following August 22, and in her first appearance, on the show *Fox & Friends* on September 6, she said she would continue to advocate for her former boss: "They still see me as somebody who is a very pro-Trump supporter," said Sanders, whose deal to write a memoir had been announced the previous day. "I'm not going to change my position."

The president approved, tweeting: "Great interview of Sarah Sanders by @foxandfriends. She is a terrific person with a great future!"

Jeff Sessions: President Trump's former attorney general, who turned seventy-two toward the end of 2018, was said in the summer of 2019 to be considering a run for his old Senate seat in Alabama. But Republican Alabama senator Richard Shelby told the *Hill* in July 2019 that he had discussed this possibility with the president, and Trump "was not on board." In September 2019, the *Washington Post* reported that Democrats on the House Judiciary Committee were negotiating with Sessions to try to secure his testimony in their impeachment investigation of President Trump. One of Sessions's lawyers told the *Post* that his client "will not appear except under compulsion of a congressional subpoena."

Dimitri Simes: Although he was not charged with any crimes related to our Russia investigation, his prominence in our report had an impact on him and his Center for the National Interest. The report noted his frequent assistance to the Trump campaign, including his offer of supposedly compromising information about Bill Clinton to Jared Kushner, his facilitating of communications between the Trump camp and Russian officials, his assistance in crafting a Trump speech, and his hosting of that Mayflower Hotel event, in which he introduced Jeff Sessions to Russian ambassador Sergey Kislyak. Given that his Washington, DC–based think tank was purported to be nonpartisan, the Center for the National Interest experienced a dramatic drop in donations, Bloomberg News and the *Washington Post* reported. Simes told the *Post* that the center also racked up $1 million in legal bills related to our investigation.

In 2018, Simes began cohosting a news/analysis show (the title translates to *The Big Game*) on a Russian television network primarily owned by the Russian government.

Sean Spicer: President Trump's first White House press secretary lasted six months on the job, resigning July 21, 2017. His inaccurate claims about the size of Trump's inauguration crowds prompted Trump aide Kellyanne Conway to coin the phrase "alternative facts." She said this with a straight face. On August 21, 2019, Spicer was announced as a contestant on the upcoming *Dancing with the Stars* season, sparking a backlash among those who argued that he should not be rewarded for a history of making false claims to the press and the American public. The president, though, offered this supportive tweet: "Just heard that Sean Spicer will be on *Dancing with the Stars*. He will do great. A terrific person who loves our Country dearly!"

Roger Stone: Judge Amy Berman Jackson, who had slapped a gag order on the former Trump advisor in February 2019 after he posted a photo of her next to a crosshairs target, issued another order on July 16, 2019, barring him from posting on such social media sites as Facebook, Twitter, and Instagram. The judge said Stone had violated the gag order by posting items about his pending case, promoting conspiracy theories, and texting a BuzzFeed News reporter to dispute a statement made by Michael Cohen.

"Once again I am wrestling with behavior that has more to do with middle school than a court of law," the judge said in court. "The goal has been to draw maximum attention."

In August 2019, the judge rejected a Stone motion to dismiss the case but allowed him access to unredacted sections of our report.

Donald Trump Jr.: We opted not to charge the president's eldest son or other Trump campaign members who participated in the June 9, 2016, Trump Tower meeting aimed at obtaining damaging information regarding the Clinton campaign (including Trump son-in-law Jared Kushner) because we could not prove that they realized what they were doing was illegal. As we put it in the report: "The investigation has not developed evidence that the participants in the meeting were familiar with the foreign-contribution ban or the application of federal law to the relevant factual context." So you might say that apparent ignorance of the law paid off in this case. Trump Jr. has continued to be a vocal supporter of his father.

Donald J. Trump: On August 12, 2019, a whistleblower in the U.S. intelligence community filed a complaint alleging that President Trump had been seeking foreign interference in the 2020 presidential election. A key element was a July 25, 2019, phone call between the president and recently elected Ukrainian president Volodymyr Zelensky in which President Trump asked for "a favor." He requested that Zelensky assist Attorney General William Barr and the president's personal lawyer, Rudy Giuliani, in investigating Democratic presidential candidate Joe Biden and his son, Hunter Biden. At the time the former vice president was considered Trump's most likely rival in the 2020 election. Prior to this conversation, the president had suspended U.S. aid to Ukraine.

Also, apparently referring to an unfounded conspiracy theory in which Ukraine supposedly helped the Democrats during the 2016 presidential election and got ahold of the Democratic National Committee server ("The server, they say Ukraine has it," Trump said on the call), Trump asked the Ukrainian president to take a call from Barr and to "get to the bottom" of that situation. Soon, media outlets were reporting that Barr had been meeting with or seeking conversations with government representatives in Australia, Great Britain, and Italy as he pursued an investigation into the origins of, yes, the Mueller Report.

On September 24, 2019, Speaker Nancy Pelosi announced that the House of Representatives would launch a formal impeachment inquiry against President Trump. "The actions of the Trump presidency have revealed the dishonorable fact of the president's betrayal of his oath of office, betrayal of our national security, and betrayal of the integrity of our elections," she said, adding, "No one is above the law."

The White House released a rough transcript of the Trump-Zelinsky conversation the following day, and the House Intelligence Committee unveiled the full whistleblower complaint on September 26. The complaint, based on "information from multiple U.S. government officials," alleges "that the President of the United States is using the power of his office to solicit interference from a foreign country in the 2020 U.S. election." It also says that senior White House officials "intervened to 'lock down' all records of the phone call [between Trump and Zelinsky], especially the official word-for-word transcript of the call that was produced — as is customary — by the White House Situation Room."

President Trump repeatedly referred to his conversation with Zelinsky as "perfect" and tweeted, among other things, that the impeachment inquiry was "THE GREATEST SCAM IN THE HISTORY OF AMERICAN POLITICS!" and "PRESIDENTIAL HARASSMENT!" In a closed-door speech captured on video and leaked to media outlets, the president referred to the whistleblower as "close to a spy" and implied violence against him: "You know what we used to do in the old days when we were smart? Right? With spies and treason, right? We used to handle them a little differently than we do now." Trump also posted tweets suggesting House Intelligence Committee chair Adam Schiff might be arrested for "treason," calling the impeachment inquiry "a COUP," and complaining that the Democrats were "wasting everyone's time and energy on BULLSHIT."

On September 27, the *Washington Post* reported that in the president's May 10, 2017, Oval Office meeting with Russian foreign minister Sergey Lavrov and Russian ambassador Sergey Kislyak — the one in which he said firing FBI director Comey had relieved "great pressure" — Trump had told the Russian officials that he was unconcerned about Russian interference in the U.S. presidential election because the United States did the same in other countries. These comments prompted such concern in the White House that access to the memo summarizing the meeting became highly restricted, the report stated.

Amid all of this scrutiny, on the morning of October 3, Trump told reporters on live TV on the White House lawn that Ukraine should investigate the Bidens, and so should China.

As of this writing, the forty-fifth president of the United States remains in office.

Index

About the Author

MARK CARO is author of *The Foie Gras Wars*, winner of the 2009 Great Lakes Book Award for general nonfiction, and author of *Behind the Laughter: A Comedian's Tale of Tragedy and Hope* (with Anthony Griffith and Brigitte Travis-Griffin) and *Take It to the Bridge: Unlocking the Great Songs Inside You* (with Steve Dawson). For more than twenty-five years, Mark covered film, food, music, murder trials, and global cities for the *Chicago Tribune* and also has written for the *New York Times*, *Chicago* magazine, and other outlets. He created the popular "Is It Still Funny?" film series in Chicago, has hosted on WGN Radio, and in the summer of 2019 launched an on-stage interview series, "Mark Caro's Talking in Space." Mark lives in the Chicago area with his wife and two daughters.